DILLY'S SACRIFICE

When Dilly's husband is left unable to work, she has to make an unthinkable decision. With four children already at home, they cannot afford to feed their new-born. The Farthing family, who live at the big house, know how it feels to lose a child. They are going through their own form of horror having just lost their own daughter to measles. Despite their grief, they decide to offer Dilly a lifeline: they'll adopt the child and employ Dilly as their maid. The consequences of this act of desperation will irrevocably change the lives of both families – and the onset of WWI even more so.

DILLY'S SACRIFICE

DILLY'S SACRIFICE

by

Rosie Goodwin

Magna Large Print Books
Long Preston, North Yorkshire,
BD23 4ND, England.

British Library Cataloguing in Publication Data.

Goodwin, Rosie
    Dilly's sacrifice.

    A catalogue record of this book is
    available from the British Library

    ISBN   978-0-7505-4283-8

First published in Great Britain in 2015 by Corsair

Copyright © Rosie Goodwin, 2015

Cover illustration © Colin Thomas

The moral right of the author has been asserted.

Published in Large Print 2016 by arrangement with
Little, Brown Book Group

Magna Large Print is an imprint of Library Magna Books Ltd.

Printed and bound in Great Britain by
T.J. (International) Ltd., Cornwall, PL28 8RW

This book is dedicated to all the people who lost their lives in the First World War fighting for our country.

Prologue

'Aw, me own darlin'. Is there no other way?'

The anguish in Fergal's voice brought tears to Dilly's eyes as she wrapped the newly born babe in a shawl and shook her head. 'You know the answer to that right enough,' she answered, more sharply than she had intended. It was a discussion they'd had many times over the last month and now that the time had come she would not swerve from her promise. *How can I?* she asked herself, as the child settled into the crook of her arm.

'I'm sorry, love,' she muttered then, as guilt, sharp as a knife, sliced through her very soul. She of all people knew that her husband blamed himself for what she was about to do and that it was tearing him apart. 'Once this little one is delivered to its new home, we needn't put Declan, Kian, Seamus and Niamh into the orphanage,' she said wearily. 'At least then we'll have the money to send them to your family in Dublin until I start work. In no time we'll have saved enough to fetch them home.'

'But it's like selling our own flesh and blood!' he choked.

She gulped. 'You know that's not true, Fergal. I've only agreed to accept enough to cover the children's fares to Ireland and this one will never want for anything. She'll live in the lap of luxury

11

and never know what it is to go hungry.'

'Unlike the others, you mean!' A note of bitterness had crept into his voice now.

She laid the child gently on the lumpy old sofa, then hurried across to him and gently took his hands. She was still weak from giving birth and felt far from well, yet she could still put him first. Fergal Carey was the love of her life and had been ever since the day she had first clapped eyes on him. 'Stop blaming yourself,' she urged softly. 'What happened to you was an accident. Until then you were a good provider and would have gone on being so.'

A lock of Fergal's straight black hair slipped across his forehead as his head drooped. Freeing one of his hands, he thumped at his useless legs. '*Why* did this have to happen? I'm no good to man or beast as I am now. How do you think it makes me feel seeing you have to do everything for me as well as work yourself almost to death? Why, I sometimes think it would have been better if that bloody tree had seen me off good and proper to be sure!'

'Don't you *ever* let me hear you say that again!' She pulled her hand away and straightened. Her mind raced back to the awful accident that had occurred. He had had a good job as a linesman at the local Trent Valley railway station and had been out on the tracks one day following a particularly bad storm when a tree had toppled on him, trapping his legs. It had taken three men two hours to free him, and for weeks his life had hung in the balance as he lay in the local cottage hospital. At last he had been pronounced out of danger but his legs had been so badly damaged that a stern-faced doctor had had to inform him that he would never walk again. It had been a terrible blow to the whole family, whose savings had gone to pay medical bills, but especially to Fergal. He had always had been an active, hard-working man, but from then on he would have to be tended like a baby. With every month that passed he had been forced to watch his useless legs wither away, and it broke his heart to see his beloved Dilly and the children struggling to survive.

Their other four children were upstairs, fast asleep in their beds, unaware of the birth that had taken place only hours before. Dilly considered that to be a blessing, although the women in the courts, like her, were brave during childbirth and rarely made a sound, intent on not distressing the rest of their brood. Dilly's four would be told that the new baby had died before it drew breath and it was doubtful that they would question it. Many babies thereabouts never saw their first birthdays but Fergal and Dilly were proud that their brood had survived, hale and hearty. Each child had been wanted and was loved but the same could not be said for this one. From the moment she had realized she was with child again, Dilly had dreaded its coming. How would she manage with yet another mouth to feed? As her pregnancy had progressed she had been able to take in less washing and ironing, and many a night they had all gone to bed with grumbling stomachs. Then, like the answer to a prayer, she had been offered a solution and had known she must seize it. Things had become so desperate that she could see no alternative but to put the children into the orphanage until she could earn enough money to feed them and pay the rent. Now not only would she have enough money to send them to Ireland to their grandparents but also a job that would enable her to earn more in a week than she could in a whole month, taking in laundry. What choice did she have? With one last glance at her husband she picked up the baby and went to the door before her resolve wavered. The promise had been easy to make while the babe had been growing inside her, but now it was here, it was much more difficult to keep. The only other person who was aware that she had given birth was Nell Cotteridge, her trusted neighbour, who had helped the child into the world, but Dilly knew that her secret would be safe with her – she would have trusted Nell with her life.

'Let me take just *one* more peek at the little mite afore you go,' Fergal begged.

She shook her head. 'Best not make things any worse than they already are.' She let herself out into the bitingly cold air of the back yard, closing the door firmly behind her. Fergal's muffled sobs came to her through it but she squared her shoulders and walked into the long, narrow entry. As she passed Madge Bunting's cottage she thought she saw the rags that passed for curtains twitch and prayed she was wrong. The last thing she needed was for Madge to find out what she was about to do. The woman had a mouth on her like a parish oven and ever since Dilly had been given the job for which Madge had also applied, Madge had resented Dilly. But there was no time to worry about that. The sooner this was done the better.

Out on the street she turned towards her destination, the baby tucked tightly against her. It was making little mewing noises and sucking its tiny fist. She felt as if her heart was breaking but her steps never faltered, even though she was still sore and light-headed from giving birth just hours before. The future of all her children depended on what she was about to do, and for their sake there could be no turning back.

The gas lamps she passed flickered eerily and cast shadows across the pavements and on the walls of the terraced cottages in St Mary's Road but the streets were deserted, as she had prayed they would be. Eventually she paused at the gates of a large house in the better part of town. Gently she twitched aside the shawl that covered the babe's face and kissed its soft cheek tenderly. 'I shall never forget you, and I shall love you for as long as there's breath in me body,' she promised brokenly. 'Please forgive me and know that if there were any other way I would never do this.'

She glanced up and down the street, to ensure that no one was about, then hurried through the gates and made her way to the servants' entrance at the back. Just as she had been told, she saw a light shining from the kitchen window and tapped tentatively at the door.

It opened almost immediately and the house-keeper, Miss Norman, an Amazon of a woman with steel-grey hair pulled tightly into a bun on the back of her head, confronted her. She must have received the note that Dilly had sent with Will, Nell's small son, earlier that evening. Dilly had heard the cook say that Miss Norman had never been married, which was hardly surprising: she wasn't the prettiest of women, but she had a kindly nature.

'Ah, you're right on time.' She nodded approvingly, keen to get the business done with, for it was past her bedtime, then spoke over her shoulder to the insignificant little woman standing behind her: 'Nanny, come and take the child up to the nursery. The mistress is already there, waiting for you. I trust you have everything ready?'

'Oh, yes, indeed I do.' The woman stepped forward, then without further ado she scooped the child from its mother's arms and bustled away, her starched white apron crackling as she went.

Dilly swayed as a coldness such as she had never felt before enveloped her. It was nothing to do with the chilly night air. But she had no time to object or even comment, for the housekeeper was pressing an envelope into her hands. 'The mistress said you should call tomorrow morning to sign the papers that her solicitor will have ready for you,' she said, then shut the door in her face.

Dilly stared at the envelope, resisting the urge that had come upon her to tear it to shreds. *But what good would that do?* The contents would ensure that her other children had a future. Turning, she staggered towards the gate and disappeared into the darkness, like a thief in the night. The deed was done and she prayed that God would forgive her.

Chapter One

December 1900

'Come along now, Niamh, we've not far to go now,' Dilly said encouragingly, as her four-year-old daughter leaned heavily into her skirt. The ferry crossing to Dublin had been rough, the sea grey and choppy, and the wind had chilled them to the bone. Darkness was falling now as she urged her brood through the back-streets towards their grandparents' home. They were all hungry and tired. Seamus, her two-year-old, was asleep across her shoulder, his thin arms dangling, and the other three were carrying the clothes she had packed for them.

'I'm thirsty an' me arms ache,' Declan complained.

'I know you are, pet, but, like I said, there's not far to go now.' Dilly's heart ached as she glanced at her first-born. Declan, with his thick mop of black hair and his startlingly blue eyes, was the image of his father and had always held a special place in her heart. Three-year-old Kian favoured his father in looks, too, but the other two took after Dilly, especially Niamh, with her deep brown eyes and coppery hair.

Fergal had chosen all of their names insisting that they should be Irish and Dilly had not objected, even though she was English. There was nothing she would not do for her husband, and as she thought of him now, alone in their tiny cottage, her heart ached, although she knew he would be well cared for in her absence. Nell Cotteridge had promised to take him his meals and help as much as she could and she would do just that. Not that Dilly intended to be gone for long. She had already booked a return passage on the ferry that would leave first thing the next morning. She tried not to think of it, for she would be without her children – but, she consoled herself, it would only be for a short time. Once she started work she would save every penny she could, and when she had caught up with the rent arrears and had a little money in the pot she would fetch them home. Meanwhile she had told the children they were coming to Dublin to have a little holiday with their grandparents and they all seemed to have accepted that, which was one blessing at least.

Now she shifted Seamus's weight on her shoulder and forced herself to go on putting one foot in front of the other.

Fergal's parents lived in Georgina Street, where they occupied the bottom half of a house that would once have belonged to someone wealthy. Years ago all the houses in that neighbourhood had been owned by solicitors, doctors and businessmen but, sadly, the area had sunk slowly into poverty, with some families forced to live five, six or even more to a single room. Fergal's parents were fortunate: there were only the two of them now that their family had flown the nest, and with his father employed at a small slaughterhouse in the next street they were able to live comfortably. Knowing how hard it must be for Dilly to make ends meet, the kindly couple had offered to care for the children for a while but even so Dilly's spirits were low as they advanced through the overcrowded streets. They were little more than slums, with ragged children playing in the gutters and beggars on each corner.

How can I leave my children here? But deep inside she knew she had no alternative. At least they would be fed and clothed until she could take them back. She trudged on. At last they came to Bolton Street, and after walking its length, they turned into Georgina Street. A short way along they passed the laundry and Dilly suppressed a shudder. It was run by the Sisters of Mercy, and her mother-in-law had told her that at least fifty single homeless women were forced to work all the hours of the day there, poor souls.

As she neared the house, she tried to be more optimistic. Georgina Street was commonly referred to as Primate's Hill, and was no more salubrious than the labyrinth of slum streets she had just passed through, but it had one saving grace: it backed onto open fields where the children could run and play, which was something to be grateful for.

Seamus had woken and was whimpering on her shoulder. Dilly's back felt as if it was breaking and waves of dizziness washed over her but she smiled at the children's pale faces as she climbed three stone steps to a front door and rapped.

It was opened almost instantly and her mother-in-law, Maeve Carey, beamed in welcome at them, then ushered them inside. She was a small woman, neatly dressed in a woollen frock that buttoned up to the neck and a snow-white apron that reached almost to the floor. Her still dark hair was plaited and wound about the crown of her head and her blue eyes, so like Fergal's, were shining with pleasure at the sight of them.

'I've been looking out for you for the last hour, so I have,' she told them, taking Seamus from Dilly's arms. 'Now come away in. I've something nice and hot ready for you and you all look in need of it.'

As Dilly followed her mother-in-law's straight back down a long, narrow passage she felt as if she had stepped into another world and began to feel a little better. Although cracked in places, the tiles on the floor shone in the gloomy light and everywhere smelt of beeswax polish. Maeve pushed open another door and they found themselves in a large, high-ceilinged room that served as a sitting-room-cum-kitchen. A large scrubbed table with six matching chairs took pride of place in the centre, and on one wall there was a huge pine dresser where Maeve's treasured, if ill-matched, china was displayed with a plaster figurine of the Virgin Mary. A fire roared up the chimney and she ushered the children towards a settee and chairs that stood on either side of it. A gay peg rug lay in front of the hearth and above the fire, suspended on a thick beam, copper pans gleamed like mirrors. Above the centre of the beam hung a picture of the Sacred Heart of Jesus, and on either side of it stood two brass candlesticks. At the other end of the room there was a large stone sink and a cooking range, from which delicious smells issued. Like the hall, the whole place was spotless – Dilly was sure they could have eaten their dinner off the floor.

Only when she had put Seamus down did Maeve turn to Dilly and hug her, saying, 'Sure, you look exhausted, lass. Come and take the weight off your feet while I dish up the dinner, eh? We can talk later when the weans are settled. I have their beds all ready for them, so I do, and looking at the state of them, they'll not take much rocking the night.'

Dilly sank onto a chair as she watched the other woman bustling about, laying dishes on the table and running to and fro with cutlery and glasses. The children watched her silently from tired eyes and every now and then she smiled at them. Soon they were all seated, tucking into a thick stew, full of large tender chunks of rabbit and vegetables swimming in rich gravy; there was fresh-baked soda bread to mop it up and Dilly was pleased to see them clear their dishes in no time.

'Well, there seems to be nothing wrong with their appetites.' Their grandmother chuckled. 'Now, who has room for a nice dish of my semolina pudding? We must save some for your granda, though. He'll be home from work any time now and he's right looking forward to seeing you all.'

The bowls were emptied in the blink of an eye, but by then the children were yawning so Maeve suggested, 'Why don't we get them ready for bed, eh? You just show me which bag their night-clothes are in and I'll see to them while you rest awhile. I reckon they can wait till morning for a wash. It won't hurt them for one night.'

Dilly rose to help her but Maeve ushered her

towards the fireside chair saying, 'No, you sit there. I've done this afore, you know.'

And so Dilly gratefully did as she was told and in the blink of an eye she had fallen into a deep sleep and didn't even get to say goodnight to them.

It was the soft drone of voices that stirred her some time later, and as she pulled herself up in the chair she saw her father-in-law smiling at her from the settee on the opposite side of the fireplace. For a moment she was disoriented and thought it was Fergal – his father looked like an older version of her husband – but then she remembered where she was and smiled guiltily.

'I'm so sorry.' Her hand rose to stroke back the lock of hair that had come loose from its pin. 'I didn't mean to fall asleep and leave everything to Maeve.'

Daniel Carey grinned as he sucked on his old clay pipe. 'You must have needed it, lass,' he said kindly. 'An' now Mother will get you a nice cup of cocoa an' you can tell us all about how our Fergal is doing and what's happening back at home.'

Minutes later Maeve had joined them and they sat sipping their drinks in the glow of the fire, Dilly's in-laws eyeing her with concern. The poor girl didn't look at all well. The weight seemed to have dropped off her, and there were large dark circles beneath her eyes, but after what she had gone through over the last year they were hardly surprised. She must have been to Hell and back, what with caring for Fergal and trying to keep the children fed and clothed.

Declan had confided to his gran'ma while she

was tucking him into bed that Mammy had lost a baby shortly before, and Maeve's heart went out to her although, tactfully, she didn't mention it. The girl would confide in her in her own good time, no doubt, but Maeve could only imagine the heartbreak it had caused her, knowing how Dilly doted on her children. She also understood how hard it must have been for Dilly to write to herself and Daniel asking for help, for Dilly was a proud, hard-working girl. But at least they were all here now and things would improve from now on. In fact, she and Daniel had been looking forward to having their grandchildren to themselves for a time.

'So,' she said, peering at Dilly over the rim of her mug, 'how is Fergal?'

'Much the same. He has good days and bad days,' Dilly admitted. 'I think the hardest thing for him is to have to lie there.'

Maeve nodded. 'I can imagine. He was always an independent young devil right from when he was small. I just wish we hadn't moved back here to live before the accident happened. Then at least we would have been there to help you.'

She and Daniel had been married for only a couple of years when Daniel had gone as a navvy to work in Nuneaton, digging out the canals, because there was no work to be found in Dublin, where they had lived at the time. He had been happy there, and eventually she and a very young Fergal had joined him in the small house he had rented. Soon after, Fergal's brother, Liam, had been born, and the years had drifted past until both boys were grown. She smiled to herself as she recalled how irate she had been when Fergal had begun to court Dilly.

'But the girl is not a Catholic and she's an orphan into the bargain,' she had blustered. But Fergal would not be swayed, and when Dilly had converted to his faith he had married her, despite his mother's protests. Slowly Dilly had found her way into their hearts, and now Maeve knew that marrying this lovely girl was probably the best thing Fergal had ever done. Finally, when their family had begun to come along, she, Daniel and Liam had moved back to Dublin to try to fulfil their dream of owning a smallholding in one of the surrounding villages.

As if picking up on her thoughts, Dilly asked, 'How is Liam doing in Enniskerry?'

Maeve beamed. 'Oh, he writes to us regularly and he says everything is going just fine. There's still a lot of work to do on the cottage before we can join him and then, of course, we shall have to save up to buy livestock, but everything comes to those that wait. We were so lucky to hear of the cottage and the land, although I'll admit at the time it stretched us to buy it, but with Father sending him money regularly, and with what Liam earns as a carpenter over on the Powerscourt Estate, we'll get there in the end. If the cottage and the land had been well maintained we would never have been able to afford it. Between you and me, I have an inkling that he's met a young lady he's sweet on in the village. She's an apprentice dress-maker, so happen there might be four of us there eventually.'

Dilly hung her head as shame enveloped her.

'You're working so hard to fulfil your dream and here's me putting on you.'

Maeve seemed to swell to twice her size. 'What nonsense!' she scolded. 'We're family, and families stick together, don't they? We'll have no more of that talk, young lady. It's a pleasure, so it is, for us to have the weans to stay so it's you that's doing us the favour, really. Isn't that so, Father?'

'Aye, it is,' he agreed amiably, as he puffed on his pipe.

Dilly rushed on, 'It won't be for too long, for I'm to start a new job next week in one of the big houses in Earl's Road. I shall be working for the Farthings, and with what I'll be earning, we should be back on our feet in no time.'

'Would that be Max Farthing?' Daniel enquired. 'The one that seems to own half the businesses in Nuneaton?'

'Yes.' Dilly nodded. 'He has shares in the brick-works and the local pit, and he owns a number of shops as well.'

'He's a decent chap, from what I heard of him,' Daniel said. 'Happen you'll be all right working there, lass. What will you be doing?'

'General maid,' Dilly told him. 'A bit of every-thing, but I won't mind that, and Nell Cotteridge has said she'll keep an eye on Fergal and the children for me when they come home while I'm at work for a few shillings a week. Speaking of which...' She began to fumble in the pocket of her dress but when she took out some change and laid it on the table. Daniel's brow creased into a frown.

'An' just what is that for?'

She flushed. 'Well ... I know it isn't much but

25

it's towards the food the children will eat while they're here. As soon as I start work I'll send you some more.'

'You'll do no such thing,' he said, sliding the money back towards her. 'Now put that away an' we'll hear no more about it! It'd be a poor world if a granda couldn't spend a bit on his own flesh an' blood from time to time.' Then, his voice softening, he went on, 'Why don't you get yourself off to bed, lass, an' have some rest afore you start back tomorrow? Maeve will show you where you'll be sleepin' an' we'll talk some more in the mornin' afore I set off for work an' afore you leave, eh?'

His kindness brought tears to Dilly's eyes. She rose and followed Maeve blindly down the passage towards a door at the front of the house.

'That's where you'll sleep, lass.' Her mother-in-law pointed towards an iron bed that stood against the far wall all made up with fresh crisp bed linen. In another bed nearer to the door Declan and Kian were curled up together looking like angels as they slept.

'We've got Niamh in a little bed in our room for tonight and Seamus will come in with me an' his granda. He'll be better than a stone hot-water bottle.' She winked and finally the tears that Dilly had held back spurted from her eyes and raced down her cheeks.

'Come on, me lass. You're fair worn out, but things will look better in the morning after a good rest. You'll see.'

Maeve pecked her on the cheek and, after blowing out the candle that she had left burning for the boys on the small chest of drawers between the beds, she crept from the room, softly closing the door behind her.

Dilly tumbled onto the mattress, too exhausted even to think of getting undressed. Her head had barely hit the pillow before she was sleeping like a baby.

Chapter Two

'Wake up, lass. I have a nice hot mug o' tea for yer.'

Dilly started awake, and as her eyes opened she found herself staring up into her mother-in-law's kindly face.

'Oh dear... I've overslept, I'm so sorry.' She struggled to sit up but Maeve pressed her back against the pillow and put the steaming mug on the small table at the side of the bed.

'There's no rush yet awhile,' she assured her, as Dilly's eyes flew to the other empty bed. 'And you've no need to fret about the little ones. They're tuckin' into their porridge an' they're bright as buttons, so they are. You lie there an' enjoy your tea. Then you'll find hot water over there in the bowl to wash, along with a clean towel. You've plenty o' time afore you have to get to the ferry.'

Dilly smiled at her gratefully as she bustled from the room, then frowned as heavy footsteps over-head echoed through the ceiling. It sounded as if a herd of elephants was thundering about but she guessed it must be the family or families who rented the upstairs rooms. Pulling herself up in the bed she stared down at her crumpled clothes in dismay, wondering why she hadn't bothered to get undressed the night before. But she had been so exhausted she could barely remember coming to bed, and as there was nothing to be done about it, she decided this was the least of her worries. After swallowing the hot, sweet tea, she clambered out of bed, her breath hanging on the air in front of her. It was bitterly cold in the bedroom, but she was used to that. At least it was warm in the kitchen, unlike at home where sometimes she couldn't even afford to light the fire.

She washed hastily and dragged a comb through her hair before pinning it back securely. Then after running her damp hands down her skirt to get rid of a few of the creases, she picked up her shawl, took a deep breath and went to the kitchen.

'*Mammy!*' Seamus lunged at her, his little face alight, and her heart twisted at the thought of leaving him. Yet he seemed quite content and, after hugging her, hurried back to the warmth of his gran'ma's lap. As she looked about she saw that all of the children were smiling. They were washed, their hair had been brushed and they were wearing the clean clothes she had brought for them. Yesterday's were steaming gently over a great wooden clothes horse in front of the fire. Dilly guessed that Maeve must have been up very early to have got so much work done already.

Niamh was just finishing a large glass of milk and grinned at her, showing off a white moustache. 'I had two whole dishes of porridge wi'

28

sugar on, Mammy,' she informed her, and Dilly stroked her soft hair.

'Aren't you the lucky one?'

The child pottered away as Maeve waved towards a large saucepan on the range telling her, 'Help yourself now, lass, an' make sure it's a good helpin', mind. You've a long way to travel an' I don't want you goin' on an empty stomach.'

Dilly did as she was told and, although she didn't feel hungry, she emptied her dish. Maeve was an excellent cook, one of those rare women who seemed able to produce a meal from nothing. The children wouldn't go hungry.

Maeve produced a large bag of glass marbles from the dresser drawer and, once the children were happily playing with them on the peg rug, joined Dilly at the table. 'I was thinkin' that seein' as it's nearly Christmas I might wait till it's over afore I enrol Declan in school. It'll give him a bit o' time to settle in. What do you think?'

Dilly nodded as Maeve lifted the heavy brown teapot and poured her out another cup of tea. 'That's a fine idea,' she agreed. 'But while the children are staying with you, you must do as you think fit. I know you'll only ever do what's best for them.'

Maeve stared into her daughter-in-law's pale face. She had told herself that she wouldn't mention the baby Declan had told her about the night before, but now she couldn't help herself. Lowering her voice, she asked tentatively, 'Is it true what young Declan was tellin' me as I tucked him in last night... that you recently lost a wean?'

Colour flooded into Dilly's cheeks as she hung

29

her head. She hated lying to her mother-in-law but how could she tell her what had really happened to the baby? Maeve might never forgive her and so she merely nodded as the other woman reached across the table to squeeze her hand.

And then thankfully the footsteps from above distracted them, and as Dilly glanced towards the ceiling, Maeve grinned. 'That's the Scully's brood yer can hear clatterin' about,' she said. 'There's nine of 'em in all. God knows how Mary, their mother, manages, but she does, bless her soul. But I don't suppose she has much choice, does she? She turns 'em out at the rate o' one a year, so she does.'

Dilly smiled but then glancing at the clock her heart sank into her shoes. In another half an hour at most she would have to be on her way, if she were to reach the ferry in time.

'I dare say we should be thinkin' o' gettin' yer things together now,' her mother-in-law said and after reaching into her apron pocket she pushed some coins across the table to her.

'What's this?'

'Our Daniel left it for yer afore he went to work this mornin'. He was hopin' to see you before he set off but you were so worn out last night that he didn't want to disturb you. An' don't go sayin' yer don't want it else you'll get me into trouble. It's only a few shillin's to make sure you an' Fergal have a decent Christmas dinner.'

Dilly opened her mouth to protest. Her in-laws were already doing far too much for them, but Maeve's determined face made her pick up the coins reluctantly and mutter, 'Thank you. I'm

30

sure Fergal will be very grateful.'

Maeve's face broke into a smile when Dilly put them into her bag. They were both distracted then again as a little scuffle broke out between Niamh and Kian,who were squabbling over a particular marble.

'Why don't you nip out into the yard an' use the jacks afore yer leave while I see to these two?' Maeve suggested.

'What's the jacks, Gran'ma?' Seamus piped up.

She chuckled. 'Why, I suppose back at home yer'd call it the privy, but over here it's the jacks. Now, let's think what we're goin' to do with ourselves today when all the chores are done. If it don't start snowin' we could all wrap up warm an' I could take yer a walk to see the ships in the docks. An' then we could go to the church an' yer could meet Father Doherty. When the weather improves me an' yer granda will take you to Enniskerry to see yer uncle Liam an' you can get yer first sight of the Glencullen River. Eh, that's a sight worth seem' sure it is. The countryside in County Wicklow must be some o' the most beautiful in the world. Would yer like that?'

Four little heads nodded in unison as Dilly let herself out of the back door and into the yard. The children seemed quite happy to spend a holiday with their grandparents and she didn't know if that made her feel better or worse. Either way, the time for her to leave them was ticking away and she dreaded it.

Twenty minutes later there were tears all round as the children clung to her skirts. They were quite looking forward to staying with their gran'ma, who spoiled them shamelessly, but they wanted their mammy to stay too.

'It's only for a little while. I shall be coming to fetch you all home before you know it,' Dilly soothed, keeping a tight grip on herself. It really wouldn't do for her to break down in front of them so the sooner she left the better. She couldn't hold back for much longer the tears that were threatening to choke her.

'Just go, pet. They'll be fine,' Maeve assured her, swinging Niamh up onto her hip and placing an arm about Declan's shoulders. It was already more than apparent that she had a soft spot for Declan, probably because he was the first-born, but Dilly was confident that she would treat all of the children fairly.

Seeing the sense in what Maeve had said, and having no wish to prolong her own agony, Dilly hugged each child in turn, planted a kiss on Maeve's cheek then turned abruptly and stumbled away, blinded by tears.

She had gone some way before she allowed her steps to slow. Leaning against a grimy wall, she fished in her pocket and pulled out a handkerchief to dry her eyes. It was then that she became aware of someone watching her and as she glanced to her left she found a small boy, probably no older than her Declan, regarding her solemnly. He was barefoot and his short trousers and shirt were so ragged that it was impossible to distinguish what colour they might once have been. There could certainly be no warmth in them and she knew that he must be freezing. His skin had a bluish tinge to it and his hair straggled onto his shoulders, lank

32

and greasy.

Instinctively, Dilly clutched her bag closer to her. Maeve had warned her to be careful; the streets were full of pickpockets and yet after surveying her solemnly for a while he said quietly, 'Don't cry, missus. If yer lost I'll show yer the way.'

The fact that this child, who must have been in dire straits, could want to help her touched her deeply. 'I'm not lost, but thank you,' she responded and with a shrug he turned to walk away.

'Wait ... do you live round here?' she found herself asking.

He shrugged. 'Most o' the time. Shop doorways an' places like that.'

'But where are your parents?' Dilly was horrified.

He shrugged his shoulders. 'Dunno ... I were left on the steps of the orphanage and I stayed there till last year when I ran away. I'm old enough to look after meself now and I get by an' sometimes if it snows Father Doherty lets me up in the church hall.'

'Do you have a name?'

He eyed her suspiciously for a moment before replying, 'I reckon it's Ben, that's what the nuns in the orphanage told me anyway but me mates call me Nipper. I'm quick on me feet, see? 'Specially if the Constabulary are after me. They wanna put me back in the orphanage but I ain't havin' none o' that. I can look out for meself, so I can.'

Dilly fumbled in her bag and after extracting two precious pennies she held them out to him saying, 'Here, have this. Go and buy yourself some hot food ... and take care.'

He stared at the coins in her palm incredulously, as if he could hardly believe his luck, then snatched the money and began to back away from her. 'Thanks, missus.' He raised a grimy hand in salute, then rushed off like a shot from a gun.

Dilly shook her head. It was hard to believe that orphans of such a young age were forced to live on the streets. Then, realizing that the time was slipping away, she hurried on, intent on catching the ferry.

Late that evening Dilly had just left the railway station in Nuneaton when the first flakes of snow began to fall and she shivered as she huddled in her shawl. But she was almost home and the thought of seeing Fergal lent speed to her feet.

It was dark so there were few people on the streets and soon she was passing through Abbey Green on the way to her small rented house in St Mary's Road. The snow had begun to fall more thickly and her feet were so cold that she could scarcely feel them, but after her encounter with Ben in Dublin she felt blessed. At least she had a home to go to, which was more than could be said for that poor little soul. She hurried down the entry and into the yard, only to come face to face with Madge Bunting.

'Got rid of all yer little 'uns now then, have yer?' she said spitefully.

Dilly gasped. 'I've taken them to have a holiday with their grandparents in Ireland, that's all,' she answered fearfully. She wouldn't have trusted Madge as far as she could throw her.

'Lucky yer could find the money fer the fares.' Madge stared at her suspiciously. 'What wi' losin' yer latest bairn an' yer man bein' crippled, I'm surprised yer can afford to eat, let alone go gaddin' off to Ireland.'

'Fergal's parents sent us the money for the fares,' Dilly answered, while offering up a silent prayer that God might forgive her for lying.

'Hmm, did they now?' Madge narrowed her eyes. 'An' where did yer say the little 'un yer just lost is buried? Can't say as I saw the undertaker callin' the night yer lost it.'

'Look, Madge... I'm really tired,' Dilly blustered. 'And keen to see my husband is all right. So I'll wish you goodnight.' Her heart was in her mouth now. If Madge should discover what had really happened to the baby and the Farthings should get wind of it her job would be in jeopardy and then all this would have been for nothing. She turned about and seconds later burst into the kitchen to see Fergal sitting close to a small fire in the grate with his legs propped up on a stool.

'Ah, thanks be to the Blessed Virgin that yer back safe and sound.' He held out his arms to her. She crossed the room, sank to her knees beside him and hugged him tightly.

'Why, you're frozen through, so you are,' he scolded. 'Now get out o' them wet clothes straight away an' into some dry ones. We'll have some tea while yer tell me how Mammy an' Daddy are an' how the weans are settlin'.'

Dilly did as she was told and after she had put the kettle onto the fire and hung her wet clothes over the clothes horse to dry, she joined him again.

It was wonderful to be back in her own home, although it felt very quiet and empty without the children – but she tried not to think of that now or of her encounter with Madge Bunting.

'Have you eaten?' she asked.

'Nell brought me a bowl o' broth earlier an' then I told her I'd wait for you to get back afore I had anythin' else. I reckon there's bread an' cheese. We could perhaps have that fer tonight, if that'd suit you?'

'It would indeed.' Dilly was so worn out that the last thing she felt like doing was cooking a meal, although she had not eaten since leaving Dublin early that morning. She cut some slices of bread from the loaf in the crock and a small chunk of cheese each. Butter was a forgotten luxury but, washed down with hot tea, the crude meal was filling and she felt slightly better after she'd had it.

Then she sat down, laid her head in Fergal's lap and told him every detail she could remember of what had happened since she had left home, including her meeting with the little orphan on her way back to the ferry. He hung on her every word avidly as his thoughts returned to the place of his birth. All the time he stared into the fire, absently stroking her hair. When she had finished, he asked, 'So you think the weans will be all right there for a while, do you?'

'Oh, yes.' She forced herself to sound positive for his sake although the lonely days without her children stretched endlessly ahead of her. 'Remember, it's only for a short while. Once I start work and we have a regular wage coming in again, I shall be able to fetch them home – and until then

36

your mammy has promised to write every week.'

'Aye, o' course she will,' he agreed, and they lapsed into silence as they stared towards the corner where the Christmas tree would normally stand. There would be no tree this year, no small presents to lay beneath it, no celebrations at all. It would be pointless without their family to share it with them. But at least there was a chance of glimpsing Olivia, as the baby had been named, when she was working at the Farthings', and that thought kept her going.

Her thoughts returned to her confrontation with Madge and she broke out in a sweat. Until that evening Dilly had thought the plan had gone like clockwork but now she was filled with dread: Madge Bunting had her suspicions, but for now all Dilly could do was pray that she would keep them to herself.

Chapter Three

September 1901
Camilla Farthing was in the nursery supervising the nanny as she got her youngest charge ready for bed. The baby had been bathed and changed into the finest clothes that money could buy. Now, taking up the child's bottle, Camilla told the nanny, 'You may go and get yourself a drink now, Nanny. I shall give Miss Olivia her bottle.'

'Very well, ma'am.' The nanny bobbed, left the room and made her way down to the kitchen, where the cook had just removed a tray of scones from the oven.

'The missus is feeding the baby,' she informed Ethel Pegs, the rosy-cheeked cook, disapprovingly. 'I wonder she lets me touch her at all. She was bad enough with the boys when they were little but never as bad as she is with Miss Olivia. She's besotted with that little girl.'

'It's understandable,' the cook replied, as she carried the teapot to the table. 'It's probably because she lost Miss Violet to the measles. It hit her hard, with her bein' the only girl.'

'Even so, she's too possessive – of them all. I wonder why she bothers to employ me sometimes. It's as if she's scared to let them out of her sight since Miss Violet died,' Nanny grumbled, as she gave the tea in the pot a good stir, then placed the cosy over it and ladled sugar into two mugs. 'The poor master seems to have taken a back seat to the children.'

'Ah, but we both know how much he dotes on the boys,' the cook said quietly. 'He brought them all in here earlier on and coaxed me into letting them have some jam tarts before they had their dinner. The missus would have been furious if she'd known.'

'I dare say you didn't take much persuading.' Nanny chuckled. Mrs Pegs made no secret of how fond she was of the four boys, and they could twist her around their little fingers.

Over at the sink, Bessie, the kitchen-cum-general maid, had her arms up to the elbows in hot water as she scoured the dinner pots, but the women knew they could talk freely in front of her. The girl had learned long ago that a word out of place at the wrong time meant a gentle clip around the ear from the cook and so always watched her Ps and Qs. Mr Farthing had fetched Bessie from the workhouse two years ago when she was just eleven years old and for the first time Bessie had discovered what it was like to have a room all to herself, albeit in the servants' quarters at the top of the house. She had formed an attachment to Mrs Pegs, who was the closest thing to a mother she had ever known and soft at heart, even though she tried to present herself as otherwise.

'I was reading in the newspaper earlier on that Toulouse-Lautrec, a French painter, has died an' he was only thirty-seven.' Mrs Pegs changed the subject. 'And it said they're goin' to be launchin' the first submarine next month. Can you believe it? A ship that can go under the sea? It makes you wonder what they'll come up wi' next, don't it.'

Nanny nodded in agreement and the two of them chatted for a while of this and that until Nanny drained her mug and declared, 'I'd best get upstairs and see what the boys are up to now. They're into all sorts of mischief if they're left to their own devices for long. Their father's with them at the moment, reading them a bedtime story.'

'Right you are,' Mrs Pegs said cheerily. 'I'll see you later for your cocoa.' And with that the two women parted.

'What's a submarine, Mrs Pegs?' Bessie piped up, the second Nanny had disappeared. 'How can a ship sail under the water?'

The cook glared at her. 'You're supposed to be

washin' up, not earwiggin',' she scolded. 'Now get on wi' what you're doin' else I'll skelp yer backside for you, me girl.'

With a grin Bessie did as she was told.

On the landing, Nanny met Mr Farthing just leaving the boys' bedroom and he smiled at her. 'Right then, Nanny. They're all tucked in and yawning.'

'All right, sir, I'll just sit in with them till I'm sure they're all asleep.'

He grinned before asking, 'Is Mrs Farthing in with Olivia?'

'Yes she is, sir. She's giving her her bottle.'

He inclined his head and went to the nursery, knowing that he needn't have asked. His wife adored the baby.

Before Violet had died, they had thrown dinner parties, visited friends and gone to the theatre regularly, but all that had changed after their daughter's death when Camilla had become reclusive. He had hoped that once Olivia arrived she would revert to her former self, but she still seemed reluctant even to leave the house. However he hoped that with time she would get over her fear of losing the child and so he remained silent and waited for things to take their course which he was sure they would eventually.

Once he reached the nursery door he tapped it then entered to find Camilla seated at the side of the fire with Olivia sleeping contentedly in her arms.

'Hello, darling.' With the firelight shining on their hair they made such a pretty picture that his

40

niggling fears were allayed for a time. 'And how is the little madam today?' he asked, tiptoeing across to them.

'Quite beautiful as always.'

She was right on that score. Ten-month-old Olivia had her thumb in her mouth and, with a mop of springy copper curls and long eyelashes curled on rosy cheeks, she looked like a little cherub. 'I fear you're spoiling her, darling.' He smiled. 'Nanny says she's growing quite crafty and doesn't like to be put down.'

'Nanny is not paid to have opinions,' Camilla retorted indignantly.

'No, of course not,' he agreed hastily. Then, on a safer note, 'Perhaps now that she's asleep you could put her in her crib and come along to say goodnight to the boys. Nanny is with them at the moment but I'm sure they would like to see you.'

'Of course.' She stood up and carried Olivia to the magnificent crib she had insisted should be bought for her in London. It was worthy of a princess, the drapes heavily trimmed with lace and pink ribbons as were all the clothes that Camilla insisted Olivia should have. She had also had the nursery completely refurbished: it had taken an army of tradesmen to bring the room up to the standard she had required. He had lost count of how much he had spent on the child since her arrival, but he begrudged not a penny if it made his wife happy. He watched her tuck the baby in then, holding out his hand, he quietly led her out of the nursery.

All was quiet when they entered the boys' room, but the instant their sons saw their mother they sat

41

up and held out their arms to her.

'Mother, will you read us the story about the big bad wolf?' Oscar, the eldest, pleaded. At six years old he was a well-built child with white-blond hair and blue eyes, exactly the same colour as his mother's.

'I'm sure Father said he had already read you your bedtime story,' she answered with a smile as she crossed the room to sit on the side of the bed. Nanny sniffed, but wisely held her tongue.

Lawrence and Samuel, the five-year-old twins who had their father's looks, with their thick brown hair and greeny-blue eyes, were in the two small beds next to Oscar's. They were as alike as two peas in a pod, and even Nanny sometimes got them mixed up, yet in nature they were total opposites. Lawrence was the quiet one, never happier than when he was looking at picture books or playing with his cars while Samuel was the more adventurous and outgoing of the two, always into some mischief or other. In the final bed was Harvey. At four he was the one who gave his parents the most cause for concern. He had the temperament of an angel and was undoubtedly Nanny's favourite but he had never been robust and was small for his age. Harvey seemed to catch every cough and cold that was going round and had to spend almost the entire winter indoors, for bad weather brought on his asthma. Of all the children he was most like his mother. He had the same soft white-blonde hair and the same fragile beauty about him.

'Have you been in the nursery with Olivia?' Harvey asked, and his mother nodded as she smoothed his unruly locks from his forehead. Like his mother, Harvey doted on his baby sister, which had surprised everyone; as he had been the youngest when she arrived, they had thought he might be a little jealous of her. But this had not proved to be the case at all. From the moment he had set eyes on her he had treated her like a doll and would spend ages just standing by her crib, talking to her and admiring her. Oscar was much the same, but the twins were typical four-year-olds more interested in their pastimes than a mewling baby.

'Are you still going to take us out on our ponies tomorrow, Father?' Oscar asked excitedly, and when Max nodded, he clapped his plump little hands with delight. Both he and Samuel had their own ponies, a Christmas present from their father, and they were never happier than when they were allowed to ride them. When asked if he would like one too, Lawrence had shaken his head. He would much sooner be indoors looking at his books. At just four years old he could say his alphabet and count to twenty without any help, which made his father immensely proud. Max would often tell him he would be the scholar of the family and already he had high hopes that Lawrence would go on to university in years to come.

Already he was looking at suitable boarding schools for them to attend when they were a little older, for he believed that children should have a good education, especially boys. Camilla was opposed to the idea but he hoped that in time he would talk her round and that she would realize how much it would benefit them. He knew that

Camilla loved all of her children but he suspected that Olivia had fast become her favourite. She had been much the same with Violet. Perhaps women felt a special closeness to their daughters? It certainly appeared so but he thanked God that at least his wife had come out of the lethargy she had sunk into after Violet's death. Their daughter had been just a few months old when she died, and until Olivia had arrived Max had feared for his wife's health and sanity.

Camilla went from bed to bed, planting kisses on the boys' cheeks and tucking the blankets up beneath their chins. Then she wished them all sweet dreams and left the room with Max.

'Mary and George have invited us for supper this evening,' Max mentioned hopefully, as they wandered along the landing. 'George said that they hadn't seen you for ages, and they're very good company, as you know. You've still plenty of time to get ready, if you'd like to go. I thought a break from the house might do you good.'

She paused outside the nursery door and stared at him from her magnificent blue eyes. 'I won't if you don't mind, darling. Nanny mentioned earlier on that she thought Olivia might be coming down with a little cold so I ought to stay close in case she needs me. In fact I think I shall just check her again now but I'll come down and join you for a drink in the drawing room, shall I?'

Swallowing his disappointment he nodded and as she disappeared off into the nursery he made his way downstairs.

Chapter Four

'Aw, come on in quick outta the cold, pet,' Mrs Pegs urged, as Dilly arrived for work one cold, blustery October morning. It had rained steadily all night and she was soaked to the skin. 'Get that wet shawl over by the fire to dry an' I'll make yer a nice hot brew afore yer start work.'

Dilly did as she was told, rubbing her hands together to try to get some warmth back into them.

'I reckon we're in fer a bad winter,' the cook said, as she bustled about.

Dilly nodded. 'Happen you're right. The leaves are coming down off the trees like nobody's business and it's enough to cut you in two out there.'

Her first job of the day was to clean out all the downstairs grates and get the fires going before the family came down for breakfast but she was sure she could spare a few minutes and the thought of a hot cup of tea was very welcome.

'So how's that handsome husband o' yours?' Cook asked some minutes later when they were both sitting at the enormous table with steaming mugs in front of them.

'Not too good to be honest at the moment, Mrs Pegs,' Dilly answered. 'Although he has no movement in his legs any more the wet and the cold cause him a great deal of pain for some reason. To be honest I hoped that it might be a good sign so

45

I called the doctor in to take a look at him but the doctor seemed to think it was normal.'

'What a shame.' Cook shook her head. 'It can't be easy for him after him bein' such an active chap.'

'It isn't,' Dilly admitted, and then longing to confide in someone she went on, 'He's changed lately ... become sort of bitter if you know what I mean? Don't get me wrong, I'm not blaming him. Fergal is a proud man and I know it must be torture for him to have to sit back and watch me become the breadwinner. I'm just hoping that now we're getting back on our feet and once I've fetched the children home he'll be back to the man he was before.' She took a long swig of her tea as Cook looked on sympathetically. Mrs Pegs could imagine how hard it must have been for her to have to take her children to Ireland and leave them there, even if it was only a temporary arrangement.

'Do you have no family over here that could have helped you?' she asked kindly.

Dilly shook her head. 'My father died when I was quite small, so I can hardly remember him, and my mother brought me up single-handed but she died, too, just before I met Fergal. She was a wonderful seamstress and it was her as taught me to sew. I was renting a room above the grocer's in Edward Street with two other girls when I met Fergal. His parents didn't approve of me. I wasn't of the same faith, you see, being Irish; they're Catholics.'

'So how did you get around it?' Mrs Pegs was fascinated. Dilly had never spoken about her private life before.

'I converted to his faith. It wasn't hard, really, because although I had been brought up as a Christian, my mam and me rarely went to church. After that, things got easier, and since we've been married his family have been so kind to me.' She stood up. 'I'd best get on. The missus won't be pleased if she comes down to a cold dining room.'

As the cook watched her go, her heart was heavy for the young woman. It must have been hard for her to take her children to Dublin, though from what Dilly had told her, the poor soul hadn't been faced with much choice. Still, at least things were looking up a little for her now. She had a regular job and seemed to have come to terms with her husband's disability.

Bessie entered the kitchen then and broke her chain of thought.

'Right, young lady, let's start the breakfast, shall we?' Mrs Pegs said, and Bessie scuttled into the pantry to get the bacon and eggs.

'Can I start to fry the bacon? I'll do it just as yer showed me,' the girl asked hopefully, and Mrs Pegs nodded. Bessie loved being allowed to tackle the easier meals, and Mrs Pegs enjoyed teaching her how to cook.

'Just so long as yer remember the master likes it crispy,' she said sternly, although her eyes were smiling.

'I'll make sure,' Bessie promised, and reached for a heavy frying pan. In no time at all they were hard at work.

Dilly was cleaning the grates and lighting the fires,

starting in the dining room. It was a messy job, getting all the cold ashes up, but she had it off pat now and soon the fire was blazing cheerfully. The ashes were in a metal bucket to the side of her and she was just about to take it outside when Mr Farthing entered the room.

'Oh, sorry, sir,' she faltered, blushing furiously.

'Please don't be.' He smiled. 'I have an early appointment at one of my hat factories in Atherstone so I thought I'd make an early start. Don't rush on my account.' He stared at her then and, as always, he saw Olivia's mother looking back at him. No matter how hard he tried, he always saw her as Olivia's mother although, to give the woman credit, she had never once tried to interfere or said anything untoward. It was quite the opposite, she had stuck strictly to their bargain. He couldn't even begin to contemplate how hard that must have been for her. To be so close to the child every day, knowing she was her own flesh and blood yet be unable to acknowledge the fact. He had noticed that she would scurry to the child's perambulator and peer at her whenever she thought no one was looking, but he had never mentioned it.

'How are the family, Mrs Carey?' he asked, and she blushed even more deeply, if that was possible. She always tried to keep out of his and his wife's way but she could hardly ignore him, could she?

'Er, the children are still in Dublin with their grandparents, sir, but I'm hoping to bring them home shortly.'

'I would consider it an honour if you would allow me to assist you. It is the least I can do, considering what you have done for my wife and myself.'

She stared at him open-mouthed as he took some notes from his pocket and held them out to her. 'I'm sure that will be enough to get the children safely home and tide you over for a few weeks.'

Her eyes became steely and her back straightened. She shook her head vigorously. 'Thank you kindly, sir, but I'm not a charity case just yet. Now, if you'll excuse me, I must get on.' With that she sailed past him, like a ship at sea, leaving him to stare after her in bewilderment. He had just offered her more money than she could earn in months but she had refused it. She was clearly a proud, if somewhat stubborn, woman. He shook his head. Women were strange creatures, there was no doubt about it, and he was sure he would never understand them if he lived to be a hundred, which was highly unlikely. But all the same he felt himself admiring the young woman's pride and courage.

Outside, Dilly hurried to the cinder path behind the stable block with the ash bucket, taking great gulps of air. Her encounter with Mr Farthing had shaken her, and now she felt rather guilty for how she had spoken to him. He had tried to be kind ... but she could only imagine what Fergal would have said had she gone home with a pocketful of money. She emptied the bucket and set off to light the fire in the drawing room.

As the morning progressed she began to feel a little better. At least working here she was in the warm, and there were such beautiful things in every room that she never tired of looking at them. The Farthings' home was a huge red-brick Victorian villa set well back from the road behind large wrought-iron gates and a neatly clipped privet hedge. The servants and the gardener kept it running like clockwork, which was just as well: Mrs Farthing never lifted a finger – she was far too busy spending time with the children and more than happy to leave the house to the servants. Although Dilly did not dislike the woman, she sometimes wondered if she ever realized just how lucky she was.

Now as she made her way back to the house with the empty bucket, Madge Bunting appeared at the door of the laundry room, enveloped in a huge white apron, her face glowing from the steam, and glared at Dilly. Before her last pregnancy, Dilly had worked for the Farthings on a casual basis for a number of years. If they threw a party she would come in either to wait at table or help in the kitchen, which had led to her permanent employment and to the bad feeling between herself and Madge. Since then Madge had worked as a laundry maid for three days a week but it was a hard, back-breaking job, stuck outside in the cold laundry room, and had made her even more resentful of Dilly.

Now, as Dilly made her way back to the house, her lips curled back from her rotting teeth in a sneer. 'Ooh, if it ain't the little favourite,' she quipped nastily.

Dilly flushed. 'You know that's not true, Madge.' She hoped to avoid a confrontation but Madge

50

was in a bad mood. Her hands were cracked and sore from the hours they spent in water and her back ached. Compared to hers Dilly's job was a pleasure.

'So 'ow come you're working in there in the warm an' I'm stuck out 'ere?'

'At least we both have jobs,' Dilly pointed out, hoping to appease her.

'Huh! We do that, but we both know I earn barely enough to live on. Makes yer wonder why *you* were the chosen one, don't it?'

Dilly hurried on, disquieted. She had felt nervous of Madge ever since she had questioned her shortly after Olivia's birth and dreaded what would happen should Madge ever discover the truth. For now she had to act normally and try not to antagonize her.

When Dilly's pregnancy had begun to show she had been at the house to wait at table when Camilla Farthing had asked to speak to her, following the dinner party she and Max had hosted. She had asked outright if Dilly would consider letting her adopt the child when it was born. At first Dilly had been horrified and indignant. But as the months went on and money was short at home, she had been forced to consider the offer. Finally she had realized that this was the only option she had to put food in her other children's bellies. She had reeled at the offer Camilla had made her but, even so, she had turned it down: she asked only for enough to get her children to Ireland. Any more than that and she could not have lived with her conscience. The deal had been struck and from that moment on everything had

51

been planned, down to the finest detail. Camilla Farthing had barely left the house since she had lost Violet more than a year before, so they had all agreed it would be easy for her to pretend that she was pregnant again. She had begun to wear loose-fitting clothes and the nursery was prepared, with only the trusted housekeeper, the nanny, the doctor and the solicitor, who would draw up the adoption papers, privy to the secret – the Farthings' sons were too young to understand that anything was amiss and it was agreed that Dilly would send word as soon as the child was born. Now the deed was done things would be a million times worse should Madge ever find out about it and she shuddered at the thought.

Sighing, she made her way back into the house just in time to see the four boys racing down the stairs ahead of Nanny.

'Boys, *please*,' the nanny huffed, as she chased after them. 'Slow down! We're not in a playground!'

Dilly smiled as she entered the drawing room to begin the dusting. It appeared that boys would be boys whatever class they came from and from where she was standing this was just as it should be. She began to take down the expensive china ornaments and silver photograph frames with pictures of the children. When she came to the latest one of the baby, in pride of place on the mantelpiece, she paused to gaze at it tenderly. Olivia was sitting up now and reminded her a little of Niamh at that age. The pain was there again, sharp as ever. Still, it wouldn't be long now until the children were all home where they belonged and she vowed that she would never send them away again, even if she had to resort to selling her body on the streets.

When she left the Farthings' house that evening the wind was worse than it had been that morning and the rain was lashing down, soaking through her thin clothes within minutes. She had not even reached the end of Manor Court Road before her hair was plastered to her head, and by the time she got home she was shivering.

Thankfully now that Fergal could get about a little in his chair he was able to keep the fire in and she crossed to it and held her blue hands out to its warmth. It was so windy that the windows were rattling in their frames and the curtains were lifting in the draughts, but for all that Dilly was glad to be home. She was feeling decidedly unwell and it had been a long day.

'You look worn out, lass,' Fergal said, with concern, as she stripped her dripping shawl from her thin shoulders. 'Sit yerself down an' I'll dish you up some o' this stew that Nell brought round earlier.'

Normally Dilly would have objected, but tonight she sat down meekly, too chilled even to get out of her wet clothes. What with Madge and the terrible weather, it hadn't been a good day.

'There's a letter come today from Mammy,' Fergal informed her.

'How are they all?' she asked.

Normally she read and reread Maeve's letters, but tonight she was so weary she could scarcely keep her eyes open. Her days started at six and she rarely got home before seven in the evening, but at least their savings were swelling, they had paid off their rent arrears and their children should be back with her and Fergal in time for Christmas.

'Mammy says Declan is doing well at the local school.'

Dilly frowned. Most of Maeve's letters were full of Declan, and she worried that it would be hard for her to let the child return home. He was clearly the favourite and, if the letters were anything to go by, the sun rose and set with him, but Dilly was determined to bring him home. Otherwise all the long months of scrimping and saving would have been for nothing. The only thing that she had spent any amount of money on was the wheeled chair fashioned by a local carpenter, which had given Fergal a small measure of independence. It was a heavy contraption but at least now he could manoeuvre himself into it and get outside to the shared privy so Nell no longer had to look after him while Dilly was at work. The cheap oil paints and blank canvases she had bought him in the spring had eased his boredom a little, although she doubted he was a talented artist.

'Mammy an' Daddy took the children to see their uncle Liam in Enniskerry last weekend,' he went on. 'She says they had a wonderful time an' by all accounts the smallholding is coming along a treat. Mammy reckons it shouldn't be too much longer before she an' Daddy can join him there. Won't that be grand, eh? I know how much they hate livin' in inner Dublin, so I do.'

The stew was simmering on a trivet above the low fire. Fergal wheeled himself clumsily into the kitchen, and returned with a dish and a spoon. He ladled some out for her.

'Did you see the baby today?' he asked, as he often did, but tonight Dilly was in no mood for his questions.

'Yes, but only when I took some coal up to the nursery just before I left. Mrs Farthing and the nanny were bathing her.'

'Is she well?'

'Of course she is. She gets the best of care. Far better than we could ever have given her,' Dilly snapped. Didn't he realize that she missed the child too? That every day being so close to her, unable to acknowledge her as her own, was sheer torture? They had struck a deal, so why must Fergal constantly keep on about it? She often felt he blamed her for their decision and regretted it, but what was to be done about it now? They had given up all rights to the child on the day she had been handed to the Farthings and there could be no going back.

Fergal stared at her, his expression sullen. Disheartened, Dilly pushed the food around the dish for a while, then handed it back to him saying shortly, 'Here, you finish it. I'm not really hungry. In fact I think I'll take the hot brick out of the oven and turn in for the night.' She was aware that a number of jobs were waiting to be done, like getting some more coal in, but this evening she was too weary to care, and as Fergal watched she stripped off her wet clothes, letting them fall into a damp heap on the floor, slid on her nightgown and clambered into the iron bed standing against one wall. They had both slept downstairs since

55

Fergal had had his accident and tonight she was glad of it; at least it was moderately warm in that room. Fergal fetched the hot brick for her, and after wrapping it in a towel, slipped it beneath the blankets by her feet. Then he felt her forehead. 'You're burning up,' he said worriedly. 'Is there anything I can get you?'

She shook her head and in minutes had fallen into an uneasy sleep.

It was the gentle pressure of Fergal's hand on her arm that woke her the next morning and she started as she glanced towards the tin clock on the mantelpiece. It stood in solitary splendour now for all the other knick-knacks of any value that they had once possessed had long since found their way to the pawn shop in Queens Road.

'It's almost eight o'clock,' she gasped in a panic. 'I'm late for work. Why didn't you wake me earlier?' She swung her feet over the side of the bed onto the cold lino but a wave of dizziness made her flop back against the pillows.

'You'll not be goin' to work today,' Fergal told her firmly. 'I've already got Nell's lad to run to the Farthings and tell them you're too ill to go in. Just lie there. I'll have you a nice hot drink ready in no time. The kettle's almost on the boil.'

'I don't want a drink,' she objected, shivering uncontrollably, but then she was asleep again, locked in a dream where she was swimming against the tide of the ocean to fetch the children home.

The next thing she became aware of was gentle hands mopping her brow with a cold cloth. She forced her eyes open and saw Nell smiling down at her. 'Ah, so you're back with us, are yer, luvvie.'

'Nell ... I'm late for work... What time is it?'

'It's two days on since the last time yer asked an' a right scare you've given us an' all,' Nell informed her.

Dilly's mouth felt as if it was full of cotton wool and there was a pain in her chest and behind her eyes as she stared up at her neighbour in bemusement.

'We've had to have the doctor into yer. Yer've had pneumonia,' Nell informed her solemnly. 'An' it's hardly surprisin' with how hard yer've been workin' yerself. Still, thank the Lord yer over the worst now an', God willin', yer'll be as right as rain in a couple o' weeks or so, if yer do as yer told.'

'A couple of *weeks!*' Dilly was horrified. 'But I can't afford to be off work for all that time. And how much did the doctor charge? We can't afford his bills.'

'Huh! If it weren't for Dr Beasley an' this here man o' yours nursin' yer round the clock, I reckon we'd be measurin' yer for a coffin so be grateful fer small mercies,' Nell scolded gently.

Fergal had wheeled his chair to the side of the bed to join them. Seeing the worry and fear etched into his face, Dilly felt contrite for the way she had spoken to him on the night she had taken ill. 'I'm so sorry, love,' she muttered, but he brushed her apology aside with a wave of his hand.

'It should be me that's sorry fer workin' yer so hard, so it should,' he ground out. Then, seeing her face drop, he added hastily, 'But you're over the worst now an' that's all that matters.' Then, to Nell, he said, 'I'll never be able to thank you enough for what you've done these past days.'

57

He and Dilly knew that many people wouldn't give Nell the time of day. She dressed a little loudly and was very fond of her rouge and powder. She didn't suffer fools lightly either and was well known for speaking her mind, but over the last couple of years she had been a true friend to them. There had been many a time she had turned up with a dish of stew or a shovelful of coal in their darkest hours, and not a day went by when they didn't consider themselves fortunate to know her.

'That's enough o' that sloppy talk,' she barked. 'An' now yer back in the land o' the livin' I'm off to cook me old man his tea else he'll not be best pleased.'

With that she ambled away, leaving Dilly and Fergal to their own devices.

Chapter Five

Over the next few days Dilly gradually improved to the point at which she could sit propped up in bed and complain of being bored. She still wasn't strong enough to potter about yet but she was used to being busy and began to feel frustrated.

'As it happens I've got a pile o' repairs that need doin',' Nell told her matter-of-factly. 'I never were much use wi' a needle an' I don't reckon my Fred's got a single shirt that ain't missin' a button or two. There's a pile o' darnin' an' all. I'll fetch the bloody lot round an' that'll keep yer occupied. Happen it'll shut yer up.' And true to her word she returned shortly after with her arms full of clothes and some needles and cottons of various colours.

Dilly found she enjoyed doing the repairs and Nell was full of praise for her work. 'Would yer look at that hem now!' She held up a skirt to the light and smiled approvingly. 'The stitches are that small and neat yer can scarcely see 'em.'

Dilly grinned. 'My mother was a seamstress. She was always sewing by the light of a candle when I went to sleep and she'd be sewing again when I woke up in the morning. I suppose I picked up a few tips from her. To be honest, I'd like nothing better than to become a seamstress but there's not much call for them round here, what with there being only one decent dress shop in town.'

At that moment their conversation was halted by the sound of horse's hooves outside and Nell shot off to the window to investigate then turned to tell Dilly and Fergal, 'Eeh, there's a spankin' pony an' trap outside the house, wi' a smartly dressed gentleman climbin' down from it. Who do yer think it might be?'

It was rare for anyone in their row to have visitors, especially in a pony and trap.

Footsteps sounded loudly in the entry and the next minute someone was rapping on the back door.

'See who it is, would you, Nell?' Dilly asked, and Nell rushed away to do as she was told.

'I wonder if it would be possible to speak to Mrs Carey for a moment, if she is well enough yet to receive visitors.'

Dilly felt the colour flood into her cheeks. It was Mr Farthing – she recognized his voice – but whatever could he be doing here? Her heart skipped a beat as a possibility occurred to her. Perhaps he had come to dismiss her because she'd had time off.

Seconds later he strode into the room and her embarrassment increased as he removed his hat and gave a slight bow. She was painfully aware of how awful she must have looked. She had not been strong enough to wash her hair since before her illness, and what would he think of her sitting in bed in her old nightgown with a shawl about her shoulders? Her home, too, left a lot to be desired, after the residence he was used to. Everything in it was second-hand and mismatched, even if it was neat and tidy. It had looked even worse since Fergal had had his wheeled chair for now everything was squashed against the walls so that he could get about easily. Now she saw the old peg rug and the overstuffed horsehair sofa through a stranger's eyes and squirmed with embarrassment. But she needn't have worried. Mr Farthing glanced towards the painting Fergal was working on. It was standing on an easel against the window, a landscape of the view from Hartshill Hayes and easily the best he had done. The visitor made no comment. Instead, after a nod of acknowledgement to Fergal, he kept his eyes trained on Dilly.

'Mrs Carey, I do hope I find you on the road to recovery. My wife and I were very concerned to hear how ill you have been and she asked me to bring these for you.' He placed a large basket on the table, full of every fruit imaginable, apples, oranges, grapes, bananas and peaches. She was struck dumb, although she didn't for a moment

60

believe that Mrs Farthing would have had anything to do with it. Dilly had the impression that the woman suffered her presence in the house only because it had been part of the agreement and she guarded Olivia jealously, whipping her away whenever Dilly strayed too close.

'I apologize for calling unannounced,' Max Farthing went on, 'and I know it isn't usual for an employer to visit his staff in their homes, but Mrs Pegs and Bessie have been concerned about you and assured me you wouldn't mind.' He glanced apologetically towards Fergal but Fergal glowered at him and looked away.

'Th – thank you very much,' Dilly stammered, and he smiled at her, appearing quite at ease as he reached into the pocket of the smart overcoat he was wearing.

'I also needed to pass on your wages, plus a little extra for anything you might need to speed your recovery,' he said.

Now it was Dilly who frowned. 'But I'm not due any wages,' she protested.

'Of course you are. When my employees are sick, with a genuine illness, I insist that they are paid. You can't help being sick. And, furthermore, my wife said that you are not even to think of returning to work until you are fully recovered. The rest of the staff are covering your job for you.'

Dilly gulped, at a loss for words. She saw Fergal's mouth compress into a thin, straight line. He was a proud man and she knew he wouldn't be happy to take money that he considered she had not earned.

'Thank you very kindly, sir,' he said, between

gritted teeth, 'but we're managing, so the money is not needed.'

Max flashed him a charming smile. 'But, Mr Carey, as I explained, all my staff are treated the same. Please accept it.' And then before Fergal could object further he placed the money on the table and backed towards the door saying, 'Now if you will excuse me I really must be going but just one more thing. I also like to pay any doctor's bills that my staff incur so if you would be kind enough to let me know the cost I will be more than happy to reimburse you. And now I will wish you all a very good day. Please do not hesitate to be in touch if there's anything you need. Goodbye.' And with that he placed his hat back on his head, gave another formal little bow and marched out as they all stared after him, open-mouthed.

Nell was the first to break the silence. 'Well, I'll be! I thought he'd come to give yer yer marchin' orders. Who'd have thought it, eh? What a kind man – handsome an' all.' She gave Dilly a cheeky wink. 'I wouldn't be kickin' him out o' bed in a hurry. I don't mind tellin' yer.'

Strangely, Dilly had never noticed before but now she thought about it she supposed that Max Farthing *was* a handsome man. He was so tall that his muscular frame had almost blocked out the light in the doorway. That, with the mop of dark hair that was inclined to curl, no matter how much Macassar oil he plastered on it, and the kindly blue eyes, made him quite striking and the realization brought a little colour to her cheeks.

Fergal's face was still set but Dilly couldn't help smiling. You could always rely on Nell to say what

62

she thought should she offend or please. Even so, she knew that Fergal was unhappy so she avoided looking at him as Nell crossed to admire the huge basket of fruit.

'Bugger me,' she gasped. 'There's enough here to feed an army. It must 'ave cost a king's ransom.'

'Well, Fergal and I will never eat it all on our own, that's for sure, so please take some home with you for the family,' Dilly urged.

'I won't say no. I can't remember the last time I got me teeth into a nice juicy peach. Lord knows where 'e managed to get 'old o' these at this time o' year. They ain't even in season.' Nell chuckled as she selected some of the fruit. Then she whooped with delight. 'Look here – there's chocolates an' all. An' a big jar o' jam an' another o' marmalade. It's like Christmas an' birthdays all come at once.'

'It was very kind of them to think of me,' Dilly said, placing emphasis on 'them'. She didn't want Fergal to be any more upset than he clearly already was. Secretly, she was vastly relieved. She had been worried about her lost wages. While she wasn't earning they had been forced to break into the small amount she had managed to save, which meant that the children's return would be delayed. Now they would be back to where they had been, although she was sure that Fergal would flatly refuse to allow Mr Farthing to pay the doctor's bills.

'Wasn't it thoughtful of them, Fergal?' she ventured, and he nodded reluctantly. He still wasn't happy about it, she knew, but beggars couldn't be choosers.

'Aye, I suppose it was,' he admitted grudgingly, and Dilly gave a small sigh of relief. She didn't feel strong enough to get into a dispute with him at the moment but thankfully he appeared to have accepted the situation, for now at least.

'Now yer know what yer know, yer needn't rush back to work if yer gettin' paid.' Nell chuckled as she headed for the door. 'I've got some bread bakin'. I'll drop yer a loaf round when it's ready an' yer can have some o' that lovely jam on it fer yer tea. An' see as yer get some o' that fruit down yer an' all. It's good fer yer.'

When she had gone Dilly couldn't help but smile. Fergal often remarked that Nell was 'as common as muck', and happen she was, if truth be told, but for all that she had a heart as big as a bucket and Dilly didn't know what they would do without her.

Fergal was still looking decidedly grumpy so she turned her attention back to the sewing and left him to come out of his strop.

Outside, Nell almost collided with Madge Bunting, who had seen Mr Farthing leave. But little got past Madge as her neighbours knew to their cost.

'Crikey, fruit from the boss!' Madge commented sarcastically. 'I wonder what little Miss Sweetness an' Light 'as done to deserve that, eh?'

'The poor love nearly died,' Nell snapped, wrinkling her nose in distaste at the ripe smell that issued from the other woman. 'Mr Farthing was merely doin' what any good employer would do an' showin' 'is concern.'

'*Huh!*' Madge sneered, showing her rotting teeth. 'I wonder if he'd do the same if it 'ad been me 'as 'ad been bad!'

Nell clamped her mouth shut, afraid she might say too much. Admittedly, Madge had a hard life: everyone knew her old man went to work once in a blue moon, and even then he usually passed most of what he'd earned across the nearest bar. Under other circumstances Nell might have felt sorry for her, but Madge was such a dirty, disagreeable woman that she found it hard to feel any sympathy for her. The Bunting children had all left home as soon as they were able to, apart from Sidney, the youngest. It was hardly surprising – when they were little they had been infested with head lice and had run about barefoot. It was a joke among the neighbours that the house was so filthy even the rats were reluctant to go into it.

Nell stuck her nose into the air and was about to walk on but Madge wasn't done with her yet and now she stopped her dead in her tracks when she said, 'Didn't it never strike yer as strange that the Careys' baby died the very same night as the Farthings had their baby daughter?'

Nell gulped deep in her throat before saying warily, 'What of it?'

With an evil glint in her eye, Madge shrugged. 'Just seems funny that I didn't see no midwife arrive nor no undertaker come to take the baby away. An' I could 'ave swore I saw Dilly creepin' out late that night carryin' somethin'.'

'You must 'ave been mistaken,' Nell replied, regaining her composure. It wouldn't do to let Madge know the true situation – she was capable of causing endless grief for both the Careys and the Farthings. 'As it happens I delivered the child,' she told the woman coldly. 'There was no time to call the midwife, an' you must 'ave missed the undertaker. You've got an overactive imagination, I reckon, Madge. But now I must gerron. Goo'day.' And with that she moved away, forcing herself to put one foot in front of the other, but her heart was racing.

Madge watched her disappear into her cottage, then hurried away, with a thoughtful expression on her face.

As promised, Max Farthing had called at Dilly's home each week after that first visit, bringing her wages and a small basket of treats from Mrs Pegs. During his second visit he had crossed to Fergal's painting, which was now finished, and asked, 'Did you paint this, Mr Carey?'

'Aye, I did,' Fergal answered guardedly. He was still not happy with the arrangement but he had remained silent each time Dilly's employer had called.

'It's very good.' Max bent to study it more closely and then shocked them when he asked, 'Would you consider selling it?'

Fergal's mouth gaped open, giving him the appearance of a goldfish. 'S-*sell* it?' he blustered. 'It's not good enough for that. It's just a pastime. I do it to keep meself occupied while Dilly's at work, so I do!'

'I have to disagree with you,' Max answered calmly. 'It's very good, and it would be nice to have a painting of a local beauty spot, especially once it has been professionally framed. Name your price.'

Fergal glanced at Dilly, bemused. Never in his wildest dreams had he thought any of his work good enough to sell, particularly not to the likes of Max Farthing.

'Why don't you make us an offer, sir?' Dilly suggested.

Max tapped his chin thoughtfully. 'Two guineas?'

Fergal was dumbstruck. It was a fortune.

'Well, Fergal, are you willing to sell it and are you happy with the offer?' Dilly asked.

Out of his depth, Fergal nodded. 'Aye, the answer is yes to both questions if Mr Farthing is quite sure that he wants it.'

'I am.' Max Farthing beamed. 'I shall be back later to collect and pay for it, if I may?' He bowed politely and departed, leaving Dilly and Fergal staring at each other in astonishment. Secretly, Max had no intention of having the painting framed. As Fergal had admitted, it was not even that good but he had felt so saddened to see the way the family were forced to live that he had seen it as a way of getting some extra money to them and saving their pride.

'Do you know what this means?' Dilly said excitedly, after Max Farthing had left. Without waiting for an answer, she hurried on, 'It means that I shall be able to fetch the children home sooner than we'd hoped to.'

Fergal nodded; even he could not argue that point.

It was three weeks later that Dilly returned to

work. Her recovery had taken longer than she had expected. Even then she did not feel completely well, but she didn't want to take advantage of Max Farthing's kindness.

'Why, yer a sight for sore eyes, lass,' Mrs Pegs exclaimed, when Dilly entered the kitchen on her first day back. Then, staring at her pale face, she asked, 'But are yer sure yer quite ready to be here? Yer still look awful pale.'

'That's because I've been shut up at home and I've had no fresh air,' Dilly assured her.

'Hmm!' The cook didn't seem convinced as she ushered Dilly to the table and poured her a mug of tea. 'Well... all the same I want yer to take yer time. No sense in overdoin' it, else you'll be back in bed.'

'I'll help yer as much as I can,' Bessie piped up, delighted to see Dilly. She had missed her while she was away.

Dilly smiled at her, 'Actually, I need to have a word with Mrs Farthing because I have to ask her a favour.'

Mrs Pegs noted that Dilly seemed worried.

'The thing is I wondered if she'd let me have Saturday and Sunday off. I know it's only my first day back but I want to go and fetch the children home. As I only work half-days at the weekend, I'm hoping she won't object.'

Mrs Pegs beamed. 'Fetch the children home! Why that's wonderful news and I'm sure the missus won't mind. They'll be home in time for Christmas – won't that be grand, eh?'

In fact it was Mr Farthing Dilly saw first when he came downstairs shortly afterwards.

'Mrs Carey, you're back!' He smiled. 'And feeling recovered, I hope. Please don't overdo things.'

'Thank you, sir. I'm much better, but I was wondering...' She gulped before going on. 'I was wondering if I might have the weekend off? I know it's an awful cheek to ask seeing as I've only just returned to work but I'm hoping to get the ferry to Dublin to fetch my children home. They've been gone almost a year and their father and I would dearly love to have them home for Christmas but I promise to make the hours up over the next couple of weeks.'

'Why, of course you can, and there will be no extra hours,' he replied. Then in a lower tone, he asked, 'Do you have sufficient funds for the journey? If not I could–'

'Oh, no, sir, thank you,' she responded hastily, as her cheeks reddened. He'd done so much for her family already.

'Very well. Why don't you finish at lunchtime on Friday? Then you could set off earlier and spend a little time with the family in Dublin before coming back.'

Again, Dilly was touched by his kindness and went about her work with a smile.

On Friday afternoon, having made sure she had all she needed for the journey, Dilly kissed Fergal and set off for the railway station with a spring in her step. It would get her to the ferry for the night crossing and she couldn't help but think that at this time tomorrow she would be with her children at last. Fergal had written to his mother the week before to let her know that Dilly would be coming, and now she could hardly wait to set eyes on them. It had hurt so much to be apart from her family, but now that she and Fergal had a regular wage coming in, she hoped they would never have to resort to such a desperate measure again.

The train journey was uneventful but the ferry crossing was another matter: Dilly spent half of it leaning over the rail depositing everything she had eaten that day in the sea. It was bitterly cold and the water was so choppy that the ferry bobbed about like a cork, and when they finally pulled into the port of Dublin, she breathed a huge sigh of relief. There had been times during the night, as the boat had risen, then dropped, like a stone, on the waves that she had been sure they were going to end up on the sea bed, never to be seen again. Yet even that had not dampened her excitement at seeing her children, and the second she set foot on dry land she was off, like a shot, through the streets of Dublin. It was still very early and few people were about, but even the darkness could not disguise the soot-smeared slums she passed. And then at last she turned into Georgina Street and her journey was finally over.

Chapter Six

As Dilly rapped on her mother-in-law's front door her heart was thudding with anticipation and her face broke into a wide smile. She could just imagine how excited the children would be to see her

70

and she could hardly wait. Suddenly the horrendous ferry journey was forgotten – she would have gone through it all again just to be standing where she was right now, with her children only yards away beyond the door.

Maeve welcomed her with a warm embrace, as neat as ever, and the familiar smell of beeswax polish greeted her as she stepped into the hallway and dropped her bag on the floor.

'They're all in the kitchen, lass,' Maeve said, as she strode ahead, and Dilly followed eagerly. When she entered the room she was so shocked by her first sight of her children that she stopped short in her tracks. They were standing in a straight line in front of the fireplace as if they were waiting to greet a stranger and had changed so much in the months since she had last seen them. They had all grown by at least a few inches and had gained weight as well. Their clothes were clearly new, and their hair shone in the glow of the fire.

Niamh's hair was tied back with a pretty red ribbon that matched the skirt and cardigan she was wearing, and the boys were neatly turned out in starched white shirts and grey trousers.

'Oh, my loves, I've missed you all *so* much,' Dilly choked out eventually, as tears welled in her eyes and she opened her arms to them. Instantly the three younger children came to her and returned her hugs but Declan crossed to his grandmother and clung to her skirts.

She beckoned to him and finally he, too, came to her, telling her solemnly, 'I'm six now, you know. Gran'ma made me a cake with candles on an' we had a little party with some of the children

71

from my school.'

'But of course I know,' she said softly. 'I sent you a card, didn't I?'

'Aye, you did.' She noticed that he had picked up an Irish accent, probably from his school mates, but she had no doubt that it would disappear once she had him home. He sidled away from her then, back to his grandmother, and Dilly felt the first stirrings of unease.

'Your daddy is so looking forward to seeing you all again,' she told them, as Maeve bustled away to put the kettle on. 'They look a picture, Maeve. I don't think Fergal and I will ever be able to thank you enough for what you've done for us all.'

Maeve waved aside her thanks. 'Think nothing of it. It's been a pleasure to have them, so it has, but, er...' She paused then, as if she was trying to find the words to say something. Suddenly she clapped her hands and told the children, 'All right, you lot. How about you go on with what you were doing while me and your mammy have a little talk, eh?'

The children scattered, and soon Maeve carried a pot of tea to the table, joining Dilly, who was watching her children as if she might never take her eyes off them again. In truth, she had expected a warmer welcome and was a little disappointed, but then she consoled herself that they would be used to living here now and might not be looking forward to the journey home on the ferry.

'So what did you want to talk to me about?' she asked her mother-in-law, as she sipped a welcome mug of tea. 'Is something wrong?'

'Oh, no, not wrong exactly,' Maeve hastened to

assure her, avoiding her eyes. 'But the thing is... Well, there's no easy way to say this, so I'll just come out with it. Declan doesn't want to come home just yet. He wants to stay on here with me an' his granda for a while longer. How would you feel about that?'

'Not very happy,' Dilly said flatly, her eyes hardening. 'Why ever would he want to stay here? He belongs at home with me and his daddy.'

'Ah, but you see he's started school now and he's top o' the class in just about every subject. Bright as a button, so he is, and it seems a shame to uproot him when he's doing so well. He's made lots o' friends, too, an' he spends most weekends over at the smallholding in Enniskerry with his uncle Liam. He loves it there so we were thinkin' you might let him stay on a while longer.'

'It's out of the question,' Dilly stated. 'How do you think Fergal would feel if I turned up at home without him? It would break his heart, and you wouldn't want that, surely. Fergal has been through quite enough as it is.'

Maeve was twisting her fingers together. Of course she didn't want to hurt her son but how was she to part with Declan? He had always been her special boy and she didn't know how she would cope without him. 'But his school...' Her words trailed away as she tried to think of a good argument to encourage Dilly to leave him there. 'He could perhaps just complete his first year there and then–'

'It's out of the question,' Dilly repeated firmly. 'We do have schools back in Nuneaton, you know, and I've no doubt he'll do just as well there. He'll make new friends, too. Children are very adaptable. Look how they settled with you.'

Maeve saw that she was losing the battle and let the subject drop for now. Dilly would not be leaving until the following afternoon so perhaps she and Daniel combined would be able to persuade her to let Declan stay.

'So how are you now, lass?' she asked. 'Fergal told us in his letters how poorly you'd been. You've been overdoing it, no doubt. There'll be lots more work for you as well once you get the little ones home, to be sure. But you don't have to answer all these questions now. We've all the time in the world to catch up, and you must be hungry after your journey. I've a nice plate o' bacon an' mushrooms keepin' warm for you in the oven, so I do, so I'll go and fetch it while you rest for a minute or two. You can have a lie-down then, for I've no doubt you got little sleep on the ferry.' She bustled away, leaving Dilly to her thoughts.

Dilly was appalled that Maeve might even suggest she left Declan with her, but even more hurt to note that Declan seemed happy with the idea. Every now and again he would glance at her as if she was a stranger, which almost broke her heart. She certainly hadn't received from him the rapturous welcome she had expected but she realized that as much as it hurt she must let him come to her now, so she sat back prepared to do just that. She was his mother, after all.

The atmosphere lightened somewhat when Daniel came home from work later that evening. He flashed a smile but told her apologetically,

'I'll not offer to give you a hug, lass, till I've had a wash. I'm afraid mine isn't the cleanest o' jobs.'

That was apparent from his blood-caked clothing and the awful smell he brought in with him. Maeve drew a curtain, shutting off the sink area, and after washing thoroughly in the water his wife had had ready for him, Daniel reappeared, his hair plastered to his head. Maeve had disappeared out of the back door to put his smelly clothes to soak in a bucket of water till morning. Niamh told her mother, 'Granda always smells when he gets home from work.'

'Well, he looks nice and clean now,' Dilly answered with a warm smile as the little girl clambered onto her lap. For the first time since she had arrived she began to relax. She had almost forgotten how wonderful it was to hug a small body close to her.

Dinner was a pleasant affair and Dilly was glad to see the children ate heartily. It would have been hard not to because Maeve's roast pork was so tender it melted in their mouths. Daniel avoided mentioning the prospect of Declan staying with them and Dilly suspected that his wife had told him not to while he was washing behind the curtain.

After dinner, Dilly helped Maeve to clear, wash and dry the pots while Daniel read the children a story. When he had finished, it was black as pitch outside so they washed and changed then into their nightclothes, then Dilly tucked them into bed. Each one kissed her soundly as they snuggled under the blankets, apart from Declan, who smiled at her politely.

'Mammy,' he began, as she turned to leave the room, 'is there no chance of me staying here a while longer with Gran'ma and Granda? I like going to mass with them, and if I come home I'll miss the nuns at me school and me friends.'

Suppressing a sigh, Dilly crossed back to him and perched on the end of his bed. 'This was never meant to be for long, sweetheart,' she explained patiently. 'Didn't I tell you when we came that it was only to be for a short while? Your daddy is missing you sorely and it's time to come home now. That's not to say you can't come back for holidays, pet. Perhaps you could come back for a while next summer. You'd like that, wouldn't you?'

Declan pouted and tears shimmered on his long eyelashes. He blinked them back bravely – only cissy girls cried. 'But what about school and me friends? And I've been helping Uncle Liam on the farm some weekends.'

'I've already arranged for you to start school in Nuneaton, and I'm sure Uncle Liam will understand that you have to come home,' his mother explained.

He turned his back on her and burrowed beneath the blankets.

Dilly rose, chewing her lip. Then, with a sigh, she quietly left the room. Declan was coming home with her and he would just have to get used to the fact. It would break Fergal's heart if he didn't.

Chapter Seven

The following morning Niamh, Kian and Seamus helped their mother to pack their clothes into the new bags their grandmother had thoughtfully bought for them. They had so much more than they'd had when they first arrived, Dilly noted. She wondered how she would ever be able to thank her in-laws for all they had done.

Declan stood glaring at her, his arms crossed and a mutinous expression on his face. 'Come on, there's still your things to pack,' Dilly said cheerfully, hoping to chivvy him out of his bad mood.

Even Maeve was embarrassed by his behaviour – as much as she adored her grandson and longed to keep him with her, she had no wish to upset his mother, bless her heart. She had enough on her plate as it was, with her crippled husband to care for and a full-time job, without this.

'Come on now, laddie,' she said. 'Did you not hear what your mother said? It's time to pack your things. And you can come back for a nice holiday before you know it, so you can.'

Daniel, who had heard the goings-on, appeared in the doorway but before he could utter a word, Declan threw himself at him and wrapped his arms about his legs. 'I don't wanna go an' leave you, Granda,' he sobbed.

When Dilly saw tears spring to Daniel's eyes, her heart sank and she knew she had lost. What was the point of forcing the child to go home if he was clearly happier here?

'I – I suppose we could let you stay here for just a *little* longer,' she forced herself to say, in a choky voice.

Instantly Declan's face lit up brighter than a ray of sunshine. 'Do yer *mean* it, Mammy? Aw, *thank you.*' He launched himself at her so unexpectedly that he almost overbalanced her and she forced a smile to her face although she felt like crying.

'He'll be well looked after, lass,' Maeve told her, as she tried to stop herself beaming from ear to ear. 'And no doubt once you've gone he'll be asking to come home in no time and when he does, either me or his granda will bring him back. Or perhaps we'll both come and see our Fergal. Won't that be grand, eh?'

Dilly swallowed, wondering how the hell she was going to explain this to Fergal when she got home, but now she had agreed to it there was no going back so she finished packing the rest of the children's clothes. Daniel carried them into the hallway for her and placed them by the front door.

Maeve had provided food for them to eat on the return journey, fresh-made soda bread and chunks of cheese wrapped in clean pieces of muslin, as well as apples and some raisin cakes that made the children hungry again just smelling them. Before they knew it, it was time for them to leave but this time Daniel accompanied them to carry the heavy bags and Declan came too.

After Dilly had thanked Maeve profusely for all she had done and kissed her, Declan skipped ahead of them on the way through the teeming streets. Dilly's spirits sank lower than ever. He was clearly delighted to be left behind, but what could she do about it? She was wise enough to know that to force him to come home with her would only have been asking for trouble. Even if he was only six years old he clearly had a mind of his own but she hoped that once he had seen them all leave he might have a change of heart and Dilly knew her mother-in-law well enough to know that if he did she would keep her promise and bring him back.

When they reached the docks they saw that the ferry was waiting and people were embarking. Daniel went aboard with them and, after depositing the bags on the deck, he kissed each of them in turn.

'Now you be a good boy for your gran'ma and your granda, do you hear me?' Dilly said as she knelt to Declan's level. 'And remember that when you're ready to come home you have only to say. We'll be waiting for you.'

He nodded solemnly and returned her kiss, then went to take his grandfather's hand. Dilly could only watch helplessly as they left the boat, then turned to wave until they were swallowed among the people swarming about the docks.

'What do you mean – he didn't *want* to come home?' Fergal raged early the next morning, when Dilly and three worn-out children finally arrived home.

'We'll talk about it later when I've settled the children,' Dilly said, as they stared fearfully at

79

their father.

'Oh, yes ... yes, of course,' he said guiltily. 'Well, aren't you weans all going to come over here and give your daddy a big hug? I've missed you all sorely, to be sure.'

The children approached him cautiously and he hugged each in turn. As they saw his delight, they slowly relaxed.

'There's a fine meat pie all ready to be heated through in the oven,' he told them. 'Nell cooked it for you earlier. She thought you might be hungry after your long journey. She's sure looking forward to seeing you again, so she is.'

Seamus yawned, and Dilly said wryly, 'I think the pie will have to wait until later. They're all so tired I doubt they'd be able to stay awake long enough for it to warm up, but they've had plenty to eat. Your mother packed enough to feed an army for on the way back so I'll just get them changed and tucked in.' Seeing the disappointment that flickered across his face, she added hastily, 'There'll be plenty of time for you to catch up on all they've been doing tomorrow when they've had a good sleep, but for now they need their beds. So do I, if it comes to that.'

He saw the strain and weariness on her face and silently cursed himself again for being so helpless. It must have been so hard for her, having to juggle heavy bags and three weans all the way home from Dublin, especially when they had to change trains. Sure, I'm nuttin' but a poor apology for a man now, he thought.

Meanwhile Dilly was fumbling in the bags. After finding the children's nightclothes, she changed them and ushered them upstairs. She had put fresh linen on their beds before leaving for Dublin and had cleaned the rooms from top to bottom, but she doubted the children would notice. They were far too tired and she had an idea they could have fallen asleep on their feet. Even so her eyes filled with tears of joy to see them tucked up in their own little beds – but her heart broke again when she looked at the one Declan should have been sharing with Kian. She felt her way down the steep staircase to find that Fergal had already heaved himself out of his wheeled chair into bed. He must have stayed up all night waiting for us to come home, she thought, but then she was tucked in beside him and had fallen asleep before she could say Jack Robinson.

It was late in the morning, when she was making her way to the shared privy, that Madge Bunting collared her.

'I saw yer were back when the little 'uns came out a while ago,' she said. 'But I didn't see owt o' your Declan. Sold another o' yer kids, 'ave yer?'

Dilly was so stunned that her mouth fell open. Madge had made many barbed remarks about the baby but she had never voiced her suspicions so openly.

'I – I don't know what you're talking about,' she stammered. 'Declan has – well, he's decided to stay on with his grandparents in Dublin a while longer. And our baby...'

'I know what yer gonna say,' Madge sneered. 'Poor little mite *died*, didn't it?'

Dilly pushed past her, her cheeks on fire. When

81

she reached the privy she sat down and dropped her face into her hands. Madge knew about the baby, or at least she had a damned good idea. But suspecting it and proving it were two different things.

The next week was not easy. Fergal had got out of the habit of having children under his feet and he became short-tempered with them, especially when he was trying to paint. Since Mr Farthing had bought the picture from him he had allowed himself to hope that this might be a way of earning his living and he spent long hours in front of his easel. Dilly had always encouraged him with his hobby because it seemed to ease his frustration, but now that the children were home, someone had to mind them while she was at work, especially Seamus, who at three was into everything. Eventually one evening they quarrelled when she came home from work to find the children running around the yard barefoot, with their hair standing on end like haystacks.

They were a whisper away from Christmas now and it was bitterly cold, certainly too cold for them to be running wild outside with no shoes on.

'What are you thinking of? They'll catch their death! And have you even bothered to take a brush to their hair today?' she ranted, as she ushered them inside. Normally she would do all she could to please him but she was tired and concerned for their family. Missing Declan didn't help, and that day she had spent a few seconds with Olivia when Nanny had left her in her perambulator in the hallway to have her sleep out. She often glimpsed the child, but today she had been able to stroke her hand and gaze at her unobserved for a few moments. She hadn't been able to stop herself – the temptation had been too great.

The more the little girl grew, the more she resembled her big sister, and it had taken every ounce of Dilly's willpower not to snatch her from the pram and run home with her. It hadn't helped when Olivia had suddenly woken and smiled up at her. But then Mrs Farthing had appeared from nowhere and grabbed the child as she glared at Dilly. To come home and find the children running riot, like little street urchins, was just too much. They had put her in mind of Nipper, the barefoot boy she had met when she had taken the children to Dublin.

'Well?' she demanded, hands on hips as she confronted Fergal, eyes flashing.

Taking his eyes off the palette in his hand, he shrugged. 'I didn't even know they'd slipped outside. Sure, they've been little demons since they came back from me mammy's, so they have. I reckon she must have spoiled them rotten.'

Exasperated, Dilly shook her head. 'But they're little more than babies, Fergal. They need careful watching.'

'Oh, meaning that's all I'm fit for?'

Her anger drained away as fast as it had come, like water down a drain. 'You know full well I didn't mean that,' she answered, as she took off her shawl. Some days she felt as if all she ever did was work; even when her long shift at the Farthings' was over, there were always jobs to be done at home. Washing, ironing, cooking, cleaning, seeing to the children's needs. The list was endless.

Crossing to the sink, she began to peel some vegetables to go with the belly pork slices she had bought from the butcher on Abbey Green on the way home. Fergal had promised her he would have the vegetables ready but he had clearly forgotten, just as he had forgotten to wash the dirty pots that were now piled high in the sink.

Later they sat down to their meal, and Dilly forced herself to be cheerful and chat to the children as they ate, asking them what they had been doing and what they might like to do on Saturday afternoon. Each week she would make time then to spend at least a couple of hours with them.

Fergal was a proud man and now, as she looked across at him, she was sorry she had lost her temper with him earlier. It couldn't be easy for him, stuck in the house with three young children under his feet all the time.

'What do you think of it?' he asked, nodding towards the canvas he was working on as he laid down his knife and fork at the end of the meal.

Dilly glanced towards it. It wasn't one of his better efforts, although she would never hurt his feelings by telling him so. He had attempted to paint the row of terraced cottages where they lived but something was lacking. He seemed to be better at landscapes than buildings or portraits.

'I'm sure it'll be fine when it's finished,' she said encouragingly.

He took her by surprise then when he asked, 'And how does the one that Farthing bought off me look now it's been framed?'

As far as Dilly knew the picture had never been

84

framed and she suspected that Max Farthing had only bought it as an act of kindness to put some money their way. But how could she tell him so? She answered brightly, 'Oh, it looks grand. It's hanging in the hallway. I must get cleared away now. Isn't Father Brannigan coming to see you tonight?'

Because Fergal had been unable to attend church since his accident, the priest was now a regular visitor to the house although he called mostly during the day while Dilly was at work. On the occasions when she saw him he would chide her for not attending mass with the children as often as she should but, as she had pointed out, her days were full as it was so she could spare the time only occasionally. Father Brannigan wasn't entirely happy about it but gave the children religious instruction when he visited their father, which Dilly felt was good enough. In truth, although she had converted to the Catholic religion before she had married Fergal, since his accident she had begun to question God. After all, what sort of God would allow a family man to be maimed and unable to care for his family, to the point at which they had been forced to give away their youngest child? But she didn't say this to Fergal, of course. She just plodded on from day to day hoping that things would improve.

As Fergal read passages from the Bible to the children, Dilly cleared away the pots, then dragged the tin bath into the kitchen from the nail on the wall in the yard and began to boil water for the children's baths. Best to get it out of the way before Father Brannigan arrived. A letter from

Dublin had arrived that morning and was on the mantelpiece waiting to be read, but she wanted to save it until the children were settled so that she could enjoy it. It might just be the one telling her that Declan wanted to come home and she tingled at the thought. She missed him terribly, but until now Maeve had written that he was settled and happy.

By the time Father Brannigan arrived the children were ready for bed, and Dilly shooed them towards the stairs saying, 'I'll get these bedded down, then pop and see Nell for a while and leave you two in peace. There's still some whisky in the kitchen cupboard if you fancy a tot.'

'Well, sure I wouldn't want to abuse your hospitality by refusing,' the priest told her. 'Perhaps just a wee drop for medicinal purposes and to keep the cold out, eh? It's enough to cut you in two out there so it is.'

Dilly found it hard to keep a straight face. Offering whisky to Father Brannigan was like offering strawberries to a donkey. It was well known that he liked his drink. So did Fergal when the priest called, although he wasn't a big drinker at any other time so she didn't begrudge him a drop now and then. The two men would put the world to rights during the priest's visits and she knew that Fergal looked forward to them.

Once the children were settled she went back downstairs and was amused to see that the men were already enjoying a generous tot of whisky each.

Fergal had made his confession to the priest

86

and received absolution, although Dilly doubted he would have many sins to confess, now that he never left the house.

Snatching her coat from a hook on the back of the door she sidled into the yard. There, she took a great gulp of the cold night air. It was always nice to have a little time to spend with her friend. Nell's husband, Fred, would no doubt have gone to the Cock and Bear Inn for his nightly tipple, and if Nell's brood were in bed the two women would be able to sit for a time over a nice hot cuppa.

Nell was just throwing some coal onto the fire when Dilly tapped at the door and came into the kitchen. 'Yer timed that nicely, I must say. I've just shooed the little buggers up the wooden hill so we can 'ave a bit o' peace an' quiet. Father Brannigan arrived, 'as 'e?'

'Yes, they're chatting away nineteen to the dozen.' Dilly slipped off her shawl and settled into Nell's fireside chair, noting that Nell looked a little concerned. She didn't seem to be her usual smiley self, and the reason for that became clear some minutes later. As they sat warming their hands on steaming mugs of tea, Nell said, 'Madge Bunting copped me again when I went out to the privy and she asked me some right funny questions.'

'What sort of questions?'

'She wanted to know whether you'd 'ad a boy or a girl the last time an' why yer 'adn't sent fer the midwife.'

Dilly frowned. Madge had asked her exactly the same thing. 'And what did you tell her?' she asked fearfully.

Nell snorted. 'I told 'er to mind 'er bloody own business,' she retorted. 'The nosy old cow. But take my advice an' watch 'er, pet. That one would slit 'er own granny's throat fer sixpence an' I wouldn't trust 'er as far as I could throw 'er.'

A cold hand closed around Dilly's heart. Madge was like a dog with a bone, even though it was now almost a year since she had given birth to her baby. What could she want of her?

Chapter Eight

Dilly was to discover the answer to her question sooner than she had thought. Two days later, as she traipsed wearily up the long narrow entry leading to her cottage after a hard day at the Farthing residence, she found Madge waiting for her.

'Madge – you made me jump,' she exclaimed, as she almost collided with her.

Grabbing her by the elbow, Madge drew her into the shadows and hissed, 'I think it's time you an' me 'ad a little talk, don't you?'

'What about?' Dilly asked, trying not to gag as Madge's foul breath hit her full in the face.

'Well, you earn a lot more than me, bein' a general maid, an' I'm strugglin' a bit so I reckon yer could afford a bit o' your wages to come my way each week to 'elp me out, like.'

'*What?*' Dilly was flabbergasted by the woman's cheek. 'And why would I want to do that? I earn my money fair and square, the same as you do.'

Madge sneered. 'Hmm, wi' a few perks thrown in, no doubt. I reckon two bob a week 'ud be a good 'elp.'

'And why would I give you two shillings a week?'

Dilly's temper was rising now, but it died instantly to be replaced by fear when Madge leaned towards her and whispered menacingly, 'Cos per'aps I know a bit more than I should about the little 'un yer reckon yer lost. I ain't daft, yer know. I saw yer scuttlin' away from 'ere the night yer gave birth, holdin' somethin' tight to you. Hardly normal behaviour, would yer say, fer someone who'd just given birth? An' I reckon that somethin' yer were holdin' were yer bairn an' you were takin' her to her new 'ome, cos the very next day the Farthings announced they'd 'ad a new baby daughter. Bit of a coincidence, eh?'

Dilly licked her dry lips as her heart raced, but Madge hadn't finished.

'Then, soon after yer start a permanent position, one I'd been after meself, you've got the money to take the kids across to Dublin when everyone knows you were strugglin' so much you'd thought you'd 'ave to put 'em in the orphanage. It'd be a shame if word were to get out that your baby was the one that the Farthings are bringin' up as their own, wouldn't it? I can't see the master takin' kindly to everyone knowin', can you? An' what would 'er ladyship say, eh? All yer little treats would stop then, I don't mind bettin', like yer fancy baskets o' fruit when yer were ill.'

'But Mr Farthing looks after all his staff if they're sick,' Dilly protested weakly.

'Does he 'ell as like,' Madge sneered. 'When I

were off work nearly dyin' wi' the fever he never even paid me me wages. Makes me wonder just what else yer do fer him to get such treatment.'

'There's nothing like that between us. Mr Farthing is a gentleman and you can't prove a thing,' Dilly said hotly, but Madge laughed – a spiteful laugh that made the hairs on the back of Dilly's neck stand on end.

'True, I can't *prove* it. But yer know what folk hereabouts are like. Once word got round they'd say there were no smoke wi'out fire an', as I said, I can't see the Farthings bein' happy about that, especially 'er ladyship. But, then, if I was to 'ave the two bob a week off yer I'd be 'appy to keep me gob shut, like. It'd 'elp me no end an' I wouldn't want to cut me nose off to spite me face, now, would I?'

'You're saying you want to blackmail me for your silence?' Dilly's mind was racing. Since Fergal's accident she had managed all the finances, for her wage was the only one coming in. They were more comfortable now than they had been for ages but two shillings a week was an awful lot of money. It would mean there would be nothing left to put a few pennies away each week for emergencies after paying the rent and the rest of the bills. *But what alternative do I have?* She was aware that Madge was vicious enough to carry out her threat, and then what would the Farthings say? How would it affect Olivia if she were ever to discover that Dilly was really her mother? The Farthings had been quite adamant that no one must ever know, *especially* the child.

As Madge watched Dilly grappling with her

conscience, she chuckled. 'So do we 'ave a deal?'

'You're wrong, Madge,' Dilly choked. 'But rather than have you spreading malicious rumours I suppose I have no choice but to pay you. But couldn't you settle for a shilling a week?'

'No, I couldn't,' Madge hissed. 'It's two bob an' that's final, unless…'

'All right,' Dilly gasped, sensing defeat. Madge had got her over a barrel and she knew it. 'But how will I get the money to you each week without anyone seeing?'

'Don't you go worryin' yer 'ead about that. I'll make sure to catch yer when no one's about,' Madge assured her, then turned and sauntered away leaving Dilly to get a grip on herself. She felt sick but she knew that somehow she must compose herself before facing Fergal. He must never, ever know about this, for if he ever did it would destroy him. But two whole shillings a week! It was more than a full day's wages, and when she thought of what that amount could do for her family she almost wept. But what would be the point? Squaring her slim shoulders she took a deep breath and moved towards her back door. It was time to start preparing the evening meal for the family. Somehow she must try to go on as normal.

One afternoon in the week before Christmas Dilly was leaving the drawing room, after making up the fire, when she became aware of Olivia sitting in her pram in the hallway. Nanny had been about to take her out for her walk, as she did each afternoon, much to Camilla's dismay – she felt it was

91

far too cold to venture out in such inclement weather – when the woman had tutted with annoyance. The boys should have been ready to accompany her but there was no sign of them. She had gone back to the nursery to hurry them along. Dilly paused as the child eyed her curiously. Then, unable to stop herself, she crossed to the pram and bent to the baby's level. 'Hello. Don't you look beautiful today?' She was rewarded with a wide smile, and when the child reached out to her, she took the tiny mittened hand, tears forming in her eyes as she resisted the urge to hold her. But at that moment the boys came pelting downstairs and Samuel almost careered into her.

'Out of the way, *Carey,*'he shouted rudely, as his father appeared from the study.

'It's *Mrs* Carey, Samuel,' his father scolded him. 'Apologize immediately!'

Samuel scowled. He had become a bit of a handful lately and sometimes Nanny despaired of him.

'We call *all* the servants by their last names and she was in my way!' he responded indignantly.

'Not in *this* house you don't, young man,' his father barked. 'You will show respect to your elders. Don't make me have to ask you to apologize again.'

As the boy saw the look on his father's face he turned to Dilly and muttered grudgingly, 'Sorry!'

Nanny had joined them, and as she grasped the handle of the pram and ushered her charges out of the front door, Max Farthing said, 'I do apologize for my son's behaviour, Mrs Carey. I'm afraid that young man is getting rather too big for his boots. I shall have to take him in hand.'

'Think nothing of it,' she answered. 'Boys will be boys, I'm afraid.'

'Quite, but even so, good manners cost nothing. Are you ready for Christmas?' he asked.

Her face clouded. 'Not yet, I'm afraid. I haven't even had time to get to the market to buy the children a tree. Sometimes there aren't enough hours in the day but I shall make time on Saturday afternoon.'

For an instant her eyes rested on the huge tree that took up a corner of the large hallway. It was magnificent, reaching almost to the ceiling, and was beautifully decorated with glass baubles and tiny candles. There was another, nearly identical, in the drawing room but she knew that even when she did manage to get into town she wouldn't be able to afford anything like either of those. She was having to make every penny count now that she was giving Madge Bunting two shillings a week. When she thought of what she might have bought for the children for Christmas she was heart-sore. But what choice did she have? Just as Madge had threatened, she had waylaid her each Friday evening as she made her way home from work and had taken the money from Dilly without a word. Fergal was unaware of what was going on and Dilly knew that it must stay that way.

Raising a smile, she inclined her head towards him, then hurried about her business. He watched her go with a thoughtful expression on his face. He had not failed to notice her wistful look as she had gazed at Olivia and felt sorry for her. The love she felt for the child was clear to see and he could only imagine what agony it must be for her to be so

93

close and yet so far away from the child. He had grown very fond of Olivia but still struggled to come to terms with the way he and his wife had come by her. And Dilly... The more he got to know her the more he found himself admiring her strength and courage. He enjoyed the rare occasions when he bumped into her about the house and they exchanged a few words. He knew his wife would disapprove of such behaviour with a servant, yet he couldn't seem to stop thinking about her and it confused him.

Camilla appeared from the direction of the morning room then and stopped his train of thought when she asked, 'What's all the commotion about? I heard you raising your voice to someone.'

'It was Samuel. He was being rude to Mrs Carey so I made him apologize.'

'You made *our son* apologize to one of the *servants?*' she sputtered indignantly.

'Yes, I did,' he said, as her eyes flashed and she flounced back to where she had come from in a swirl of silken skirts.

Turning about he went back into his study and yanked on the bellrope that dangled down beside the fireplace.

'Yes, sir?' Millie, the housemaid, asked with a bob of her knee when she appeared a few seconds later.

'Millie, I wonder if you would ask Mr Jackson to come to me for a moment, please.'

'Yes, sir. I reckon he's in the kitchen at present, having a cup o' tea with the cook.'

She scooted back the way she had come and

seconds later, Jackson, the gardener, appeared in the doorway. 'Yer wanted me, sir?'

'Yes, I did, Mr Jackson. I wondered if you might be kind enough to run a few errands for me.'

The elderly man nodded obligingly and Max Farthing began to tell him what he wanted him to do. 'And, Jackson,' Max cleared his throat uncomfortably, 'I, er, I'd rather you didn't let the mistress know about this, if you don't mind.'

'Right y'are, sir.' Jackson tipped his cap and he left the room.

As Dilly hurried up the entry that evening she shivered. A thick hoar frost was already forming and the blades of grass were standing to attention, like little white soldiers, crunching beneath her feet as she walked across them. The entry was acting as a wind tunnel and she couldn't wait to get to the warmth of her kitchen. Her lips twitched into a smile as she reached the back door. The children were clearly in high spirits and their laughter was echoing about the yard.

She hurried inside, shutting the door firmly behind her to keep out the cold. In a corner of the room a Christmas tree was stood in a sturdy bucket of earth and the children were happily decorating it with paper chains they had made that afternoon.

'Where did that come from?' she asked in astonishment. Her husband, she saw, was looking none too pleased.

'The Farthings' gardener delivered it this afternoon,' he told her grumpily. 'And that weren't all. There's a hamper over there on the table an' all.

95

Sure, he must think we're not capable of feeding our own weans. When I think of all the vegetables I used to grow,' he said regretfully. 'Everything has gone to seed now.' Fergal had always loved his garden and many a weekend he would come in with the children, carrying so much fresh produce that they would never have been able to eat it all. Dilly had supplied some to Nell.

'Oh, I'm sure he was just trying to be kind,' Dilly said hastily, hoping to stop him getting maudlin as she crossed to the hamper. As she glanced inside, it was all she could do to hide her delight. There were several of Mrs Pegs' home-made mince pies and a large Christmas pudding, which would feed them all for at least two days. There were sweets and chocolates for the children, as well as fruit and vegetables, a selection of nuts and other treats.

'He said you're not to get a turkey either,' Fergal went on resentfully. 'He's going to deliver one to us on Christmas Eve. I told him not to bother, that we were quite capable of getting our own, so we were. But he said that it was already ordered.'

'That's grand, then.' Dilly kept her smile fixed firmly in place. 'It'll save me no end of running about so I'll be able to spend more time here with you and the children, won't I? I shall have to thank the Farthings kindly when I get in tomorrow.'

She passed him the newspaper, which she bought him religiously each evening on her way home, hoping it might cheer him up. He might not be able to get out and about any more but he liked to keep abreast of what was happening in the world and would read it from cover to cover.

'Hmph!' Fergal crossed his arms and stared into the fire but Dilly went about her business and ignored him. The children were subdued too and Seamus sneaked into the kitchen to whisper, 'Daddy's in a bad mood, Mammy. He shouted at me today when I knocked one of his pictures over.'

Dilly bent to kiss his forehead and smooth back a lock of his unruly hair. 'Daddy just gets frustrated with being trapped inside all the time, sweetheart. Try to be patient with him. He doesn't mean to be angry.'

Seamus swiped a fat tear from his cheek as annoyance surged through her. She would be having words with Fergal, that was for sure.

Ushering Seamus back into the scullery, she beckoned to Fergal. Once he had wheeled himself closer to her, out of earshot of the children, she said, 'You really shouldn't take your frustration out on the children, Fergal. I *know* how hard things are for you but I do my best. The last thing I need is to come home to upset after a hard day's work.'

'What mood am I supposed to be in when Mr Farthing keeps sending reminders that he can provide more for my family than I can?' he hissed back. 'And why does he look after *you* so well? I don't see hampers being delivered to Madge and she works for him too.'

Dilly's shoulders slumped as a picture of Olivia flashed before her eyes. 'I think we both know the answer to that, don't you?' she replied. They seemed to have been arguing more and more lately, but tonight she was just too tired. Turning away, she began to prepare their dinner.

It was later that evening when the children were tucked into bed that she glanced towards the easel and gasped. 'Did you do that, Fergal?'

On the canvas was a scene of a bluebell wood and she fell in love with it on sight.

'Niamh did it. It's good, isn't it? I reckon she'll make a fine little artist.'

'It's excellent considering she isn't even six yet. She must take after you.'

Pleased at the compliment, Fergal smiled for the first time that evening. He seemed to be mellowing now. Careful to avoid the Christmas tree or the hamper, Dilly went on to chat about other things until Fergal began to stroke her hair. She forced herself not to stiffen as she realized what this might lead up to. Since Olivia's birth they had rarely come together – she was too afraid of falling for another child – but he had so few pleasures in his life now. How could she deny him his rights? She still loved him dearly, although he had changed greatly. She could understand it, but the happy-go-lucky, caring man she had once known had long gone and now he had days when he would sink into a deep depression. She knew a lot of his moods were caused by the griping pain he still felt in his legs, and sometimes when she saw him juggling himself into bed from his chair she could have cried over his wasted limbs. Bed sores were becoming a problem now, too, although she washed his legs in warm salt water every night. Now she raised her hand to stroke his, and soon after they were side by side on the bed and she tried to make him feel that he was still the man she loved in the only way she could.

Chapter Nine

January 1902

'What do you think of the idea then, Father Doherty?' Maeve kept a watchful eye on the priest as she pushed another of her fresh-baked scones across the table to him. The first had disappeared in the flash of an eye.

The priest scratched his head. 'Well, to be sure, it could be the making of the child,' he admitted. 'And far more of a life for him living in Enniskerry with you and Daniel than roaming the streets. The good Lord knows how many times I've found him a home in the orphanage only for him to run away. And to be sure that wee lad can run! No wonder they call him Nipper, for neither the Constabulary nor meself can catch the little tyke if he don't want to be caught. But, then, I dare say at the end o' the day the final decision will have to lie with him.'

'Aye.' Maeve nodded. 'In that case I'll ask him what he thinks o' the idea this very evening. I told Declan to bring the wee lad home with him for some dinner after school.'

Father Doherty spread a generous amount of butter on his scone, followed by a dollop of Maeve's home-made jam. He ate it in two big bites, then washed it down with a second cup of tea.

'Ah, that sure hit the spot, so it did,' he said

appreciatively, as he patted his full stomach. 'But I must be away now. I have a meeting with the nuns at the laundry about one of the girls they have taken in who is near her time.'

Maeve made the sign of the cross on her breast. 'Poor wee lass,' she muttered. Everyone knew how hard it was for the lasses who ended up there. They got little sympathy or kindness from the nuns and were worked almost to death until the hour they gave birth, only to have their babies whipped away from them. Then they were turned out onto the streets. Some of the more fortunate ones were allowed to return to their families once their disgrace was no longer in evidence. Many of the others ended up selling their bodies on street corners after dark and laying their heads wherever they could.

Maeve followed Father Doherty to the door, reminding him, 'I'll not be seeing you again for the next couple of weeks. I think I mentioned that I'm taking Declan for a surprise visit to see his mammy and daddy in England.'

'Rather you than me,' Father Doherty replied. 'Sure I wouldn't fancy bobbing about on the Irish Sea in January.'

'Well, needs must!' Maeve crossed her arms. 'We love having wee Declan with us but I know from the tone of their letters that his parents miss him. I thought he'd be asking to go home by now but instead he's excited about moving to Enniskerry with us, which is why I decided to take him for a wee visit to see his family before we go. You never know, once he sees them again he may decide he wants to stay there with them and I'd not stand in his way.'

'I doubt that. The lad seems happy as Larry with you and Daniel. Safe journey. Goodbye, Maeve.'

Maeve closed the door behind him, then hurried away to start the dinner. If young Nipper was coming she wanted to make something that would stick to his ribs. The poor mite looked like he could do with a bit of meat on him. She could still clearly remember the day she had first met him some months before. He and Declan had become firm friends at school and one afternoon he had walked Declan home. She found it strange that the wee chap attended school yet refused the priest's offers of a home, but he was a bright little spark and she knew that the teachers were fond of him and often gave him food, which was probably one of the attractions. It had just so happened that she had been scrubbing the outside step when they had arrived. Her heart had gone out to the poor barefoot waif and she had invited him in for a meal. For a moment Nipper, which was the only name she had ever known him by, had seemed about to refuse her offer but when Declan pleaded with him to join them he had accepted. She smiled now as she thought back to how much food he had put away. He had eaten even more than Daniel, which had amazed her, for sure the child wasn't as far through as a broomstick.

That had been the start of it, and since then Maeve had shown him many kindnesses. For a start, she had insisted he should have the boots and coat that Declan had outgrown, and from what she could see of it they had never been off him since even if they were a little tight on him.

When it was bitterly cold she had encouraged him to stay on a straw mattress in Declan's room and he was now a regular visitor.

Daniel had also taken a great shine to the lad and had been the first to suggest he might like to move to the small-holding with them. After all, as he had pointed out, Nipper was a wiry wee chap and an extra pair of hands about the place in return for his keep would be more than welcome. Now that she had Father Doherty's blessing, all she could do was put the idea to him and she found she was looking forward to it.

It was later that evening when they had tucked into a hearty meal of mashed potatoes and Irish sausages that Maeve said, 'So, how would you feel about coming to live with us in Enniskerry when we go, Nipper? Daniel here was only saying the other night what a fine strong lad you are and sure we'd be glad of your help about the place, so we would.'

Nipper looked up from the game of cards he was playing with Declan. He was rendered temporarily speechless but then he managed to mutter, 'What? You mean come an' live with you *proper*, like?'

Daniel, in the process of filling his pipe as he sat in the fireside chair, chuckled. 'Aye, lad, that's exactly what we mean but don't go thinking we're offering you any favours. It would be you helping us out for I'm under no illusions. Working a farm, even a small one, is hard work and you'd be expected to pull your weight, so you would.'

Declan's face lit up as he stared at his friend. 'Crikey! Think how good that would be, Nipper,' he said excitedly.

But Nipper was far more cautious. 'What about school?'

'Of course you'd go to the village school in Enniskerry with Declan,' Daniel informed him. ''Twould only be in your free time you'd be expected to help.'

'And where would I sleep?' Nipper asked warily.

Daniel tamped down the tobacco in his pipe. 'You'd share a bedroom with Declan,' he answered, as he held a spill towards the fire to light it.

Nipper was still undecided. Living on the streets of Dublin was all he could remember since he had run away from the orphanage at a very young age and he wasn't at all sure he could adapt to living in a proper home with a real family.

'I'll think about it,' he mumbled, and Daniel grinned as he held the lighted spill to his pipe and drew on it. He was an independent little so-and-so, there was no doubt about it. 'You do that, son, and perhaps you can let us have your answer when Maeve and Declan get back from the visit to his parents.'

Nipper nodded but said no more. He had a lot to think about.

'I wonder now if I shouldn't have given them some notice that we were coming,' Maeve fretted, as she pressed a change of clothes for herself and Declan into a large jute bag.

'Stop worrying,' Daniel told her. 'Sure it will be a wonderful surprise for them all when you just turn up out of the blue, so it will. I only wish I

103

could come with you but I can't afford to have time off work and risk losing my job till Liam lets us know the cottage is ready.'

Maeve's stomach was in a knot. She had never travelled so far on her own before and suddenly she wondered if she was doing the right thing. But it would do Fergal a power of good to see his son, Dilly too. In every letter she received from her, Dilly asked if Declan was ready to come home yet, which made Maeve feel bad. Now she looked across to her grandson, who was warmly wrapped up in his fine new coat and a thick woollen scarf she had knitted for him, and asked, 'Are you ready, lad?'

'Aye, Gran'ma, I am.'

Daniel pressed the money for their fares and a little bit extra into her hand, though she had no idea what she might need it for. For a second her teeth nipped at her lip. This money should have been going into the pot for things they would need when they moved to the country but, as if he could read her mind, Daniel told her, 'Now off you go and don't be mitherin' about a few shillin's. Give them all my love and have a good time now. Are you sure you don't want me to carry your bag to the ferry for you?'

'I'm hardly a weakling, Daniel Carey,' she said sharply, yet her eyes betrayed the great love she felt for him. 'You finish getting yourself ready for work and earn some more money to put back in the pot. I'll see you on Tuesday at the latest. I shall only stay a couple o' nights.' She kissed his whiskery cheek, then shooed Declan towards the door.

Outside she was shocked to see Nipper waiting

for them. It was very early in the morning and he looked frozen. 'Whatever are you doin' here?' she asked.

Nipper bowed his head and kicked at a stone with the toe of Declan's cast-off boot. 'Thought I might come an' see you off on the ferry,' he mumbled.

'Right, then, we'd best be off,' she answered, although her heart ached for him. They walked along in silence for a time and it wasn't long before an idea occurred to her. She quickly calculated how much his fares would cost, then asked casually, 'I don't suppose you'd care to come along with us, would you, Nipper? You could help Declan with this bag when it gets too heavy for me.'

She watched his eyes widen. Nipper had never set foot on a boat in the whole of his life, or even outside Dublin.

'How long are you goin' for?' he asked, trying hard to stop his voice betraying his excitement.

'Only a couple of nights. I couldn't stay longer else my Daniel will starve to death, so he will. I swear that man could burn water.'

'In that case if you need a hand wi' your bag I suppose I could do,' Nipper said nonchalantly. 'Just to help you o' course.'

'Of course,' Maeve agreed solemnly and as they went on their way she was suddenly glad of the extra money that Daniel had given her.

The crossing was every bit as rough as Father Doherty had warned it might be, but as Maeve clung to the rail, grey-faced, the boys appeared to be loving it. The ferry pitched and turned, and every few seconds the Irish Sea spat ice-cold water into their faces. But at last they sighted land, and as they alighted from the ferry, Maeve breathed a sigh of relief.

Nipper was just as excited about the train journey and pressed his nose to the window as the fields flew by, determined not to miss a thing. They ate the griddle scones, ham and bread that Maeve had packed for them, and drank from the bottle of water, until at last the train drew into Trent Valley station.

'Here we are, me fine boys,' Maeve said, as she grasped the handles of her bag. 'Let's be having you. I could kill for a nice hot cup o' tea.'

Nipper stared at everything with interest as they passed over the bridge under which the River Anker flowed and Declan pointed out places to him.

'The cattle market is through there,' he said, waving in the general direction. 'On market day the farmers bring all their animals to sell. There's chickens, cows, sheep, pigs and everythin' yer could think of. There are stalls that sell all manner of other things as well. An' if yer walk that way yer come to Attleborough an' past that is Coton. They're parishes,' he added importantly, as they passed beneath the gas lamps that were throwing eerie shadows across the pavements. Nipper found it hard to imagine the place being busy: it was very quiet, compared to Dublin town.

At last they came to Abbey Green and within minutes had turned into St Mary's Road.

'Our cottage is just along here,' Declan informed Nipper, as they turned into the entry.

At the end, as they turned into the yard, they

were confronted by Madge Bunting, who was just off to the pub to get a jug of ale with some of the money she had taken from Dilly that night. She peered at them in the darkness, then chuckled. 'Well, I'll be blowed. If it ain't young Master Declan,' she crowed, 'the prodigal son returned to the fold, eh?'

Maeve took an instant dislike to the woman and ushered the children ahead of her as Madge shuffled away.

'Sure, I thought that were a witch,' Nipper whispered to Declan, who giggled.

Truthfully, Maeve didn't think Nipper looked much better but all the same she said encouragingly, 'Well now here were are at last, let's go in and give your mammy and daddy a nice surprise, eh, Declan?' and with that she opened the door and they all trooped into the kitchen.

Fergal was sitting by the fire reading his newspaper and Dilly was at the table darning a pair of Niamh's thick woollen stockings by the light of the lamp when the door opened. As the icy air blasted into the room Dilly jumped, jabbing herself with the needle as shock coursed through her. And then suddenly she let out a cry, and before anyone had time to speak, she was across the room, laughing and crying at the same time as she clasped Declan to her. 'I can't believe it! I thought I was seeing things for a minute there!' she cried joyously, as she covered his face with kisses. Declan squirmed, painfully aware that Nipper was witnessing all this. Kisses were for cissy babies and he was wondering what his mate would think of him, but he was very pleased to see his mother.

'I thought it'd be a nice surprise for you.' Maeve bent to hug her son, then pointed to Nipper, who was still standing self-consciously by the door, 'And I hope you don't mind but I thought I'd bring Declan's young friend along as well.'

Tearing her eyes away from her son, Dilly glanced at their visitor and got the second surprise of the night. 'Why, bless me, it's young Nipper, isn't it?'

Nipper grinned. Dilly had never forgotten the young orphan she had briefly met in Dublin and had often wondered how he was faring. Now here he was, large as life, in her own kitchen.

'You're the lady who once give me twopence,' Nipper said. He clearly hadn't forgotten her either and was shocked to discover that she was Declan's mammy.

'You two know each other?' Maeve gasped.

Laughing, Dilly went on to tell her how they had met. 'The little ones are all fast asleep in bed,' she told Declan and Maeve then. 'But won't it be a wonderful surprise when they get up to find you've come home?'

The smile slid from Declan's face as he glanced nervously towards his father. His mammy had misunderstood why he was there and he knew he had to put her right straight away. 'It's only for a visit, Mammy. We'll be staying for two nights an' then I'm goin' back to Dublin with Gran'ma an' Nipper.'

'We'll see,' Dilly said cheerfully. Now that he was home she was sure she would be able to convince him to stay. This was where he belonged, after all.

'Are you sure there's room for us?' Maeve asked. She'd forgotten how small the cottage was.

'Of course there is,' Dilly assured her. 'You can hop into bed with Niamh and the boys can go in with Kian and Seamus. It'll be a bit of a squeeze but we'll manage just fine.' And then she filled the kettle and put it on to boil as they all caught up on what they'd been doing.

Chapter Ten

Just as Dilly had predicted, the other children were delighted to see their brother and grandmother there the next morning when they came down for breakfast. Declan was crouching in front of the fire toasting bread on a long brass fork but he put it aside and there were kisses and hugs all round as Nipper stood well away from it. He had never been shown any affection so he didn't know how to respond to it, although something rather strange happened when Niamh appeared. Her thick, shining hair was loose about her shoulders, and in her white nightgown Nipper thought for a moment that she was an angel and his heart did a funny little flip. She was easily the prettiest little girl he had ever seen and he felt embarrassed for the first time in his young life when he looked down at his ragged clothes. He had never much cared about them before but suddenly they mattered and he wished he could disappear.

Niamh, however, didn't seem to mind, and when they were introduced she smiled at him, making colour flame into his cheeks.

'Have yer come home for ever?' a delighted Kian asked his brother, and when Declan shook his head, his small face clouded.

But, still, Dilly was determined that nothing should spoil the day and now she whispered to Fergal, 'I'm going to nip next door and get Nell's Will to run round to the Farthings with a message for the housekeeper. I'll tell him to say I can't come in this morning but that I'll make the hours up next week.' It was a Saturday, when she worked a half-day, so she couldn't see Miss Norman having any objections. She had never missed a day except when she had been ill.

The family spent a pleasant morning chatting. Maeve was full of the impending move to Enniskerry and confided to Fergal, 'We've asked young Nipper if he'd like to come along with us. Poor little mite's never had a proper home and I reckon the fresh country air will do him a power of good.'

As Fergal nodded, Maeve looked at him long and hard. Her son seemed to have shrunk since the last time she had seen him and his legs beneath the blanket across his knees were little more than sticks. When she thought back to what a strong, powerful man he had once been she could have cried. It was then that she voiced an idea that had recently been growing in her head. 'Would you, Dilly and the wee ones not consider coming to live with us when we move? It wouldn't be straight away, of course, for Liam and Daniel would have

110

to build a house for you all. But it's something for you to think on, is it not?'

Fergal looked at Dilly and saw the confusion in her eyes. Should Declan return to Dublin with his gran'ma, it would solve a problem for they could be with their first-born again, but it would mean leaving Olivia. Even though they could never claim her as their own, he knew Dilly drew comfort from being close to her, able to watch her grow.

Dilly's mind was also racing. There was Madge to consider and Dilly couldn't see her taking kindly to them leaving and her money drying up. The woman would probably go through with her threat of telling the Farthings that she knew Olivia's true parentage. Dilly couldn't risk that happening. She felt as if she was caught between the devil and the deep blue sea.

'It's something we'll think on,' Fergal told his mother tactfully. 'For sure it would be a huge up-heaval for the whole family to up sticks and move so far away.'

'Rubbish!' Maeve told him. 'Why, the little ones loved their holiday with me an' their granda, so they did, and I think they'd be even happier once we moved. It would be better for you, too, for you'd have your daddy and Liam to get you out-side into the good clean air instead of being cooped up inside all the time.'

'Well, as I said, we'll think on it,' Fergal told her, and with that she had to be content for the time being.

In the afternoon, Maeve and Dilly wrapped the children up warmly and they took a stroll around the marketplace. It was far too cold to think of venturing into the wide open spaces of the park but Maeve enjoyed herself, happy to peruse the vast amount of goods on display on the stalls. It seemed there was nothing you couldn't buy from one or another of them and had her purse been full, she could have spent a fortune. She wasn't so keen when they came to the cattle market, though, where the beasts were penned as red-faced farmers haggled over them.

'You'll have to harden your heart once you move to the smallholding,' Dilly chuckled. 'You'll not be able to look upon the animals as pets then.'

'I know that, sure I do,' Maeve admitted. 'And that's the bit I'm least looking forward to.'

It was then that they saw Olivia's nanny threading the pram through the crowds as she came towards them. Dilly's heart sank.

'Good afternoon, Mrs Carey,' Nanny greeted her, drawing the pram to an abrupt stop.

'Good afternoon.' Turning to her mother-in-law, Dilly said awkwardly, 'This is Mrs Perkins, the Farthings' nanny, and the child is Miss Olivia, their youngest.'

'How do you do?' Maeve greeted her, then stepped towards the pram and peeped down at the infant, who was fast asleep beneath a layer of blankets with her small thumb jammed into her mouth.

Maeve's eyes seemed to grow to twice their size. 'Goodness me, what a beautiful wee girl,' she said quietly, as Dilly felt her cheeks grow hot.

'She is,' Nanny agreed, with a glance at Dilly. 'And good as gold into the bargain. But now I

112

must get on, if you'll excuse me. Mrs Farthing gets irate if I keep her out in the cold for too long. Good day.'

'Good day,' the women chorused, as Nanny grasped the handles of the pram and moved on.

Maeve watched her go. 'She's a bonny wee thing, isn't she? How old did you say she was?'

Dilly was almost squirming. 'I didn't,' she answered shortly, 'but I reckon she's just over a year old now.'

'Hmm. She puts me in mind of our Niamh when she was that age.'

Just then a shout went up from Kian, who had found a litter of kittens in a cage. The women hurried over to him and the rest of the children, who were staring at them. 'Can we have one, Mammy, *please?*' Kian begged.

'I like that one there, the ginger one.'

'Well, I like the tabby one,' Seamus piped up.

'Not today, sweethearts,' Dilly told them firmly, glad of the distraction. 'We'd have to ask your daddy how he felt about it first. They do need feeding and caring for, you know. Now come along. If we stand here for long we'll freeze.' She managed to prise the children away and they moved on.

All too soon it was time for Maeve to leave. Declan was still adamant that he was returning to Dublin with her and nothing either Fergal or Dilly said to him would change his mind.

Dilly resorted to tears but that just made the situation worse.

'I do love yer both, Mammy,' a teary-eyed Declan assured her, 'but I'm happiest in Dublin and I'll be happier still when we move to Enniskerry. Uncle Liam has already put my an' Nipper's names down at the village school, and when we ain't there we'll be helpin' on the farm. An' you'll be able to come an' see me whenever yer want, won't yer, to be sure?'

In that moment Dilly realized that Declan might never come home and, much as it hurt, she had to accept it. She didn't tell him that the visits would have to be few and far between; her every waking minute was taken up with looking after the family and working. Instead she forced a smile and stroked his beloved face, then walked with him, Nipper and Maeve to the train station.

'Just remember, should you ever need anything you have only to ask. And promise me you'll think on what I said, about you all coming to live with us in Enniskerry,' Maeve urged, as the train drew onto the platform, with a hiss of steam and smoke.

'I will,' Dilly said, but the older woman had an idea that Dilly had already made up her mind. Hasty goodbyes were said, then Maeve pushed the boys gently onto the train and opened the window so that they could all lean out and wave.

'Goodbye – have a safe journey.' Dilly was blowing kisses and Declan was blowing them back, much to Nipper's amusement.

The guard was marching along, slamming the doors. Then he raised his flag, blew his whistle and the train began to chug away. Dilly ran alongside waving until she felt her arm might drop off. Then the train had gone round a bend in the track and her shoulders sagged. There was no need to keep the smile in place now: her son was gone. Crossing to a bench, she sank onto it, buried her face in her hands and sobbed as if her heart would break.

The instant she got home, Fergal noticed her red-rimmed eyes and opened his arms to her. 'I'm so sorry, lass. But, you know, we *could* go to Enniskerry as me Mammy suggested.'

When she raised her face to his, he saw her answer writ clear and knew in that moment that despite her brave talk about giving their child up for adoption being the best thing, she felt the loss as keenly as he did and there was nothing more to be said.

Chapter Eleven

August 1909

'Off out again, are you, darling?' Max Farthing asked, as he left his study to find his wife jabbing a hatpin into her latest purchase.

'Yes, and I don't know what time I shall be home so don't wait dinner for me,' she answered coolly.

Keeping his voice level to hide his irritation, he said, 'You're not off to one of those ladies' meetings again, are you?'

'I am, as a matter of fact, and why shouldn't I?' She stared boldly at him in the mirror as she pulled her gloves on. 'What else is there for me to do now that you've sent the boys to boarding school?'

Max sighed. Camilla and a few of her friends had lately formed a small group that met once a week, sometimes twice. They were all really bored women who had nothing better to do with their time and Max opened his mouth to tell her, but thought better of it and promptly clamped it shut again. It would only end in another disagreement.

'You can't even *begin* to imagine what it's like for me now that I have only Olivia,' she went on resentfully.

'But we've been through this dozens of times,' he answered wearily, as he swiped a hand across his eyes. 'And you know I only did it because I want to give them the best education I can. In any case, a bit of discipline will be good for Samuel. He was getting out of hand.'

'That is only your opinion,' she snapped. 'I never had any trouble controlling any of my sons and I shall *never* forgive you for sending them away, especially Oscar, who really didn't want to go.'

'That was only because he didn't want to leave Olivia – those two were almost inseparable as you know, but he's doing well now.'

'Oh, yes, and what's your excuse for sending Lawrence and Harvey too? You know that Harvey isn't strong. How can I look after him when he's so far away?'

'Lawrence wanted to join his brothers,' he pointed out, doing his best to keep his patience with her. 'As for Harvey, well, they do have a doctor at the school, should he need one. You and they will all thank me one day when they go into their chosen careers with good qualifications.'

Her lips set in a grim line before she lifted her

116

bag and changing the subject abruptly asked, 'Will you be going to your club tonight?'

When he nodded, she turned towards the door.

'And are you still going to the rally at Pendine in Carmarthenshire at the weekend?' Her words were heavy with meaning and he flushed as he nodded again. She was probably insinuating that what was good for the gander was good for the goose but he had no intention of missing this particular event. It was the International Car Rally at which the cars would race along the beach to try to set new speed records. He was looking forward to it.

'Very well. This might be a good time for me to ask Millie to move your things into another room upstairs,' she informed him coldly. 'It will be so much more convenient if we each have our own room now, don't you think? We shan't have to worry about disturbing each other if we come in late. Goodbye, Max.'

When his jaw dropped, she raised her eyebrows and left without another word, leaving him to stare sadly after her.

Once the front door had slammed behind her, Camilla blinked to hold back tears. Since the day Oscar had been shipped off to boarding school in Harrow four years ago at the age of ten, protesting loudly, her relationship with Max had gone steadily downhill. Oscar had been joined three years later by Samuel and Lawrence and she knew that Max had been relieved to see Samuel go: he had turned into a rebellious, argumentative child and Max had hoped that strict discipline would temper his ways. Deep down, Camilla knew that her husband was right but that didn't assuage the overpowering loneliness she had felt as the boys had left. Harvey had joined his brothers two years ago, and now that they were all at boarding school, time hung heavily on her hands. She had begged Max not to send them away, especially Harvey – she worried about him. He was still only eleven and her heart ached each time she thought of him so very far away. But on the subject of their education Max would not be swayed, and she couldn't forgive him. She had begged and pleaded with him, saying they could be tutored at home as Olivia was. But he had stood his ground.

As each of them had reached the age of ten he had driven them to the school in his Crossley motor car, another bone of contention with her. She hated the new-fangled vehicles, insisting that they were dangerous. She much preferred to use the horse and trap. They seemed to disagree about so many things nowadays, although when she had told him that she no longer wished to share a bedroom with him, he hadn't put up an argument. That had hurt her deeply and shown her just how rocky her marriage had become. *Still,* she consoled herself, as she strode along, *at least I still have Olivia.*

In the hallway, Max's gloomy thoughts were interrupted when Olivia flew down the stairs, her shining copper curls bouncing on her shoulders. She was wearing a blue dress and over it a pretty white pinafore, trimmed with broderie anglaise. She looked delightful, even if the ribbon he knew

Nanny would have fastened in her hair that morning had long since disappeared.

'Hello, Daddy. Has Mummy gone out?' She flashed him a smile that would have melted ice.

He returned it. 'Yes, she has, sweetheart, but why aren't you at your lessons in the schoolroom?'

'Miss Blake said I could have a break to get a drink so I'm going to see if I can scrounge some lemonade from Mrs Pegs.'

Max grinned. He doubted she'd have much trouble doing that. The entire household doted on the child and she had them all wrapped around her little finger. Not that she ever took advantage of it. She had a sunny disposition and was as happy as the day was long.

'That sounds like an excellent idea,' he replied. 'If I come with you, do you think I might be able to scrounge a cup of coffee?'

'Oh, yes, Daddy.' She gripped his large hand with her small one and they walked towards the kitchen. As they reached the door, Dilly came through it with a bucket of water and a scrubbing brush. She had been about to scrub the step outside the front door but she smiled and stood aside as they passed her.

When they were out of sight the smile slid from her face and she sighed. She had been feeling ill for weeks, but it was only a few days ago that she had realized the truth. She was pregnant again. The thought terrified her. She worked just three days a week for the Farthings now. Since the boys had left for school there wasn't so much to do and she had suggested to Mr Farthing that she might

119

cut her hours: she had been offered a job at Miss Mode's, the finest dress shop in the town where she worked in the sewing room at the back for three days. Now she had a whole day off each week on Sunday with the family. She had hardly been able to believe her luck – sewing had always been one of her passions and she had thought that things were finally going in the right direction. But then she had found she was with child again and knew she would never be able to give another away. It would rip the very heart out of her. But if it was born, what alternative would she have? She wouldn't be able to work for a while with a new baby to care for, and then what would they do for money? Admittedly, Kian had recently started at one of the local pits Mr Farthing owned and he gave her part of his wages each week, but his contribution was nowhere near enough to pay the rent and all the bills. And so she had come to a difficult decision; somehow she must get rid of the new life growing inside her. Of course Fergal must never find out. He was a staunch Catholic and believed that any woman who aborted her child would go straight into Hell's flames. Should he ever have an inkling of what she was planning to do he would never forgive her. A shiver went through her.

She and Fergal made love so infrequently now that she could remember clearly the night the baby must have been conceived. It had been one evening in June. She had had a bath in front of the fire and when she climbed out of the water to dry herself she had recognised the look in Fergal's eyes and cringed. She had avoided the act whenever she could, terrified of falling for a child – she was still only thirty-three, after all. Yet, up to a point, she had been lulled into a false sense of security: it had been nine years since she had given birth to Olivia and she had prayed that her childbearing days were over. She had given herself to Fergal willingly, but look where it had led!

Still, after tonight it would all be over. She had confided her predicament to Nell, who had told her of a woman in Bermuda village who could help her. After work one evening Dilly had paid her a visit. She could feel the two guineas that it would cost lying heavy in her apron pocket and her hands trembled as she thought of what lay ahead. Although she had converted to marry Fergal she had never been a staunch Catholic, as he was, but she hated herself for what she was about to do.

The rest of the day passed slowly but at last Dilly collected her shawl from the kitchen and set off for Bermuda village on legs that felt like jelly.

'Please forgive me, Lord, for what I am about to do!' she prayed, as she climbed the hill to the bull-ring and set off along Heath End Road. Eventually she took a left turn and, after walking on for some way, she saw the old woman's cottage standing alone in the dip of the valley.

The breath caught in her throat as tears sprang to her eyes and her hand dropped unconsciously to the slight swell of her belly. But then she steeled herself and began to move on, for deep down she knew she must put the rest of her family first and she had no choice.

When she reached the cottage she looked this way and that to make sure no one was about, then

121

pushed open the rickety gate and walked up the weed-strewn path. Maggie Kemp would never win any awards for cleanliness, that was for sure, she found herself thinking, but then she raised her hand and rapped on the door before she could change her mind.

Maggie had obviously been waiting for her because the door opened immediately. After glancing up and down the lane, as Dilly had done, the woman grasped her elbow with a scrawny hand and yanked her inside.

Dilly blinked in the gloomy light as Maggie demanded, 'Did yer bring the money?'

'Y-yes. I have it here.' Dilly fumbled in her pocket. Then, after handing it over, she watched silently as Maggie checked it before dropping it into the pocket of the grimy apron she was wearing. To take her mind off the reason she was there, Dilly tried to guess what age Maggie might be but found it impossible. Her hair, which was pulled back into an untidy bun at the nape of her neck, was snow-white, or it would have been, had it been clean, and there were more lines on her face than on a map of England.

'Did anyone see yer come 'ere?' Maggie demanded, and Dilly started, then shook her head.

'Right, then, an' yer quite sure you ain't more than nine or ten weeks gone?'

Another shake of the head.

'Good. Then let's get this over wi'. Foller me.'

Maggie led her up a wooden staircase and pushed her into a tiny bedroom with a leaded-light window under which stood a bed. There was nothing else in the room, apart from a small table.

A dish of some kind lay on it but Dilly couldn't see what was inside for it was covered with a none-too-clean rag.

'Strip off from the waist down an' hop on there,' Maggie ordered. She was clearly as keen to get this over and done with as Dilly was.

Self-consciously, Dilly did as she was told, then left her clothes in a heap on the floor. There was nowhere else to put them.

Seconds later she lay down on the grimy mattress, which was lumpy and uncomfortable although she was so nervous that she barely noticed.

'Draw yer knees up an' let 'em drop open,' Maggie instructed as she removed the cover from the dish and lifted a lethal-looking steel knitting needle from it. 'Yer goin' to feel a sharp pain but don't go cryin' out, mind. We wouldn't want anyone passin' by to hear yer. It'll only last fer a few seconds, then it'll all be over.'

Dilly's teeth were chattering with fright and tears coursed down her cheeks. Maggie bent towards her and a pain the like of which she had never known tore through her. She had to stuff her fist into her mouth to stop herself screaming. The few seconds that Maggie had mentioned seemed to go on for ever but at last she straightened and wiped the blood from the knitting needle with the cloth.

'Lie there fer a minute, then yer can get up an' gerroff,' Maggie informed her. 'You'll start to bleed heavily an' hopefully by bedtime it'll be done.'

Keen to get away, Dilly attempted to rise, but when a wave of dizziness washed over her, she dropped back onto the mattress and closed her eyes, trying not to think of the sin she had committed. She knew that for as long as she lived she would never forgive herself for this day. She felt dirty and unclean.

Some fifteen minutes later Dilly walked unsteadily from Maggie's cottage, her head bowed at the shameful thing she had done. Maggie had given her a grubby cloth to pad out her drawers until she got home, for the bleeding had started already.

She was walking unsteadily along St Mary's Road when she became aware that someone had fallen into step beside her. Glancing to the side she almost groaned aloud when she saw it was Madge Bunting, the very last person she wanted to see at that moment.

'I 'ope you ain't forgot it's pay day,' Madge remarked. 'I've been keepin' an eye out fer yer fer the last hour. Why are yer so late?'

Ignoring the question, Dilly fumbled in her pocket for her purse while gripping her stomach with the other hand. She was bleeding profusely and in total despair as she blinked back the tears.

'Don't forget we agreed it's to be 'alf a crown a week from now on,' Madge gabbled greedily, as her eyes fastened on the purse.

Dilly was too weak to argue and merely handed over the money without a word. Tonight she felt so ill that she would have given Madge her last penny just to get rid of her.

'Ta.' Madge snatched the money and dropped it into her pocket before smacking her lips. 'Right, I'll see yer next week, then. I'm off to wet me whistle at the Cock an' Bear now. Tara.'

By the time Dilly staggered up the entry to her cottage she had griping stomach pains and hurried down the yard to the privy, where she sat for the next half an hour. By then she knew it was all over. The baby was gone but she was light-headed with pain. Even so, she knew she must cover up the evidence so she staggered from the privy to return moments later with a shovelful of ashes, which she threw into the pan to conceal the blood. She tried to straighten but barely managed the short walk to her back door.

'Eeh, lass! Yer look like death warmed up, so yer do,' Fergal exclaimed, when he caught sight of her.

'I'm all right... It's just ... women's things,' she muttered, as she held on tightly to the back of a chair. 'But I wouldn't mind a lie-down.'

'O' course. Come an' hop into bed an' I'll put a brick in the oven to warm for you to put by your belly,' Fergal said. 'I'll warm you up a drop of Indian Brandee an' all an' put a bit of sugar in it. That usually does the trick, so it does.'

He wheeled himself away as Dilly drew back the bedclothes and dropped gratefully into bed. Despite the pain she soon fell into a restless sleep.

'What's up wi' Mammy?' the children asked, when they came in from playing outside shortly after.

'Ssh now!' Fergal put a finger to his lips. 'She has a poorly tummy, so she does, so we'll get a meal on, shall we, ready for when Kian gets in from his shift?' And for the rest of the evening they all crept about and Dilly slept on.

The following morning, Dilly woke at the usual time and clambered weakly out of bed. The pain was much easier now but she was still bleeding heavily and felt shaky and tired. Still, she was determined not to miss work so she set off for the Farthings'.

Nell hurried out for a quick word as she left. 'Is it all done, pet?' she asked anxiously, keeping her voice low for fear of Fergal hearing.

'Yes,' Dilly said dully.

'But yer really shouldn't be turnin' in to work today,' Nell fretted. 'Could yer not take the day off and rest?'

Dilly shook her head, patted Nell's arm and went on her way.

Max Farthing was about to climb into his car as she walked up the drive to his house and he paused to say, 'Good morning, Mrs Carey.'

'Morning, sir.'

She made to pass him but he frowned as he noticed how pale she was and asked, 'Are you feeling unwell, Mrs Carey?'

'I'm fine, thank you, sir.'

She walked on and he watched her go, with a frown on his face. The poor woman looked worn out, but it was hardly surprising, with all she had to contend with, a house to run, a crippled husband, a young family to care for and two jobs.

Unbidden he found himself comparing her to Camilla, who had never had to lift a finger in her life. Raised by wealthy parents, pampered and spoiled, she had continued to live in much the same way when she had married him, yet she could always find something to complain about, even more so of late. Dilly Carey just seemed to accept her lot for what it was and get on with things. She was fiercely proud, and an attractive woman – with the right clothes, he thought, she could be stunning. He wondered if Fergal Carey realized what a very fortunate man he was.

By mid-morning Dilly felt so ill and weak that Mrs Pegs couldn't help but notice, although Dilly was trying to carry on as if this were just any other day.

'Why don't yer get yerself away home, pet, an' take the rest o' the day off?' she suggested kindly, as she peered at Dilly's chalk-white face. 'Bessie can see to anythin' else that needs doin'.'

Dilly opened her mouth to refuse but Mrs Pegs was having none of it. 'Go on now,' she said firmly, after fetching Dilly's shawl for her. 'I'll clear it wi' Miss Norman an' we'll see you tomorrow, if yer feelin' better, eh? We can manage, can't we, Bessie?'

When Bessie nodded, Dilly's shoulders slumped. The offer was tempting and she would love a lie-down. The blood was still flowing and happen a rest might slow it down. 'Very well,' she agreed. 'Thank you, Mrs Pegs.'

She set off for home, but her footsteps dragged as she relived the terrible thing she had done the night before. Because of her, a child would never be born, never have the right to life. It weighed heavy on her conscience.

Suddenly she saw her life stretching before her. Endless weeks of working, only to hand a portion of her hard-earned wages to Madge Bunting. But worse than that, she now had three children to

127

miss, Declan, her first-born, who was still living happily with his grandparents, working the farm in Enniskerry, Olivia, whom she had been forced to give away within hours of her birth, and finally the poor wee soul she had murdered the night before. She had no doubt that she *had* murdered it, just as surely as if she herself had plunged the knitting needle into it. It was a heavy cross to bear and she knew it always would be.

Chapter Twelve

April 1911

'So where's our Declan, then?' Maeve asked as Daniel and Nipper came into the kitchen. 'It's not like him to be late for his snap. I swear that lad's got hollow legs.'

Daniel laughed as he washed his hands at the sink. He dried them and took a seat at the table. 'He's up in the top field with one of the ewes that's lambing,' he informed her, as he began to carve a thick wedge from the freshly baked loaf on the table and plaster it with butter. 'I doubt he'll be in till he's seen the lamb safe delivered. You know what he's like with the beasts.'

'Aye, I know all right.' Maeve chuckled. Sixteen-year-old Declan had taken to the farming life like a duck to water and was never happier than when he was out in the fields. Nipper was much the same, although he was more ambitious than Declan. She glanced at him now as he joined her husband at the table. It was hard to believe he was the same scrawny young lad who had come to Enniskerry with them just a few short years ago.

It had been hard for him to adjust to a normal family life and to living indoors when they had first arrived, yet now he loved his home comforts. He and Declan had attended the village school but now they worked full time on the smallholding, and Nipper spent every spare minute he could at the forge in the village with Sean Mc-Loughlin, the elderly blacksmith – he was keen to learn the trade.

Maeve had felt hurt when he had first confided to her his dream of becoming a blacksmith, for she thought of him as a member of the family and had imagined he would always be there, at least until he wed. He had been quick to reassure her that she and Daniel were the closest thing to a family he had ever had and he would always stay close but wanted a measure of independence.

Maeve was inordinately proud of him. Until he had come to live with them he had only ever known himself as Nipper or Ben, the name the orphanage staff had given him when he had been abandoned there. After making enquiries through Father Doherty, Maeve had set the date he had arrived there as his birthday and she had insisted he take their surname, so he was now known officially as Benjamin Carey. Maeve thought it had a nice ring to it and, as she had pointed out, you could hardly call a man who owned a business Nipper. It wouldn't do and, knowing him as she did, she had no doubt he would fulfil his dream one day. As he had said, people would always need blacksmiths

129

for they did much more than shoe horses, and with all the neighbouring farms thereabouts he would never be out of work.

She looked at him now, his strong, muscled arms and shining hair, and thought it was no wonder that half the lasses in the village had set their caps at him. At seventeen he was still but a youth but he looked set to become a very handsome young man indeed. He showed no interest in the lasses who chased after him, for he was too intent on making something of himself. He saved every penny of the small wage they paid him so that eventually he would stand on his own two feet.

Declan, on the other hand, was quite content to spend all his time on the farm and, unlike Nipper, he had an eye for the girls, which amused Maeve and Daniel no end. He was a lovely-natured lad and they adored him, but Maeve still felt guilty that he had chosen to live with them and not his parents. She knew how hard it was for Dilly in England and made sure he visited them at least once a year, although sometimes she had almost to force him to do so. It was strange – he clearly loved his parents but she had accepted the situation for what it was long ago. She just wished that Fergal and Dilly would join them in Ireland. She was certain that the good clean air would do Fergal and the weans the world of good, but whenever she suggested it, Dilly would make an excuse and change the subject.

She moved to the kettle, which was bubbling on the range, and as she poured the boiling water into the teapot she spotted Liam heading into his own cottage which had been tacked on to the end of

130

the existing one. Daniel had started to build it in his spare time with the help of the three boys the year Liam had wed young Shelagh Connelly from the village so that the young couple could have some privacy. It had worked well. Liam was now the proud father of Patrick, a bonny two-year-old boy with another wean due any day. Maeve adored the little chap but was secretly hoping that the next one would be a lass. She had always longed for a daughter but a granddaughter living close by would be the next best thing. Had she been honest with herself she would have admitted that this was another reason she wished Fergal and Dilly would join them. She would be able to get to know Niamh better, rather than seeing her for just a few days a year as she did now.

All in all, though, she was content. The small-holding was thriving and they now had a flock of sheep, as well as pigs, cows and chickens, thanks to Daniel's careful breeding programme and hard work, and with each year, the smallholding became more profitable. As her eyes swept the comfortable kitchen she felt a glow of satisfaction. No one would have believed that just a few short years ago the place had been almost derelict. Now it was cosy and welcoming. The large scrubbed table and six sturdy chairs that they had brought with them from Dublin took up the centre of the room and behind it was a large dresser containing her prized china, used only on special occasions. Gay peg rugs were strewn across the flagstoned floor and comfortable armchairs stood at either side of the fireplace. Maeve had stitched bright flowered curtains for the windows and made cushions for the chairs with the scraps of material that were left over. Beneath the window that overlooked the yard was a deep stone sink and a wide wooden draining-board, and Maeve never tired of standing there, watching the chickens pecking among the cobblestones in the yard.

The pigsties lay at the far end of the yard next to a barn where they stored the animals' fodder in the winter. Between that and the kitchen was the dairy, where Maeve churned milk from their cows into butter and cheese. Now that the cows were so productive she often had enough to take some into the village on market day and sell it, and the money she made from this went into her savings pot, 'For a rainy day,' as she often informed Daniel. There was also a large laundry room, housing a copper, a dolly-tub, another deep stone sink for rinsing the clothes and a mangle. Next door to that was the outside privy and behind it the cinder path that led to the orchard.

Inside the house a door leading from the kitchen led into an airy parlour kept immaculate at all times and used only on high days and holidays. Another door led to the staircase and three good-sized bedrooms, one for herself and Daniel, another for Declan and Nipper, and the third for the grandchildren when they came to stay.

'Here, woman, how much longer is that tea going to be?' Daniel demanded, with a twinkle in his eye. 'A man could die of thirst while you stand there daydreaming at the window, so he could.'

'Oh sorry... I was miles away.' Maeve quickly carried the pot to the table and poured out two large mugs of tea and after Nipper and Daniel had drained them they went about their work leaving Maeve to tackle a large pile of ironing.

Up in the top field Declan heaved a sigh of relief as he helped the sheep to deliver the lamb she had been struggling to bring into the world. It had been born in the breech position and Declan had feared they might lose it, but it was a healthy little thing, and as he cleared its mouth it began to bleat and its mother turned towards it protectively and began to wash it.

Declan grinned as he wiped his bloody hands on the grass and stepped back. His job was done; it was up to the ewe now. He felt a measure of satisfaction as he looked about the field at the lambs that were gambolling about, chasing their mothers, kicking their legs in the air and bleating. It was a fine sight indeed and touching to see how the ewes cared for their young. Unbidden, a picture of his own mother flashed into his mind and the all-too-familiar guilt set in. The truth was that he couldn't bear anything to do with illness. The sight of his father's legs withering away had made him feel nauseous, and he had known he couldn't stay there, young though he had been. But he could never admit that this was why he had preferred to stay in Dublin. He was too ashamed.

Now that the lamb was safely delivered he set aside his gloomy thoughts and went down the field to rejoin Nipper. They had been rebuilding some of the dry-stone walls that surrounded the fields, a job Declan enjoyed. He was aware that he had probably missed his afternoon snack but decided he could wait till dinnertime. His gran'ma set a fine table so she did, and he would make up then for what he had missed.

'Mr McLoughlin let me shoe me first horse tonight,' Nipper told them proudly that evening as they sat around the fireplace enjoying a mug of cocoa. 'I'm thinking that by the time he's ready to retire I'll be ready to buy the business from him. If I can afford it, that is,' he ended glumly.

'Doesn't a cottage come with the business?' Maeve asked uneasily. She hated the thought of losing him but was wise enough to know that all the chicks might want to spread their wings and leave the nest some day. If he did buy the black-smith's business at least he wouldn't be far away.

'Aye, it does,' Nipper answered. 'It's only a wee two-up-two-down place but it would suit me fine, so it would, and I'd still be close at hand to help here if I was needed.'

Touched, Maeve reached out and squeezed his hand. 'Happen if it's meant to be then it'll be,' she said philosophically. 'I'm a great believer that our paths are mapped out for us by Him above. Now drink your cocoa and get yourself to bed, lad.'

And Nipper did just that.

At that moment in Dublin, Father Doherty was enjoying a last tot of whisky when his housekeeper tapped at the door. 'There's a lady here, Father, wishing to speak to you.'

He sighed wearily. It had been a long day and he had come home late after reading the last rites to one of his parishioners, whom he doubted would last the night. He had been looking forward to re-tiring but he said, 'Very well, Mrs Brogan. Would you kindly show her in?' It would probably be some poor soul fallen on hard times who was seeking a bed for the night. He rose to meet his visitor, but when she walked in some seconds later he was taken aback. This was a lady, if he wasn't very much mistaken, certainly not someone in need of shelter. He judged her to be somewhere in her mid-thirties.

'Thank you for seeing me at such a late hour, Father Doherty.' The woman extended her hand. Moving forward, he shook it, taking in at a glance her well-cut travelling costume and her plumed hat. Everything about her spoke of class. It wasn't often he saw ladies dressed as elegantly in these parts.

''Tis no trouble at all, Mrs ... er...' He turned back to the housekeeper. 'Would you kindly bring in a tray of tea, Mrs Brogan? To be sure, I was thinking I might like a cup before turning in.'

The housekeeper left the room, closing the door softly after her, and the priest ushered the woman towards the fireside chair opposite to the one he had been sitting in.

'I – I am aware that it is inconsiderate of me to call without making an appointment,' she said, clearly ill at ease, 'but I hope that when I tell you the reason for my visit you will find it in your heart to forgive me. My name is Elizabeth McFarren.'

He noted her Irish surname, which was at vari-ance with her perfectly modulated English accent.

'My husband was Irish,' she went on, as if she had been able to read his mind. He nodded, more

135

curious by the minute as she perched uncomfortably on the edge of the seat. She took off her gloves and folded them, then clasped her hands primly in her lap and he recognised a troubled soul, whatever her breeding. 'So, Mrs McFarren, how may I help you?' he asked kindly, hoping to ease the tension in her. The silence seemed to stretch for ever but eventually, her eyes downcast, she said, 'I have come to enquire about a baby that was left on the steps of the Nuns of Mercy orphanage some years ago.'

Father Doherty frowned. 'I'm afraid I have known of many such weans over the years. Could you not be a little more specific?'

There was a tap at the door and, when the housekeeper appeared with the tea, the conversation was halted. Once Father Doherty had prepared the cups and they were alone again, he encouraged, 'Do go on.'

'It ... it was a boy child. He would be seventeen years old now. Almost a man.'

'Was it yours?' he asked, in a voice that was little above a whisper.

When her head bowed he had his answer. 'Yes... he was mine. But there was no way I could have kept him... If I could go back to the beginning and explain you might understand why.'

Father Doherty remained silent as he handed her a cup of tea but her hand was shaking so badly that he placed it on the small table to the side of her.

'My husband is ... was... a great deal older than me. He recently passed away, which is why I felt able to come here now. I met him when I was holidaying in London with my parents and I suppose I was swept off my feet. He was a sea captain, a very dashing figure back then, and in no time at all we were married. I came to live with him at his home in Dublin. We had been married for just over a year when I gave birth to my first son, Lionel, but then my husband had to go abroad. He often had to spend long periods away from home. Anyway, he was gone for almost two years, to India, and while he was away I became lonely. I'm ashamed to say I – I had an affair with a young man. Well, it wasn't even an affair, really, just a moment of madness. My husband had been gone for almost eight months when I discovered that I was with child. I was frantic with worry. My husband was a kind, generous man and I couldn't bear to hurt him. It would have broken his heart – what I had done was unforgivable. It was my trusted maid who suggested that we might travel for a few months until after the baby's birth, so when I could no longer hide my condition, I left Lionel in the charge of his nanny and told the staff that my maid and I were going to England to visit my parents for a few months. On the night the child was born my maid wrapped him warmly and delivered him to the steps of the orphanage. I pinned his name, written on a piece of paper, to his shawl. I called him Benjamin, and I can truly say that I have never known a day's peace since. That has been my punishment for abandoning him.

'As the years passed, my maid would travel regularly into the city to get a glimpse of him or take the donations I sent to the orphanage so that

137

she might be allowed inside. But one day when she asked after him a nun told her he had run away and was living on the streets. He was just a child and I was sick with worry, but what could I do, Father? I was terrified of my husband finding out what I had done and I had no way of knowing where the child might have gone.'

As comprehension suddenly dawned, Father Doherty stroked his chin. 'Seventeen years ago, you say it was, and a boy? He was just a wean when he took to the streets?'

She nodded miserably.

'Then I think I may know who you are talking of. It would be young Ben. I thought that was the name the nuns had given to him but he liked to be known as Nipper.'

As hope shone in her eyes the Father noticed how pretty she was. She had the same colour hair and eyes as Nipper, now that he studied her a little more closely. In fact, the resemblance was uncanny.

'I – I tucked a large sum of money into his shawl that would pay for his keep for years to come when the maid took him to the orphanage,' she rushed on. 'I have prayed that the nuns passed it on to him so that when he left he might be able to survive.'

The priest frowned. It was the first he had heard about any money, but Sister Monica would probably have put it into the charity box to benefit all of the orphans. He would certainly be speaking to her about it. That money should have been kept for Ben.

'If you have an idea who the child was, do you

138

know what became of him?' she asked now.

He nodded. 'I do right enough,' he told her. 'The lad was taken in by a good Catholic family who now run a smallholding in Enniskerry. He's officially known as Benjamin Carey – they gave him their name – although he still likes to be called Nipper. He is there with them and I can tell you he's grown into a fine, strong young man. A son any mother would be proud of.'

The woman's fist flew to her mouth and she stifled a sob as tears streamed from her eyes. 'Th-thank you. I know how badly you must think of me, but it means the world to know that he is safe.'

Father Doherty's eyes softened. It was clear to see how much she was suffering. 'We all do things we are ashamed of in this life, and I believe your first concern was to save your husband's feelings so it was not an entirely selfish act,' he told her. She was trying to compose herself, he could see. When she became a little calmer he asked, 'Are you here because you are wanting to meet the young man now that your husband has passed away?'

She shook her head vigorously. 'Oh, no, Father. I lost that right on the night I gave him away. I am here because I am hoping to make the rest of his life a little easier.' She fumbled in her bag and withdrew a sum of money that had the priest's eyes popping. 'There is five hundred pounds here,' she told him solemnly. 'I was wondering if you would pass it on to him for me. Perhaps there is a path that he wishes to pursue. If so, this may help him.'

'As it happens I know that he's training to be a blacksmith and this would certainly help him attain his dream. But where would I tell him it came from?'

Bemused, she stared at him. 'Could you not say it was left with you to give to him when he reached his twenty-first birthday by someone anonymous but that you feel he should have it now? I know it would be lying but surely if the lie was to someone's good the Lord would forgive you.'

Sweat broke out on Father Doherty's forehead. What she was asking him to do was a sin against God. 'Why do you not go and give it to him yourself?' he suggested. 'To know who his mother is would mean more to him than any amount of money, to be sure.' He could have told her of all the times he had held Ben on his lap when he was a wee boy and watched the child cry as his friends had been chosen for adoption and he had been left at the orphanage. 'But me mammy *will* come back for me one day, *won't* she, Father?' Ben had asked hopefully, and the kindly priest had thought his heart would break.

'My husband may be gone but I'm afraid I have to think of my other son,' Elizabeth McFarren answered. 'What would it do to him to know he had a brother I had given away all those years ago? And what would he think of me?' She shook her head. 'No, Father. I'm afraid I can't do it to him, especially so soon after losing his father. His father bought him a post in the army and he is away training to be an officer at the moment.'

Father Doherty steepled his fingers. He eyed

140

the money she was holding out to him as if it might bite him. And then he reached a decision. 'I cannot do as you ask. It would be a mortal sin to tell such a blatant lie ... but,' he hurried on, as he saw her face drop, 'I can give you Nipper's address in Enniskerry. Then perhaps you can come up with a way to get the money to him.'

Before she could argue he crossed to his desk and quickly scribbled down the Careys' address. He then moved back to her and pressed the piece of paper into her hand saying, 'May God go with you, my child. And may you one day find peace.'

She pushed the paper and the money back into her bag then after putting on her gloves she rose to face him.

'Thank you, Father, and bless you too,' she said quietly then without another word she left the room leaving him to stare down into the flames of the fire.

There goes one troubled soul, he thought, and offered up a silent prayer for her and one for Nipper, too, who even now was to be denied the right to know his true parentage.

Chapter Thirteen

'It's as true as I'm sitting here,' Maeve told her captive audience. 'I was out working in the dairy when this posh pony and trap pulled up in the yard. I went outside to find out what they were wanting. A lady, she looked like a ladies' maid, got down from the trap and asked me which way it was to the church so I gave her directions and off she goes. I went back into the dairy and never gave it another thought, but when I'd done churning the butter, I went back to the kitchen and found this big envelope addressed to Benjamin Carey on the doorstep. It's a good job I found it when I did, else the chickens would have pecked it to pieces, so they would.' She chuckled before going on. 'Anyway I thought it was strange there were no stamps on it but I just put it on the dresser and forgot all about it till later that evening when I suddenly remembered it and passed it to Nipper. You can imagine how shocked we were when all this money tumbled out across the table. *Five hundred pounds* no less! For a start off Nipper was having none of it, but eventually we persuaded him that whoever had sent it had intended him to have it. To be sure it was his name on the envelope so there could be no mistaking who it was meant for. And now the lad is set up for life if he spends it wisely, God bless him! He's already agreed to buy the blacksmith's business from Sean Mc-Loughlin when he retires and he gets a fine wee cottage that comes with it.'

'Well, I'll be... How wonderful for him,' Dilly said, as her mother-in-law paused for breath. 'But our Declan will miss him when he goes, won't he? They've become like brothers over the years.'

'They have that,' Maeve agreed. 'But he'll only be a few miles down the road so they'll still see a lot of each other, so they will.'

'And you think it might have been the woman who asked for directions that left it?'

Maeve shrugged. 'Who else could it have been? We're stuck out there and sometimes see no one for days. I can think of no one else who might leave it. Nipper tried to make Daniel take some of it to buy some more beasts in repayment for us taking him in but Daniel wasn't having a bar of it, and rightly so. The lad's like a son to us, so he is – why would we want to take his money from him?'

As Maeve looked at her son she saw that his eyes were drooping and she whispered to Dilly, 'Do you not think we should be getting me laddo to bed? He looks weary, so he does.'

'I'm not tired yet,' Fergal snapped, much to his mother's astonishment. She had thought he was almost asleep but his quick burst of temper told her otherwise. '*Why* must you talk about me as if I'm not even in the room? Me body might be failin' but me mind ain't!'

Dilly sighed as the children instantly became silent and crept away to their rooms. They always made themselves scarce if they heard their father working himself up into a temper.

'Even so your mother's right. It's time you had a rest,' Dilly said patiently, laying aside the skirt she had been hemming. She often brought work home from the dress shop if Fergal was unwell. It was no hardship as she was never happier than when she was sewing. Lately she had even begun to suggest ideas for designs to Mrs Ball, the owner of the shop, who had soon discovered that Dilly had a real flair for fashion as well as sewing.

Maeve looked shocked but silently helped Dilly to transfer her son from the chair to his bed, crying inside at the sight of his poor shrivelled body. He had once been so strong and vibrant.

'Would you like a drink before you settle down?' Maeve asked, but Fergal shook his head, his eyes dark and brooding.

'Wouldn't I ask for one if I did?' he snapped.

Maeve straightened. Then, hands on hips, she scolded, 'To be sure there's no need to talk to me and your wife like that!'

Fergal had the good grace to look contrite and turned his face to the wall as Maeve took Dilly's elbow and led her out into the yard.

'Is he often like that?' she asked.

Dilly nodded wearily. 'Yes, but we're all used to it. He calms down eventually. Happen it's just frustration that makes him that way.'

'Frustration or not, he has no need to talk to you like that,' Maeve said indignantly, shocked at her son's behaviour.

A letter from Dilly informing her that Fergal had deteriorated had brought her from Ireland. They were into June now, and although it was early evening it was still bright and balmy outside. Maeve had been fretting about the smallholding, and how they would manage without her, but now that she had seen the change in her son she was glad she had made the journey, even if she could stay only for a couple of nights. She had not visited since the time she had arrived unannounced with Declan and young Nipper and she was heart-sore to see how ill he was. He had caught a cold in the spring that had settled on his chest and since then, no matter what infusions or tonics Dilly forced on him or how much grease she applied to his chest,

144

he hadn't improved.

Thankfully, Maeve had noticed that, at fifteen, Niamh was now a great help to her mother. She had had another shock at first sight of her granddaughter: she was turning into a rare little beauty. Her glorious copper-coloured hair, which no amount of ribbons would hold in check, tumbled down her back and her deep brown eyes were heavily fringed with long black lashes that her gran'ma declared were beautiful enough to tempt the ducks off the water, much to the girl's embarrassment. She was now working as a trainee teacher at Chilvers Coton School, attending evening classes two nights a week and an art class on another evening; she helped with the housework when she was at home, which had shifted at least some of the burden Dilly's shoulders. Maeve had been astonished by how much her grandchildren had grown up. Kian, who looked like a younger version of his brother Declan, was still working at Nowell's colliery in Whittleford, although he made it no secret that he didn't particularly like it. Still, it was regular work and he stuck at it, keen to do his bit for the family. He was still working above ground for he was only fourteen but he was looking forward to going below when his wages would increase.

Then there was Seamus who, although he was still at school for another wee while, dreamed of becoming a doctor. Maeve doubted he would achieve his ambitions: although the family were a little better off financially, medical school was expensive – how would they afford it? Dilly was holding down two jobs but Maeve suspected that much of her wages went on Fergal's doctor's bills. She wished with all her heart that she could help, but although the smallholding was thriving, most of their profits were ploughed back into buying more beasts and equipment to lighten the men's workloads. There was her 'rainy-day' money, though, and she mentioned this now. 'I don't have a lot put by, lass, but you're welcome to what there is if it would help with doctor's bills and such.'

Tucked away on her smallholding in the beautiful Irish countryside, Maeve felt sheltered and safe from harm, but when she visited the English Midlands she was always shocked to see how quickly the world was changing.

Dilly thanked her but waved aside her offer, insisting that they were managing fine. She fetched two chairs into the yard and the two women sat down side by side.

Maeve was enjoying a glass of stout when Madge Bunting appeared out of her cottage. She eyed her warily. She had seen her on a few previous visits and didn't like the look of the dirty baggage. The woman looked as if a change of clothes and a good wash would do her the power of good.

'Entertainin' our in-laws, are we?' she said sarcastically and Maeve noticed the way Dilly lowered her head and flushed. 'Aye, she is, and it's right lovely to be here,' Maeve answered sharply, wondering why Dilly didn't tell her to mind her own business.

'Must be nice to see *all* your gran'kids growin' up fit an' strong.'

Maeve narrowed her eyes, wondering what the woman was implying. 'Aye, it's always grand to see them all, so it is,' she answered, as civilly as she could.

Madge cast a look at Dilly, which Maeve couldn't interpret, and went on her way with a snigger.

Maeve frowned. 'I don't understand why you give the likes of her the time of day,' she said, but Dilly merely shrugged. It was almost as if she was afraid of the woman, Maeve mused.

'I have to live here,' Dilly answered dully. 'So it's best to say nothing for the sake of peace.'

'Ah, but you *don't* have to live here and put up with the likes of that trollop,' Maeve said heatedly. This was the opening she had been waiting for. 'You could all come to Enniskerry, as I've told you before. The lads could work on the farm. The good Lord knows Daniel, Liam and Declan would be glad of the extra hands, and Niamh could get a job in the village, I'm sure. There's a lovely little village school with only one teacher to run it and I've no doubt she'd jump at the chance of letting Niamh continue her training there. The men could build on another extension for you all to live in so that you had your own space. Just think how wonderful it would be for all the family to be together and how much better it would be for Fergal. Why, the good clean air could blow fresh life into him, so it could, and improve his mood into the bargain!'

'And how do you think we would manage to get him there?' Dilly asked. 'He hasn't the strength to even wheel himself about the cottage any more, let alone tackle getting on and off trains and ferries.'

Maeve wagged her finger. 'Now don't you be using that as an excuse,' she scolded. 'Sure if you'd

147

only agree to come, Declan and Daniel would come over to get Fergal safe home, so they would. Think of it, *please*, Dilly. I worry meself sick wondering how you're coping and how me lad is.'

Could she have known it, there was nothing her daughter-in-law would have liked more than to join the family in Enniskerry. Sometimes Dilly dreamed of waking up to birdsong and the sound of cattle lowing, instead of factory hooters, and of having someone to help her care for Fergal. As Maeve had now witnessed there were days when she and the family crept about the place for fear of disturbing him; days when they barely dared speak for fear of having their heads snapped off. But much as she wanted to she knew she could never think of leaving Olivia, even though she only glimpsed her each week. That was enough. To see her growing and hear her voice kept Dilly going.

And Dilly was still convinced that if Madge got wind that she was about to lose the money she extorted from her each week she would spread the word about whose child Olivia really was, and what would that do to the girl? Dilly shuddered. Olivia would hate her for giving her away at birth, and she knew she could never bear that. Every single day Dilly felt as if her family was incomplete and the only time she was truly happy and at peace was when she was near to the girl. Even then the yearning to reach out and tell her just how much she loved her was almost unbearable. But now she was too weary to argue so she reached across the short divide and squeezed her mother-in-law's hand affectionately and the action made

Maeve clamp her lips shut. The poor lass had enough on her plate after all, without her nagging her.

Fergal was having a bad day when it came time for Maeve to leave. She drew Dilly aside and whispered, 'Is there nothing more they can do for him, lass?'

'The doctor did say that amputation of his legs would stop the pain,' Dilly said, with a worried glance at her husband, who had decided not to get up that morning. 'But the problem is there could be complications and the doctor told us in no uncertain terms that the risks could be high. Fergal might not even survive the operation so what are we to do?'

Maeve chewed her lip, seeing Dilly's predicament. The thought of her lad with no legs was heartbreaking, even if it might bring an end to his pain, but not at the risk of his life. 'That must be for you two to decide,' she said eventually, 'but I feel bad running away and leaving you with so much on your plate, so I do.'

'You're needed at home and I can manage,' Dilly told her, with a fond smile. 'You must be coming up to your busiest time of year on the farm so finish packing that bag and be off with you. It's not as if I have no help. Niamh is here to lend a hand.'

Niamh would have done far more if Dilly had allowed her to, but her mother didn't wish her to miss out on her social life so she bore the brunt herself. Niamh would be young only once, and she had no wish to turn her into an old woman before her time.

'I'm working at the dress shop today so I'll walk

149

as far as the town with you,' she said then, as Maeve crammed the rest of her things into her jute bag. She herself rushed about, ensuring that Fergal would have all he needed to hand before she left and after Maeve had bade him a tearful goodbye, they set off together in the misty early morning.

'Well, I shall have to leave you here or I'll be late,' Dilly said, as they came to the edge of the town. 'Have a safe journey home, Maeve, and do give my love to everyone... Please tell Declan I miss him.'

Maeve dropped her bag and hugged her fiercely, 'Sure I will,' she promised huskily. 'And isn't it time, after all these years, that you started to call me "Mammy"?'

As Maeve stared at her she thought the woman was a marvel. Dilly was now almost in her mid-thirties but she still looked little more than a girl. Her thick hair still shone and, with her slim figure and clear skin, she could easily have been taken for ten years younger.

'Thank you, I will ... Mammy,' Dilly answered.

Then Maeve was snatching up her bag and, with a last wave, she was off in the direction of the station. Dilly watched her go, then hurried on her way.

Her spirits rose as she walked back to Miss Mode's. Camilla Farthing had an appointment to bring Olivia into the shop to choose material and be measured for two new day dresses and Dilly was looking forward to it. Mrs Ball had told her she might attend to them.

At eleven o'clock promptly the bell on the shop

150

door tinkled and Mrs Ball called Dilly from the sewing room, where she was putting the finishing touches to a gown that a client would collect later that day. 'Mrs Farthing is here, Dilly,' Mrs Ball said. 'I might take a short break while you attend to her and her daughter, dear.' She disappeared into the back room as Dilly smiled a welcome.

Camilla Farthing looked none too pleased to find that Dilly would be serving them but Olivia's lovely face broke into a smile of welcome, making Dilly's heart race with pleasure.

'Hello, Mrs Carey. Isn't it a lovely day?' Olivia said brightly, already eyeing the many rolls of fabric with excitement. 'Mother says I may have something a little more grown-up today. What would you suggest?'

'Well, if it's day dresses you're wanting you will need something practical although, of course, it can still be pretty.'

Trying to ignore the malicious glare Mrs Farthing had focused on her, Dilly crossed to the large shelves that housed the bales of fabric and selected a blue cotton, covered with tiny sprigs of forget-me-nots. 'This would go well with your colouring and be perfect for the summer. If you liked it, we could trim it with the pale green colours of the leaves or white. What do you think? I have a pattern in this book that would be perfect for this fabric and it would look lovely when it's made up.'

As the three of them looked at the pattern Dilly was suggesting, Camilla had to accept grudgingly that it was indeed a wise choice and Olivia certainly seemed delighted with it, although as Camilla watched their two heads bent across the pattern book a surge of jealousy washed through her, like iced water. They were so alike that every time she saw them together it was a constant reminder of where Olivia had sprung from.

She had been hugely relieved when Dilly had cut the hours she worked at the house but now she was serving her in a dress shop! It seemed that there was no getting away from her. Perhaps in future she might persuade Olivia to shop in Coventry. Had it been left to her, Dilly would have been dismissed from her employ many years ago, but Camilla knew her husband would never contemplate going back on their agreement. He seemed to like the woman, which was yet another bone of contention with her.

She watched Dilly and Olivia examine a rather fine bale of autumn-coloured fabric, and again she was forced to admit that it was an excellent choice. Once it was decided on, she stood aside as they consulted the pattern book once more, nodding her agreement when Olivia turned to ask her opinion.

Next came the measurements, and as Dilly expertly took Olivia's details, Camilla felt another ripple of jealousy. They seemed so at ease with each other and she felt left out.

'My brothers are coming home from school next month for the summer holidays,' Olivia rattled on. 'Oscar is sure to notice how grown-up I look in them. Do you think you might be able to get the dresses done by then, Mrs Carey?'

'I don't see why not,' Dilly answered indulgently, 'as long as you are able to get to the shop for fittings.'

'I shall make sure of it,' Camilla said imperiously.

They turned their attention to the ribbon that the dresses would be trimmed with.

'Very well, Olivia, we really must be going now,' Camilla said finally. She had the idea that the girl could have stayed and chatted to Dilly Carey all day. She certainly seemed to be enjoying herself. 'Mrs Hetherington-Smythe is expecting us for luncheon and we don't wish to be late, do we?'

As Camilla Farthing turned to lift her bag from a chair, Olivia pulled a face. It was all Dilly could do to stop herself laughing. The girl clearly wasn't looking forward to the luncheon and certainly had a lively sense of humour.

'Goodbye, Mrs Carey, and thank you for all your help.' She had paused at the door. 'Just let us know when you want me to come in for my first fitting.'

Then she was gone, leaving Dilly bereft as she carried the material Olivia had chosen to the cutting room. With Mrs Ball's permission she would make Olivia's dresses a priority.

Chapter Fourteen

July 1913

'Are the bedrooms aired and is everything in readiness for the boys, Miss Norman?' Camilla enquired excitedly, as she took yet another peep from the drawing-room window.

'Oh, yes, madam,' the housekeeper assured her. 'And I've prepared a room for Master Oscar's friend. May I ask how long he will stay?'

'Oh, a couple of weeks or so, I should imagine.' Camilla surveyed the room, straightening a slight crease from one of the cushions. The house was gleaming from top to bottom and Max had left the evening before, intending to stay at a hotel so that he could pick the boys up bright and early from Harrow and bring them home for the summer holidays. Now that Oscar was eighteen he would not be returning to school but would start to work for his father. He would manage the books of Max's many businesses; when he was fully trained Max intended to make his eldest son a partner in readiness for when he inherited one day. He was extremely proud of Oscar, who had worked hard at school. Lawrence and Harvey were doing well too and achieving excellent reports, but unfortunately the same could not be said of Samuel, who was always in trouble. Camilla had lost count of the number of times they had been summoned to the school to discuss his behaviour. There had been times when they had feared he might be expelled, but they had managed to avoid that up to now and could only hope that, as he grew older, he would settle down.

Today, though, she wasn't thinking about Samuel. She was excited about the arrival of Oscar's friend. William Buchanon-Green came from a very good family indeed. His father was a wealthy man with a huge country estate outside Ledbury and was just the sort of person with whom Camilla wanted her children to mix. The year before Oscar had stayed with William's family and when Camilla and Max had travelled there to bring him home, she had been beside herself at her first glimpse of the place. An added attraction was Georgina, William's seventeen-year-old sister, who appeared to be besotted with Oscar. In the short time they had been at the house, Camilla had seen how Georgina's eyes followed Oscar adoringly, and now she had high hopes that they might make a match. She had written to Georgina's mother requesting that she join Olivia and the boys for a short break.

'Imagine having the Buchanon-Greens as in-laws,' she had said to Max, when they were at home, and he had chuckled.

'Why, Camilla, I didn't realize you were such a shameless match-maker,' he had teased. 'Georgina is a nice enough girl, from what I saw of her, but they're so young.'

'Not too young to feel attracted to each other,' Camilla said. 'If we encourage the friendship, who knows where it might lead? I suppose *some* good should come of you sending my children so far away from me! A good marriage is just as important as a good education. I don't want any of my children marrying down.'

Max had sighed and returned to his newspaper, but since then Camilla had invited William to their home at every opportunity. Now Georgina would be with them, too, and Camilla intended to throw Oscar and the girl together at every opportunity. In fairness, Oscar had shown no interest in her but Camilla was sure she could change that.

It was almost an hour later when the car pulled up on the drive. After checking her hair in the hall mirror, Camilla rushed out to welcome them all, closely followed by Olivia.

'Oh, boys, it's lovely to see you,' Camilla gushed. 'You too, William.' She embraced each of them. Camilla was annoyed to find that she had to wait her turn with Oscar for, as usual, Olivia had got to him first, but she kept her smile in place. Oscar had always adored his little sister and Olivia worshipped the ground he walked on. Camilla had found it endearing when they had both been children but lately she had found it slightly unnatural. They were older now and should be conducting themselves in a more adult fashion.

'It was a bit of a squeeze with three of us in the back,' Lawrence informed her, with a cheeky grin, as he walked to the back of the car and began to untie their luggage. 'Still, I suppose it's better than having to come back on the train, like Samuel and Harvey. What's for lunch? We're starving, aren't we, chaps?'

Camilla laughed as she ushered them inside. 'Don't worry. Mrs Pegs has everything ready for you. She knows what an appetite you three have and she's been baking solidly for the last week. But why don't you take your cases up to your rooms? I will show William his room.'

The boys lifted their suitcases and trailed inside after her, Olivia close to Oscar's side. His white-blond hair was cut short, as the school insisted, but she thought it suited him – she was sure he had grown at least another couple of inches since the last time she had seen him. To Olivia he was the handsomest young man in the world and always had been.

He in turn was noticing the changes in her. At twelve and a half she was at that curious stage where she was neither a child nor a young woman. She seemed to be all legs and arms and her huge dark-lashed eyes seemed almost too large for her heart-shaped face. But she also looked set to turn into a great beauty and Oscar smiled as he imagined all the beaux who would be hammering on the door for her in the not too distant future. He couldn't imagine his mother being happy about that but, now that he came to think of it, he wouldn't be either. He had always been fiercely protective of her and couldn't imagine that this would change.

The house was suddenly full of laughter and chatter, and Max smiled as he watched his children rush off to their rooms.

Upstairs, Camilla threw open the door next to Oscar's room and told William, 'I thought you might like to be next door to Oscar, dear. I do hope that you'll be comfortable.'

'It's quite charming, Mrs Farthing, thank you,' the young man assured her. Little did he know that, in his honour, Camilla had had the whole room refurnished in solid mahogany and redecorated from top to bottom. As she had pointed out to Max, 'The boy is used to the best and I don't want him going back and telling his parents that he had to slum it while he was with us.'

Max had sighed as he sifted through the stack of bills she handed to him. After the amount of money she had spent on the room he was sure that the King himself could have slept there and not found it wanting. She had done the same to the room earmarked for Georgina, but he could hardly complain – he had recently spent a substantial amount of money when he had changed his car for the very latest bullnose Morris Oxford.

As it happened, Olivia was quite taken with the room that had been decorated for Georgina and intended to claim it as her own, once the guest had gone. As she had pointed out to her mother, she was too old to be confined to the nursery floor and this room had a much more feminine theme, with chintz curtains and a flowered carpet. She could scarcely wait for Georgina's visit to be over so that she could move in.

As Camilla was settling their guest in, Olivia was perched on the end of Oscar's bed chattering away excitedly. 'It'll be such fun now that you're home to stay,' she told him.

He grinned ruefully. 'I doubt you'll see that much more of me,' he warned. 'Not with the amount of work Father has lined up for me.'

'Ah, but you won't be working on Sundays,' she pointed out. She clearly had it all planned. 'We'll be able to go out together.'

He reached across to ruffle her hair, then took her hand and led her down to the dining room.

Lunch was a merry affair, everyone laughing and chatting, and the food was delicious. Mrs Pegs had cooked a joint of beef and served it with a red wine sauce, some crispy roast potatoes and a selection of vegetables. This was followed by a choice of desserts, and once everyone had finished, Olivia declared that she wouldn't be able to eat another thing for at least a week.

'I wish I had a pound for every time I've heard you say that,' Lawrence teased her. 'I've never seen a girl eat as much as you do.'

William found that hard to believe. Olivia was so slim she looked as if a strong gust of wind might blow her away. She seemed to have grown up enormously since the last time he had seen her, and as he noticed how pretty she was, he found himself blushing. He covered his embarrassment by dabbing at his mouth with his napkin. When he next glanced up Oscar was watching him closely, which made him blush again.

Georgina arrived two days later, in a car driven by her father's chauffeur. Olivia was delighted to have another girl for company, even if Georgina was somewhat older than her – she had always wanted a sister. After a very short time she found Georgina wasn't quite as much fun as she had hoped she would be. Unlike William, whom Olivia thought

159

was quite handsome, Georgina was plain, with large features and mousy hair, which she pinned back in a severe bun on the back of her head. Her clothes were drab too, although they were of excellent quality, and she was quite shy and retiring. Her eyes were by far her best feature: they were a striking shade of blue that reminded Olivia of the bluebells she had seen in the woods and were heavily fringed with the longest lashes she had ever seen.

Shortly after Georgina's arrival, Olivia gave up her attempts to befriend her, finding her dull, and transferred her attention to her brother, who was much more fun to be with. It didn't matter because Camilla was clearly going all out to impress the girl and would whisk her off at every opportunity, visiting friends she had long neglected or taking her shopping. When they were at home she pushed her towards Oscar at every chance, insisting they sit beside each other at mealtimes or that they play cards together in the evening, much to Olivia's disgust. In no time at all Olivia was thoroughly disgruntled.

'It must be nice for you having another girl to chat to,' Dilly said to her one morning, as she came out of the drawing room with her polish and dusters. The boys had gone out with Max to visit one of his hat factories in Atherstone, and Camilla had whipped Georgina off to visit the shops in Coventry and show her St Michael's Cathedral.

Glancing around to make sure that no one was about, Olivia confided, 'She's quite boring, actually, Mrs Carey. To be honest, I shall be glad when she's gone so that I can move my things into her room. Mother wanted me to go with them this morning but I don't want to traipse around shops and visit a stuffy old cathedral.'

Dilly stifled a grin. You could always trust Olivia to tell the truth. It was a trait she had acquired from Max, and it often got her into trouble with Camilla, who was trying to teach the girl etiquette. 'Have you no lessons today?' she asked.

Olivia grinned. 'No, I persuaded Father to make Mother let Miss Travis visit her family in Rugby for a few weeks. It didn't seem fair that the boys were on holiday and I still had to work.' Miss Travis was the governess that the Farthings had employed some years before to teach Olivia. She was a quiet, insipid little woman, unlike the former governess, Miss Blake, who had left when the last of the boys started school, and Dilly was aware that Olivia could run rings around her.

'Good for you. But what are you going to do with yourself if everyone else is out?'

'I'm going to take Spirit, Oscar's horse, for a gallop across the Weddington Fields,' Olivia said. She knew she wasn't supposed to take the horses out on her own in case of an accident, but if she went now her parents would be none the wiser, and what they didn't see couldn't hurt them.

'Well, you be careful,' Dilly advised and she watched the girl go on her way with a smile on her face and an ache in her heart.

That evening after dinner, as Oscar and William sat playing chess in the library, William commented, 'I reckon my little sister has a crush on you, old chap.'

161

Oscar looked shocked. 'Of course she hasn't. You must be mistaken.' He suspected that William had a crush on Olivia and he wasn't keen on the idea at all.

'I think you'll find she has.' William chuckled. 'You must have noticed the way she watches you.'

'I haven't, as a matter of fact,' Oscar responded, slightly embarrassed. Georgina was a nice enough girl but he had never felt drawn to her. Come to think of it, he hadn't felt particularly drawn to any girl, although lots of his school mates, including Samuel, had been sneaking out of school at night for secret liaisons with the local girls. One had even got a girl into the family way and had been expelled. Oscar had always been content to study, but he supposed that now he had left school he might consider the odd little romantic liaison if someone caught his eye. It certainly wouldn't be Georgina, though.

'Anyway, let's get on with this game,' he said, hoping to change the subject. 'I reckon you're just trying to put me off because I'm winning!'

'I was doing no such thing! Just passing a comment, that's all,' William teased but he let the subject of his sister drop. He didn't want to make Oscar feel uncomfortable.

One morning, Samuel and Georgina found themselves alone in the house. Olivia and Oscar had taken the horses for a gallop, Harvey was visiting a friend and Lawrence was in bed feeling rather unwell as he had come down with a heavy summer cold. Camilla had gone somewhat reluctantly to one of her ladies' meetings that had been prearranged and concerned raising funds for the church roof, and William had gone to explore the marketplace. Georgina was at a loose end when Samuel found her browsing the books in the library.

'Oh, sorry – I didn't know you were in here,' he said, when she glanced up from the book she was holding.

'It's all right. I wasn't really reading it,' she told him, and suddenly he noticed how magnificent her eyes were. Admittedly she was a plain Jane but Samuel was bored and supposed any company was better than none.

'I was just looking at that photograph of the baby on the mantelpiece,' she said then. 'She's very pretty. Who is she?'

Samuel crossed the room and lifted it down. 'My sister, Violet. Sadly she died shortly after this was taken and my mother has never really got over it.'

'How awful for her, and all of you, of course,' she said sympathetically.

He stared at her for a moment, then asked. 'Would you like to see her room? It's just as it was on the day she died. Mother flatly refuses to get rid of anything that belonged to her.'

Georgina frowned, although she was consumed with curiosity. It was such a sad story. 'I don't know if I should,' she said doubtfully but Samuel waved aside her concerns and crossed the room and took her hand.

'Mother wouldn't mind you looking at it,' he assured her, and led her from the room. All girls seemed to go soppy about anything concerning a baby. Upstairs he slipped into his mother's room and found the key to Violet's room. He knew where she kept it and also knew that she wouldn't be pleased if she knew he was going in there but hopefully she would never find out. He led Georgina along the landing and paused outside a door. 'This was Violet's room, next to Mother's. She loved her so much she wouldn't hear of Violet being stuck up in the nursery.'

He pushed open the door and Georgina walked past him into the room. Crossing to the lace-trimmed crib, she stroked it as Samuel watched her. Actually, she wasn't quite as plain as he had first thought – in fact, she was beginning to look quite attractive. She was at the dressing-table now and lifted a tiny silver hairbrush with soft bristles that still contained strands of soft downy hair.

He walked up behind her, and when he put his arm about her she started. 'It's all right,' he whispered, forcing himself to look heartbroken. 'It's just that I always get upset when I come in here.'

Georgina was a kind-hearted girl and instantly laid a hand on his arm. 'Oh, you poor thing.'

His arm tightened about her, and she tried to wriggle free, evidently uncomfortable at his close proximity. 'I, er ... think we ought to go back downstairs now, if this is upsetting you so much,' she said, raising her voice, and then thankfully the door suddenly opened and Max stood there frowning in surprise to see their guest clutched to his son's chest.

Samuel immediately stepped away from the girl, who shot past Max and disappeared in the direction of her bedroom as fast as her legs would

164

take her looking decidedly upset.

'What's going on here?' Max demanded.

'Oh, I was just showing Georgina Violet's room,' Samuel said glibly as he headed for the door. Without another word he passed the key to his father and after brushing past him clattered away down the stairs.

Max had never known Samuel to show an interest in his late sister's room before and Georgina had looked uncomfortable when he had come upon them. He glanced sadly around his baby daughter's bedroom, then quietly closed the door and made his way downstairs, feeling quite uneasy.

William and Georgina stayed for another two weeks, during which time Max noticed that Georgina gave Samuel a very wide berth.

On the day they left, Olivia wasted no time in transferring her things to the newly decorated room and claiming it as her own. Once she had suggested that she might move into Violet's room, but her mother had become so upset that Olivia had never suggested it again. The room was kept as a shrine to the daughter Camilla had lost, and Olivia knew she occasionally went in there to make sure that it was properly aired and in order. Olivia thought it was spooky; Violet's tiny clothes still hung in the wardrobe – she knew because she had crept in there once when Mrs Carey had left the door unlocked after cleaning. Her toys were still positioned in the cot she had slept in and on the chair beneath the window. It was as if her mother expected Violet to appear at any minute.

She supposed that if her mother could take comfort from going in there it was no bad thing, although she often wondered why she and the boys had slept on the nursery floor when they were younger while Violet had been close to her parents. But at least she felt much more grown-up now that she was on the same floor as her brothers and would frequently pop along to Oscar's room for a late-night chat.

Lawrence was still confined to bed. No surprise there, for since starting school he still seemed to catch every ailment that was going. On top of that his eyesight was very poor and he was forced to wear thick-lensed spectacles – as did Harvey – which made his twin tease him relentlessly. No one would have guessed that Samuel and Lawrence were twins: they were as different as chalk from cheese in both looks and nature. Samuel was tall and clearly took after their father while Lawrence was slight and more like their mother. Even so there was a special bond between them, and sometimes if one felt really ill, the other would suffer similar symptoms.

Next to Oscar the brother Olivia was closest to was Harvey. He was mad about animals and his ambition was to become a vet, much to his mother's distress.

'But, darling, it's such a – a *dirty* job,' she had remonstrated, but now she had given up. Harvey had made up his mind and as his father thought it was an excellent profession to go into, he was determined to pursue it.

Olivia had said that she would like to be a nurse, which had horrified her. Admittedly more women worked nowadays, to bring in a little extra money, but there was no way she wanted her daughter to do that.

'Young ladies of your class do not *need* to work,' she had told her primly. 'You will stay at home with me and your father, and one day you will meet a nice, respectable young man from a good family and you will marry – someone like William Buchanon-Green, hopefully.'

Olivia had pulled a face behind her mother's back, which made her father disappear behind his newspaper with a grin. The girl was still very young but she had spirit and he had no doubt that, when she was older, she would have her own way. And good luck to her. The way Max saw it, she should be allowed to follow her dream, and when she was old enough he would help her to do it, if that was what she still wanted.

Camilla was a great one for attending ladies' meetings and supporting women's causes, yet at heart she was still of the old school and not moving with the times, especially when it came to her children.

'Why don't you let me take you out to the new Prince of Wales Theatre that's opened in town?' Max asked her one evening. She had been so much happier since the boys had been home and he thought she might enjoy it. 'I'm told they have some splendid acts. George Robey was there recently and a chap at the club was saying that Charlie Chaplin and Harry Tate will be performing there soon.'

Camilla wrinkled her nose. 'How *very* distasteful. It's almost as bad as that new Picturedrome

167

that's opened and that terrible aerodrome in Attleborough. The aeroplanes are such noisy unnatural things. Worse than motor cars, if you ask me. And, anyway, why would I want to go anywhere when my boys are at home? I have to make the most of their company while I can.'

Max sighed and gave in. If he didn't they'd be back to the old argument, about him sending them away to school. He loved having them at home as much as she did but he still felt he had done the right thing in ensuring they had a good education.

That summer was one that Olivia was to remember for the rest of her life. She and the boys rode their horses or went for long walks. They played games, argued and laughed together. Dilly was pleased to see her looking so happy. Even so, all was not right with the world, as rumours of unrest abroad appeared in the newspapers.

Fergal would read pieces aloud to her each evening when she got home from work but she let most of it go over her head. She couldn't see what the fuss was about. After all, how could what was happening in other countries affect them? She had more than enough to worry about closer to home, what with holding down two jobs and keeping the house running, so she went on her way, blissfully unaware of what was just over the horizon.

Chapter Fifteen

June 1914

As Max Farthing entered his club on a balmy evening in June he was waylaid by one of his long-time acquaintances, Richard Bowling, who was just leaving. 'Have you seen the newspapers, Max?' he asked.

Max shook his head. 'Not today – I've been visiting three of my factories. Why do you ask?'

'Read that.' Richard thrust a newspaper into his hand as he headed for the door. 'The heir to the throne of Austria-Hungary, Archduke Franz Ferdinand, has been assassinated in Sarajevo. This could trigger war.'

Max frowned, fearing he could be right. 'Do you think we might be dragged into it?'

Richard nodded gravely. 'Can't see how we'd avoid it. But I must be off. My wife is throwing a dinner party tonight and you know what the ladies can be like if we're late for such things.'

Max ordered a drink from a passing waiter, then, after finding a seat in a comfortable leather chair in a far corner where he would not be disturbed, he read the newspaper report for himself. The thought of war terrified him. Not because he was a coward – he would gladly fight for his country if need be and if he wasn't considered too old. It was the thought of his four young sons enlisting that worried him. When the waiter returned with his drink, he folded the newspaper and pushed aside his anxious thoughts. There was a chance it would come to nothing and there was no point in worrying unnecessarily.

An hour later, when he got home, Camilla was getting ready to go out. 'Mrs Pegs is keeping your dinner warm,' she told him. 'I'm sorry, I have to dash. It's my turn to arrange the flowers for the church but I shouldn't be gone for long. Oscar and Olivia are still in the dining room, if you'd like to join them.'

He nodded at her before heading for the dining room where he found Olivia and Oscar enjoying some of Mrs Pegs's delicious lamb.

They smiled a greeting, then Oscar asked, 'Have you heard about the assassination in Sarajevo, Father?'

'I called into my club on the way home and read about it in the newspaper,' Max replied.

'The men were saying in the factory today that they think it could lead to war.'

Oscar looked so young that Max's heart did a flip at the thought of him having to become involved in it.

'But even if it did lead to war there's no reason it should include us, is there?' Olivia piped up. 'It's all happening miles and miles away. Why should Britain have to become involved?'

At thirteen and a half Olivia was an intelligent girl but she clearly didn't have a great grasp of politics. The way he saw it, that was no bad thing. He didn't want her worrying about something that, as she rightly pointed out, might never happen. 'Let's hope you're right,' he said brightly.

'And now where's my dinner? I'm starving. How did you get on at the factory today, Oscar? Are the books balancing?'

The conversation turned to other things and, for now, they tried to forget about the black cloud that seemed to be looming over them. That proved easier said than done: over the next few days, talk of the assassination was on everyone's lips as the possibility of war drew closer. The archduke's death had set off a diplomatic crisis and Austria-Hungary had delivered an ultimatum to the kingdom of Serbia. Now all everyone could do was wait to see where it might lead. Britain and Germany began to increase their fleets and the Kaiser took offence as Britain tried to mediate between the already warring factions. Taking courage from this the Austrians declared war on Russia, then France and Germany responded with orders to their own troops. The tsar ordered the mobilization of his armies and war seemed inevitable.

'But the boys won't have to go, will they?' Camilla asked Max fearfully one Sunday morning as they sat enjoying a leisurely cup of tea.

Max eyed her for a moment, then chose his words carefully. He had no wish to alarm her, yet he wanted to be truthful. He believed that it was just a matter of time now before war was declared, as did many of the men he knew. 'I shouldn't think any of our boys will be forced to enlist immediately, although there will probably be a recruitment campaign. Hopefully, even if it does happen, it will all be over in no time.'

Camilla nodded unconvinced.

171

Upstairs, Olivia was perched on the edge of Oscar's bed as he prepared to go riding. 'What will you do if we go to war, Oscar? I heard Mrs Pegs and Mrs Carey talking about it in the kitchen and they reckon all the young men will be called up. Mrs Carey is worried about her sons, but they won't force anyone to go, will they?'

'I shouldn't think so. At least, not straight away.' He had already decided that he would enlist, if need be, but he didn't want to frighten her so he kept his voice light as he went on, 'Why don't you get changed and come with me? It's a grand morning and a gallop will do the horses good.'

Instantly cheered, Olivia hopped off the bed. 'You're right. It's far too nice to be stuck at home. Give me ten minutes, will you?' With that she scooted off, leaving her brother to finish getting ready.

Fifteen minutes later they rode Spirit and Flame down the drive and turned towards Abbey Green. Children were playing on the grass and they waved to them as they passed. The sun was shining from a cloudless blue sky and it was hard to believe that there was trouble in the world. From the corner of her eye, Olivia watched her brother. His blond hair had grown since he had left school, and he was so handsome that he was attracting more than a few admiring glances from the local lasses as they passed.

Things will be all right, Olivia told herself. She didn't know how she would bear it if Oscar was called up to fight so she pushed the thought aside, determined to enjoy the day.

In Ireland the thoughts were just as gloomy and Maeve was beside herself with worry. 'Our lads won't have to go and fight if war's declared, will they?' she asked Daniel anxiously.

He sighed. 'I wouldn't think so. If you work the land you can claim exemption. But the lads might want to go, and if they do, we'd be hard pressed to stop them.'

'Hmm. You just watch me,' Maeve said. 'I don't believe in fighting. Why don't they try to bring a peaceful conclusion to all this trouble?'

'It may have gone beyond that, to be sure,' Daniel said sadly. 'But there's no point in worrying about it. What will be will be, and there's nothing we can do to stop it. In the meantime let's just go on with our lives and try not to worry about it.'

At that moment, Dilly was uttering the same words to Fergal. He had read about what was going on in the newspapers each day and feared the worst. She knew he was ashamed that if local men were called up to fight he would not be able to go with them and was terrified of being branded a coward. Dilly had had many heated words with him on the subject, pointing out that there was no point in whipping himself about something that could not be changed, but even common sense could not make him feel better. Now she had given up talking about it.

Eventually, on 28 July, the Austro-Hungarians fired the first shots as they prepared for the invasion of Serbia. Russia mobilized as Germany invaded neutral Belgium and Luxembourg, then moved on towards France. The British people knew it was only a matter of time before they must become involved.

The terrible news came on 4 August, on a hot, sultry day when there seemed to be no escape from the heat.

'Well, it's fair to say that we knew it would happen, so it's hardly come as a surprise,' Max said to Oscar. 'It says in the newspaper that recruiting offices are springing up all over the place so hopefully enough chaps will volunteer to make sure that it's all over for Christmas. We can just carry on as usual.' He didn't like the frown that creased Oscar's brow, as he left the room without a word, and prayed that he wouldn't do something silly. But his son was nineteen and knew his own mind...

Over the next few days the town seemed to go mad as young men flocked to the recruitment offices. Many had been trapped in dull jobs and the thought of being shipped abroad to fight for their country promised to be a big adventure. There were no uniforms or weapons available to them yet and no proper training centres set up, so they drilled in local parks as things were organized. The local people cheered them as they passed and already the lads' chests were puffed with pride. But the Germans were advancing on Paris and the training would be short as the Hun had to be stopped.

'I'm sure the poor young things don't have a clue what they're letting themselves in for,' Dilly told Fergal, as she prepared their evening meal. 'You'd think the lads were about to go on holiday rather than to fight a war. I heard Mr Farthing tell his son that he'd heard almost all of the lads that have just finished at King Edward's Grammar School have signed up, and them little more than babes in arms!'

It was then that she saw Kian bow his head and a terrible sense of foreboding stole through her. She felt as if someone was gripping her heart with an icy hand. 'You – you haven't gone and done anything foolish, have you, son?' she croaked.

Shame-faced, Kian shrugged. 'All depends what you call foolish,' he muttered. 'I've signed up, if that's what you're asking.'

Dilly gripped the back of a chair as the colour drained from her face.

He raised his head and looked at her defiantly. 'Well, I've never made a secret o' the fact that I'm not happy workin' in the pit. At least this way I'll get to see a bit o' the world!'

'Oh, aye, you'll see a bit o' the world, all right,' she stormed. 'From the bottom of a muddy trench with guns firing across your head! Why didn't you come an' talk to me and your daddy before you did it, Kian?'

'Because I knew I'd get this reaction,' he snapped back. 'I'm not a baby any more, Mammy. I'm old enough to make me own mind up.'

'But you're not even old enough to go,' she argued. 'You should be eighteen and you're only seventeen. You should have had our permission to join!'

'What's the point o' worryin' about a few months? Loads o' the lads are lyin' about their age. Some are even younger than me. Anyway, it's done now so what's the point of arguing about it? I've arranged for me pay to come here so you and Daddy will be none the worse off for me going.'

'As if I *care* about the money!' Dilly was openly crying now, as she gazed at her handsome son. He was a broad, strapping lad, and anyone could have mistaken him for nineteen or twenty, at least. Sometimes when she looked at him now she saw Fergal as he had been when she'd first met him. With his clear blue eyes and mop of black hair, Kian was never short of admiring glances from the local lasses and lately he'd taken full advantage of the fact, to his parents' amusement. He was turning into a heartbreaker, was their lad, yet he had a lively sense of humour and a ready smile so no one thought any the worse of him.

'Well, I – I shall go and see them at the recruitment post and tell them you've lied,' Dilly said desperately.

Until this point Fergal had said nothing but now from his bed he stated quietly, 'Oh no you won't, lass. The lad has made up his mind and he should go with our blessing, if that's what he really wants to do. I'm proud of him, so I am, and you should be too. You will be, I know, when you've calmed down a bit.'

Dilly spun round and gaped at him open-mouthed, then stuttered, 'Fergal, this isn't a picnic he's going on. He could be *killed!*'

'I'm all too aware of that,' he said sadly. 'But he's doing what he feels is right, and I'll tell you now, if it weren't for these damn legs o' mine I'd be going with him, as you well know.'

Dilly's temper seeped away and her shoulders sagged as she asked brokenly, 'When will you

176

have to leave?'

'The day after tomorrow. We're being taken to Warwick to train and from there we'll no doubt be shipped to France.'

Dilly sat down heavily before her legs gave up on her. The day after tomorrow! It was so soon, but she knew in that moment that she had to accept it. She had no choice. Kian was set on going and go he would.

Kian went out soon after to say goodbye to his friends and Dilly's spirits were low as she set about the rest of the chores before banking the fire down. The others had gone to bed and Fergal was already fast asleep so, slipping quietly out of the back door, she set off for the privy. The yard was pitch black but she had gone no more than a few yards when a voice hissed at her from the darkness startling her.

'I thought I'd catch yer if I waited late enough!'

Dilly stilled a groan. She had been sure that the day could get no worse but it looked as if it was about to. 'What do you want, Madge?' she asked wearily. She'd only paid the woman a few days ago.

'Well, my Sidney's gone an' joined up.'

'My Kian has too,' Dilly whispered, for fear of being overheard. 'But what do you expect me to do about your Sidney?'

'Nothin',' Madge said flippantly. 'But once he's gone I'm goin' to be strapped for cash, see. Yer know his dad's neither use nor ornament. Even when he does do a day's work, which ain't very often, his wages allus end up over the bar o' the Crystal Palace or the Cock and Bear. So I got to thinkin' you'll have to give me a bit more each week from now on, startin' tomorrow.'

'But I can't afford to,' Dilly gasped. The rank smell of Madge was making her gag and she was in no mood for this tonight. 'I'm stretching myself now, working two jobs, to give you what I do.'

Madge sniffed as she crossed her arms beneath her sagging breasts and hoisted them up. 'You'll just 'ave to work a bit 'arder, then, won't you?' she said threateningly. 'I'll see yer 'ere this time tomorrow night. Another two bob should see me clear to the end o' the week. Otherwise...'

'I know, I know,' Dilly said fearfully, as she tried to think how much money she had left in her purse. Madge grinned, her black teeth gleaming darkly in the gloomy yard and then with a malicious grin she sauntered away as Dilly sagged against the wall and began to cry softly. She'd not be sad to see the back of this day, that was a fact.

In the Farthing household the atmosphere was also charged but for a different reason.

'He's being expelled and I'm to fetch him home as soon as possible,' Max fumed, as he read through the letter he had received that morning from the housemaster at Harrow concerning Samuel.

'Perhaps it's no bad thing,' Camilla shocked him by saying. 'At least if he's at home we'll know he's safe. In fact, I'd like you to bring all three of them back now that there's a war on. I'm sure you can find them plenty to do in your businesses.'

Max stared at her as if she had taken leave of her senses, but then, as another thought occurred to him, he frowned. Lads were racing for the recruit-

178

ment offices as fast as their legs would take them, from what he could see of it, and some would no doubt be his employees, which could lead to a staff shortage. Perhaps Camilla's suggestion wasn't such a bad one. How he was supposed to keep everywhere running smoothly without enough staff levels he didn't know.

'Do you think the lads might agree to work for me? I mean, they all have ambitions and it isn't what they'd planned.'

'I don't see that they have much choice,' Camilla said. 'None of us planned to be at war, but now that we are, I suppose the boys will just have to put their ambitions on hold.' Suddenly the fact that they were at war didn't seem quite so bad if it meant that her boys would be coming home.

A tap at the door interrupted their conversation and they smiled as Oscar stepped into the room. He looked worried and his mother asked him, 'Is everything all right, my dear?'

'Yes... Well, no, it isn't really.' He rushed on, 'I've just come back from one of the hat factories in Atherstone and I should warn you that at least four of the lads who work there signed up today, Father.'

Max sighed. It was just as he had feared. And if four had gone already from just one place how many more of his businesses might suffer?

'The thing is...' Oscar went on tentatively. 'I ought to sign up as well. I wouldn't like the chaps to think I was a coward.'

'You'll do no such *thing*,' Camilla cried, before Max had had a chance to say a word. 'It's going to be hard enough as it is for your father to keep the businesses running without you deserting him too. Those businesses are your and your brothers' inheritance, Oscar, and you owe it to your father and me to stay here and try to keep them ticking along.

Besides, everyone is saying the war will be over for Christmas, so you may as well stay put.'

Oscar looked uncomfortably between the two of them, feeling torn down the middle. Half of him wanted to stay and help, yet the other wanted to do his bit for his country.

'Why don't we give it a few weeks to see what's going to happen?' Camilla suggested, her heart pounding.

Oscar nodded reluctantly, as Olivia breezed into the room. She stopped in her tracks as she noticed their serious faces before asking, 'What's wrong?'

'Oscar wants to go and fight,' her mother informed her, and the colour left the girl's cheeks.

'You can't, I won't let you,' Olivia snapped at Oscar. 'We need you here!'

Knowing he was beaten, Oscar let out a sigh. He would wait for a few weeks to see how the war developed, as his mother had asked, but then he had every intention of reassessing the situation.

Chapter Sixteen

'Oh, dear Lord, Dilly says that our Kian has joined the army,' Maeve gasped, as she read the latest letter from England. 'He's gone off to train in Warwick, so he has. Oh, me poor wee lad! Whatever possessed him to do such a thing? His parents must be beside themselves with worry, to be sure.'

From his seat at the side of the hearth, Daniel sighed as Nipper and Declan looked on.

Maeve had suffered a slight stroke two weeks before and the lads had carried her bed downstairs so that she could still be among them. The doctor had said that if she rested and did as she was told she could make a full recovery. But Maeve was not a good patient, as they had soon discovered. It went against the grain with her to have Shelagh and the menfolk waiting on her and seeing her house looking less than perfect. The women from the surrounding farms had been as good as gold, popping in whenever they could with meals for the family and taking the dirty laundry away, but the main burden had fallen on Shelagh, Liam's wife. The poor lass was doing her best, in and out all day long doing what she could, but it wasn't easy with two wee weans to see to. Maeve was fiercely independent and could have cried at the dust settling on her furniture. The stroke couldn't have happened at a worse time: the men were busy harvesting, keen to get it done before the weather changed.

'I'm sorry to hear that,' Daniel answered. 'Does it say if Niamh is prepared to come here for a wee while and help out with the chores until you're recovered?'

Maeve shook her head. 'No. The letters must have crossed in the post.' She hadn't been happy when Daniel had taken it upon himself to write and ask Dilly if she could spare Niamh for a few weeks, but the dear soul was out of his mind with

181

worry for her. He knew that if help didn't come soon Maeve might refuse to rest...' I dare say they'll write again soon as the letter arrives,' Maeve added dully. Much as she longed to see her granddaughter she couldn't think of anything worse than to have to lie there and let the girl look after her. Not that she had much choice in the matter – she felt as weak as a kitten. Each time she tried to get out of bed a wave of dizziness washed over her and she would be terrified that she was going to have another stroke.

At that moment the door opened and Liam walked in, still in his work clothes, just as he did each evening to check on how his mammy was.

Maeve told him about Kian enlisting, then felt uneasy as she saw a meaningful glance pass between him, Nipper and Declan. 'I hope none of you are thinking of doing anything so foolish,' she snapped.

Eager not to distress her, the three shook their heads in denial.

'Course we ain't, Mammy,' Liam assured her. 'Who'd do the work about this place if we was to go?'

'Hmm.' Maeve leaned back against her pillows. 'That's good. Everyone knows that folk who work the land won't have to go. They're needed to grow food. But have you eaten yet, lad? Shelagh will have your dinner keepin' warm, so she will. Go on, get off with you and spend some time with that lovely wife of yours and the weans afore they go to bed.'

Liam grinned. 'Well, that's fine.' He chuckled. 'You're sendin' me away afore I've barely set foot through the door.'

'Aye, well, I don't need checking on. I ain't on me deathbed yet,' Maeve told him, with a twinkle in her eye.

Liam hurried away to do as he had been told. He had learned long ago that it was pointless arguing with his mother.

'Aye, and we'd best go out and get the chickens away for the night,' Declan said, then he and Nipper left together. Declan was finding it hard to cope with his grandmother's illness, and although he adored her, was keeping out of the way as much as possible.

Once they were a distance across the yard, Nipper commented, 'This war couldn't have happened at a worse time, could it, what with us bein' in the middle o' harvesting?'

'You're right.' Declan sighed. 'I can't see us being able to sign up for a while, what with Gran'ma being ill and us having so much work on. There's no way Granda would manage on his own... but I still feel cowardly not joining up. I know a lot o' the lads from the village have enlisted already.'

Nipper nodded in agreement. 'All we can do is get the harvesting done and see how things go. If your sister does come out for a while to help Maeve till she's back on her feet, that will be a weight off everybody. And it's always quieter in the winter. Perhaps some of the older chaps from the village who're too old to fight might lend a hand where it's needed. If it isn't all over by then, that is. Everyone seems to think it'll be done and finished in no time.'

'Then let's hope they're right.' The two young men separated to set about the last tasks of the day before turning in.

The following night Camilla was waiting for Max when he returned from Harrow. As he entered the house she saw at a glance that he was in a bad humour, although he had brought all the boys back with him, as she had requested.

'So,' she said, addressing Samuel, who was clearly in a sulk, 'you've really done it this time, young man, haven't you? I'm ashamed to have to admit that a son of mine has been expelled from school.' Secretly she was thrilled to have him home although she couldn't show it, of course.

Samuel shrugged. 'Me and a few of the other chaps only left the school for a few drinks,' he said pettishly. 'It was hardly a hanging offence!'

'It is when you all come back roaring drunk,' Max snapped, as he threw his hat onto a chair.

'And I don't know why you insisted we had to come home too,' Harvey piped up. 'It'll be years before I can train to be a vet now.'

Lawrence was the only one of the three who remained silent, looking worriedly from one to the other. He was a gentle soul and hated confrontations.

Olivia burst in then and the mood lightened a little. For whatever reason she was always happy to have her brothers at home. She went from one to the next, giving each a hug. 'Mrs Pegs has a meal all ready for you, if you'd like to go through to the dining room. She thought you might be hungry when you got back.'

184

'I'm starving,' Harvey announced, and promptly followed his sister, as did the other two.

Looking at Max, Camilla urged, 'Don't be so upset. I'm sure you'll find more than enough to keep them busy. This might have been the best thing that could have happened. At least we know they're safe at home now.' Max could only shake his head, as she tripped off to the dining room, wearing a broad smile.

'Daddy has written to ask if Niamh could go to Enniskerry to help out for a while,' Fergal told Dilly, the second she set foot through the door after work a few days later. 'Mammy has had a stroke.'

Dilly saw the fear in his eyes.

'He says it was only a slight one and the doctor thinks she'll recover so long as she rests,' he went on. 'But do you think Niamh will agree to go?'

Dilly frowned. This was turning out to be a nightmare of a week, but she knew how hard it must have been for Daniel to write and ask for help – he and Maeve were so independent that they must be in desperate need to go to such lengths. 'I'm sure she will when we explain the situation to her,' Dilly told him. She wished that she herself could go but that was out of the question. 'I'll talk to her the second she comes in,' she promised.

Niamh readily agreed to go and help on the smallholding when she heard about her gran'ma's stroke, so that night Dilly wrote back to Daniel and told him that Niamh would join them that very weekend. She just hoped that the letter would reach them before Niamh did so that there would be someone to meet her from the ferry in Dublin. Niamh hurried away to post the letter so that it would be collected first thing the next morning.

That night as Dilly lay beside her husband's sleeping figure, her head was in a spin. She was still desperately upset about Kian enlisting in the army. He had looked so young when they had gone to see him off from the station on the day of his departure. A lot of young men had been going with him and the platform had been full of wives, mothers, sweethearts and sisters. The lads had been in a high good humour as the crowds waved Union Jacks and cheered, but Dilly hadn't been able to raise so much as a smile. Didn't anyone realize that those boys might be going to their deaths?

Then, of course, she had the added problem of Madge Bunting, who had lain in wait for her and taken yet more money, as she had threatened. Sometimes Dilly wondered where this blackmail was going to end. She lived in fear of Fergal finding out what was going on. Or the Farthings, for that matter. Just the thought of what it might do to Olivia if she was to discover her true parentage still sent a cold shudder up her spine. Madge's demands were worsening but what could she do about it? Sometimes Dilly felt like giving up and running away but she knew she never would, not while Fergal and the family were dependent on her and while she could still be close to Olivia. And now she had to face being without Niamh as well as Kian. Deep down she worried that Niamh might settle in Enniskerry. What shall I do if she decides she wants to stay there? she asked herself. The answer came back all too soon: there would be nothing she could do about it. Hadn't Declan done the same? For a while there would be just herself, Fergal and Seamus, and she would have to get used to it.

The following Saturday found Dilly once more on the railway platform, this time to wave to Niamh.

'Don't worry, Mammy. I shan't be gone for long,' the girl assured her, as she had picked up on her mother's fears. 'Soon as ever Gran'ma is back on her feet I shall be back, never you fear.'

Dilly hugged her fiercely and pushed a lock of the girl's shining hair across her shoulder. The recent sunshine had bleached golden highlights into the copper tones, and as Dilly looked at her she saw her for the first time as a young woman. Niamh was now eighteen with a temperament to match her looks. Soon some handsome young man might take a shine to her and whip her away for good. Somehow it made the parting a little easier – after all, each of her children was entitled to a life of their own. She kissed her daughter soundly and pushed her gently towards the train. 'Be off with you, then. Take care now. Your granda should have received the letter to tell him you were coming but if by any chance he hasn't you've more than enough money to catch a ride to Enniskerry.'

'I'll be fine, Mammy.' Niamh swung her bag up and, after dropping another kiss on Dilly's cheek, she clambered aboard the train. As it drew away, Dilly waved until it was gone from sight, then wearily made her way through the town to the dress shop.

It was early evening when Niamh arrived in Dublin, and as the ferry pulled into the port she peered anxiously across the rail for a sign of her granda, hoping he had received the letter saying she would be arriving. The crossing had been pleasant, the sea as calm as a millpond and the sun sparkling on the water.

Once the ferry was anchored, the gangplank was lowered and the passengers streamed down it. Hoisting her bag, Niamh followed them, still glancing about. Then someone called her name and there was Declan, racing towards her with a broad smile. 'Niamh!' He picked her up and swung her in the air, as if she weighed no more than a feather. Then, taking her bag, he clasped her hand and led her away. 'I've got the pony and trap over here. Gran'ma's so excited about you coming – we haven't been able to do a thing with her all day, to be sure.'

'I thought perhaps Granda would come to meet me,' Niamh commented.

Declan shook his head. 'He doesn't like to be too far away from Gran'ma at present,' he confided. 'She gave us all a rare old gliff when she had her stroke, I don't mind telling you. Still, she's on the mend now, and seeing you will be a better tonic than any the doctor could prescribe for sure.'

They had arrived at the trap by then and after slinging her bag up he lifted her up too and hopped into the driver's seat. Soon they were rattling across the cobblestones through the teeming streets of Dublin at a rare old rate, and occasionally Niamh shut her eyes tight, convinced that another vehicle would crash into them. She remained silent as Declan steered the trap through the narrow streets, but at last they left the mayhem behind and were trotting along country lanes.

'You'll find a basket behind the seat,' Declan told her. 'Gran'ma made Shelagh pack it up for you. She thought you might be hungry.'

'I'm starving,' Niamh admitted, as she reached behind him to lift the basket. It was covered with a crisp white linen cloth, and when she lifted it her mouth watered. There were chunks of fresh-baked bread and cheese, slices of thick-cut ham and juicy red apples from the orchard.

'I'll never eat all this!' she said, and her brother chuckled.

'Send some it my way, then. I never say no to a feed, sure I don't.' Niamh smiled to herself. Declan's Irish accent would take some getting used to but it was to be expected. He had spent far more of his life in Ireland than he had at home. They rode on, munching the tasty treats. Niamh relaxed as they passed through the beautiful Irish countryside and began to understand why her brother had chosen to stay in Ireland rather than return home. It was like another world here, with nothing but birdsong to be heard and miles of lush green fields stretching away to either side of them, with not a single pit chimney belching soot or a motor car in sight.

'You'd never believe there was a war on when you're here, would you?' she remarked, then, 'I think Mammy's worried that you might be going to join up too.'

Declan sighed. 'Between you and me I have thought of it, to be sure, but then I realized it wouldn't be fair to leave the others to cope on their own,' he admitted. 'The sad fact is Granda isn't getting any younger.' He didn't mention that Nipper was planning to go when he felt the time was right.

Niamh sighed with relief and contentment. Her belly was full, her journey almost over. She gave an enormous yawn.

'Why don't you hop in the back?' Declan suggested. 'There are some sacks there that you could lie down on and shut your eyes for a wee while. We've got a good way to go yet an' Gran'ma won't be best pleased if you're away to your bed the second you set foot through the door.'

'I'll do that,' Niamh agreed, swinging her leg over the seats and dropping lightly onto the sacks. They smelt of the apples and plums that were loaded into them each week to take to market. 'But I won't go to sleep. I'll just rest my eyes for a while.' But despite what she said within minutes she was fast asleep and, peeping over the seat at her, Declan grinned and went on his way.

When Declan nudged her awake as they reached the smallholding Niamh felt brand new and keen to see her grandparents.

'You go in,' he told her. 'I'll fetch your bag for you.'

Niamh hopped lightly down from the trap and dashed inside. It was dark by then but an oil lamp in the centre of the kitchen table threw a soft glow about the room.

'Why, bless me!' Maeve gasped from the bed at first sight of her granddaughter. 'Look at you, lass! You're all grown-up, so you are.'

She held out her arms and Niamh flew into them as Daniel looked fondly on. Maeve is right, he thought. Niamh has grown up and a right pretty young lass she is an' all.

Once Niamh had hugged her gran'ma, she hurried over to do the same to her granda. Then he rose, saying, 'I bet you'll be dying for a nice hot cup o' tea after all that travelling.'

Niamh pressed him back into his chair. 'It's all right, Granda. I'll make it. That's what I'm here for – to help.'

She had just filled the kettle when the back door opened and Nipper appeared, having locked away the chickens. They stared at each other in amazement. The last time Nipper had seen Niamh had been before when she had been a little girl, easily the prettiest he had ever set eyes on – but what a beauty she had turned into! She was remembering a lanky young lad, all arms and legs with two left feet, who was prone to trip over anything and everything, yet here was a handsome young man, with muscled arms, and eyes that would have charmed the ducks from the water.

'So...' Nipper was the first to speak. '...you're here, then.'

'Aye, I'm here,' she responded, with a cheeky grin.

Maeve watched the interaction between the two with amusement. The last time she had seen that look in a man's eyes had been the night she had met her Daniel. Could it be, she wondered, that she was watching the start of something beautiful? She hoped so, for she loved Niamh and Nipper dearly and she could think of nothing better than the two of them making a match of it. But she wisely remained silent as she watched them. What would be would be.

Chapter Seventeen

Kian had been gone for two weeks and they had been the longest Dilly could ever remember. They had received one letter. Well it had been more of a note, really – he had never been a great one for setting pen to paper. In it he had told them he was missing them and that the training in Warwick was going well. There had been nothing since and Dilly was constantly worrying about him.

The house seemed emptier than ever, now that Niamh was gone too, so her spirits were low as she made her way home from work one evening in early September. Mrs Ball's dress shop was making uniforms for the troops now, and although Dilly approved of that, there wasn't the excitement in producing the same garments over and over again as there had been in making gowns. Still, she supposed it couldn't be helped. She had begun to take different routes for Madge Bunting's demands were becoming ridiculous but the woman still managed to seek her out. Even so, as she entered the kitchen that night her heart raced with joy. Kian was standing there, all grown-up and heartbreakingly handsome in his uniform.

'Kian!' She dropped her basket and was across the room in a second, clasping him to her. 'I thought I was seeing things. But what are you doing here? I thought you were still training and–'

'*Whoa!*' He laughed and held up his hand to stem her words. She suddenly realized that she was actually looking up at him. When had he grown so tall?

'They've given us all three days' leave,' he explained, and her smile slipped a little.

'Only three days? But why do you have to go back so soon?' And what had they done to his lovely hair? It was cropped so short that it seemed to be standing on end. It made him look older.

He glanced at his father. 'We're being shipped out to France the day after we go back.'

Dilly sat down heavily on the nearest chair, her pleasure at seeing him turned to ice-cold terror. 'S-so soon?' she muttered fearfully.

'Now don't get worrying,' he answered, as if he were the adult and she but a child. 'I'm a big lad now and it'll take more than them Jerries to get me.'

'Course it will, son,' Fergal agreed, as he watched the different emotions flitting across his wife's face.

Dilly forced a smile. 'Have you seen anything of Nell's Mickey? He joined up just after you and he's training in Warwick, too. Nell only has Will at home now, bless her.'

'He was in Warwick,' Kian answered, 'but he's home on leave too. We're being shipped out together.'

'I see.' Dilly was at a loss. She knew that Nell was as upset as she was about losing her son. 'In that case we'd best make the most of the next three days, eh? And we'll start by having some of this lovely steak and kidney pie that Mrs Pegs sent for us. While it's warming through, I'll do us a nice pan of mashed potatoes to go with it.'

She bustled away to peel the potatoes as Kian took a seat beside his father's bed and began to tell him about his training. Dilly kept her eyes on what she was doing but her ears strained to hear what her son was saying.

'I thought I was fit, but I'll tell you now, Daddy, come evening after being on assault courses all day, I'm fair worn out. We've been having arms practices as well. It's not so hard to aim at a target, but I don't know how I'll feel when I have to aim at another living being.' Kian went on, 'It was bad enough being at school but that's a picnic to being in the army. They yell at you if you put so much as a foot wrong. The sergeant in our hut had one young chap make his bed four times until he got it right. And another one had to clean his boots again and again until the sergeant could see his face in them.' He shook his head. 'I ask you, why do we need to know how to make a bed or wear shiny boots when we're going to be wading in mud?'

'I dare say it's all part of being disciplined and learning to do as you're told,' Dilly heard Fergal say.

Despite the seriousness of the situation she had to smile. Kian had never been the tidiest of people and she couldn't imagine him making a bed, let alone polishing his boots. But at least she could spoil him for the next three days.

After dinner, Kian popped out to see his friends and Dilly began to feel a little better. At least she had seen him before he was shipped off to France and she was grateful for that.

Once Seamus had gone to bed she dimmed the lamps and, seeing that Fergal had dropped off to sleep, hurried out to the privy. But she had gone no more than a few steps across the yard when she became aware of someone coming up behind her. Whirling about, she found herself face to face with Madge Bunting again.

'If you've come to ask me for more money, Madge, I'm afraid you're out of luck,' she said. 'I've not a penny to spare till payday and this has got to stop. You're bleeding me dry. I do have my *own* family to see to, you know!'

Madge glowered at her. 'I shouldn't get *too* cocky if I was you. Your precious little family could be torn apart in the blink of an eye if I was to open me trap an' tell what I know.'

Dilly's shoulders sagged as she asked despondently, 'Are you *ever* going to give me any peace, Madge, or do you intend to go on blackmailing me for ever?'

Madge had no chance to reply for at that second Nell appeared saying, 'What's this, then?'

Nell could see that Dilly was agitated and wondered what was going on. It wasn't the first time she had seen Madge corner her and she wondered if she'd just heard aright.

'Oh, er, it's all right, Nell,' Dilly said hastily. 'I

195

was going to the privy when I bumped into Madge.'

Disgruntled, Madge pulled her grimy shawl about her shoulders and set off down the entry.

'They reckon she's on the game now,' Nell confided, 'though who'd pay for the use o' her body I've no idea. There must be them as do though cos she's been seen regular standin' outside the Cock and Bear, waitin' fer the men to come out o' the pub – I dare say they can only face her when they're pissed up. One bloke gave 'er a backhander the other night by all accounts for harassin' him!'

She peered at Dilly and frowned. There was something wrong here. Whenever Madge was about, Dilly was like a cat on hot bricks. One thing was for sure, if Nell were to find out Madge was upsetting the lass she'd strangle the baggage with her own hands. Dilly had enough on her plate and Nell was fiercely protective of her. But whatever it was, Dilly clearly wasn't going to tell her just yet so with a sigh, Nell went on her way, wishing Madge Bunting could just fall off the face of the earth. She certainly wouldn't be a loss to anyone.

On the morning Kian was due to go back to camp, Dilly wept bitterly. She had a bad feeling deep in her gut and couldn't rid herself of it, but then she supposed that every mother waving her son off to war must feel the same so she dried her tears and kissed him tenderly begging, 'Please don't go taking any unnecessary chances. I want you back all in one piece – do you hear me?'

'Loud and clear!' Kian said, as he swung his kitbag onto his back. He shook hands with his father, and in no time he was gone, leaving Dilly bereft. Kian was putting a brave face on it, but she knew her lad like the back of her hand and had sensed he was as nervous as a kitten.

'He'll be fine,' Fergal assured her, as Dilly raced about getting ready for work. 'He'll be back before you know it.'

'Of course he will,' Dilly said to humour him. 'It's just me being daft. But now I must be off or I'll be late. See you later, love.'

Out in the yard, Kian took a deep breath and hurried to Nell's door. She answered it and smiled as he pressed an envelope into her hand. 'Would you keep this somewhere safe for me, please, Mrs Cotteridge, and make sure that my mammy gets it if anything should happen to me?'

'I will, lad,' she promised. 'But hopefully I'll never need to deliver it. Our Mickey's just gone. He said he'll see you at the station. And ... take care.'

He nodded as he moved away. Kian was feeling as bad as his mother was as he strode towards the station. All the excitement of joining up had long since died away in the training camp and now he was ashamed to admit that he was terrified of what lay ahead. Still, he had made his bed and now he must lie on it, so he strode on with a smile fixed in place.

The following Friday, Dilly kept a watchful eye open for Madge as she made her way home from work. Madge always managed to waylay her on payday but, strangely, tonight Dilly reached the entry with no sign of her. *I bet she's waiting for me in the yard,* she thought, but all was quiet, with no sign of Madge anywhere. Dilly hurried inside. She'd no doubt Madge would collar her before the night was out.

Nell was inside, speaking to Fergal, and when Dilly entered she heaved herself to her feet. 'There y'are, pet. I were just sayin' to Fergal that I ain't seen Madge fer a couple o' days.'

'Do you think we ought to go and check? Perhaps she's ill,' Dilly said, although she shuddered at the thought.

'Do I 'ell as like!' Nell stated emphatically. 'Her old man's still about an' if owt were wrong no doubt he'd 'ave said sommat, though he's in an alcoholic stupor most o' the time. Anyway, I'll be off now, night both.'

Dilly frowned, wondering where Madge might be. She'd turn up eventually, like a bad penny. Unfortunately she always did.

Chapter Eighteen

One evening, early in October, when the harvesting was over, Daniel said, 'I heard there was going to be a social with a band playing at the village hall this Saturday. Why don't you go? The Lord knows you've earned a night out and it would do you good. There's been enough doom and gloom lately, if what we read in the newspapers is anything to go by.'

Niamh flushed. Her granda was right. Daniel read the papers religiously and kept them abreast of the war. She lived in constant fear of something happening to Kian, who was in France. She suspected he had been shipped out in the summer, along with seventy thousand other men of the British Expeditionary Force, to join their French and Belgian comrades – every night she prayed to the Lord to keep him safe. It would be grand to have a night out and try to forget everything for a while. But then she realized she wouldn't be able to go. She had brought nothing suitable to wear.

Maeve was now able to sit in a chair at the fireside of an evening for a couple of hours and glancing across at Niamh she asked, 'Don't you fancy it, pet?'

'I haven't got anything to wear, apart from my work clothes,' Niamh admitted sell-consciously.

'If that's all it is, it's soon sorted,' Maeve declared. 'Nipper's going into town for the beasts' fodder tomorrow. You could go with him. There's a canny little dress shop, so there is. I'm sure you'd find something you like.' When Niamh blushed, she added quickly, 'And I shall treat you to a new outfit, so I shall. Why, I really don't know what we would have done without you the way you've kept this place going so it'll be my pleasure.'

'Oh, no, Gran'ma, there's no need for that,' Niamh protested, as the colour in her cheeks deepened.

But Maeve was having none of it. Turning to Nipper, she asked, 'It'd be no trouble, would it, lad, if Niamh came along with you?'

'None at all,' he assured her, with a grin, then bit

into a thick slice of soda bread smeared with creamy butter. 'Sure I'll be in the town for at least a couple of hours so she'll have plenty of time to look around.'

'But who will look after you and see to everything while I'm gone?' Niamh protested.

'I shall be fine on my own for a time, so I shall. I'm getting better every day and the whole place is gleaming. I couldn't keep it better myself. You having a few hours off is neither here nor there. So, that's settled,' Maeve said, with satisfaction. 'And while you're choosing a dress you'd best choose some new shoes or boots to go with it. You can hardly go in those you're wearing. A new bag wouldn't come amiss either.'

Niamh grinned, as she glanced down at her worn boots. She supposed her gran'ma was right and she knew better than to try to argue with her when her mind was set on something. 'Thanks, Gran'ma. I'll look forward to it.' Then she hurried away to heat some milk for their last drink.

'She's a grand lass, is she not?' Daniel remarked, when the young people had retired to bed. 'We shall miss her when she goes home.'

Maeve's face clouded but she knew that it must come about. She had already brought up her eldest grandson and had no wish to keep Niamh from her parents for longer than she had to. In fact, she was hoping she would be well enough for Niamh to return home in time for Christmas.

'She is that,' she agreed. 'And between you and me I don't think we're the only ones who think so. Have you seen the way Nipper watches her?'

'Can't say I have.'

Maeve sighed. Men could be so blind. It was as plain as the nose on her face that Nipper was drawn to the lass, but that was men for you, not that she would have changed a single hair on Daniel's head. He might not be prone to saying romantic things but his kindly gestures and gentle touches told her every single day how much he valued her.

Liam and Shelagh clearly shared the same closeness and she guessed that Shelagh would miss Niamh when she went home. It had been nice for her to have another young woman about the place and the weans adored Niamh. They would miss her too. 'I wonder if Shelagh could go into town with Niamh for a couple of hours,' she said thoughtfully. 'The lass never gets a break from the weans. Could you find time to help me watch them if she were to go too?'

Daniel laughed. 'The whole family will be going at this rate,' he said. 'But, yes, I'll help with them gladly. It'll be nice not to see them just in passing. They're usually abed by the time I've done of a day.'

'Perhaps Liam and Shelagh could go to the social too,' Maeve added. 'And Declan.'

'Why not?' Daniel placed some peat on the fire to keep it burning overnight and Maeve settled into the bed contentedly. She loved the mossy damp smell of it. It was like bringing the outdoors inside. The straw was safely stored in the barn for the winter and the smallholding was fast becoming a farm. If only it hadn't been for this damn war everything would have been perfect, but there was always the niggling worry about Kian in France.

She offered up a prayer that the Holy Mother would watch over him, then let out a sigh. Seconds later she was fast asleep.

The same couldn't be said for Niamh, who was lying in her bed beneath the eaves, staring at the moon through the tiny window. There was a little bubble of excitement in the pit of her stomach and it wasn't all to do with the fact that she would be going into town for a new outfit tomorrow. It was the thought of being able to spend some time with Nipper. She had never admitted to herself before that she was drawn to him but now that she had she couldn't deny it. The Sunday before they had taken a walk together across the fields. Since her arrival they had only really seen each other at mealtimes or in passing, for harvesting the cereal was one of the busiest times of year next to the spring, when lambing took place. Daniel, Liam, Nipper and Declan had spent long hours and days on neighbouring farms helping to gather in the harvest and the other farmers had helped them. That was how it was done in Enniskerry, and Niamh had been rushed off her feet keeping the men supplied with sandwiches and tea. She had loved carrying the heavy baskets of food to the fields for them. Surprisingly she had hardly missed her teaching job but, then, she had rarely had time to. She had enjoyed her stay and knew that she would miss the place and the people when she returned home. It would be hard to settle into the little back-to-back cottage again, now that she was used to the wide-open spaces and the emerald-green fields. But return she would: it would be wrong to leave the care of her daddy solely on her mammy's shoulders.

Her mind drifted back to the Sunday before and she pictured Nipper as they had kicked off their shoes and splodged in the crystal-clear stream that cut a swathe through the hillside, giggling and splashing like two wee weans. They had wandered through the woods, enjoying the sunshine as it shone through the trees that formed a canopy above them, and then, as the sun began to fade on the way back to the farm, he had bent and plucked a four-leaf clover from the grass. 'There,' he'd said handing it to her. 'Keep that safe and it will be lucky for you.'

It was now pressed among the pages of her Bible, and Niamh knew she would never part with it. It had been as he was handing it to her that their fingers had brushed and she had felt an unfamiliar tingle ripple through her. She thought Nipper must have felt it too, for he had flushed and looked away quickly. After that they had walked far apart and a silence had settled between them. She wondered if he might ask her to dance at the social and the tingle was there again. Then she thought of the new dress she might find tomorrow and when she drifted off to sleep, her mind was full of happy thoughts.

The next day dawned fine and clear, and after breakfast Maeve pressed a sum of money into Niamh's hand that made her gasp. 'Go on, away with you and buy yourself something nice. Granda is in Liam's with the weans and Nipper will be off into town soon. Shelagh's coming with you to help you choose. Now, away you go – you don't want to end up walking in.'

'But I haven't washed the breakfast pots yet,' Niamh objected, glancing towards the dirty crockery piled in the sink.

'That'll wait, so it will.' Maeve waved her away. 'Go and get your bag and coat – there's a nip in the air – and put that money away safely.'

Niamh pecked her on the cheek and skipped off to do as she was told. She was relieved that Shelagh would be going with them. She had been tongue-tied with Nipper for the last few days but Shelagh would ease the tension.

In fact, the ride into town was filled with laughter as Shelagh told them what the weans had been up to. By the time they drew into the marketplace, they were all in a good humour.

'How long have we got?' Shelagh asked, as she clambered down from the high seat at the front of the cart.

'I've got a list as long as your arm but I've been instructed by the gaffer that I'm not to rush you so take as long as you like,' Nipper answered, with a cheeky wink. 'I can always go for a pint at the inn or see Sean McLoughlin. The business will be mine when he retires so I've got to keep me eye on it, haven't I?'

He tethered the horse and sauntered away. Then Shelagh took Niamh's arm. 'Come on, let's get started. Liam has given me some money and told me I'm to get myself a new dress, too.' Shelagh loved her husband and weans to distraction, but it was nice to have a little time to herself and she intended to make the most of it. Women with baskets on their arms were shopping for food but

Shelagh steered Niamh into the narrow cobbled back-streets and soon they came to Miss Kelly's Fashion Emporium. The sign that hung outside swung gently in the breeze, and in the window there was a selection of clothes and shoes. It certainly didn't look big enough to be classed as an emporium but the items in the window were very fashionable for a small town.

'She has some nice things inside,' Shelagh informed her as she pushed the door open. 'Not so much choice as you'd get in Dublin but I'm sure we'll get sorted.' The bell above the door tinkled as they entered and an attractive middle-aged woman appeared through a door behind the counter with a bright smile. She was tall, slim and beautifully turned out. Her fair hair was caught up in an elegant chignon at the back of her head and her eyes were a lovely soft grey.

'I don't suppose you two young ladies would be after an outfit for the social on Saturday, would you?' she said teasingly. Then, pointing towards the dress rails, she told them, 'Why don't you have a browse through those and see if there's anything that catches your eye? If not, I have some new stock at the back that I haven't brought through yet.'

The girls did as they were told, and it wasn't many seconds before Shelagh held a pretty blue dress aloft saying excitedly, 'Oh I like this one. Isn't it a lovely colour? And it's my size too. Do you think I should try it on?'

'Of course,' Niamh told her. There was nothing that had caught her eye yet but she was keen to see how the dress looked on Shelagh.

The young woman disappeared into the fitting room and when she came out Niamh beamed. 'Why, it could have been made for you. It's perfect and the exact same colour as your eyes.' The dress was fitted to the waist, with long sleeves and a pretty white-lace collar, while the skirt fell in pleats to her ankles. It showed off Shelagh's slim figure to perfection.

'It does look lovely,' the shop owner agreed. 'But before you make up your mind finish going through the rails. Half the fun of having a new dress is trying a few on, and there might be some more that you like as well. If they're not in your size I can always alter one for you.'

She was very obliging so Shelagh did as she was told, enjoying herself enormously. By the time she had gone through the rails she had found another two she liked so she tried them on too, then decided that she still liked best the one she had tried on first. At home she had a pair of shoes and a bag that would be just right with it.

'Well, that's me done,' she said happily, after she had paid for her purchase, which she was delighted to find was a very reasonable price. 'But what about you, Niamh?'

'I haven't really found anything yet,' Niamh admitted glumly. 'Although this one is quite smart.' She held up a dress in a light dove grey, trimmed at the neck and cuff with darker grey ribbons, but Miss Kelly shook her head.

'That's far too old for you, lass,' she said kindly. 'It might be fine for going to mass but it certainly isn't right for a dance. You want something young and frivolous. Now, let me think...' She tapped her lip thoughtfully with a forefinger, then grinned and disappeared through the door behind the counter.

When she reappeared a dress in a lovely shade of green, with an autumnal pattern, hung over her arm. 'I think this might be just perfect for you. The green will match your lovely eyes and the autumnal colours will show off your hair. Do try it on.'

Niamh eyed it doubtfully. Indeed it was a beautiful dress, but the material was so fine and shimmery she feared it would be highly impractical.

'Oh, go on,' Shelagh urged. 'It's so lovely.'

Niamh went obediently into the fitting room, and once the dress was on she stared at herself in the mirror in disbelief. It was the most beautiful dress she had ever seen and she felt like a different person in it.

'It's the very latest fashion from London,' Miss Kelly assured her. 'But do come out and let us see you in it.'

Niamh had never had the chance to try on ready-made clothes before. At home new clothes had to be ordered and made by a seamstress, although Niamh had never had to resort to that because Dilly was so good with a needle. She had always made Niamh's clothes, and thinking of her now brought a lump to the girl's throat. Niamh knew that Dilly would approve of this particular design – in fact, she would probably copy it when Niamh eventually returned home. Her mammy had a flair for knowing what would suit any particular person. And perhaps one day everyone would be able to enter a dress shop and try outfits on without having to have them made. These off-the-peg dresses were another indication of how the world was changing and Niamh guessed that Dilly would approve of the idea.

Now she swished the curtain aside and stepped into the shop. Shelagh and Miss Kelly gasped.

'Why ... you look absolutely gorgeous,' Miss Kelly told her, and Shelagh's bobbing head told Niamh that she thought so too.

She twirled about to look at herself in the mirror again and couldn't stop smiling. The dress was semi-fitted to the waist, where there was a wide belt of heavy silk embroidery to match the russets and golds in the pattern, then flared out to her ankles with a dipped hem. The sleeves were full and transparent, caught at the wrist with the same band of embroidery as around the waist. The material, Miss Kelly informed her, was chiffon and it swirled about her legs at the least movement she made. The cut of the dress was actually very simple, but that was what made it so stunning.

'It's just perfect for you.' Shelagh smiled. 'Why, to be sure, you'll be the belle of the ball. But we must find you some shoes to go with it. You can't go in those heavy great things you're wearing now.'

Miss Kelly went away again and returned with various pairs for Niamh to try on until they found some that were just right. They were a very soft fine leather in a warm russet colour with fairly high heels and a little strap across the instep and exactly matched one of the colours in the dress.

Niamh wasn't used to dainty shoes or heels and wobbled dangerously across the shop to look at them in the mirror. 'I love them,' she admitted, with a grin. 'But what if I can't walk in them? And would I ever wear them again? I can hardly see me chasing the chickens across the yard in these!'

'Oh, away with you,' Shelagh said airily waving her concerns aside. 'Sure you're only young once and you'd never find a more perfect match if you were to search the length and breadth of Ireland. In fact, I don't know of anywhere else that stocks ready-made clothes come to think of it. You can always have a practice at walking in them of an evening before the dance.'

'I could, couldn't I?' Niamh said, not needing very much persuading. 'I'll take them.'

She gulped a little when Miss Kelly told her what the dress and the shoes amounted to, and felt slightly guilty at spending so much money on one outfit, but then, as Shelagh pointed out, that was what her gran'ma had given her the money for, so why not spend it on something she truly loved?

'I shan't be able to afford a bag to go with them,' Niamh said regretfully, as Miss Kelly was carefully parcelling her purchases.

'Ah, well, I may be able to help you there too,' the kindly woman told her. 'We had a little flood in the storeroom last year and I'm sure I have a bag out there that would match. It might have a wee water stain on the bottom but no one would see that and I could let you have it at a very good price if you liked it.' She hurried away to fetch it.

As she had said, it was a perfect match for the shoes, very dainty and feminine. 'It's lovely, but I can't find a water mark on it,' Niamh told her, as she examined it admiringly. It was just about the prettiest bag she had ever seen.

Miss Kelly winked at Shelagh. 'Sure it must have dried out then, but I still couldn't sell it as perfect.' She named such a ridiculously low price that Niamh's eyes popped.

'I'll take that too, then,' she said quickly. 'And thank you very much.'

'It's been a pleasure. Do come again.' Miss Kelly watched the two young women leave with a broad smile on her face. It was always good to see a satisfied customer leave the shop and the two that had just left had surely been a pleasure to serve.

Nipper was just throwing a large bag of chicken pellets into the back of the cart when the two rushed towards him. 'You've never got sorted already?' he gasped incredulously. 'Maeve told me to be patient as women were awful for losing track of time when they got shopping.'

'Not these women,' Shelagh answered smugly. 'We were sorted in no time. But let's not go back just yet, eh? We could go to the tearoom for a cup of tea. Let's push the boat out a bit. My treat. We'll be back at home working soon enough.'

An hour later, after a visit to the tiny tearoom in the town square, they piled back onto the cart and set off for the farm in high good humour.

'So can I see what you've bought?' Nipper asked, as they trundled along the leafy lanes. Niamh was clutching the bag containing her purchases as if it contained the Crown Jewels.

'Not so much as a peep till Saturday night,' Shelagh told him firmly. 'But I will tell you this. Niamh will knock your eyes out when you see her in her new outfit, so she will. She'll be the prettiest girl at the dance.'

Nipper thought Niamh would be the prettiest girl anywhere, no matter what she was wearing. She could wear a sack and still look beautiful as far as he was concerned but he didn't say so and they went on their way, happily contemplating their night out.

Chapter Nineteen

As Niamh was trying on clothes, Kian blinked to keep himself awake as he crouched ankle deep in a muddy trench. He'd long since lost all feeling in his feet and dreaded to think what they would look like when he eventually took off his boots. He prayed he hadn't got trench foot. He had seen men in agony with their toes rotting away and couldn't think of anything worse, apart from getting shot that was.

It seemed a million years ago that he had set off for France, packed like a sardine into a tin alongside the other chaps. There had been only the most basic of amenities on the boat and the stiff khaki uniforms and heavy boots were uncomfortable, yet the atmosphere had been charged with enthusiasm. They had been convinced they could conquer the world. What chance did the Germans stand against them? they asked each other, as they were tossed about like matchsticks on the choppy sea.

When they had landed in Boulogne they had found a French brass band playing to welcome them and had filed down the gangplank to rapturous applause. The French people had been eager to embrace them, shake their hands or kiss their cheeks, surging forward, like a tidal wave, as the sergeants barked commands and tried to get the men into order. The soldiers had all looked so young, only the colour of their closely shorn hair distinguishing one from another. Even so, the French had clearly seen them as their saviours and crawled over them like flies. Women of every age threw flowers at them or hung garlands about their necks, and chaos reigned as the new recruits lapped up the attention. Eventually they had made their way through the crowds to the lorries that were waiting to take them to their barracks and scrambled into them to sit shoulder to shoulder again as their uniforms rubbed their skins raw and blisters popped up on their feet.

The 'barracks' proved to be a sea of tents in a field of mud, and even from there they could hear gunfire and screaming.

One of the largest tents had been set up for dining, and after taking their kitbags to their designated sleeping areas, which proved to be little more than narrow wooden bunks, they were marched away to eat. The food was almost inedible and Kian had stared in horror at the unidentifiable slop that was his main meal of the day. At some stage he supposed it might have been some sort of vegetable but it had been kept heated for so long that it was little more than mush in a thin greasy gravy.

'Come on, lads, eat up!' a sergeant roared, seeing the disgust on many faces. 'You didn't expect *à la carte,* did you!'

Plates of thick grey bread had been placed at intervals along the narrow trestle tables and Kian found that by dipping chunks into the slop he could force it down. 'We feed our pigs better than this at home,' he grumbled to the young private next to him. He noticed that the lad was very pale and tearful but was hardly surprised. It was hard to make himself heard above the roar of distant gunfire and he wondered how the elation of such a short time ago could have changed so quickly. Everyone was apprehensive and fearful now. They were then served with lukewarm, unsweetened stewed tea but everyone drank it. No one knew when they might eat or drink again and they supposed they should try to keep their strength up.

They were marched back to their tents and ordered to put away their things. Next to each bed there was a small wooden locker and they unloaded their kitbags into it. A grey blanket was folded at the end of each bed and there was also one pillow each, but other than that the tents were bare. Wooden boards that were already slippery with mud from their boots formed the floor and Kian thought he had never seen anywhere so bleak. The sergeant appeared through the tent flap again and took them to show them the latrines. Again they found themselves squelching through thick mud. It seemed there was no escaping it in that hell hole.

'That is the hospital tent,' the sergeant told them, pointing to a far corner of the field. 'The injured are taken there first before being transported to hospitals or shipped home, depending on how serious their injuries are. And I want *no* fraternizing with the nurses,' he added, directing a glare at them all. 'That tent over there is the mess tent. You can use that for writing letters home when you're not on duty. There are dominoes and a dartboard in there, if anyone wants to use them.'

At that moment a horse and cart clopped towards the hospital tent and nurses appeared as if by magic. Some of the stretchers that were laid on the back were rushed straight inside. Kian saw others being carried into the tent next door. Following his eyes the sergeant told them, 'That's what we use as a morgue until we can identify the bodies and inform their families.'

'Will they be shipped home for burial?' Kian dared to ask.

The sergeant shook his head. 'There's no time for that. Some of the soldiers will take them to a burial ground not far from here and bury them later today.'

It was then that the true horror of what he had let himself in for sank in, and Kian shuddered as he watched the body of a young man, probably no older than himself, being carried into the morgue. His uniform was red with blood and Kian was horrified to see that one of the arms dangling limply over the side of the stretcher was missing a hand. Blood dripped from the severed limb, turning the mud beneath it scarlet. It was a sight he would never forget but, sadly, was the first of many such tragedies he would see, as they all would.

Kian swallowed as he swatted away a fly from his cheek. There seemed to be millions of the damn things everywhere and this, added to the cloying smell that hung in the air and the unpalatable meal he had just forced himself to eat, made him feel nauseous. He wasn't the only one: suddenly a new recruit just behind him was violently sick on the mud.

'Smell gettin' to you, is it, laddie?' the sergeant barked unsympathetically. 'You'll soon get used to it. It's blood an' death you can smell. We bury the corpses each day, if we can, but sometimes they have to lie in the morgue for a bit, hence the stink. It's a flies' and rats' picnic round here!'

His words made the young private retch again and Kian averted his eyes. This wasn't how he had imagined it to be.

'Right, the rest o' the day is yours,' the sergeant shouted. 'There'll be another meal in the dining tent for you all at six o'clock sharp. I suggest you get as much rest as you can because you'll be up bright and early tomorrow. After a day in the trenches you'll be able to call yourself real soldiers.'

He marched away, his back straight as a rod, and the young men glanced at each other.

'I'm going to write to me mam to tell her we've arrived,' one chap said dejectedly, and gradually they all drifted apart.

As Kian turned a young man beside him said, 'I reckon we're in the same tent, mate. I'm Johnny Webster. I live in Bedworth. What about you?'

Kian stuck his hand out and they shook. 'From Nuneaton. The name's Kian Carey.'

'Irish?'

'Me daddy is,' Kian told him. 'And I do still have

family in Enniskerry, near Dublin, but I was born and raised in Nuneaton in the Midlands.' It was quite nice to meet someone from the same neck of the woods as him. Bedworth was only just up the road from Nuneaton, as the crow flew. So far he hadn't had a glimpse of Mickey Cotteridge but at least fifteen boats had brought them here. Mickey could have been on any of them and taken elsewhere.

As they entered their tent Johnny said gloomily, 'Ain't the poshest o' places to kip, is it?'

'Huh!' Kian snorted. 'That's a bit of an understatement if ever I heard one.'

The two young men grinned at each other and their friendship was formed.

The evening meal was slightly more palatable than what they'd been given earlier. They were served with sandwiches consisting of the same dry grey bread that they had eaten before but at least the cheese inside was tasty. Everyone was tired and most retired early, but Kian couldn't sleep for the constant buzz of flies and the echo of gunfire.

'Christ almighty,' one chap shouted from the darkness. 'Doesn't that bloody racket *ever* stop?'

'We're in a war zone in case you'd forgotten, mate,' some sharp whip retorted, but eventually they slept out of sheer exhaustion.

The next day they were issued with rifles and frogmarched to the trenches.

As Kian slopped through the stinking mud a large rat suddenly ran across his foot and he shuddered with disgust as he looked about and saw that they were everywhere. The noise of the gunfire was deafening and he felt sick with fear. Some way

216

along the trench a grim-faced officer was waiting for them.

'Right, you lot,' he barked. 'We never know when the Germans are going to attack but when they do I shall give the order and you all climb out of the trench and form a line. Then we meet the buggers head on. It's you or them, remember. There's no room for yellow bellies here. Do you understand?'

Some of the lads looked as if they were about to burst into tears but he showed them no sympathy. Sympathy cost lives.

'On my command you all cock your rifles and make sure they're fully loaded and don't be afraid to use the bayonets on 'em if need be. Those bastards will use 'em on you, given half a chance, believe me!' He looked sternly about at the sea of pale faces before going on, 'You also need to remember that if the chap next to you goes down you carry on and step over him, even if he's your mate. Soon as the battle's over the stretcher-bearers go out and try to bring back those that are still alive but that isn't your job. Your job is to shoot the Germans. Lastly, we shall be watching each and every one of you, and I'll tell you now, if you turn coward and try to run back we'll bloody shoot you ourselves. We've no room for cowards here. If you should be injured just lie still and play dead till it's all over. Then, hopefully we'll be able to get you back to the hospital tent. Any questions?'

One young man asked tentatively, 'When do you think the next attack will be, sir?'

'Huh!' The officer snorted. 'Your guess is as good as mine, laddie. It could be early morning,

217

noon or twilight. The swine attack when they feel like it. You could be waiting here for ten minutes or ten hours. No time of day is sacred to them. Any more questions?'

Heads shook as the officer took a packet of cigarettes from his pocket and lit one. 'Right, then, at ease till I give the command but just make sure you're ready when I do.' With that he marched away, leaving them to glance at each other.

'Ugh!' They all started as a young private shook his leg, sending a huge rat slamming up the side of the trench before it scurried away, red eyes glowing in the early-morning light. 'The bastard tried to bite me – look,' he cried, pointing towards a hole the filthy creature had made in his trouser leg just above his boot. 'And did yer see the red around its mouth and dried in its whiskers? Where do yer reckon that come from?'

Most of them had a good idea but no one said anything. It didn't bear thinking about – but it might explain why the rats were so huge: bodies were left on the muddy field to rot. The rats were clearly better fed than they were.

A few of the lads, Kian and Johnny among them, began to walk along the trench and explore. Here and there the sides were shored up with wood and occasionally they came to a dug-out where they could stand together side by side. The floors had once been planks but the wood had long since disappeared beneath the cloying mud.

Kian dared to peep over the side of the trench. In the distance he could see a stretch of woodland with rolls of barbed wire in front of it.

'The Germans are on the other side,' a lanky

youth informed him. 'When it's dark some of our men sometimes go and try to cut through it or set mines to blow it up so we can get to them more easily. When they do attack they come from either side of it.'

He seemed to be much more knowledgeable about things than most of them, and Kian asked, 'How long have you been here?'

The man lit a cigarette and blew a smoke ring. 'A month or so now. Couldn't tell you exactly. After a while you lose track of time. One day runs into another.'

Kian saw now that his uniform was caked with dried mud and he smelt pungent, which was no surprise to Kian, now he had seen the inadequate bathing facilities they had been shown to that morning: jugs of cold water on a trestle table, which had to be shared between them, with scum floating on the top and slivers of greasy soap.

He returned his attention to the field above the trench and realized then that the gunfire they could hear, although close, was coming from the other side of the wood.

'It'll be our turn next,' the youth informed him grimly. Dropping his cigarette butt into the mud, he shouldered his rifle and wandered on.

The sun rose slowly in the sky as the men paced anxiously up and down. Others, who had been there longer, took the opportunity to lean against the sides of the damp trenches and rest as best they could. At around midday the men from the Catering Corps came with baskets of sandwiches and bottles of lukewarm water and they all drank thirstily. They were hot and uncomfortable and

219

many had taken off their tin helmets.

The sound of gunfire ceased abruptly, the sudden silence unnerving.

'Stand by your bed, chaps,' one bright spark shouted. 'It'll be our turn next.'

Small wooden ladders appeared from nowhere and were propped up the sides of the deep trenches. Kian was surprised he hadn't noticed them before. The idle hours had lulled them all into a false sense of security but now the air was tinged with a sense of waiting, for what he wasn't sure but he was aware that his skin had broken out in goosebumps beneath the itchy material of his uniform and his brow was sweating. A tall gangly lad with goofy teeth and the worst case of acne Kian had ever seen began to sob and an officer poked him sharply in the ribs with the butt of his rifle commanding, 'Pull yourself together, lad! You won't last ten minutes up there if you don't get a grip on yourself!'

Kian rammed on his helmet as the others were doing and cocked his rifle then suddenly they were all spurred into action when a shout went up. 'Onwards, men!'

They swarmed towards the ladders, and he was suddenly above ground, gasping as he saw a surge of Germans in a straight line heading towards them. He tried to run but the mud sucked at his boots, making each step an effort as he raised his rifle and pointed it towards the enemy.

Suddenly machine-gun fire rattled out. The smell of cordite burned his nostrils and the man in front of him suddenly jerked, like a puppet on a string, and fell face first into the mud. Kian hesitated but, remembering what the officer had said, he stepped over him. Smoke burned his eyes and throat but he forced himself to lift one foot then the other as the enemy came closer.

Then he had been face to face with a German and they had raised their rifles to fire at each other. He was looking into the eyes of a man no older than himself and saw fear in them as his finger squeezed the trigger. The bullet had found its mark. The boy's eyes had opened wide and he toppled forward and jerked convulsively but Kian had had no time to dwell on it because someone was lunging at him with a knife. He had raised his bayonet and thrust it forward. Seconds later it sliced through the German's uniform and slid into his gut. Blood had spurted from the man's mouth then as gracefully as a ballet dancer's. The man's arms flew out and he had slid to his knees, dropping sideways, his eyes staring sightlessly up at the sky...

There had been many such attacks since and Kian had lost track of how many Germans he had killed. Many of the chaps he had travelled with had lost their lives. Some of their bodies had been taken to the mortuary tent and hastily buried in shallow communal graves with small white wooden crosses to mark the spot. Others had been left on the field because there wasn't enough time to retrieve them.

Kian was amazed that he and Johnny were still alive. But for how much longer? It could only be a matter of time now. Their luck wouldn't hold for ever. He had forgotten what it was like to feel clean and how it felt to sleep in a comfortable bed, his mother's kiss when she wished him a good night, or the sound of laughter. There was nothing but death and destruction all around them here. But in a few hours' time he would go back to the barracks, such as they were. He had done his two days' shift and soon he would be able to sleep. There was talk of them being transported further up the coast but there would be other fields to tramp across, other Germans to face, and now he was only too aware that any time soon he might be facing the longest sleep of all. His luck couldn't hold for ever.

Chapter Twenty

'Look at you!' Maeve gasped on Saturday evening, when Niamh appeared in all her finery. The outfit had been hidden from prying eyes until the big night arrived and Niamh felt as if she was floating on air. The dress wafted about her legs and the new high heels made her seem tall and sophisticated.

Shelagh had been round a little earlier to do her hair and now it was pinned into loose curls on top of her head, showing off her slim neck and shapely shoulders.

'Eeh, I don't think I've seen a bonnier lass since your gran'ma was your age.' Daniel choked, feeling strangely emotional. He had always looked upon Nianth as a little wean but now here she was, a beautiful young woman. It made him wonder

222

where the time had gone. They had received a letter from Dilly that morning and Daniel wished that she and Fergal could be here to see their daughter now.

Niamh did a little twirl, her face flushed with excitement. At that moment the door opened to admit Nipper and Declan, all togged out in their Sunday best.

Nipper had clearly tried to tame his thick curly hair with Macassar oil but already it was springing up again. Even so he was still very smart in a navy-blue pin-striped suit with wide lapels, a crisp white shirt and a pale blue tie. He couldn't remember ever making so much of an effort with his appearance, but when he caught a glance of Niamh he was glad that he had. She was so stunning that she almost took his breath away. He felt awkward as he shuffled from foot to foot, although he had no idea why. Declan was smart, too, in a pale grey suit that set off his jet black hair, although Maeve clicked her tongue disapprovingly when she caught sight of his shoes.

'Get the polish and the shoebrush from under the sink and give those the once-over,' she ordered. 'To be sure you can't go to a dance in dirty shoes.'

Declan grinned as he rubbed one down the back of his trouser leg. 'You're too fussy by far, so you are, Gran'ma.' He chuckled. 'The lights will be low and, anyway, who will be looking at me shoes?'

Maeve couldn't help but smile back. She could never stay annoyed with Declan for long, and he knew it. 'Well all right then, go as you are. But you'll only have yourself to blame if the lasses pass you by for someone smarter!'

'I doubt there'll be much chance of that happening. There'll be twice as many lasses as lads, after so many have joined up.' Instantly he wished he could take back the remark as everyone's faces had become solemn.

But then Shelagh and Liam appeared and the atmosphere lightened again as Shelagh sashayed up and down the room to show off her new dress. 'Now, the weans are fast asleep in bed and you shouldn't be hearing a peep out of them,' she told Daniel. 'I've made up the fire and the tea things are laid out ready for you.'

He grinned as he headed towards the door with a pile of newspapers under his arm. He was looking forward to a night in front of the fire with nothing to do but read and keep an ear open for the weans. 'They'll be right as rain with me, so they will. Get off with you and have a good night. And don't rush back, mind. I shall kip as well in front of the fire as in bed.'

The girls began to pull on their coats as Liam hurried away to bring the pony and trap to the door – they couldn't be expected to pick their way across the cobbled yard in the shoes they had on.

Niamh and Shelagh kissed Maeve's cheek. Then she watched them go, as excited as two schoolgirls.

Once they were all seated in the trap, two in the front and the other three in the back, which was quite a squeeze, they were on their way. The nights were fast drawing in and there was a nip in the air, but it was a fine clear night and, as the horse clip-clopped along, Niamh's excitement grew. She had never been to a proper dance before and just hoped she could remember all the dance steps that Shelagh had spent the last few nights teaching her.

They were almost in Enniskerry when she suddenly thought of Kian and wondered if he was safe. It was a harsh reminder that the world was at war but even so she tried not to think of it, determined that nothing should spoil this special night. Liam let them down outside the door while he drove on to make the horse comfortable in the local inn's stable.

They trooped inside and Niamh looked about. Tables and chairs were ranged around the walls and an elderly band were tuning up on the stage. Just as Declan had forecast, there appeared to be more women than men but already the room was quite full and the wooden dance floor shone in the dull light in front of the stage.

'What would you ladies like to drink?' Nipper asked. Then, with a wink at Declan, 'I dare say they'll have a drop o' poteen behind the bar.'

'I reckon me and Niamh will have a port and lemon,' Shelagh said, with a grin at Niamh. 'Might as well push the boat out, eh, lass?'

'Well ... I don't usually drink,' Niamh said uncertainly, but Shelagh waved away her concern.

'A couple won't hurt you. Now, come on, let's go and find a seat while the men get the drinks in.'

Niamh discovered that port and lemon was quite pleasant, and within half an hour she was having the time of her life. She was in great demand with the young farm workers and barely had time to sit down between dances before someone whisked her onto the floor again.

Soon the room was hazy with cigarette smoke that swirled about the ceiling like ghosts in the dim light. The band was belting out all the popular tunes and Niamh couldn't stop smiling.

Over the rim of his glass of Guinness, Nipper watched her as he tried to pluck up courage to ask her to dance. He wasn't keen to see her dancing with anyone else but was afraid she might refuse him.

It was as Shelagh and Liam returned to the table after a dance that Shelagh followed his eyes and suggested, 'Why don't you go and ask her for a dance?'

Dull colour crept into his cheeks. 'She looks happy enough where she is.'

'Well, sure faint heart never won fair lady,' Shelagh told him. 'And I've an inkling that Niamh would love to dance with you. Hasn't she been peeping at you all night from the corner of her eye – as have most of the other girls here, may I add!'

Nipper glanced at Declan, who was waltzing the daughter of a neighbouring farmer round the room. Now he came to think of it, Declan had been dancing with her almost all evening so he supposed Shelagh was right. The worst Niamh could say was no. He waited his chance, and once Niamh was returned to the table, he asked, 'Do you fancy doing a turn round the floor with me, then? I can't promise I won't stand on your toes, though.'

'I'd love to,' Niamh answered shyly, as he rose and took her hand.

Shelagh grinned as she watched them go. Leaning towards Liam, she whispered, 'I reckon those two have a soft spot for each other.'

Liam laughed. 'And you wouldn't be trying to move things along now, would you, you little match-maker?'

Shelagh raised her eyebrows and smiled at him innocently. 'As if I *would*. But come on now. They're playing a waltz.' She grabbed her husband's hand and as they reached the dance floor he took her in his arms and she soon forgot all about Niamh and Nipper.

Nipper was holding Niamh awkwardly about the waist at arm's length. He could feel the heat of her through the floaty material of her dress and the closeness of her was making him experience sensations he had never felt before.

Niamh was struggling for something to say – for once she was tongue-tied. 'It – it's a grand dance, isn't it?' she managed eventually.

'Aye, it is,' Nipper answered. 'And... sure you're looking fine tonight, Niamh.'

They stumbled on until a young spark who had indulged in a little too much poteen bumped into them, almost knocking them over. Nipper instinctively pulled Niamh to him to stop her falling as the youth apologized and bumbled on his way.

Suddenly he felt her heart beating and smelt the clean sweet scent of her hair. When she relaxed into him he tightened his grip. It felt the most natural thing in the world to hold her tight, and when she smiled up at him it was all he could do to stop himself kissing her there and then.

'It's mighty hot in here,' he said. 'Shall we step outside for a breath of fresh air?' He was embarrassed that she might feel the effect she was having on him.

'I'd like that,' she answered, and when he took her hand to lead her towards the exit she went willingly.

'Look,' Shelagh hissed delightedly at Liam, as she spotted the two young people wending their way towards the door. 'Didn't I tell you those two were smitten with each other?'

'Aye, you did.' He laughed as he clutched her to him. 'But now forget about those two and concentrate on your husband, woman! It isn't often we get time together without the weans so let's make the most of it.'

Outside, Niamh shivered. After the heat of the hot, stuffy room the cool night air struck cold, not that she minded. At that moment she would have walked through solid ice to be with Nipper.

He thoughtfully slipped his jacket off and hung it about her shoulders and then before they knew it they were in each other's arms and he asked softly, 'Would you mind very much if I kissed you, Niamh?'

Niamh gulped. She had never had a proper kiss before and she was nervous, but she wanted it now, more than anything in the whole world.

When she nodded he lowered his head and suddenly she felt as if a million butterflies had taken flight in her stomach as his lips gently found hers.

The kiss was tender, but as he felt her respond it became more ardent and they clung to each other as if it was the most natural thing in the world. In that moment Niamh discovered how it felt to be in love and Nipper knew there would never be another girl to match the one in his arms for as long as he lived.

Other courting couples were standing in the shadows kissing and giggling but for Niamh and Nipper, in that short precious time, there were only the two of them in the whole world and she wished that time could stand still.

'I think I've been wanting to do that since the very first second you walked into the kitchen when you arrived,' Nipper told her, when they came up for air.

Niamh giggled. 'I remember thinking how grown-up you looked and how handsome, but I didn't know what you thought of me.'

'Well, you do now,' he whispered, as he stroked her cheek. Their lips joined again and they lost all sense of time as they stood wrapped in each other's arms.

'Ah, so here you are. We thought you'd got lost, so we did,' a voice interrupted them some time later.

The two young people sprang apart guiltily. Shelagh was grinning from ear to ear as she said, 'I wondered how long it would be before you two realized what was growing between you. It was clear to everyone else, so it was, unless they were blind. But come away in now. You're missing the dance and it's chilly out here.'

The two trooped reluctantly back inside, but Nipper kept a tight grip on Niamh's hand, and for the rest of the night he made quite sure that she

229

had time to dance with no one but himself.

All too soon the band was playing the last dance and as the sweet strains of 'Love's Own Sweet Song' floated on the air, Nipper led her onto the floor and they swayed together in time to the music.

When it was finished they made their way reluctantly back to the table as Shelagh hurried off to fetch the coats. There was no sign of Declan. He had walked a young lass from the village home, Liam informed them, but he was sure he'd make his own way back when he was good and ready, so they all went outside to wait while Nipper fetched the horse and trap from the inn's stable.

In the front, Liam steered the horse with Shelagh at his side while Niamh snuggled up to Nipper in the back. It was very romantic, with a million stars shining down on them, and she knew she would remember this wonderful night for as long as she lived.

'You were the bonniest lass in the whole place, to be sure,' Nipper whispered into her ear, and she shivered with delight, wishing they could stay just as they were for always. There was nothing to be heard but an owl hooting in the trees and the clip-clop of the horse's hoofs. For a time, they could almost forget about the war.

When they reached the farm, Shelagh wished them goodnight then hurried to her cottage. Liam led away the horse to bed him down for the night in the stables, as Nipper and Niamh went into the cosy kitchen.

Maeve was sitting up in bed, waiting for them,

with a book, *The World Set Free* by H. G. Wells, laid open on her lap. One look at their star-struck faces and the way they glanced at each other told her all she needed to know.

'Had a good time, did you?' she asked coyly, and Niamh flushed to the roots of her hair.

They were both glowing as if they had been lit from within and could scarcely keep their eyes off one another.

'It was a grand do,' Nipper told her, as he crossed to the bed to kiss her. Over the years Maeve had become the mother he had always dreamed of knowing.

'Yes, it was.' Niamh came to perch on the edge of the bed. 'The band played all the popular tunes and I barely sat down all night. I also had my first taste of port and lemon,' she admitted, 'but only two glasses.'

'Well, it's clearly done you no harm and a little drop won't hurt you now and then,' Maeve replied, as she stroked the girl's hand. 'But now perhaps you'd both best think of getting to bed. There are still beasts that will need seeing to first thing in the morning.'

Daniel joined them. 'Patrick and little Bridie have been as good as the day is long,' he informed them with a smile. 'Not a peep have I had out of either of them all night.' He yawned. 'All the same I'm ready for me bed, so I am.'

Taking the hint Nipper and Niamh stood up, wished each other goodnight and went their separate ways to their rooms.

'Did you see the way those two were carrying on?' Maeve asked her husband, as he shrugged off

231

his braces. 'Talk about lovesick! Why, they could hardly keep their eyes off one another.'

'And is that a bad thing?' Daniel asked seeing the look on his wife's face.

'Not exactly – in fact, I think they'd make a fine couple. To my mind they're perfectly suited. It's just... I suppose I'm concerned that if anything comes of this Niamh would move here to live. How would our Fergal and Dilly feel about that?'

As Niamh undressed, she was wondering precisely the same thing. Already the first doubts were creeping in, not about Nipper, no, never about him: he was perfect in every way – but how would her parents react to the news? She knew how keenly they had felt the loss of Declan after he had chosen to live with his grandparents, so what would it do to them if she, too, were to decide to stay in Ireland? She was painfully aware that her father was very sick, and if she didn't go home there would be only Seamus to help her mother with him. Yet as her fingers stroked her lips she closed her eyes and remembered how it had felt when Nipper had kissed her. Her whole body had felt as if it was on fire and she knew already that she would never love anyone else as she loved him. Deep down she supposed that she had loved him since the minute she had set eyes on him after Declan had brought her here from the ferry. She had never allowed herself to believe that someone as handsome as Nipper would ever look her way so she had kept a check on herself. But now she knew that he had feelings for her, everything had changed. With a sigh she hung up her lovely new dress and slid into bed with a yawn. What was it her mother was fond of saying? 'It will all come out in the wash.' On that happy thought, she drifted off into a deep sleep.

Chapter Twenty-one

'I'm bored,' Olivia complained, as she slouched on the sofa in the drawing room.

It was so unlike her daughter to complain that Camilla, who was embroidering, raised her eyebrows. Olivia had not been the same since the horses had been taken, leaving only Dancer to pull the carriage. The army had left her because she was too old to be of much use to them. Nearly all the horses left in England were old now; the army had taken all the young ones. Olivia had sobbed on the day they had come for Spirit and Flame, feeding them sugar lumps and stroking their silky manes until they were led away. Everyone knew there was very little chance of them coming home. It was well known that many of the horses used in battle did not fare well; she had been inconsolable for days after they had gone.

'Why don't you do some sewing?' Camilla suggested.

Olivia sighed and shook her head. 'I don't feel like sewing,' she answered sulkily. 'I want to do something useful. Women are taking over the jobs the men did now that so many have gone to war. Why can't I have a job?'

'Because you're only thirteen and there's no need for you to work,' her mother answered patiently.

'I shall be fourteen soon,' Olivia argued. 'And lots of girls are working by the time they're my age. My brothers are, too, so why can't I?

'It's different for boys,' Camilla said. 'Young men are expected to learn a trade, and where better than in their own father's businesses? But it isn't seemly for young ladies to work.'

'Oh, Mother, you're *so* old-fashioned.' Olivia groaned. 'I don't want to sit here being waited on until some young man that you and Father approve of turns up and marries me. I want to *do* something with my life!'

'Nonsense, dear,' Camilla snapped. 'Only the working class work. You have been brought up as a lady.'

'Well, I don't *want* to be a lady!' Olivia pouted. 'Lots of girls are VADs or going into munitions factories.'

'Yes, they are,' her mother answered. 'And those in the factories have skin that is turning yellow from all the awful chemicals they're working with whilst the VADs are being shipped off to live and work in terrible conditions as they nurse the soldiers abroad. Is that really what you want?'

When Olivia remained mutinously quiet, Camilla pursed her lips. 'You have to be sixteen to become a VAD so I really don't know why we're having this conversation. By the time you're sixteen this war will hopefully be over, so concentrate on your lessons for now.'

Olivia stormed out of the room, almost colliding with Dilly, who was polishing the hall floor.

As always, Dilly smiled at her. Then, noting the girl's glum expression, she asked quietly, 'Is everything all right, pet?'

That was the thing about Mrs Carey, Olivia thought. She always had time for her and spoke to her as if she was a young woman rather than a child. If only her mother could be the same.

'No, it isn't really, Mrs Carey.' She tossed her head in frustration. 'I was just saying to Mother that I want to do something to help the war effort but she won't hear of it. She says I'm far too young. Honestly – anyone would think I was still a little girl with no mind of my own! Just because we're women doesn't mean we aren't capable of working. Loads of women in the town are already doing the jobs their husbands did before they went off to war, so why shouldn't I be allowed to?'

It was one of the rare occasions when Dilly agreed with Camilla wholeheartedly but she had no wish to upset the girl she loved so much. Choosing her words carefully, she said, 'Well, she has a point. You are still very young.' Then when her comment brought forth a glare, she hurried on, 'Perhaps you could do something without becoming actively involved, in preparation for when you're old enough.'

'Such as what?' Olivia asked, slightly pacified.

'Well, you could perhaps join a first-aid class. I know the Red Cross are running them of an evening at the St John's Ambulance hall. Even if the war is over before you can join in, you'll have learned something useful. They're glad of all the help they can get at the moment because, as well as teaching first aid, they're asking for volunteers to go in and roll bandages for the troops.'

'Hmm,' Olivia said, staring thoughtfully into space. 'You may be right. I don't think even Mother could object to that.' Then, the smile back on her face, she leaned in unexpectedly and kissed Dilly's cheek. 'Thanks, Mrs Carey. I'll talk to her about it, but not till Daddy's about. He listens to me much more than she does. Goodbye for now.' She disappeared up the stairs, leaving Dilly to finger the cheek she had kissed. She's so like I was when I was that age, she found herself thinking, and her heart broke afresh at all she had lost. At least she still saw her, which was much more than most mothers did when they gave up their children for adoption. There was no use crying over what could not be changed, yet the feeling of loss had not lessened over the years and Dilly had accepted that it never would.

When Olivia put the idea to her parents that night over dinner, her mother frowned but her father said, 'Actually, it's a very good idea, sweetheart. In fact, I'm proud that you want to do something. What do you think, Camilla?'

'Well, I certainly wouldn't want her walking there and back on her own, these dark evenings,' Camilla fretted.

'I could help there,' Oscar offered. 'I'd be happy to take her and bring her back.'

'Then I have no objection.' Max smiled, and although Camilla was far from happy with the idea she knew when she was outnumbered.

Olivia was delighted. Not only would she roll bandages and learn the basics of first aid but she would have her brother to herself for a short while too. They hadn't spent so much time together since their horses had been taken and she had missed their riding. Now she had something to look forward to and she could hardly wait to begin.

It was early November and the nights were cold and dark, but on her first visit to the St John's Ambulance hall, Olivia was in high spirits as Oscar walked her through the town.

'Are you sure you don't mind coming back to take me home?' she asked chirpily, as she tucked her arm through his.

'Not at all. I'm meeting Paul Whetton for a few games of snooker,' he assured her, and they strolled on, happy in each other's company.

Olivia enjoyed her first evening immensely and finally felt she was doing her little bit towards the war effort.

She was met at the door by a Red Cross worker, who set her to work rolling what felt like miles of bandages but Olivia didn't mind. Everyone had to start somewhere, she decided, and set to work cheerfully. After all, she wouldn't be rolling band-ages for ever!

'I'm going to enrol as a VAD, no matter what Mummy says, as soon as I'm old enough,' she informed her brother, when he came to collect her later that evening.

He had no doubt that she would. She could be a stubborn little madam when she set her mind to something.

'It isn't looking like the war is going to be over by Christmas, as everyone hoped it would be, if what the Red Cross ladies were saying is right,' she said solemnly, as she tucked her arm into Oscar's.

'No, it doesn't,' he agreed. 'If anything, it seems to be escalating. I read that after the German march on Paris was stopped, both sides have been digging trenches that run right from the Belgian coast to the Swiss mountains. Neither side can outflank the other apparently, so we're having to attack front on. We've lost so many lads from Nuneaton already.'

'The ladies at the first-aid group were saying that there's talk of Weddington Hall being turned into a hospital for wounded soldiers,' Olivia told him, as they hurried through the dark streets. The pavements were coated with frost and she clung to him to prevent herself slipping.

'I heard that too,' Oscar replied, then confided, 'I feel really bad about not joining up but every time I so much as hint at it Mother flies into a panic and upsets herself. Then she makes me feel guilty by telling me that Father needs me here and I'd be letting him down if I went. But I'm afraid that the older men still working for him must regard me as a coward.'

'That's utter rubbish!' Olivia objected, terrified at the thought of him going.

He shrugged. 'Well I may not have much choice soon, if it continues as it is. They're going to need every man they can get, from what I can see of it. The prime minister is calling for more volunteers and I think joining up will be compulsory soon. The fact that Mother has started holding dinner parties for everyone who has an eligible daughter since she read about Georgina's engagement doesn't help,' he ended glumly.

Olivia's happy mood was shattered and they were silent for the rest of the way home, each engrossed in their own thoughts. She loved her other brothers and her parents, but she had long ago realized that Oscar was the most important person in her world – she would have walked through fire for him. She couldn't envisage life without her brother in it.

Chapter Twenty-two

The letter that arrived from Enniskerry early in December had Dilly dancing a jig around the kitchen as she told Seamus and Fergal joyously, 'Niamh is going to be home for Christmas. Listen to this!

'Dear Mammy and Daddy,
I am pleased to say that Gran'ma is now feeling much better and has decided that within the next couple of weeks she will be able to manage again without my help. I am planning to return the second week in December, though I can give you no definite date yet as I haven't booked the ferry. You'll also be pleased to know that Declan will be coming with me. It is a fairly quiet time on the farm so Granda has told him that he should come back with me for a short holiday. Shelagh and Liam send their love. Patrick and Bridie are

239

growing like weeds now and I shall miss them. They are such lovely little souls, though Granda says they're little demons, always up to some mischief. I hope Seamus is well? I've missed him and am looking forward to seeing you all again.'

Dilly did another little jig around the kitchen table, but then her face became serious as she said quietly, 'If only our Kian could be home for Christmas, too, it would be perfect, wouldn't it? I wonder where he is now.'

There had been no word from him for more than a month, but sometimes the letters took a while to get through and two or three would arrive at once. In the last he had told them that he was still in France but the letter had been so heavily censored that they had no idea whereabouts he was. She had posted him a parcel containing warm socks, chocolate and underwear to Mons, the address where all the troops' letters were sent from, but she had no idea whether it would ever reach him. She worried about him constantly, even more so since telegrams had begun to arrive for parents in the town whose sons had been casualties of the war. Dilly could not begin to imagine how she would cope if anything should happen to Kian, but all she could do was take each day as it came and pray. She had been attending early-morning mass each Sunday at Our Lady of the Angels Church in Riversley Road where she would plead with the Holy Mother to keep him safe, and light candles for him. Then there was Madge or, rather, her absence. No one had seen her for some time but Dilly was still nervous that she would turn up out of the blue to demand payment. She had been putting the woman's money away weekly and every time she stepped out of the door she expected Madge to confront her. It was all very nerve-racking.

Still, the letter from Niamh had cheered her up, and as she served the evening meal, she was in a lighter mood.

Fergal now had his meals on a tray in bed; he was no longer able to get about, even in his wheeled chair, and Dilly tried not to notice his deterioration. It was as if he had lost the will to live. His once-powerful arms were now thin and sagging and the skin on his haggard face had taken on a greyish tinge through lack of fresh air and being confined to one room. Over the last few months she had been forced to call in the doctor to him on a number of occasions, but there was little more the doctor could do. Work in the dress shop now consisted solely of sewing uniforms for the troops, and while Dilly knew she was doing her bit for the war effort it was monotonous. Many women had now taken on the jobs their men had done before joining up and the town was proud of what its menfolk were doing. Her biggest fear was that Seamus might decide to join up too. He was now sixteen, although his height made him appear much older. Having him at home had kept her going over the last months. He was working at the same local pit as Kian had, and had an eye for the girls, much to his mother's amusement. With his copper hair and blue eyes, he was never short of a lass to walk out with and was earning himself a reputation as the area's Casanova although there wasn't an ounce of harm in him. That night, when he came in at the end of his shift, he smiled as his mother told him the good news and chatted to him as he washed in the water she had ready for him.

'That's grand. I've missed her,' he said, dropping his work clothes into a heap on the kitchen floor. His mother scooped them up, took them out into the yard and beat them against the wall, sending a flurry of soot into the frosty night air, just as she did each evening. Back in the warmth of the kitchen she folded them neatly for him to put on the next morning. When he was washed and dressed, he seated himself at the table as she fetched from the oven the meal she had been keeping warm for him.

'It'll be nice to see our Declan again,' he commented to his father.

Fergal nodded. 'Aye, it will that, lad. And it'll be nice to have our little lass back an' all.' Fergal had missed Niamh and could hardly wait for her to be home. She was usually back from the school where she worked much earlier than Dilly came in, and she had been company for him.

Dilly had gone back to reading the latest letter from his mother again, now that Seamus was eating his meal, and she told Fergal, 'Niamh says your mammy is almost back to her old self again and feels confident that she'll be able to manage with a little help from Shelagh when she comes home. That's grand to hear, isn't it?'

'Aye, it is that.'

'I reckon I'll go down the market and treat us to a little Christmas tree nearer the time,' Dilly babbled on. 'We can just about stretch to it and it would be nice for Niamh to come home to a house that's cheery. She'll be back in time to go to midnight mass with me on Christmas Eve an' all.' She saw a flicker of despair flare in Fergal's eyes. Before his accident they had always gone to midnight mass together and it was one of the many things he missed.

'I've ordered us a fine goose off Walter Bradley,' she hurried on, 'and Mrs Pegs has us a Christmas pudding soaking in brandy so we'll be dining like kings this year.'

Fergal ate barely enough to keep a bird alive nowadays; as he pointed out, he did nothing to build up an appetite, but that didn't stop her cooking tasty treats to tempt him.

'Anyway, here's me babbling like a brook when there's work waiting to be done,' she went on, pushing the letter deep into her apron pocket. She would read it again from beginning to end later that evening when she was tucked up in bed by the glow of the fire. 'I'm going to get these dirty dishes washed and dried and then I'll get the flat iron heated...' She bustled away, leaving Fergal to stare morosely into the fire.

In Enniskerry, Niamh was also tackling a sink full of dirty dishes, with Nipper on hand to dry them. They were rarely apart when he wasn't out of the farmhouse and while she was looking forward to seeing her younger brother and her parents again, she wondered how she could bear to be parted from him as the time drew closer for her to leave.

Outside, the wind was whipping the trees into a

frenzy and the smell of snow was in the air but inside all was warm and cosy, with a great peat fire blazing in the grate. Maeve's bed was now upstairs again and each day she was able to take a little more of the housework off Niamh's shoulders. Even so, everyone was concerned that she didn't overdo it. She tended to tire easily and had taken to retiring early at night, which gave Nipper and Niamh a little time alone together.

This was the time of day that Niamh had come to love best, when they would sit cuddled close on the sofa before the fire in the flickering candlelight, talk of what they had done that day and plan their future. But that was still a way off, and once the dishes were stacked away, she told Nipper, 'I'm away to feed the pigs. Will you get the chickens into their coops?'

'You've no need to ask,' he answered, with a cheeky wink, as he went to the door and slid his stockinged feet into his boots before putting his heavy coat on. 'But make sure you wrap up now. It's enough to cut you in two out there, so it is.'

'I will.' Minutes later, Niamh stepped out into the backyard, lifted the full pig bucket and set off for the stone pig pens at the far end of the yard.

The sow and her newborn family came snuffling and grunting to meet her as she stepped into the sty and deposited their supper on the ground. Within seconds the cabbage leaves and potato peelings had disappeared as if by magic and Niamh smiled with pleasure as she eyed the fat pink piglets. There were five of them, all healthy and eager to feed from the sow. The timing of their arrival had been perfect, just as

Daniel had planned it, for the winter months could be lean in Ireland. Should food run short, some of them could be sold at market or slaughtered for their own table. Niamh shuddered at the idea, then made her way quickly back to the warmth of the kitchen. Nipper reckoned it would snow as soon as the wind dropped, and it was so cold that she could well believe it.

Inside, she stared up at the rafters as she slipped off her boots. Boards were laid across them and on one of these she had placed the last of the apples from the orchard, making sure that there was air between them so that they would keep. On another board there were potatoes, and on yet another a selection of winter cabbages, turnips and swedes that she had collected from the kitchen garden. Sacks of flour were piled at one end of the room alongside a great smoked ham that dangled from a hook in the broad beam. With the bruised fruit that was not worth keeping, Niamh had made numerous pots of apple and plum jam. They were now lined up in a neat row on a shelf in the pantry. With all of this, and the eggs that the chickens produced, she hoped that the family would have enough to see them comfortably through the winter.

Maeve had popped into the adjoining cottage to say goodnight to the weans and Niamh took this as a good sign, for she couldn't have attempted it just a few short weeks ago. It showed how well she had recovered from her stroke. Daniel was settled beside the fire with his pipe and his newspaper and smiled at her fondly as she came to warm her hands.

'You've been a little godsend to us these last couple o' months, so you have, *alanna*,'he told her affectionately. 'You know what your gran'ma's like – she'd have tried to do all the work herself, so she would, if you hadn't been here to help. She can be a stubborn woman.'

'And you wouldn't have her any other way,' Niamh teased, as she smiled into his eyes.

When Nipper and Maeve joined them she began to heat the milk for their cocoa. Declan had gone into the village to meet the young lass he had met at the dance so there would be just the four of them tonight. No one expected Declan to return before bedtime – he had gone out all togged up in his Sunday best.

'Me an' your granda were sayin' earlier,' Maeve began tentatively some minutes later, as she warmed her hands about the steaming mug, 'that it might be best if you set off for home next week, lass. I've a feeling it won't be long now afore we're snowed in, if the sky is anythin' to go by, an' I'd not want to deprive your mammy an' daddy of your company at Christmas, to be sure.'

'But you're not quite ready to take on all the work on your own just yet,' Niamh objected, with a desperate glance at Nipper.

'Sure I am.' Maeve smiled. 'And it's not as if I haven't got Shelagh close at hand to help till I'm properly back to normal. No, you get away home an' don't you be fretting about me. You've been an angel, so you have, but it's time for you to go back to your own life now. Your granda thought he might take you to meet the ferry next Monday before the bad weather sets in.'

Niamh took a great gulp of her cocoa to cover her confusion, burning her throat. She'd known she would be home for Christmas but she hadn't reckoned on going so soon. Suddenly the thought of leaving Nipper was unbearable but she knew it would be useless to argue if her gran'ma had made up her mind so she stayed silent until the old couple had drained their mugs and wished her and Nipper goodnight.

'Well,' she said quietly, when the sound of her grandparents' bedroom door closing echoed down the stairs, 'I didn't think I'd be going home for at least another couple of weeks.'

Nipper took her hands and stroked them tenderly. 'Neither did I,' he admitted. 'But it won't be for ever, lass. We agreed it was right you should go home when Maeve was well again but soon as this war is over you can come back. Old Sean will have retired by then, and we'll get wed and live in the blacksmith's cottage. You know there's no other girl for me, Niamh... that's if you'll have me?'

'Oh, I *will!*' she said ecstatically.

His face became serious as he played with her fingers. 'But there's something I should be telling you...'

She frowned, sensing that he was about to say something that she didn't want to hear.

Nipper ran his tongue along his dry lips. 'The thing is... I've decided that after Christmas I'm going to join the navy.'

Niamh whimpered with distress but he shook her hands up and down saying, 'Now don't be taking on. It's something I've had a mind to do for some long time now. There's never so much work

247

to do on the farm in the winter so Daniel, Liam and Declan will manage without me. And I – I suppose I want to feel I'm doing me bit. Try to understand. There's young men from the village have gone already, as you well know.'

A great fat tear squeezed from beneath her lowered lashes and ran down her cheek as he gathered her into his arms. 'It won't be for long. And just think of the future we'll have ahead of us when I come home. You'll be the blacksmith's wife. We'll have a fine life and a houseful of weans, if I have my way.'

'But what if you don't come home?' she whispered fearfully. She could not contemplate life without Nipper now.

'Huh! To be sure I will.' He laughed. 'I have too much to live for to let the Jerries get the better of me but I want to be able to hold me head up, do you see?'

She nodded reluctantly, knowing there was nothing she could say to make him change his mind. 'But you will write to me?'

'Every single day if I get the chance.' Then, fishing in his pocket, he produced a tiny box. When he snapped open the lid she found herself staring at a sapphire surrounded by tiny diamonds that flashed all the colours of the rainbow in the firelight. He had bought the ring with some of the money that had been addressed to him and only wished that he could have found an even fancier one. 'It's not as grand as I'd like,' he admitted, 'but it was the best I could find the last time I went into Dublin. Perhaps it will do for now, and when the war is over I'll buy you a diamond as big as a saucer.'

'You most certainly will not. It's the prettiest ring I ever saw and I wouldn't change it for the biggest diamond in the world.'

'So it's official, then? You'll be my girl and wait for me?'

'For ever, if need be,' she promised, as she held out her hand. When he had slipped the ring onto her finger she kissed him soundly on the lips.

'I was going to wait and come over to ask your daddy for permission to court you properly before I gave it to you,' Nipper said, 'but it took me by surprise, knowing you'd be going so soon, and I don't want you to leave without knowing for sure how I feel about you. Do you think your mammy and daddy will be angry?'

'They'll love you as much as I do when they get to know you properly,' she said, but he shook his head.

'That couldn't be a fraction of how much I love you,' he whispered. He felt he had missed out on so much in his life, never having known who his parents were. But now he had a future to look forward to, and he vowed that when his own weans arrived they would never have to suffer the pain of rejection as he had. He wondered again who might have left such a large sum of money for him, but as he saw Niamh admiring her ring with a dreamy look in her eyes, thought himself a very fortunate man indeed. Wasn't he going to be marrying the most beautiful girl in the world?

Just as Maeve had prophesied, the wind dropped the next day and within the hour the snow was falling steadily from a silver-grey sky. The men-folk spent all day outdoors herding the sheep and the cows down to the field next to the barn so that they might have shelter.

'Would you just look at it?' Maeve said, as she stared from the kitchen window. 'Why, the snow-flakes are the size of dinner plates, so they are! Thank goodness we've all the winter food in for ourselves and the beasts.'

Niamh went to stand beside her, secretly hoping it would settle so deeply that she'd be unable to reach the ferry. But her wish went unheeded when the snow stopped later that day. It was inches deep but not deep enough to leave them cut off from the world.

'Not yet,' her granda told her gravely, when she said as much to him, 'but I fear this is just the tip o' the iceberg, lass. Look at that sky! It's full of it. There's a lot more to come, you just mark my words.'

The day of Niamh's departure arrived in the blink of an eye and she stood with tears streaming down her cheeks as she said her goodbyes. Nipper had insisted on taking her and Declan to the ferry and the whole family had gathered in Maeve's cosy kitchen to see them on their way.

'Sure I'm going to miss you something terrible, so I am.' Shelagh sniffed as she hugged her tightly.

'I'll miss you too.' Niamh kissed her cheek, then bent to the weans and tickled them under their chins. Patrick had his finger jammed in his mouth and baby Bridie was fast asleep on the sofa, looking like a little angel.

'I dare say she'll be toddling about before I see her again,' Niamh said wistfully. She pecked Liam on the cheek and turned to her grandparents.

Maeve was openly crying and Daniel looked very bright-eyed too.

'Come along now, else you'll be missing the ferry, so you will,' Daniel said hoarsely, blowing his nose noisily on a grubby white handkerchief. He hated goodbyes.

'Aye, your granda's right, lass,' Maeve croaked. 'But thank you so much for all your hard work. I don't know how we'd have coped without you.' She nudged Niamh gently towards the door and, outside, Nipper lifted her and swung her into the front of the trap as if she weighed no more than a feather, whilst Declan scrambled into the back.

'Giddy-up there,' Nipper commanded, twitching the reins, and they were off. Niamh clung to the seat with one hand as she waved to her family, who were assembled outside the farmhouse, with the other.

Once they were lost to sight she sighed as she tucked her arm through Nipper's. 'I'm surely going to miss them all.'

'Ah, you'll be back again before you know it,' he told her encouragingly.

They fell silent, each savouring the precious time they had left together. Neither knew when they would meet again.

The snow was falling once more as they reached the outskirts of Dublin and Niamh's teeth were chattering, despite the warm blanket Nipper had insisted she should have across her legs. 'I'm afraid you're in for a cold crossing,' he said.

'No doubt, but at least the sea is calm so I won't be pitched about all over the place.'

Very soon he drew the horse to a halt, threw a sack across his back and attached his nosebag, then tethered him to a railing. He helped Niamh down and retrieved her bag from behind the seats. Hand in hand they went across the quay towards the ferry, as Declan discreetly walked ahead to give them time to say goodbye in private. People were already boarding and they knew that they must make the most of every second now.

'Stay safe, me darlin' girl,' Nipper said softly, as he took her face and kissed her tenderly. 'And just remember it won't be for ever. Till then we'll just say that what you're wearing is a friendship ring, as we agreed. Then, soon as I'm home, I'll come and see your daddy and we'll make it official, all right?'

Niamh was unable to speak for the lump in her throat that was threatening to choke her. Then she found her voice: 'Pl-please be careful,' she implored.

They had decided that he would not tell Maeve and Daniel of his decision to join the navy until after the holiday. He had no wish to spoil what might be their last Christmas together for a while. He led her towards the boat and gently pushed her onto the gangplank saying, 'Go on now. May the Holy Mother watch over you and keep you safe till we meet again.'

She grasped the rope that served as a rail and climbed onto the ferry, blinded by tears. On the deck she joined her brother at the rail and waved until she felt her arm was going to drop off. Then the boat chugged slowly away, but a part of Niamh's heart stayed with Nipper, the dear man with whom she wanted to spend the rest of her life.

Declan seemed subdued, too, and once the boat was well under way, she asked tentatively, 'Are you not looking forward to seeing Mammy and Daddy again, Declan?'

He sighed, 'Aye, I am ... but I always struggle wi' seeing Daddy so...'

'Crippled?'

When he nodded she slid her hand into his. It was the nearest he had ever come to admitting why he preferred to live in Ireland, and she didn't hold it against him.

Chapter Twenty-three

'Is everything all right, darling?' Camilla asked her son, as she stared at him across the dining table. 'You're looking very glum tonight and you've been very quiet.'

Lawrence flushed as his twin brother sneered.

'Go on then, tell them where you've been today and why you're so quiet,' Samuel goaded him.

Lawrence glared at him, but his mother wasn't going to let the matter drop now. 'So where *have* you been today, Lawrence?' she asked tartly.

Max saw colour rise in the boy's cheeks and cast his wife a warning glance, which she chose to ignore.

'If you must know I went to enlist in the army,' Lawrence answered quietly.

'You did *what?*' Camilla gasped, as she dabbed at her mouth with a starched white napkin.

'Oh, don't worry, Mother,' Samuel said spitefully. 'He isn't going anywhere – are you, Lawrence? He failed his medical, you see. Poor eyesight, they said.'

Lawrence wished the ground would open up and swallow him as shame surged through him. Samuel would never let him live it down. Lawrence had been forced to wear thick spectacles for some years now but he had never dreamed it would stop him enlisting.

'Why didn't you tell me what you were planning to do, Lawrence?' Max asked quietly hoping to defuse the situation.

Lawrence shrugged. 'It was something one of the chaps at work said,' he muttered miserably. 'I overheard him talking to some of the other older men during break this morning and he was saying it didn't seem fair that my brothers and I could stay at home just because we were your sons while their lads had had to go off and fight. I'd been thinking about it for a while, and I dare say that was just the spur I needed to make me do something about it.'

Olivia reached across the table to squeeze her brother's hand with tears of sympathy in her eyes. Poor Lawrence. He had never been as robust as Oscar and Samuel and she knew he was ashamed of it. But Camilla was furious and her eyes flashed as she said acidly, 'Well, thank goodness they didn't accept you. It was a foolish thing to do. Have you *any* idea how many young men are being killed in this war? You could quite easily have been one of them, had you gone.'

All four of her sons were now helping their father to run his businesses, no mean feat with almost a third of his work force already at war.

But Max felt for the lad. 'At least if they say anything else you can tell them now that you tried to join up. It was highly commendable of you.'

Camilla rose from the table, throwing her napkin down in temper. 'I knew you would take his side,' she hissed. 'Would you still have thought he was brave when the telegram came informing us that he had been killed in action?' She stormed from the room, leaving the door swinging open behind her.

Samuel chuckled. 'Not really been your day, has it?' he quipped.

Max rounded on him. 'Why don't you leave him alone?' he ground out. 'He's done nothing to be ashamed of. I sometimes think a stretch in the army might do *you* the world of good. You're not at work half the time and a bit of strong discipline might make you a better man. You have an allowance and wages yet you still can't manage – and I happen to know you're always leaching money out of your mother. So where does it go, eh?'

Samuel stood up so abruptly that his chair tottered precariously. He wasn't smiling now. 'What I choose to spend my money on is no concern of yours, Father,' he retaliated and with that he too strode out of the room, leaving the other three to stare after him.

Glancing at his first-born, Max asked, 'Has he been trying to get money out of you, too, Oscar?'

255

Oscar avoided his eyes as he put down his knife and fork and Max had his answer, but he knew Oscar was too loyal to get his brother into trouble so he didn't press the point. The lovely meal that Mrs Pegs had gone to such pains to cook for them was only half finished but everyone seemed to have lost their appetite so Max told them, 'You may all leave the table, if you have had enough.'

Oscar and Harvey stood up and left the room, but Olivia scooted around the table, sat on the chair next to her father and took his hand, 'Don't be upset, Father. Lawrence was only doing what he thought was right.'

He smiled at her sadly. 'I know he was, dear, but he should have talked to me about it first.'

'He wouldn't do that because he knows that Mother would never have allowed it,' she answered. 'She's terrified of the boys joining up. She doesn't even like me doing my first-aid training. But when I'm old enough, if the war isn't over, I *shall* go and become a nurse.'

'I rather think you will, whatever I and your mother say.' He grinned ruefully. 'Between you and me, I fancy Oscar would like to go, too, but he stays out of loyalty to me. I must admit that he, Lawrence and Harvey have been a wonderful help to me but if Samuel was to go I doubt I'd miss him. He makes it very clear that he isn't happy working for me. But I don't think he'd be happy working for anyone. I'm afraid he's a law unto himself and I can see trouble ahead. I fear your mother has spoiled him.'

'Mother has spoiled all of us but we're not like Samuel,' she pointed out. 'The thought of war is always terrible but it seems so much worse at Christmas, doesn't it, with all our young men fighting so far away?'

'Yes, it does, my dear. I read in the newspaper that the suffragettes have sent an open letter to the women of Germany and Austria asking that a truce be called for the Christmas period. We can only pray that it will do some good.'

'I know it would make Mrs Carey feel a little better,' Olivia said. 'She told me that the thought of her son, Kian, being so far away from home and fighting at Christmas is unbearable.' She wondered if she dared suggest an idea that had been in her head for some time. She knew it wasn't the ideal time but while she had her father alone she'd try it anyway. The worst he could say was no.

'I was wondering...' she began. '...how you might feel about allowing Mrs Pegs to throw a little supper party for the staff and their families? It would be held in the kitchen, of course, some time between Christmas and New Year. Do you think Mother would allow it?'

'It's an excellent idea, my dear. And leave your mother to me. Tell Mrs Pegs to arrange it. I will supply the food and drink as a little bonus from me to them.'

'Oh, thank you, Daddy! You're so kind.' Olivia threw her arms about his neck. 'I shall ask Mrs Pegs what evening will suit her best and then I'll invite them all.'

'Do remember, though,' her father cautioned, 'that Mrs Carey's husband is an invalid. She may not wish to attend a party without him.'

'Oh, she will when I've finished with her,' Olivia

gurgled excitedly. 'She can bring her daughter and son. It'll be such fun. And don't worry about Mother being in a bad mood. Miss Travis upset her this morning when she handed in her notice so that she can go and live on the coast.' She grinned impishly. 'Between you and me I'm glad she's going,' she confided. 'I'm far too old to have a governess now.'

He smiled at her indulgently although his heart ached. She was clearly very fond of Dilly Carey, but how would she feel should she ever discover their true relationship? He sighed as Olivia tripped from the room. He was proud that Lawrence had tried to enrol but Camilla, instead of trying to understand why he had done it, had only looked at it from her point of view. Lawrence had grown into a responsible young man as had Oscar and Harvey – but Samuel!

Max lit a cigar and leaned back in his chair to savour it. He had heard whispers that his wayward son was heavily into gambling and card games. How to catch him at it was the problem. He wasn't at work half the time, if what he had heard the staff at his various businesses muttering was true, and he had no doubt that when he wasn't at the office Samuel was up to no good. Of course, none of them had dared tell him so to his face: Samuel was the boss's son. Still, Max had no doubt that if he gave Samuel enough rope he would hang himself eventually, and when he did, he intended to come down on him like a ton of bricks.

The next morning when Dilly arrived at work she found Olivia waiting for her in the kitchen. She knew that Camilla frowned on Olivia spending too much time with the servants and looked at her warily. 'Is anything wrong?'

'Oh, no, Mrs Carey, quite the opposite.' Olivia was beaming from ear to ear as she looked at Mrs Pegs, who was flipping bacon in a pan at the stove, and Bessie, who was loading the trays to take into the dining room. 'It's just that I have a little surprise for you... Well, for all the staff, really. Father has agreed that Mrs Pegs can put a party on for you and your families between Christmas and New Year. We just have to decide when. Won't it be grand? I shall meet your children properly at last.'

Not wanting to dampen the girl's enthusiasm or appear ungrateful, Dilly chewed her lip as she hung her shawl on a nail on the back of the door. 'It's a grand idea and I'm sure everyone will enjoy it,' she said, as tactfully as she could. 'But Mr Carey is very unwell – I don't think I would feel comfortable going off to enjoy myself and leaving him at home all alone.'

'I spoke about that to Father this morning before he left,' Olivia told her hurriedly. 'He thought you might say that so he's going to send some whisky and cigars to your house so that Mr Carey can have a treat while you're gone. I'm sure he wouldn't want you and the rest of the family to miss an evening out!' Seeing that Dilly was still hesitating, she rushed on, 'Mr and Mrs Jackson, Bessie and Millie will be coming and Miss Norman of course. Nanny will be here too. Miss Travis won't though because she's retiring and going to live with her sister in Bournemouth. The boys and I wouldn't miss it – oh *please*, say that you'll come!'

Dilly felt as if she had been backed into a corner. 'It sounds lovely and it's very kind of you all to arrange it, but let me have a word with Mr Carey before I give you my answer, would you?'

Olivia nodded, guessing that it would be pointless to press her.

Dilly reached out and squeezed her arm. 'It's a lovely thought,' she told her. 'Just leave it with me, eh?'

'She's a good-hearted girl and she means well,' Mrs Pegs commented, when Olivia had left the room.

'I know that,' Dilly agreed. None more than me, she thought sadly, and after collecting the ash bucket, she hurried off to start the fires in the downstairs rooms.

All day, Dilly's mind was on Olivia's invitation. She could think of nothing she would enjoy more than spending a whole evening with the dear girl, but she couldn't imagine that Camilla would be happy with the idea. The woman bristled with jealousy every time she saw Dilly so much as look at her. Her possessiveness hadn't waned over the years so Dilly doubted it ever would now.

On that, she wasn't far wrong. When Max mentioned the party to his wife that evening she went red in the face with rage. 'A *party* ... for the *staff*?' she gasped, as she stared at him incredulously. 'Whatever are you thinking of, Max? We give them a bonus at Christmas – surely that is enough!'

'It was my idea, actually, Mother,' Olivia piped up. 'And they'll be in the kitchen so you probably won't even know they're here. It's not even going to be a party, really – more of a little get-together ... and perhaps a leaving party for Millie. She'll be gone in the new year when she gets married.'

'It's a fine idea,' Oscar said, smiling at his sister. Then, looking towards his mother, 'Imagine what your friends will say when they know how generous you've been to your servants. I don't doubt some of them will want to do the same.'

Camilla could see the sense in that but she hated the thought of Olivia spending a moment more than was necessary with Dilly Carey. Had it been left up to her, the woman would have been given her marching orders years ago, but Max still wouldn't hear of it. 'We promised her a job for as long as she wanted one,' he reminded her. 'That was part of the bargain you struck and now you have to abide by it.'

Camilla bit her tongue and didn't argue but she still seethed with jealousy every time she saw Olivia even speak to the woman. 'Very well, then,' she agreed reluctantly. 'But just make sure they stay in the kitchen.'

Olivia gave her father a triumphant smile and the rest of the meal passed without further comment on the subject.

Fergal was none too happy with the idea either. 'Why would they decide to throw a party for the staff now?' he asked. 'Sure they've never bothered to do anything like it before.'

'I think it's a lovely idea,' Niamh said, as she laid the table for dinner. 'I've always wanted to take a peep inside the house.'

'So have I,' Seamus agreed, as he buttoned his

clean shirt.

'Mr Farthing is having some whisky and cigars sent round for you so that you can have a treat too,' Dilly told her husband, as she fetched a large cottage pie from the oven and plonked it in the middle of the table. 'But if you're really against the idea then of course we won't go. I've no wish to upset you.'

Fergal instantly felt guilty. He couldn't remember the last time Dilly had left the house, other than to go shopping, to work or church.

'I dare say it's only for one night,' he said grudgingly. 'You go, lass. I'll be fine. But perhaps you and Niamh might need to be taking a little money from the pot for some new clothes. It's been a while since either of you had anything new to wear, to be sure.'

Niamh beamed from ear to ear. Dilly made most of their clothes for them or they were bought from the second-hand rag stall off the market, not that anyone would have guessed it by the time her mother had cut them down and remade them.

'That's a grand idea,' she said, 'but I have the lovely dress that Gran'ma bought me. It would be nice for Mammy to have something new, though. Are you sure we can afford it, Daddy?'

'It's almost Christmas so why not treat yourselves, *both* of you?' Fergal answered, in a rare good humour. 'Though from what you've told me about the state the shops are in, I've no doubt you'll have trouble finding much to tempt you.'

'In that case I'll catch the train to Birmingham and get us some material from the rag market,' Dilly said. 'We could go on Saturday afternoon,

Niamh. Then I've time to run us something up. I'm sure Mrs Ball wouldn't mind me taking the fabric into work and using the machine in my dinner hour.'

And so it was agreed.

The shopping trip was a huge success, although Niamh and her mother were shocked to see the difference the war was making to the country. The names on the railway stations had been removed or painted over, and when they arrived in Birmingham, stalls that were usually crammed with fabric now offered only a scant selection to choose from; for many of the material factories were producing only fabric for army uniforms. The same scarcity could be seen on the fruit and veg and ready-made clothes stalls. Earlier in the month the newspapers had reported that two German battleships had anchored close to shore in Scarborough and a bombardment had claimed many innocent lives. The church overlooking the harbour where people were praying had taken the first hit, closely followed by the Royal Hotel, which was a firm favourite at the holiday resort. The popular town had been devastated – and suddenly the war was not just overseas but frighteningly close to home. The sound of war planes droning overhead was all too common now, and far from being over in time to celebrate Christmas, as people had initially hoped, it was getting worse. It had upset Dilly to hear of such a beautiful town being bombed, for she had happy memories of it: she and her mother had taken their only holiday there when she was a child.

Even so the war didn't stop them enjoying their brief respite from everyday life, and on the train home they admired the material they had bought. Niamh had again pointed out that she could quite easily wear the beautiful dress her grandmother had bought her in Enniskerry but Dilly had insisted she should have a new outfit as a Christmas present. With her mother's help, Niamh had chosen a soft woollen fabric in a lovely shade of blue, which Dilly said she would make into a fashionable jacket and skirt. Dilly had also bought some navy-blue piping to complement it and thought it would be perfect with Niamh's best white cotton blouse. Niamh would never have made that particular choice but, knowing her mother's talent as a seamstress, she trusted her taste implicitly. For herself, Dilly had found some very fine needlecord, remarkably inexpensive yet so soft it felt almost like velvet, in a lovely russet colour that Niamh was sure would enhance her hair and eyes. Already Dilly had an idea for the dress she would make with it.

The train was packed with soldiers, some returning home for a short break and others to their units. Dilly couldn't help wishing that she might spot Kian among them but she kept her thoughts to herself. She and Niamh rarely had the chance to spend any time alone together and she was determined that nothing should spoil it.

'We're going to look the bee's knees when the outfits are done,' Niamh said excitedly. 'You're so clever with a needle that I know they'll be beautiful.'

'Ah well, I have my mother to thank for that.

Your grandmother taught me well. Her stitches were so tiny they were almost invisible. I just wish she could have lived to see you. She would have loved you as she loved me for she was a gentle soul.' Dilly smiled at her daughter. She had been rather quiet since returning from Ireland and sometimes she had seen see a dreamy look in Niamh's eyes as she stared into space. She rarely ventured out of the house any more, except to go to the school where she still taught, and spent the majority of her leisure time painting.

Dilly had a feeling it might have something to do with Nipper. She had noticed the sapphire ring Niamh wore and had asked her about it but Niamh had said it had been a present. Wisely Dilly hadn't pressed to know more. She was sure Niamh would confide in her when she was ready. Dilly had fond memories of the little orphan she had met on the streets of Dublin so many years ago, and from what Maeve said about him in her letters he had grown into a fine young man, although Dilly found it hard to envisage what he might look like now. According to Maeve, he was handsome, kind and considerate, and well set up financially. If that was so, Dilly could see no reason why he and Niamh shouldn't make a go of things. The only problem was that if Niamh should marry him she would most likely make her home in Ireland, and the thought of that almost undid her although she would never have stood in her daughter's way. All the chicks would have to fly the nest at some point, as Dilly was painfully aware.

Her thoughts turned to Declan as she stared at the fields from the train window. He had returned to Ireland the day before but it had been grand to see him, if only for a couple of days. She knew that his first sight of his father had shocked him for Fergal had deteriorated since Declan's last visit. She'd had an idea that her lad had been glad to go back to Ireland, loaded with the small presents she had bought and carefully wrapped for the family across the sea.

As she fingered the new material she thought of more practical issues. She would have a job to get both outfits finished within less than two weeks but she was determined she would do it, even if it meant staying at the dress shop till midnight every night. Niamh and Seamus were looking forward to the party and she would let neither of them down. The day before she had given Seamus some money from the savings tin to go to the tailor in town and buy himself a new suit for the occasion. He had set off at the same time as she and Niamh had that morning with a spring in his step. It wasn't often that any of them had brand-new clothes so now all she had to do was make her own outfit and Niamh's.

To pay for all the treats Dilly had dipped into the money she would owe Madge when she re-appeared, but she tried not to think of that. For now she was determined that nothing should spoil their day.

Chapter Twenty-four

'You've done *what?*' Max Farthing stared aghast at his wife across the breakfast table.

'I've invited the Merrimans and their daughter for a light supper this evening,' Camilla answered calmly. 'Penelope is a delightful girl. I thought Oscar might like to get to know her a little better,' she ended innocently.

Oscar stifled a groan as he glanced at Olivia, who lowered her eyes, sensing trouble.

'But why would you do that? You know the staff are having their party this evening,' her husband snapped.

Primly Camilla laid down her knife and fork. 'Don't trouble yourself about that,' she said airily. 'Mrs Pegs has already agreed that she will lay on a cold supper for us in the dining room so it shouldn't affect their party at all.'

'But surely you could have planned it for another evening? And why must you parade yet another of your cronies' daughters in front of Oscar? I'm sure when he's ready he'll be able to choose a wife for himself!'

'But, Max, the Merrimans are very rich. Frank Merriman owns almost as many businesses as you do, and you must admit that Oscar doesn't seem to be in any hurry to make a match. I'm just pointing him in the right direction.'

'From what I've heard, Penelope Merriman has

a face like a horse's,' Samuel snorted gleefully. 'Rather you than me, old man!'

'Oh, shut up!' Oscar retorted. Then addressing his mother he added angrily, 'I'm not even twenty yet, Mother. Are you really in such a tearing rush to get rid of me?'

Olivia scraped her chair back from the table, flung down her napkin and rushed from the room, unable to listen to any more.

'Now look what you've done!' He glared at his mother as he rose to follow his sister. Without another word he, too, stormed from the room.

'Well done,' Max said scornfully. 'I have to say that your timing for this supper party is atrocious! Couldn't you have invited your friends for some other evening – or have you done this deliberately to spoil the party for the staff? Poor Mrs Pegs must be rushed off her feet.'

He detected a hint of malice in his wife's eyes as she answered, 'Of course I didn't do it for that. There's no reason why any of us should attend the servants' do. I'm sure they'll be quite capable of entertaining themselves, given enough beer. And, furthermore, I'm entitled to invite my friends here whenever I please.'

Max shook his head in disgust. Leaving his half-finished breakfast, he rose and walked away, Lawrence following. Only Camilla and Samuel remained in the room.

'Oops, Mother, you've upset everyone.' Samuel chuckled as he speared another juicy sausage. He knew his mother quite well enough to know that she had probably deliberately timed her supper party to spoil the servants' party. She had never made a secret of the fact that she wasn't keen on the idea of entertaining the staff and he had no doubt this was her way of showing it.

'I really didn't give it a thought,' she said, straight-faced, then turned her attention back to the meal in front of her. But Samuel noticed a little smile on her face and knew that he had been right.

In the Careys' cottage, on a cold and frosty morning, Niamh was carefully pressing the creases out of the lovely costume her mother had made for her with the flat iron.

'I can't believe it's almost New Year,' she commented, not taking her eyes for a second from the job in hand. 'Christmas just seemed to pass in a blink, didn't it?'

'It did,' Dilly agreed. They had enjoyed a grand festive season, thanks to the generous hamper Mr Farthing had sent round with Mr Jackson. Now she was chopping carrots to add to the stew she was making for their lunch but had no time to say more – they heard footsteps in the entry and a shadow passed the window.

'I wonder who this can be,' she said, as her heart began to race. She still expected Madge to return daily and dreaded it, but the knife fell from her hand as the back door opened letting in an icy draught of air.

'Kian!' Dilly was across the room in seconds but when she flung her arms about her son he winced. She stepped back hurriedly saying, 'Oh, I'm sorry. What are you doing here? Have you been injured? Are you home for good–'

269

She stopped abruptly as she stared into his pale face, then led him towards the chair by the fire where he lowered his kitbag to the floor. Everyone seemed to be holding their breath as he took a seat wearily, but at last he said, with a forced grin, 'I'm back for a break. Got stabbed in the shoulder while we were fighting but it's not too bad. Just needed a few stitches and it'll be as good as new in a couple of weeks, so the nurses said.'

'Oh, son!' Dilly's heart was pounding as she thought of what might have happened. Nearly every street in the town had received telegrams informing families that one of their loved ones had been killed in action and she broke out in a cold sweat each time she saw the telegram boy cycling along St Mary's Road. That Kian was home for a while was only a temporary reprieve and she knew he wasn't out of danger, not by a long shot. Still, at least he was here now and she would make the most of every second.

'I'm just making a nice pan of stew and dumplings for our dinner,' she told him. 'But I can do you some bread and cheese to tide you over while it's cooking. Then I want you to go upstairs and have a rest. You look worn out.'

'Aye, you do, lad, to be sure,' Fergal piped up from the bed. 'Get a good hot cup of tea inside you, then do as your mammy says. You'll feel all the better for a lie-down, so you will. There'll be all the time in the world for a catch-up later on.'

Niamh had already hurried away and returned with the tea which she pressed into her brother's hand saying, 'It's so good to see you, Kian.' She was both thrilled and terrified at the sight of him, for he was deathly pale and hardly resembled the brother she had carried in her heart.

He smiled at her gratefully and leaned back in the chair with a sigh as they all glanced worriedly at each other. Dilly bustled away to fetch him a snack, and when she returned, he cleared the plate in seconds. 'I reckon I will go and have a lie-down, if you don't mind, Mammy.'

'Of course I don't. Wasn't it me that suggested it? I'll pop a brick in the oven and bring it up to you when it's warmed through,' she told him, keeping her voice cheery. 'It's mortal cold upstairs – if I'd had warning you were coming I'd have had the bed warm for you.' She was having trouble recognizing the stranger who had appeared in place of her son; he seemed to have had all the stuffing knocked out of him and had lost the sparkle that had made him the lad he was. Hauling himself out of the chair, he headed for the stairs without another word, and once they heard his bedroom door shut, Dilly said worriedly, 'Do you think his injuries are worse than he's letting on?'

Fergal shook his head. 'Not his physical injuries, no. It's more what's happening to him up here that's the trouble.' He tapped his head to lend emphasis to his words. 'If the rumours flying around are anything to go by it's a bloodbath out there and the lad's probably seen sights that could drive a man mad. But give him a little time and happen he'll open up to us. What he needs more than anything at the moment is a little peace and quiet to be sure and a little space to get his thoughts in order.'

She nodded, seeing the sense of his words, then went to pop a brick into the oven. Minutes later when she took it up to him, she found Kian flat out and fast asleep on the bed still dressed in his khaki uniform. She laid the brick at his feet, tucked a blanket around him and tiptoed quietly from the room.

It was late afternoon and already dark before Kian put in another appearance and his mother was relieved to see that he looked slightly better, although there was still a haunted look in his eyes. He finished his dish of stew in record time, then settled down beside the bed to enjoy one of the fine cigars that Max Farthing had sent for Fergal.

'That'll put hairs on your chest, lad, so it will,' Fergal said lightly, as Kian blew out a plume of blue smoke and coughed. It was much stronger than his usual cigarettes.

During the afternoon Dilly and Niamh had bathed and washed their hair in front of the fire, and Niamh began to tell her brother about the party. 'Why don't you come too?' she asked. 'Seamus is coming and it'd be lovely if you did an' all.'

'Aye, why don't you, lad?' Fergal encouraged him. 'A bit of a knees-up might do you the power of good. Seamus is in the kitchen washing and you'd be company for each other.'

Seamus appeared then and, after giving his brother a hearty slap on the back, which made Kian wince, he added his pleas to everyone else's. 'Come on,' he said. 'There's gonna be far more women than men an' you'd be doin' me a favour.'

'In that case I'll come, but I may not last the night,' Kian warned. 'I'll have to have a bit of a

272

clean-up first.'

An hour later they were ready to leave and Dilly's chest swelled with pride as she eyed her brood. The lads were so handsome and Niamh looked beautiful in the new costume she had made for her, as she was quick to tell her.

'You don't look so bad yourself, lass.' Fergal eyed her admiringly, and just for a moment the magic that had been between them before his accident was back and she blushed like a schoolgirl at the compliment.

Patting the skirt of her new dress, she laughed. 'Get away with you now, you smooth-tongued devil.' She made sure he had everything he would need for the evening close at hand – a pile of newspapers, the whisky and cigars Mr Farthing had insisted he should have, and a plateful of pork pie and crusty bread should he get hungry.

'Are you quite sure there's nothing else you want?' she asked, for at least the tenth time in an hour. 'Nell will be popping in to see you in an hour or so.'

'Then I'll not be short of visitors for Father Brannigan's coming too, when he's done evening mass,' Fergal informed her with a chuckle. 'I reckon it might have something to do with the fact that I mentioned the whisky and cigars. But now off you go. I shall be as right as ninepence, to be sure.'

Fergal was in a rare good humour so Dilly ushered the young people towards the door and soon they were striding through the frosty streets.

'I reckon we're in for some snow,' Seamus commented, glancing down at the trousers of his new suit. The crease in them was so sharp he could have cut butter with it.

Dilly wished Kian had come home in time for her to buy him a new outfit too, but she supposed there wouldn't have been much point if he was returning to the front in a couple of weeks' time. Although he was pale and had lost weight, he was still very handsome in his uniform and she noticed many of the local lasses peeping at him as they marched along.

When they arrived at the Farthing residence, Dilly led them to the back entrance, and as they entered the kitchen she was amused to see young Bessie's eyes almost pop out of her head at the sight of Seamus. The girl had gone to great pains with her appearance and Dilly scarcely recognized her in her pale lilac dress, her hair freshly washed and hanging loose about her shoulders. Bessie would never be considered pretty in the conventional sense but she looked very attractive and she wondered if Seamus might add her to his list of conquests. Mr Jackson and his wife were there, all done up in their Sunday best, as was Miss Norman, who was already on her second glass of sherry, her nose glowing. Mrs Pegs had made an effort too, and looked quite different without her customary white cap and apron.

'Well, now, Dilly, what a handsome family you have, and how wonderful that Kian arrived home in time to join us,' she said, with a broad smile, as Dilly introduced them to everyone. 'What would you all like to drink? Mr Farthing has done us proud – there's a fine assortment here. There's sherry or port for the ladies, a selection of wines from the cellar and ale for the men, if they prefer it. There's even a bottle of Scotch whisky for those who fancy it, so what will you be tempted to?' As she bustled about, making sure that everyone's glass was full, Dilly looked admiringly towards the table, which was covered from edge to edge with all manner of treats. Mrs Pegs had been busy. There were meat pies and pickles, fresh-baked bread and sausage rolls, as well as thick sponge cakes oozing jam and cream, fruit cake and pastries.

'That looks good, Mrs Pegs,' Dilly told her, when she joined her.

The cook frowned. 'Aye, I hope it does. It didn't help when the mistress said they were having guests tonight an' all,' she said grimly. 'Still, at least she said they'd settle for a cold supper and serve themselves, so they've got the same as us. Between you and me, I don't reckon the master were any too pleased with her about it,' she confided, in a hushed tone. 'I heard Miss Olivia and Master Oscar talkin' earlier on an' it seems the missus is tryin' to set him up wi' another young lady.' She shook her head. 'The lad's only nineteen, for goodness' sake. He's all the time in the world to meet his match, though he ain't shown much interest up to now.' Her eyes strayed to Bessie who was listening to something Seamus was saying with a star-struck look in her eyes.

'If I ain't very much mistaken our Bessie's got a crush on your Seamus.' She grinned. 'But it's hardly surprisin'. He's a handsome young whip, ain't he?'

Following her eyes, Dilly nodded. 'It looks like

you could be right.' She smiled. 'But I hope she hasn't because Seamus has a reputation for being a bit of a heartbreaker and I wouldn't want him to hurt Bessie. She's a lovely lass.'

At that moment the door into the hallway opened and, to everyone's surprise, Olivia entered the room, breathtaking in an ivory satin dress trimmed with gold beads. She was closely followed by Samuel, who made a bee line for Niamh. Dilly saw Kian's eyes travel to Olivia and her heart sank as she saw his interest. This was her worst nightmare come true and suddenly she lost all interest in Seamus and Bessie and rushed across to stand at Kian's side, keeping a close eye on Samuel and Niamh at the same time. Everything was getting a little too complicated for her liking.

'Hello, Mrs Carey. You're looking lovely tonight,' Olivia said pleasantly. 'And this must be Kian, your son who's in the army.'

'Yes ... yes, it is,' Dilly agreed, all of a quiver. 'He, er, arrived home this afternoon unexpectedly, but he has to rejoin his unit again in a couple of weeks' time – don't you, pet?'

Kian nodded, although his eyes never left Olivia's face. He knew from what his mother had said that she was only fourteen but she was already beautiful and he had no doubt that she would be stunning when she had grown up. He wondered what it was about her that seemed so familiar and then he realized – she was remarkably like Niamh to look at, although she was some inches shorter and not quite as rounded as his sister.

'How do you do, Kian? Thank you so much for coming,' Olivia said, holding out her hand in a

276

friendly fashion. When they'd shaken, she lowered her voice and said, on a giggle, 'I feel so sorry for poor Oscar. Mother is in there relaying his many virtues to Penelope Merriman. She seems quite taken with him, poor girl, but Oscar clearly isn't interested. I do wish Mother wouldn't keep trying to play match-maker. On the other side of the room Father and Mr Merriman are talking business and it's *so* boring! That's why I thought I'd slip in here to join you. I'm sure I won't be missed.'

'In that case may I get you a drink, miss?' Kian said gallantly.

'It's all right, pet,' Dilly butted in. 'I'll get it – just a cordial, of course. I'm sure Mrs Farthing wouldn't want Olivia drinking anything stronger. She's only fourteen, aren't you, miss?' By now the kitchen was echoing with laughter as the staff ate and drank and forgot their worries for a while, but Dilly was fervently wishing they had never come as Kian and Olivia chatted as if they were lifelong friends and Samuel commandeered Niamh. He was also glancing lasciviously towards Bessie from time to time. Dilly shivered. She didn't know what it was about that young man but she couldn't take to him – she wouldn't have trusted him as far as she could throw him. A short while later the situation altered when Oscar appeared, flustered and uncomfortable.

'Give me a glass of that ale, would you, Mrs Pegs?' he asked, as he yanked at his shirt collar. 'I've had to escape for a while. It's awful in there. Mother has all but got Penelope and me married off!'

Mrs Pegs chuckled as she poured some ale into a glass and handed it to him. 'Well, I can think o' worse fates, Master Oscar,' she teased him. 'I've heard tell the young lady's father is rollin' in money and she seems a nice enough girl.'

'She is,' Oscar admitted ruefully, glancing apologetically towards Kian, who was listening intently. He leaned towards him and muttered, 'But she has a face like the back end of a bus!'

Kian laughed, as Olivia caught Oscar's hand and shook it, scolding, 'Don't be so cruel, Oscar. Poor Penelope can't help it.' Suddenly they were all chatting and Dilly relaxed a little. Oscar's arrival had distracted Olivia from Kian, for which she was truly thankful.

Mrs Pegs, meanwhile, was watching them closely. Leaning towards Dilly, she whispered, 'I don't mind admittin' I worry about those two.'

'Why is that?' Dilly asked, as she took a sip of her port.

'Well ... I've heard o' brothers an' sisters bein' close but those two are just a little *too* close, if you get my meaning.'

'Whatever do you mean?' Dilly was horrified.

'It's nothin' I can put me finger on exactly but they're never apart when they're both here an' at their ages I don't think it's natural. They should be out an' about, minglin' wi' people their own ages now.'

Dilly nearly choked as she took another long swallow of her drink and wondered if this evening could possibly get any worse. She soon discovered that it could, when Max Farthing put in an appearance shortly after.

'I thought I'd pop through and make sure you have everything you need,' he told them, with a smile. The kitchen was ringing with the young people's laughter, and when he turned to Dilly and looked at her admiringly, she blushed to the roots of her hair.

'Why, Mrs Carey – or may I call you Dilly? You're looking very charming this evening,' he told her, with a gallant little bow. Dilly's heart was hammering against her ribs, like a barn door in a gale, and she gulped as her hand rose self-consciously to her hair. She normally wore it in a neat bun at the back of her head, but this evening Niamh had encouraged her to tie it up and let it fall in flattering curls about her face.

Max had only ever seen her in drab clothes but tonight the colour of her dress enhanced her eyes and he realized, with a little shock, that she was a beautiful woman.

'Er ... thank you,' she said, thinking how handsome he was in evening dress, his thick hair shining in the light cast by the oil lamps dotted about the room. And then she felt guilty. Here she was, behaving like some lovestruck girl and her a married woman! He looked away and as her eyes followed his she saw that Niamh and Olivia had introduced themselves and were laughing together. Without a word being said, she knew what he was thinking. The similarity between the two girls was quite striking and she fervently prayed that no one else in the room had noticed it too.

Niamh and Olivia joined them then and, thankfully, the tense moment passed as Olivia said, 'Niamh was just telling me you made the outfits you're both wearing, Mrs Carey. How very talented you are, but then I already know that after the lovely ones you made for me.'

'Oh, Mammy is a great seamstress,' Niamh said proudly. 'Her mother taught her. She loves working in the dress shop, don't you, Mammy? Or, at least, she did until they started to sew uniforms. Still, that won't be for ever, will it?'

Max frowned, wondering why Dilly hadn't chosen to work in that profession full time if she had such a flair for it, but then, as he saw her smiling at Olivia, it struck him why she had worked at the house for so long. It was so that she could be close to Olivia and the thought saddened him.

He remarked on the weather then and her family, and when he moved away to speak to the rest of the staff, she heaved a sigh of relief and took a great gulp of her drink. Now I'm going to be tiddly on top of everything else, she thought, feeling light-headed. She wished she had never agreed to come but it was too late to do anything about it now. All she could do was bide her time and whip her family away at the earliest opportunity.

Chapter Twenty-five

'Mr and Mrs Merriman have invited us to a New Year party at their home,' Camilla told her family at breakfast the following morning.

Oscar groaned. 'Oh, *no*, Mother! Surely I won't have to go.'

'But of course you must, darling,' she simpered. 'We're all invited and it would be rude not to. I've heard that their parties are very lavish so I've no doubt we shall all enjoy it immensely. Anyway, Penelope would be so disappointed if you weren't there. You got on so well last night.'

'Well, *I* shan't be going,' Samuel muttered sullenly. He had a card game planned for New Year's Eve and had no intention of missing it for some stuffy dinner party.

'I'm not keen on the idea either,' Lawrence added nervously. He had never been one for social get-togethers and could see no reason why he should go. He had important things to do today, and if everything went to plan, he would have news for his family by dinner time.

'Considering I couldn't even persuade you to have a dinner party or go out until recently you're suddenly very keen to socialize,' Max told his wife caustically. He wasn't keen on the Merrimans and could think of far better ways to spend New Year's Eve than in their company.

'Ah, but the children were younger then,' Camilla said serenely. 'Now that they are older it's important we ensure they mix with the right people.'

'You mean people you consider good marriage material,' Oscar quipped grumpily.

Camilla shrugged. 'If there happen to be some very eligible young ladies and gentlemen at these events, what is wrong with that? Your father insisted that you boys should have the best education possible, and he is well regarded in the town, so I want you to meet and marry someone suitable.'

'You can forget about trying to marry *me* off,' Olivia stated boldly. 'I shall become a nurse when I'm old enough. I shan't get married and have babies for years and years!'

'You may think so now but when you're a couple of years older and some handsome young man sweeps you off your feet, you'll change your mind,' her mother answered. 'Anyway, I haven't given up hope of finding a suitable finishing school for you. I realize that France, my first choice, is out of the question now but there must be somewhere in England.'

'Oh, Mother, you really are *quite* unbelievable,' Olivia snapped. 'There's a war on, yet you can still think of sending me to a finishing school! Why should I go to one of those places when you were so against the boys going away to school?'

'They were little more than babies but you are fast becoming a young woman,' Camilla replied, dabbing her lips daintily on a linen napkin.

Max decided not to comment when he saw the mutinous expression on Olivia's face. Since the boys had returned from school, Camilla had tried to control them, with little success. She still attended the odd ladies' meeting and lately she had become involved in preparing Weddington Hall for the first influx of wounded soldiers who were expected there in the near future by ordering bed linen and curtains, although she faithfully refused to do anything that would mean getting her hands dirty. She was going there later that day and had agreed that Olivia might accompany her. Max was pleased to see her venturing out but had long since accepted that theirs was now a marriage in name only. Camilla had made it clear on the day she had had his clothes transferred from their room into another that there would be no more physical contact between them. Being the gentleman that he was, Max had accepted it, but he had been deeply hurt. Now he was still fond of his wife – she was the mother of his children, after all – but no longer gave the matter much thought. His children and his work were his life, but for all that he was no doormat and was determined that he would not allow his wife to coerce any of his children unwillingly into a marriage.

'I don't think any of these young people should be forced to go to the Merrimans' if they've no wish to, Camilla,' he told her now, in no uncertain terms. 'They are all young adults and should be respected as such. Times are changing and you must accept that. Since the war broke out women are doing men's jobs, and it's highly commendable that Olivia wants to go into nursing.'

A hint of pink appeared in Camilla's cheeks as she glared at him. 'Some things should never change,' she told him, through gritted teeth. 'A woman's place is in the home and different classes should never mix. It's a recipe for disaster.' Then, turning back to her children, she told them firmly, 'I have accepted the Merrimans' invitation on behalf of us all. Please do not let me down. Olivia, please get ready to come to Weddington Hall with me, if you still wish to go. Jackson will be bringing the trap round to the front shortly.' With that she rose and marched out of the room as they stared numbly after her.

Shortly afterwards Oscar and his father left the house together, Max to visit his factories in Atherstone and Oscar to visit the pit.

Oscar had barely entered the office there when he saw a large white envelope with his name handwritten on it propped against the inkpot on the desk. So many of the employees had joined the army that the pit was operating on a skeleton staff now, which meant the output of coal had decreased.

'Have you any idea who put this here, Miss Ransom?' he asked the woman who managed the secretarial work. She was as old as Methuselah but highly efficient.

'I'm afraid not, Mr Farthing,' she replied, balancing her gold-rimmed spectacles on the end of her beaky nose. 'It was already there when I arrived at work this morning.'

Oscar sat down, picked up a paperknife and carefully slit open the envelope. Then his face paled as a solitary white feather floated out of it to land on the blotter on the desk in front of him. His lips set in a grim line yet strangely he found that he wasn't upset. It was probably just what he had needed to spur him on to do what he felt he should. And it would solve the problem of Penelope. Since the families had dined together she had clung to him like a limpet, making it more than clear that she was his for the taking. In fairness he felt sorry for the girl: she was nice enough in her own way but she was also fearfully dull. She couldn't hold a light to Olivia. He shook himself mentally, horrified. Olivia was his sister, for Christ's sake! Why could no other girl he met

284

ever measure up to her? Perhaps it was time, for all their sakes, that he went away for a while.

That evening at dinner Camilla appeared to have put the morning's disagreements behind her. She smiled at her family as she took her seat and laid her napkin neatly across her lap.

Max carved the leg of pork Mrs Pegs had roasted, and they helped themselves to vegetables as his wife asked pleasantly, 'So, what have you all been up to today then?'

Lawrence cleared his throat noisily before saying, 'Actually I went back to the recruitment office. I know I can't join the army as a soldier because of my poor eyesight but they have agreed to take me on as a stretcher-bearer. Hopefully I shall be leaving for France next week.' There, he had said it, and felt all the better for getting it out of the way.

'I have some news,' Oscar said. 'I've joined up too.' There was a stunned silence as he glanced apologetically at his father. 'I hope you'll try to understand but I couldn't continue to sit back and not do my bit.'

'You've both done *what?*' Camilla screamed, standing up so suddenly that she almost overturned her chair. Her face had paled to the colour of bleached linen but Max merely glared at her.

'Sit down, woman. Screaming like a fishwife isn't going to change anything,' he said harshly, then to Oscar, 'I do understand, my boy, and whilst I can't say I'm happy about it, I'm proud of you. You too, Lawrence.'

He looked towards Olivia, who was sobbing,

285

and said softly, 'Don't upset yourself, darling. You should be proud of your brothers.'

'I might enlist too, now that I'm seventeen,' Harvey said, and everyone looked at him in amazement. Harvey was such a quiet, studious soul that they could almost forget he was there for most of the time.

Samuel curled his lip. 'You must all be stark staring mad,' he told them acidly. 'They're calling the lads going out there "cannon fodder". They're mown down like blades of grass. Where's the glory in that, eh?'

'Well, at least they aren't cowards like *you!*' Olivia blazed. She dashed from the room with tears streaming down her cheeks. Camilla followed her. Funnily enough, it seemed that only Samuel had an appetite now. Max wasn't surprised; nothing seemed to concern Sam for long and he doubted he would have to worry about him enlisting. Just for an instant he found himself heartily disliking his son.

'Oh... good evening. What are you doing here?' Niamh asked, later that evening, when she stepped out of Chilvers Coton School to find Samuel Farthing leaning against the wall, waiting for her. She had offered to go in for a few hours to help the headmistress mark the children's work ready for next term and was shocked to see him there.

'I heard your mother tell Olivia last night that you'd be coming here this evening and as I was passing I thought I'd walk you home. Can't have a good-looking young lady like you wandering about in the dark on her own, can we?'

Niamh felt a shiver of apprehension run up her spine as she fell into step with him. She didn't have much option without appearing blatantly rude.

'You'll never believe what Oscar and Lawrence have done today,' he said, as they walked towards the Coton Arches. 'They've only gone and enlisted. Oscar's joined the army and Lawrence is going to be a stretcher-bearer. Harvey's going to do the same tomorrow too. They must all be mad if you ask me.'

'I think they're very brave,' Niamh answered, and her heart ached as she thought of Nipper. Any time now he would be enlisting too.

'Well, I won't be volunteering to go out there and get my head blown off,' Samuel said matter-of-factly. 'Dead heroes aren't much good to anyone to my way of thinking. But it'll all be over soon, no doubt.'

'I don't think so, if what we're reading in the newspapers is anything to go by,' Niamh retorted. She hadn't taken to Samuel and wished he would go away and leave her alone. They appeared to have nothing in common at all.

'We could take a short cut through the Pingles Fields and Riversley Park, if you like,' Samuel suggested, as they came to the entrance, but Niamh shook her head.

'I'd prefer to stick to the road, if you don't mind. It's bad enough here with no streetlights but it'll be black as pitch in there. We won't be able to see a hand in front of us.'

That was exactly what Samuel had been hoping for but, not wishing to upset her, he followed her beneath the Arches into Riversley Road. Niamh was feeling very uncomfortable, even more so when he took her hand and tucked it into the crook of his arm. 'Just in case you slip on the frosty pavements,' he told her. If anyone were to see them she was sure they would seem to be a courting couple, rather than two people who had only met properly for the first time the night before.

'What are you planning to do on New Year's Eve?' he asked then.

'Stay at home with my family. Kian is only with us for a couple of weeks so I want to see as much of him as I can. What about you?' She didn't really care what Samuel was planning to do one way or another but she supposed that she should at least make an effort to be polite.

'Oh, I shall be all over the place... Popular, you know!' he bragged, and her dislike of him grew. He really was very full of himself, unlike his brothers, whom she had found very pleasant. Once they reached the bottom of Edward Street Niamh removed her arm from his and said, 'I'll be off, then. I shan't be sorry to get home this evening. It's very cold, isn't it?'

'Oh, but I don't mind walking you the rest of the way,' Samuel told her. He wasn't used to being given the brush-off. Girls usually fell at his feet, especially when they found out he was the son of one of the wealthiest men in town.

'No really, there's no need for you to go out of your way.' Niamh took a determined step away from him.

Not wanting to push his luck, Samuel shrugged. 'Very well, but how would you like to come to the music hall with me one evening?'

Niamh wanted to tell him that she was already spoken for and not interested, but as she hadn't even told her family yet, that wouldn't be a good idea.

'That's very kind of you,' she said, 'but I don't get a lot of free time, what with helping Mammy look after Daddy and work.'

She saw a flash of irritation in his eyes but then it was gone as quickly as it had been there and he was all charm again. 'Very well, but I shan't give up asking. Perhaps when the nights are lighter and you're not so busy, eh.'

She merely inclined her head and walked away, as he stood there and fumed. Just who did the stuck-up little madam think she was, refusing him like that? And she had nothing to be stuck-up about! He had never been turned down before yet, strangely, it made him want her all the more. I shall just have to try a bit harder, he told himself, and stuffing his hands into his pockets he marched on.

When she reached the warmth of the cottage Niamh hung up her coat and hurried to warm her hands at the fire. Kian and Fergal were discussing the progress of the war and her mother was black-leading the grate but she smiled at her. 'There's some tea in the pot if you want a cup to warm you up, and I've left some bread, pickles and cheese on a plate in the larder for your supper.'

'Thanks, Mammy, but I'm not hungry. I'll have a cuppa, though,' Niamh answered, with a preoccupied expression on her face.

Dilly frowned, but held her tongue. She knew there was something on her daughter's mind but she'd wait for the right moment to approach her, probably when the men were asleep, which wouldn't be long now. Fergal rarely stayed awake beyond nine o'clock and Kian was eager for an early night. Seamus was out with his friends so there'd be time for a talk before he came home.

Just as she had thought, by a quarter past nine Fergal was snoring and Kian had disappeared upstairs, so Dilly made herself and Niamh some cocoa. When they were sitting at either side of the fire she asked gently, 'What's bothering you, pet? And don't say "nothing", because I know you better than that.'

Niamh shifted uncomfortably in her seat, then confessed, 'Samuel Farthing was waiting for me when I came out of the school this evening. He walked me part of the way home. He said he was just passing and that he'd heard you tell Olivia last night that I'd be working this evening so he waited for me.'

The sick feeling was back in the pit of Dilly's stomach but she kept her voice light as she answered, 'Then perhaps that's all it was.'

'I – I don't think so,' Niamh said. 'He made me tuck my arm in his and I didn't want to, but then again, I didn't want to appear rude. He asked me to go to the music hall with him as well, but I made an excuse. I don't like him, Mammy,' she admitted. 'Oscar, Harvey and Lawrence are nice, and so is Olivia, but there's something about Samuel that makes my skin crawl.'

'I know what you mean,' Dilly agreed. 'I reckon

there's a bad streak in that young man. Just keep your distance and don't give him any encouragement. He'll soon tire of chasing after you.'

'I didn't give him any encouragement,' Niamh said indignantly. Then, taking a deep breath, she said, 'The thing is, you see ... me and Nipper have an undertaking. We fell in love while I was staying with Gran'ma and Granda but we decided it might be for the best to wait until the war is over before we do anything about it.'

Dilly sighed. She wasn't surprised.

'Are ... are you angry, Mammy?'

Dilly looked at the daughter she adored. She was dressed in the new calico skirt Dilly had sewn for her, and her white cotton blouse was tucked into the waistband, showing off her blossoming figure to perfection. For the first time her mother saw her as a young woman rather than a girl, and her voice was tender as she answered, 'No, pet. I'm not angry with you. I've had a sneaking feeling about it ever since you came back from Ireland. I think Nipper fell in love with you the very first time he set eyes on you in this kitchen when you were just a wee thing. And I can well see why. Now you've turned into a beauty. All the same, I think it wise to wait until after the war. 'Tis a terrible thing, and who knows what the future holds for any of us?'

Niamh rested her head on her mother's shoulder as she let out a long sigh of relief. It was nice to share her secret, although she was worried about Nipper. Now that Christmas was out of the way he might already have joined the navy but all she could do was wait for a letter from him and pray that the Holy Mother would watch over him.

291

Chapter Twenty-six

'Are you quite sure you have everything you need, lad?' Maeve asked tearfully, as Nipper swung his rucksack onto his shoulder.

'Aye, I have, to be sure,' he answered, gazing at the woman who had been like a mother to him since the day she had taken him in off the streets of Dublin. He had the urge to hug her but he still found it hard to show affection, probably because he had received very little as a child – until Maeve had taken him in.

The whole family was there to see him off and now, as he looked at their familiar faces, he realized that they were *his* family now and had been for some long time.

'Be careful,' Shelagh whispered huskily, stepping forward to plant a kiss on his cheek. Then Liam was shaking his hand and Nipper was shocked to see tears in his eyes too. Even the weans were grizzling after picking up on the sombre mood. Nipper was painfully aware that Daniel was waiting outside in the trap to take him to the ferry. Then he would travel to England and his training station in Portsmouth. Maeve had taken the news badly when he had told her he had enlisted yet she had seemed to understand it was something he had to do and had given her blessing. But that was Maeve all over; selfless to a fault.

Suddenly she lurched towards him and they

clung together as her tears dampened his great-coat. 'Go on,' she said, chokily releasing him and pushing him towards the door. 'It took the three of you to clear the snow from the lane this morning, and if you don't get a move on it'll be settled again and sure you'll be stuck here, so you will.'

He stroked her cheek, unable to speak for the lump that had formed in his throat. Then he strode away, closing the door quietly behind him, without looking back as those left behind wondered if they would ever see him again.

Things were no happier at the Farthing residence and, as what remained of the family sat at breakfast, Camilla picked at her food. Oscar, Lawrence and Harvey had left for training the day before. Harvey had enlisted to look after the army horses, a job they all knew he would love as he longed to become a vet. They had all been issued with army uniforms and old Lee Metford rifles and, along with other recruits, they had been given a roaring send-off at the station by the local people. Even the mayor and mayoress had turned up to wish them God speed.

Olivia was as deathly pale as her mother, but Samuel tucked into his food without a care in the world.

'I wonder how the boys are,' Olivia said, suddenly voicing the thought that was in all their minds.

'They'll be fine.' Max smiled at her, hoping to put her mind at rest. Olivia had been beside herself when Oscar had left. It had come as no surprise to him because the two had always been close. His eyes rested on Samuel then and a frown creased his brow. Little did he know it yet but his brothers' departure was going to place a lot more work on his shoulders. As Max saw it, the lad had got away with far too much for far too long, but that would change now. It was time for Samuel to stop gallivanting and take over some responsibility for some of the businesses. With so many men away fighting, Max couldn't do it all himself. Even some of his most trusted managers had gone now, leaving women to oversee the works as best they could.

'I thought you could spend today in the pit offices, checking the books. There are some deliveries to be arranged as well,' Max informed his son.

Samuel's eyes widened with horror. Of all his father's many businesses, the pit was the one he hated most. It was such a filthy place. Even in the office, which was comparatively clean, he could taste the soot particles in the air and he always felt grubby there. 'Do I *have* to?' He groaned. He'd planned to lunch at the club his father favoured in town.

'Yes,' Max answered sternly. 'Now that the others have gone, it's up to us to keep the businesses going as best we can.'

'Come on, Sam, we all have to do our bit,' Olivia said, and Camilla glared at her.

'Do you have to shorten your brother's name, Olivia?' she snapped. 'It's so ... so *common!*'

'I would think you had more pressing things to concern yourself with than scolding her for such a trivial thing,' Max barked. 'Three of your sons

294

are at this very moment being shipped to God knows where!'

All three boys had joined the 1st Royal Warwickshire regiment, but that didn't guarantee that they would stay together. Once they were shipped abroad they could be miles apart. Of the three, Max was most concerned about Harvey. He had never been robust and he prayed that the hard physical work he faced wouldn't prove too much for him.

Camilla removed a flimsy lace handkerchief from the pocket of her dress and glared at him. 'It's strange that you're so concerned now yet you didn't mind them being sent away to school,' she said sarcastically.

Max was amazed. 'There's a huge difference between going off to risk their lives and being educated,' he answered coldly. Camilla had changed so much over the last few years that he scarcely recognized her. All she seemed to care about was her social standing in the community, yet she had once been so warm and loving. It hit him then that, apart from sharing mealtimes, they did nothing as a couple any more. Hadn't for many years, if it came to that, and strangely as he gazed across at her he realized with a little shock that he didn't even miss their closeness any more. With a sigh he rose and left the room without so much as another word and Camilla didn't try to stop him.

During the second week of January, Fergal read in the newspaper of the start of the Battle of Soissons. Kian's recall papers had arrived the day before and he was due to rejoin his regiment at the end of the week. Dr Beasley had checked his shoulder and announced that it was healing well.

'Looks like they'll be sending me there, then,' he said, without enthusiasm. He wasn't looking forward to going back to the trenches.

Seeing the haunted look settle again in his son's eyes, Fergal asked, 'Is it really awful out there, son?'

'"Awful" doesn't even come near it,' Kian snorted. He had said very little about his experiences since his return but now he lit a cigarette and stared into space, remembering. 'The worst time for me was Christmas.' He shuddered. 'A truce was called and the Germans were coming onto no man's land and shaking our hands. I dare say anyone would think that was a good thing, but it made it worse somehow, knowing that very soon you might be facing the same person and putting a bullet or a bayonet into them. When I got this,' he tapped his shoulder, 'I found myself looking down the barrel of a rifle. A young German chap was standing straight in front of me and he looked as terrified as I felt. We were knee deep in thick mud and so cold that we couldn't feel our hands or feet. Anyway, in a split second I knew it was either him or me. His finger was on the trigger yet even when I drew my bayonet back and lunged at him he didn't pull it. When the knife went in he looked a bit surprised before he went down and I wanted to cry. He wasn't any older than me, someone's son, and I had killed him. I just stood there watching him sink into the mud. That was when another German crept up on me and I got this. Served me right, really. I'd frozen with shock. It's

296

all right pulling the trigger when you can't see their faces but when you're right in front of each other, like we were, it's different. Luckily my mate, Johnny Webster from Bedworth, was right behind me and he helped me back to the trench. He got a bollocking for doing it, though. We're supposed to move on even if it means stepping on injured or dead bodies. Anyway, they took me to the holding tent – that's like a sort of hospital – and after the doctor had stitched me up they sent me to a proper hospital in the nearest town before sending me home. That journey was like a nightmare. There were chaps with limbs blown off or horrifically burned. Some didn't even know what time it was, let alone who they were. I was one of the lucky ones. My injuries were minor, compared to theirs.'

'Ah, son.' Fergal was choked with emotion as he thought of what his son had gone through. 'I wish to God you didn't have to go back, sure I do!'

Kian shrugged. 'No choice, Daddy. They shoot deserters and if I'm to die I'd rather die as a hero than a coward.'

Fergal held his tongue. There seemed no fitting answer to that.

Dilly appeared to be in an ill humour when she arrived home that evening and the reason became clear when she told them, 'Mrs Ball said today that she intends to retire. Her husband is very ill and she wants to be with him. If no one buys the shop it will close and that will be half of my wages gone. Still, I dare say I can always ask Mr Farthing if I can start full time again at the house. I doubt he'd refuse me.'

Fergal frowned. He doubted Max Farthing would refuse his wife anything. He had noticed the way he looked at her when he delivered treats for the family, and would fume with jealousy for days after. Not that Dilly had ever given him cause to feel so. Yet he couldn't help it. What use was he to her now? She was more his nurse than his wife, still a fairly young woman and attractive at that. 'No point in worrying about it just yet,' he told her. 'Wait and see if Mrs Ball manages to sell the place first, eh?'

Dilly clamped her mouth shut. This was one of the few times when she wasn't willing to take her husband's advice. She needed to work full time to keep their heads above water, and she would speak to Mr Farthing at the earliest opportunity.

She began to prepare the evening meal when the back door swung open and Nell appeared, all of a fluster. 'Did yer hear all the rumpus in the yard just now?' she gasped.

Dilly shook her head, 'No. What's happened?'

The police have just told Stan Bunting they've found a body an' they think it might be Madge. They've taken 'im to the morgue to try an' identify it, or what's left of it. It were found in reeds under the Cock and Bear bridge an' had been there fer some time.'

'Oh, my God!' Dilly's hand flew to her mouth and she had to swallow the bile that rose in her throat. Madge had been missing for months now. Yet always in the back of her mind she had been waiting for her to reappear, glancing over her shoulder and starting whenever she heard footsteps behind her.

'I'll bet it were one of 'er payin' customers that done 'er in,' Nell went on. 'She were askin' fer it, weren't she? An' Stan never even reported 'er missin', which says somethin' fer what 'e thought of 'er, don't it.'

'E-even so, what a terrible way to die,' Dilly stammered, as a mixture of emotions flooded through her. If it *was* Madge they had found, her nightmare would finally be over.

'What will happen now?' she forced herself to ask, as Fergal and Kian looked gravely on.

Nell shrugged. 'I suppose if Stan can say it is 'er they'll start to look fer whoever it was as done it,' she stated flatly. Had it been anyone else, Nell would have had a measure of sympathy for them but she had never pretended to like Madge and wouldn't be a hypocrite now.

'Anyway, I'd best gerron. I'll let yer know if I 'ear any more.' And with that she left Dilly to stare into space.

By bedtime the lane was alive with news of the body that had been found. Fergal was already in bed and Dilly was in her nightgown, damping down the fire, when Nell tapped on the door and slipped into the kitchen.

'It *was* Madge's body they found,' she whispered, drawing Dilly away from the bed so as not to disturb Fergal. 'An' they've only gone an' arrested Stan fer the murder of 'er!'

'No!'

'They 'ave, I'm tellin' yer, if the rumour's true. But I'll tell yer summat, I don't believe 'e did it, not fer a minute! He might be drunk but 'e's as

299

soft as a brush is Stan. The fact that 'e didn't report 'er missin' went against 'im, apparently. The police think that's suspicious. Whoever did it, it weren't a robbin'. There were money in 'er pocket by all accounts.'

Dilly felt sick. Madge had gone missing shortly after their final confrontation when she had forced more money out of her. It might well have been her money that they'd found in the dead woman's pocket. And a fat lot of good it had done her.

Guilt sliced through her because she could feel nothing but relief that Madge was now out of the way. And Olivia would be safe from discovering who her true parents were. She felt as if a great weight had been lifted from her shoulders, but once Nell had left she said a prayer for Madge's soul.

The opportunity to speak to Mr Farthing came the next morning when she met him coming out of the dining room. Despite what had happened to Madge, life had to go on.

'Ah, sir, I was wondering – could I have a quick word with you?'

'Why, of course,' he answered amiably. 'Come in here and tell me what's on your mind.'

Dilly followed him into the dining room, relieved to find no one else in there, and began tentatively, 'Is there any chance of me coming back here to work full time? I know you may think there's no need now that the three young men are no longer here but Mrs Ball, the owner of the dress shop where I work for the rest of the week, has said she intends to sell up and retire. Then I'll only be working part time and...'

'Ah, I see your predicament,' he answered, stroking his chin thoughtfully. 'Of course you may come back. But why not wait and see if the shop sells first? I know how you enjoy working there.'

'Thank you.' Dilly heaved a sigh of relief. That was a crisis averted as far as she was concerned. At least they would still be able to manage financially if she stayed in full-time employment, whatever it was.

She bobbed her knee and went about her work.

Shortly afterwards, Max took up his hat and left the house.

'Has Mrs Ball sold the shop, then?' Fergal said, two evenings later.

Dilly's eyes shone as she nodded. 'Yes – and all of us who work there are to keep our jobs.'

'Why that's good then, sure it is,' Fergal answered, as she set about laying the table for tea.

'Who's bought it?' he asked but Dilly couldn't tell him.

'Mrs Ball hasn't told us yet. Apparently the new owner will be coming in to meet us at the end of the month so we'll know then but it's good news.'

That evening Niamh had stayed late at the school and Kian had gone to say goodbye to the few pals who hadn't joined up yet. He was due to leave the next day, and Dilly was dreading it, not that she would dream of telling him so. She knew it was hard enough for him to return to his regiment without her making it worse for him.

She had bought some mutton chops from the butcher and they were gently sizzling in a pan on

301

the range alongside some winter cabbage. Fergal barely ate enough to keep a bird alive now, and that was reflected in his skeletal frame. His eyes looked too big for his face and his skin was a ghastly grey. Dilly frequently tried to tempt him with whatever tasty titbits she could get her hands on but nothing seemed to help.

The back door flew open and Nell appeared, white-faced and clutching a piece of paper in her hand.

'Nell! Whatever is the matter?' Dilly took her arm and led her to the nearest chair as Nell pushed the paper towards her.

Her heart sank as she saw it was a telegram and as she read it her mouth dried.

REGRET INFORM YOU PRIVATE MICHAEL COTTERIDGE KILLED IN ACTION ON 11 JANUARY AT SOISSONS STOP

'Oh, Nell ... *no!'* Tears spilled down Dilly's cheeks, yet Nell was dry-eyed and clearly in shock.

'I-I'll get you a cup of hot, sweet tea. It's supposed to be good for shock.' She looked desperately towards Fergal for help. Her words had sounded so inadequate but she could think of nothing else to say. This was every mother's worst nightmare come true.

'Aw, lass.' Fergal had pulled himself up to lean on one elbow in the bed. The effort had made sweat stand out on his brow. 'I don't know what to say, that's a fact. 'Tis terrible.'

'There ain't nowt to be said,' Nell answered dully. 'It's there in black an' white an' there's nowt goin' to bring him back, is there? I can't even lay him to rest, bless his soul.'

'No, but perhaps Father Brannigan could help us there. I'm sure he'd do a memorial service for him and say a mass, if I asked him to.'

'But I ain't a Catholic, an' I can't remember the last time I set foot in a church.'

'That doesn't matter,' Dilly put in. 'It might bring you a little peace. We can light some candles for him, too, if you like.'

Kian walked in then and instantly picking up on the tense atmosphere he asked, 'What's to do here then?'

Dilly gulped. He was to return to the front the very next day and she couldn't begin to imagine how this was going to make him feel. The timing couldn't have been worse. Not that there was ever a good time for terrible news like this. 'It – it's young Mickey... He's been killed,' she muttered, as she wrung her hands.

Kian sat down heavily on the chair beside Nell as he tried to take in what she had just said. Images were flashing through his mind. Images of him and Mickey discarding their clothes and diving naked into the blue lagoon – a water-filled quarry popular with local young people – on a hot summer's day, of them listening to musicians playing in the bandstand in Riversley Park on a fine Sunday afternoon; of the two of them kicking a football across the cobbles in the lane or scrumping apples in the priest's garden. Father Brannigan had almost caught them once, and as they had scaled the wall to escape, laughing, they had left a trail of stolen fruit behind them. Kian had known that the priest had recognized them, and for days he had expected to get a walloping off his daddy, but Father Brannigan had never told. And now Mickey was gone, just another casualty in this bloody senseless war.

'It should have been me,' he muttered brokenly. 'Mickey were a good lad whereas I'm... Well, I ain't never going to get to Heaven, that's for sure!'

'Don't say such a thing,' Dilly told him, but he wouldn't be comforted.

His hands screwed into fists as he choked back a sob. His mate was gone for good, and as he sat there, he wondered when it would be his turn.

Chapter Twenty-seven

January was a terrible month. On the 15th, the Royal Navy attacked the Dardanelles and Niamh was terrified as she thought of Nipper, who might be a part of it. She had received two letters from him in the last fortnight but neither had told her very much, for they had been heavily censored. She tied them together with a ribbon, placed them beneath her pillow and every night before she slept she prayed that he was safe. A few days later she and the whole country were plunged into panic when the first Zeppelin raid hit Great Yarmouth. Thankfully, they soon learned that British battleships had scotched the Germans' plans to bombard the east-coast towns and the mood lightened again. The Germans had been spotted off the coast of Yarmouth but their ship the *Blücher*, reported to be the largest battle cruiser in the world, had rolled over and capsized on the Dogger Bank. By far the worst news came at the end of the month when poison gas was used for the first time at Bolimov.

'They reckon it drives the men mad,' Fergal told Dilly soberly. 'It affects their lungs an' eyes an' all, the poor buggers.'

Things were going from bad to worse. Niamh was a nervous wreck, fretting about Nipper, who had been involved in the Dogger Bank battle and, early in February, Germany declared the waters around Great Britain a war zone.

As Dilly made her way to the dress shop one blustery February morning her spirits were low. Stan Bunting was still being held for Madge's murder, although there had been no charges yet and the whole town was talking about it. Few believed Stan was capable of murder. In fact, most people were saying that Madge had only got what she deserved and there seemed to be little sympathy for her.

When Dilly stepped into the shop, her mouth fell open in amazement.

'I thought it was time you all met the new owner.' Mrs Ball smiled. 'Mr Farthing has bought the shop and it'll be his by the end of the week, if my solicitor gets a move on with the papers.'

Max smiled at the four women sitting at their machines before informing them charmingly, 'You have nothing to worry about, ladies, I assure you. Things will continue just as they were before, with just a few small changes.' Motioning to Dilly he went on, 'Mrs Carey will take on the role of manageress, if she wishes to, that is,' he said. 'And on the days when Mrs Carey isn't here, Mrs Boyd will act as assistant manageress. Does that sound acceptable to you?'

''Ere, does added responsibility mean extra wages?' Bertha Boyd piped up cheekily.

'But of course, dear lady,' Mr Farthing answered smoothly, and Bertha blushed like a schoolgirl. She had an idea she was going to like working for Max Farthing.

'How do you feel about this arrangement, Mrs Carey?' he asked.

'Well, I er... I suppose it will be fine, if you think I'm up to it,' she stuttered, as she tried to compose herself.

'Of course you are,' he assured her. 'And I promise there will be very little interference from me. You ladies clearly know what you're doing, but if you'd like to come through to the office, Mrs Carey, we will discuss what your duties will be and decide your wages. And when we've finished, perhaps you would like to come through, Mrs Boyd?'

'Not 'alf!' Bertha said enthusiastically. Just fancy, her as assistant manageress! She could hardly wait to get home to tell her old man.

In the small room at the rear of the shop, Max Farthing ushered Dilly towards a chair, then handed her a set of keys. 'From now on I would be grateful if you could arrive before the others and open up. I have had another set of keys cut for Mrs Boyd, and on the days when you are not here she will do it, but if there are any problems, I shall give her permission to come to my house to see you.'

306

Dilly nodded, as she sat with her hands folded in her lap and he went on.

'And now to wages. How does three pounds a week sound?'

'*Three pounds!*' Dilly croaked. It was a fortune. 'That's too much for just three days' work, sir.'

'Nonsense. You're taking on extra responsibilities and that should be reflected in your wages. You are happy with this arrangement, aren't you, Mrs Carey?'

Dilly's heart was racing and her eyes were shining as she tried to conceal her excitement. It was a dream come true! Manageress of the dress shop!

'I'm very happy.' Her voice came out as a squeak and his eyes twinkled with amusement.

'Very well. Perhaps you wouldn't mind staying behind tonight so that we can go over the books together. Could you manage that?'

'Oh, yes, sir,' she said.

He smiled. 'Good. If there are ever any problems, just come and see me. Now you'd better send Mrs Boyd in and I'll see you this evening.'

'Thank you.' Dilly left him in a daze. Three whole pounds a week! She would be able to save some of that and treat Fergal to a few luxuries. With a spring in her step, she made her way back to her machine and soon she was busily sewing.

That afternoon, as Niamh stepped out of the school she groaned inwardly when she saw Samuel waiting for her.

'I was beginning to think I'd missed you,' he said cheerfully, as he advanced on her and took her elbow in a familiar way. This was the second

307

time that week she had found him outside, and suddenly she knew she had to stop it before he tried to take it any further.

'Well, I'm glad you're here,' she told him, as she discreetly removed his hand. 'I think you should know that I'm spoken for.'

Today she was dressed in a long blue gabardine skirt that her mother had recently made for her with fabric she had bought from the rag stall on the market. It had originally been a dress with a ragged collar and cuffs but Dilly had cut it down and made it into a very presentable garment. Over the skirt she wore a long navy coat, which Dilly had also reworked, and on her head perched a rather nice hat with two feathers to the side – Niamh had treated herself to that. All in all she looked very smart and pretty, and now she watched as Samuel's mouth opened and shut, giving him the appearance of the goldfish Niamh had seen on a rare trip to the fair that sometimes came to town.

'What do you mean exactly?' he asked eventually, falling into step with her.

'Exactly what I say. I have a friend in Ireland. Well, he was in Ireland, he's in the navy now, and after the war we plan to get wed.'

'Aren't you a little young to be thinking of settling down? You should be going out and enjoying yourself.'

'I *do* enjoy myself,' Niamh said stoutly. 'I have my work at the school, and in my spare time I like to paint.'

Samuel looked a little deflated, but he wasn't beaten yet, not by a long shot. 'What happens if this friend of yours doesn't come back?' he said churlishly.

Niamh glared at him. 'That was rather tactless, don't you think?' she said acidly. 'But I'll answer you anyway. There's only one boy for me and that's Nipper. His real name is Ben.'

Samuel stuffed his hands into his pockets and pouted. 'And there's nothing I can say to persuade you to come out with me?'

'I'm afraid not.'

'Well, you know where I am if you change your mind,' he snapped, and walked away without another word, leaving Niamh to sigh with relief. Hopefully he would leave her alone now that she had put him straight.

As promised, Max Farthing arrived back at the dress shop as the women were leaving and ushered Dilly into the office to go over the books that Mrs Ball had left out for them.

'Of course, everything will change after the war when the shop reverts to dresses rather than making uniforms,' he said.

She nodded, her face glowing. 'I understand that, and I have such ideas for the place. For a start I love the idea of the ready-made garments that are becoming so popular now. Imagine a woman being able to walk in off the street and leave with a dress ready to wear. Of course, I will still want to offer a personal service to those who prefer to have their outfits made ... if that's all right with you, of course.'

He laughed. 'I'm more than happy to leave that side of things to you, Mrs Carey,' he assured her.

'I'm afraid I have no idea what women want but you clearly do, and you sound as if you're looking forward to it.'

'I can hardly wait,' she admitted, flashing a smile that made his heart miss a beat. Suddenly he found himself wishing that Camilla was more like her.

The books balanced perfectly and once they'd finished poring over them he remarked, 'It's a bad do, that woman from your street being found dead, isn't it?'

'Madge Bunting.' Dilly nodded. 'They're still holding her husband but no one believes him capable of killing her. I heard that hardly anyone went to her funeral, apart from her children, but even they hadn't bothered much with her once they'd left home. She wasn't too popular.' She might have gone on to tell him of all the years Madge had blackmailed her, but she didn't.

'And how are Fergal and the family?' he enquired. He knew how much she worried about her son at war, just as he did about his boys.

'Fergal is much the same,' she said. 'And every day I pray that Kian will stay safe in France.'

'It's not much better here now, though, is it, what with all the bombing that's going on in London? The war has badly affected my businesses. Many of my factories are operating on a skeleton staff but the women who have stepped into the men's shoes are doing a sterling job, keeping everything ticking over.'

'Times are changing for women – for everyone, if it comes to that,' Dilly agreed.

For the next half an hour they chatted easily of

310

everything from their families to politics, and Max thoroughly enjoyed it. Dilly was an intelligent, beautiful woman and he knew, without a doubt, that he had done the right thing in buying Mrs Ball's business. Dilly would make an admirable manageress and he was looking forward to working with her.

That evening Niamh chuckled as she told her mother of her conversation with Samuel.

'Let's hope he'll leave you well alone now,' Dilly said, and hurried on to tell her daughter about her new position. She had made two large pans of rabbit stew, one for themselves and one for Nell's family: since the news of Mickey's death had reached them, their kindly neighbour hadn't been herself at all. She had done so much for them in the past that Dilly felt it was time she looked after Nell for a change. She had also treated Fergal to some Everton mints and a cream cake from the bakery to celebrate her new role as manageress.

It was as she was ladling the stew into bowls that Seamus arrived home and she knew instantly that something was troubling him.

'I'll just pop this pan of stew over to Nell,' she told them, as he stripped off and began to wash at the sink.

They were eating when he put down his spoon and said quietly, 'Mammy ... I have something to tell you...'

Dilly's heart cartwheeled. She had a terrible feeling that she knew what was coming. 'You've joined up, haven't you?'

'Aye, I have.'

'And when do you go?' She didn't protest; she knew that there would be no point.

'They said within the next two weeks. I've already given notice at the pit, and until I leave, I'll be training locally. They'll pay me and the rest of the lads that signed up with me a shilling a day till we go.'

'I see.' All the excitement of the day was gone and she was numb inside. Now there was another to worry about.

Dilly took to her new post as manageress of the dress shop like a duck to water. If truth be known, she was glad of the extra responsibility, for while she was busy she didn't have time to fret about Kian and Seamus. The days when she was in the shop meant leaving home a little earlier each morning to open up and leaving a little later after the others had gone but she didn't mind that. After the constant whirr of the sewing machines all day, she liked the peace and quiet as she set about putting everything to rights and making sure that the premises were safe. Seamus had been gone for two weeks now but, as yet, she had heard nothing from him or Kian. The house seemed ridiculously empty without the boys.

One day Nell rushed in to tell her that Stan Bunting had been released without charge. 'They'd got no evidence to pin on 'im,' she added. 'But no one's seen hide nor hair of 'im. He's just cleared off, though I don't suppose yer can blame 'im.'

'What will happen now?' Dilly asked.

Nell shrugged. 'I dare say they'll just carry on

lookin' for whoever did it, though I doubt they'll ever find 'em.'

In March, when the newspapers reported that the army had launched an offensive at Neuve Chappelle, Dilly's spirits sank to an all-time low. She had the dress shop running like clockwork and Max Farthing had taken to popping in occasionally of an evening when the rest of the staff had gone to check that she had everything she needed and go over the accounts ledger. They would talk at length of the war reports and share their concerns about their sons, and Dilly saw what a kind and considerate man he was, always the perfect gentleman with her.

Samuel was still making a nuisance of himself with Niamh, but the girl seemed to be handling the situation well so Dilly didn't mention it to his father, hoping that in time he would give up trying to woo her and turn his attention to someone else.

The bombing raids that were still targeting London had shocked the country, causing many deaths and casualties, but the British people still held firm to the belief that one day they would win the war. Even though Dilly had never been particularly religious she continued to attend church each week, when she would light candles for her boys, and Father Brannigan would hear her confession before mass. But the one thing she never confessed were the feelings she was developing for Max Farthing, for she hardly dared admit them even to herself. Somehow the war seemed to have wiped away the class difference between them, and now she found herself able to speak about her fears more freely to him than she could to her husband, which made her suffer all manner of guilt. When she was at the house they still addressed each other formally but when they were alone at the shop they had begun to call each other by their Christian names and she looked forward to his visits. One evening Max confided that he was less than happy with Samuel since his brothers had enlisted. He had hoped his son would become more involved with the family businesses, but up to now his hopes had come to nothing. Max was beginning to despair of him. 'All he seems to want to do is gad about enjoying himself and spending his allowance,' he told Dilly miserably.

'Perhaps it's time you stopped the allowance and made him work for it,' Dilly suggested. 'After all ... he's more than old enough now to be independent, if he had a mind to be.'

The next day, having given Dilly's suggestion some thought, Max told Samuel at breakfast that he intended to stop his allowance.

'But you can't!' his wife spluttered. 'Samuel is a young man. He should be enjoying himself at his age.'

'I've nothing against him enjoying himself,' Max stated calmly, helping himself to devilled kidneys from a silver dish on the sideboard, 'but life cannot be all about doing what we want. The money to enjoy ourselves should be earned. I was having to earn my living when I was his age, and so was my father before me. So, from now on he will work for a wage. A generous wage, I may add, but there will be no more hand-outs.'

Samuel's hands clenched into fists beneath the tablecloth and his face flushed an unbecoming shade of red.

'I shall write a rota, telling you what I want you to do and where I want you to be each day,' Max continued. 'Then you'll know where you stand and there can be no confusion.'

'And do I have any say in this new arrangement?' Samuel ground out, from between clenched teeth.

'Not if you want money in your pocket.'

Realizing that his father was not going to be swayed, Samuel rose abruptly and stormed out of the room as Olivia kept her eyes firmly on her plate. Secretly she felt that Samuel had had his comeuppance. Money ran through his fingers like water down a drain. Why should he be given it for nothing when the rest of her brothers were fighting the Kaiser for a pittance? Even so, she knew better than to voice her opinion, and as her mother and father started to argue she left her seat and hurried from the room. It was all they seemed to do now.

Far away Oscar was crouched in a trench waiting for the signal to begin yet another attack. It was just before dawn and all around him his comrades were resting as best they could, their backs against the walls of the trenches in the stinking mud. The last weeks had been far harder than he had expected, but he had never thought it would be a picnic. The trenches stretched for miles – there seemed to be no end to them. When he had first arrived he had helped with the digging and by the end of the second day his palms had been raw. The

315

clay was stiff and unyielding, and he was unaccustomed to manual labour so his hands had fared worse than many of his companions'.

'Come on, nancy-boy, put yer back into it,' his sergeant had roared, when Oscar had stopped momentarily to wipe his bloodied hands on his trouser legs. His upper-class accent had set him apart from many of the other chaps, but he had soon proved he was as willing to work as any of them and slowly he had gained the sergeant's respect. It was bitterly cold at night, although they were almost into spring, but Oscar was used to that now, although he still found it difficult to sleep before an attack. The day before Ricky Mann, a chap the same age as him from Atherstone, had trodden on a landmine as they tried to penetrate the miles of barbed wire that the grenades had failed to destroy. Even though they had been told to ignore casualties, Oscar had rushed to him and dropped to his knees in the mud. He had held him as tears slid down his cheeks. He had recognized Ricky shortly after arriving as one of his father's employees from the hat factory and they had become friendly. The noise around them was deafening, the smoke so thick that he swallowed it every time he opened his mouth. Ricky stared up at him and smiled ruefully.

'It ... looks like the bloody Hun's done fer me, matey,' he choked out, as blood bubbled from his mouth and nose.

'Of course he hasn't,' Oscar said desperately. 'Just lie still and try not to talk. The stretcher-bearers will come for you soon.' He was trying desperately to ignore the fact that Ricky's shredded trouser legs were empty and the mud beneath him was crimson. The poor bugger was lying in a great pool of it and there was nothing that Oscar could do to help him, other than offer a few words of comfort.

'I ... if yer get home ... will yer go an' see me lass an' tell her I were thinkin' of her?'

Ricky's eyes were glazing now and a strange rattle came from his throat. 'Of course I will...' he began, then realized that Ricky could no longer hear him. He had gently laid his pal down, and somehow he had got through the rest of the day in a blind rage. He had even taken pleasure in seeing his bullets find their target or feeling his bayonet sink into the stomach of a German. He had no idea what had happened to Ricky's body. He doubted that the stretcher-bearers would have managed to retrieve it. Their first aim was to get the wounded to the hospital tents, and there were so many of them that often the corpses of those who were beyond help stayed in the mud, carrion for the rats, the flies and any wildlife that dared venture to the field. It was no wonder the rats were so huge, he thought, as he gazed at his comrades, some resting, others smoking or scribbling notes to loved ones that they knew might never reach them. He thought of his brothers then, and wondered how they were faring. He hadn't glimpsed either of them since they had arrived and hoped they were all right. Finally as the ladders were raised up the sides of the trenches, and just before the command to attack, he thought of Olivia and felt slightly better. Somehow he had to survive this for her sake. He knew how upset she would be if anything were to happen to him. Grasping his rifle, he placed his foot on the first rung of the ladder and climbed up to to face another day of a living Hell.

Chapter Twenty-eight

Early in May as Niamh made her way home from an evening mass, Samuel appeared from nowhere and fell into step with her.

Swallowing her annoyance, she moved on. She'd made it more than obvious that she wasn't interested in him, yet still he persisted in seeking her out and she had no idea what she could do about it.

She had been worrying about Nipper ever since she had read that the *Lusitania* had been sunk by a German U-boat. At least 1,200 lives had been lost and she was beside herself with fear. What if he had been on that ship? She had no way of knowing: the infrequent letters that she received from him were always so heavily censored that they gave no clue as to where he was or what ship he was on.

So, that evening she was in no mood for Samuel's flirting and she asked bluntly, 'What do you *want*, Samuel? I'm rather tired and I'm afraid I'm not very good company this evening. I just want to get home and go to bed, so if you'll excuse me...'

She had never been openly rude to him before,

but rather than walk away, he said, 'In that case it sounds as if you're in need of a bit of cheering up. Why don't you let me take you for a nice meal somewhere? We could try that eating house in the marketplace.' He could easily afford it because he'd had a good win at cards the night before. It was just as well, he thought, because the wages his father was dishing out were not generous. How he expected him to keep up the lifestyle he was accustomed to Samuel didn't know, and they'd had bitter words about it. But Max had been adamant.

'It's only fair that you start on the same wage as the other staff,' he'd told him coldly. 'It wouldn't do for them to see me giving you preferential treatment, especially when they're having to work so much harder because we're short-staffed. The harder you work and the more you learn about the businesses, the more I will pay you. That's my final word on the matter. You'll thank me one day when you and your brothers own it all.'

Samuel doubted that very much. He had no intention of working a fraction as hard as his father did – he didn't tell him so, of course – but for now he would have to try to toe the line, as hard as it was.

Niamh raised her eyebrows with annoyance and marched on. Samuel clearly hadn't listened to a word she'd said. Either that or he had skin as thick as that of a rhinoceros!

'So, what do you think?' he pressed, smoothing his hand down the smart new waistcoat his mother had treated him to.

'I *think* that I want you to go away and leave me alone!' There, she had finally said it and felt all the better for it.

Samuel's face darkened at her blatant rudeness.

'In that case I'll do just that until you're in a better humour,' he pouted and to her relief, he turned about and strode away.

Stuck-up bitch, Samuel thought, as he headed for the nearest inn. Just who the hell did the baggage think she was? She was only the daughter of one of their servants and should have been flattered that he was showing an interest in her. In the bar of the Rose he shuffled through the sawdust on the floor and ordered a jug of ale. Once he had downed it, he ordered another, then another. Slowly his humiliation at being rejected seeped away. She wasn't the only girl in the world, after all, and there were many who would be glad of his attentions.

By the time he staggered home, at gone midnight, he could barely put one foot in front of the other, but he was still sober enough to know that there would be ructions if his mother saw him in that state. He made his way carefully round to the back door. The servants would be in bed by now, and if he was quiet enough he might get to his room without anyone hearing him. Thankfully the back door was unlocked, as he had hoped it would be, and he crept into the kitchen, feeling his way in the dark. The only light in the room was from the dull glow of the fire, and as his eyes slowly became accustomed to the gloom, he suddenly became aware of a white-clad figure standing by the sink.

The figure jumped, then squeaked, 'By, Mr Samuel, yer give me a gliff then, I don't mind tellin' yer.'

'Bessie!' he hissed. 'Christ, you scared me too. I thought you were a bloody ghost.'

She inched away from the sink. 'I were thirsty so I came down for a drink o' water. Sorry if I startled yer.'

She was standing in front of the fire now, and he could see her shape through the almost transparent cotton nightgown. Her nipples were straining against the fabric and he felt himself begin to harden.

'It's all right, Bessie.' His hand dropped to stroke his stiffened member through the thick material of his trousers and as he remembered the humiliation of Niamh's rejection earlier in the evening his jaw tightened. She might not want him but he had no doubt Bessie wouldn't be averse to a bit of attention. She was no beauty queen, but she wasn't ugly either, and he felt if he didn't get release soon he might burst.

Bessie was staring at him with frightened eyes – she reminded him of a little bird about to take flight. Which was the last thing he wanted her to do, so he said, coaxing, 'Why don't we sit down together for a little while, eh, Bessie? Everyone is asleep so we won't be disturbed.'

She crossed her arms over her breasts protectively as she whispered, 'Best not, Mr Samuel. Mrs Pegs will lay into me if she catches me down here wi' you in me nightie. It ain't right, see?'

'It looks *very* right from where I'm standing, Bessie,' he said as he took a step towards her. 'I never realized before how lovely you are.'

Her head began to shake as he drew closer. 'I'll be away to bed now, then.'

She made to walk past him but he caught her wrist and after giving it a vicious little yank he pinned her to him.

She could feel the hardness of him through her thin nightdress and began to panic. Bessie was inexperienced with men but she was no fool. She knew from things that she had heard whispered between Millie the parlourmaid and Mrs Pegs what went on between men and women, and she also knew that those things shouldn't happen unless you had a ring on your finger.

He had one arm tight about her but now the other arm caught her breast, pinched it spitefully and she yelped with pain.

'Come on, you little prick-tease! You know you want it,' he said, his hot beery breath on her neck.

'No! No I don't!' She was squirming now and trying to get away but with one movement he flipped her onto her back and she landed so heavily on the flagstoned floor that the breath was knocked out of her. As she struggled to breathe again, he yanked her nightdress over her hips and she heard a rip. Before she knew what was happening his hand had closed over her breast. Lowering his head he began to suck and bite her nipple. Tears of shame spilled from her eyes as she fought back vomit.

She opened her mouth to scream but as if sensing what she was about to do he clamped a hand over it and threatened, 'You make one sound and I'll tell whoever comes that you were waiting up for me and begging me to fuck you. What'll happen to you then, eh, Bessie? It'll be back to the workhouse for you cos no one will ever take your word against mine. Is that what you want?'

'N-no,' she whimpered, believing every word he said.

'Then shut up and lie still.' He raised his hand and struck her cheek so hard that she tasted blood. He was panting now as he undid the buttons on his flies. 'You might even find you enjoy it.'

Bessie lay still, too terrified and dazed to do anything else, and watched in horrified fascination as his stiff penis sprang from his trousers. Then he roughly parted her legs with his knee and before she could say another word he had dropped his weight on top of her and one hand was roughly kneading her most tender parts as his other fist pummelled her.

'Pl-ease don't!' she breathed but then suddenly he rammed his member into her and pain tore through her. She felt as if a red-hot poker had been pushed inside her and bit her lip to stop herself crying out. He was bucking up and down making disgusting grunting noises. With every thrust the pain increased and she wished she could die of shame there and then. No man would want her now. She would end up an old maid after this. But if this was what married life entailed she would never want to marry.

His hands were all over her tender breasts, bruising them as he kneaded them roughly. Then he let out a gasp and she felt something hot and sticky before he growled and collapsed on top of her. She could feel his heart hammering against hers and complete despair washed over her.

She lay there, concentrating on the flickering shadows on the ceiling, terrified to move in case he did it again, but eventually he rolled off her and corrected his clothing as if nothing had happened. Then, with a last contemptuous glance at her, he left the room.

Bessie was too afraid to move. She lay there, listening to his footsteps receding, then drew herself into a tight ball whimpering with shame and fright. She felt as if someone had punched her all over but eventually she dragged herself to the sink where she managed to light a candle. It took three attempts, for her hands were shaking so badly that she kept dropping the matches, but at last she did it. Instantly she saw that the beautiful lawn nightgown Mrs Pegs had bought her for Christmas was ripped almost to the waist. It had been the finest thing she had ever owned yet she knew that even if it hadn't been ripped she could never have worn it again. It would always have reminded her of what had happened this evening.

The next thing she saw was bloodstains on it and she gasped with fear, wondering if he had damaged her internally. Then rationality took over. She grabbed a cloth, soaked it in cold water and systematically began to scrub every inch of herself. She repeated the process twice, even though she soon realized she was wasting her time. She could scour herself till she stripped the skin from her body but she would never feel clean again, not if she lived to be a hundred years old.

Finally she dragged herself off back to her little attic room, stripped off her nightgown, bundled it into the corner of a drawer and pulled a clean one over her head. Then she huddled in her bed and sobbed until at last she fell into an exhausted sleep.

The next morning when Mrs Pegs entered the kitchen she tutted with annoyance. Bessie's first job of the day was to get the fires alight in the kitchen for breakfast but there was no sign of her and the fires were almost out. She laid some kindling on the glowing embers and blew on them with the bellows until some tiny flames appeared. Then she threw on a few nuggets of coal, and did the same to the fire in the range. Coal was like black gold now and they were having to be careful how much they used, even though Mr Farthing owned the local pit. The fires in the library and the day room were no longer lit unless he specifically requested it, which he rarely did unless the mistress was expecting visitors. Food was getting harder to find too, now that the boats bringing it in from abroad were being intercepted by the Hun. Sighing, she glanced at the clock on the kitchen wall. Twenty past six! Bessie should have been up an hour ago. In fairness, Mrs Pegs had to concede that it wasn't like the girl to let her down. In fact, she couldn't remember her sleeping in before. Deciding she ought to check that she was all right, she went towards the door that led upstairs to the servants' quarters just as Miss Norman appeared.

'I'm afraid the tea will be a bit late this morning,' Mrs Pegs told her. 'Bessie ain't up yet an' I've only just got the fires lit. I'm going up to her now. It ain't like her to let us down.'

The cook set off up the steep wooden staircase,

reached Bessie's door and tapped. When there was no answer she cautiously inched it open. She could just make out Bessie's shape in the narrow iron bed but she appeared to be fast asleep.

'Bessie... are you all right?' she whispered into the gloom.

Bessie sat bolt upright. 'Oh... What time is it? Have I overslept? I'm real sorry, Mrs Pegs. I-I'll be right down.'

Ethel Pegs frowned as she stared at Bessie's swollen split lips and the massive bruise on her cheek.

Bessie's hand rose to cover her face self-consciously as she stuttered, 'I er – got up for a drink o' water in the night an' tripped over the kitchen chair leg in the dark. I cracked me face on the sink as I fell.'

'Did yer now?' Mrs Pegs didn't believe a word of it. The kitchen table and chairs were too far from the sink for Bessie's words to ring true but she didn't say as much. The girl was as jumpy as a kitten as it was. 'Well, yer made a right mess o' your face, gel. Why don't yer lie in for a while? Yer lookin' right peaky.'

'I... If yer quite sure?' Bessie was hugging the blankets beneath her chin, and even in the gloomy room Mrs Pegs could see that she was as pale as wax.

'I'm sure, lass,' she said quietly. 'You stay there an' I'll fetch you a nice cup o' tea up when it's brewed.' She left the room, frowning. She had never known Bessie to be untruthful but she would have bet her life that the girl was lying now. But why? What could have happened to her?

Deciding that Bessie would probably tell her in her own good time, she set off for the kitchen. There was breakfast to cook for the family and standing about here wouldn't get it done.

Once Mrs Pegs had gone, Bessie pulled herself painfully to the edge of the bed and, holding her ribs, swung her feet onto the cold floorboards. She had never known she had so many places to ache. As she groaned her split lip opened up and she felt blood trickle down her chin. When she tried to stand the room swayed, so she clutched the rail at the end of the bed until the dizziness had passed, then slowly made her way towards the washstand. With difficulty she managed to pull off her nightgown and caught sight of herself in the mirror on the wall. She gasped. There was hardly an inch of her that wasn't bruised and, even though she had scrubbed herself thoroughly the night before, there was dried caked blood between her legs. Her cheek was black and purple, one eye was almost shut and her lip was swollen. She poured water into the bowl and somehow managed to wash herself again, but it took her a long time to get dressed, for every movement was painful. Even so, through sheer determination she managed it and dropped gratefully back onto the bed. She would rest for a while, then go down to the kitchen and start work. Somehow she had to go on as if nothing had happened although how she would do that she had no idea.

Chapter Twenty-nine

The next few months passed uneventfully as people waited anxiously for news from the front. Before they knew it they were into August.

'Phew, open that door a bit wider, would yer?' Mrs Pegs asked Bessie, as she lifted a large rack of lamb from the oven. It was a beautiful day, far too nice to be indoors.

Mr Jackson was in the garden pruning the late roses, and the heady scent was wafting about the room. Dilly was in the dining room, setting the table for lunch for Mrs Farthing. Samuel and his father were out and Olivia was practising her first aid so the house was peaceful.

As Bessie ran to do as she was told, Mrs Pegs watched her out of the corner of her eye. Something was still not right with the girl, she'd bet her soul on it. She hadn't been right since the night she reckoned she'd fallen, back in May, but whatever it was, Bessie was staying tight-lipped. If Mrs Pegs asked, she would close up tight as an oyster.

'Go an' fetch that jug o' lemonade from the shelf in the larder,' Mrs Pegs told her, once the lamb was on a plate in the middle of the table. 'A glass o' that might cool us all down a bit.' As Bessie bustled away she lifted her voluminous apron, wiped the sweat from her brow and sank onto a chair for a moment's rest.

The atmosphere in the house was strained.

Bessie was far from her cheerful self and Dilly seemed at a low ebb today: she'd had a letter from Seamus who was in a field hospital after being injured. As usual the letter gave no indication as to where the hospital might be but he had assured Dilly that his wounds were not serious and he would write again soon.

What he considers "not serious" and what I consider "not serious" could mean two completely different things,' she had fretted to Mrs Pegs.

'Now get a grip on yourself,' Mrs Pegs had said soothingly. 'He was able to write the letter and they ain't planning on sending him home, so what does that tell you, eh? If he was seriously hurt they'd be shipping him back, once he was fit enough to travel, now, wouldn't they?'

'I dare say you're right,' Dilly said grudgingly, although she still couldn't help but worry. With the sun shining, it wasn't hard to imagine how awful it must be for the troops stuck in the trenches in the sweltering heat. The British hospitals were bursting at the seams with casualties, some with such serious wounds that they would never be the same again. Their only consolation was that for them, at least, the war was over but now, as cripples, many would face a war of another kind, as her Fergal had been forced to. The hot weather was not suiting him at all – the cottage was cold in winter and like a furnace in summer. Unable to get out and about he would usually be moithered and sweaty by the time she got home, although he insisted on keeping his legs covered with a sheet. Niamh was no happier – she constantly watched for the postman and worried about Nipper. But at least the family in Ireland seemed to be faring well, if their letters were anything to go by, and Dilly supposed that was something to be grateful for.

As she entered the kitchen after polishing the furniture in the dining room, Mrs Pegs waved her towards a chair saying, 'Come an' take the weight off yer feet for a minute or two, lass, an' have a cool drink. I swear we'll sweat to death at this rate.'

Dilly gratefully did as she was told and, glancing at Bessie, Mrs Pegs whispered, 'Somethin's still not right wi' her, I know it. She ain't been herself ever since the night she reckoned she had that fall, not that I believed her for a second. I just wish she'd talk to me if somethin's troubling her.'

'She hasn't been her usual cheery self,' Dilly agreed. 'And she doesn't look at all well, does she? Would you like me to have a word with her?'

Mrs Pegs sniffed. 'I dare say yer could try. But it'll have to wait till later. She's just off to do a bit o' shoppin' fer me.'

'Don't worry, I'll choose my moment,' Dilly promised and soon after a dejected-looking Bessie set off with her basket and Mrs Peg's shopping list gripped in her hand.

Once she was clear of the house, Bessie sighed. It was a relief to get away, for every time she'd glanced up lately she'd found Mrs Pegs watching her and she was terrified that she would guess the awful secret she had been forced to keep to herself. It was almost three months since the night Samuel had forced himself on her, but instead of coming to terms with the nightmare it had got

330

worse: she feared now that she was with child and she didn't have a clue what to do about it. When she had missed her first course she hadn't been too concerned. After such a brutal attack it was normal, perhaps. But when she missed the second she had become fearful. Then her breasts had begun to feel sore, and for the last two mornings she had had to rush to the outside privy to be sick before she had even had time to get dressed. She had seen lots of girls in this condition in the workhouse. They would be treated abominably, as if they had committed a mortal sin, and forced to work right up until they gave birth. Then their babies were torn away from them and many of the little souls were placed into what they termed the nursery, never to reach their first birthday.

Bessie couldn't bear to be sent back to that awful place. On the day Mr Farthing had fetched her out of it, she had felt as if she had died and gone to Heaven. Over the years the Farthing residence had become her home, even if she was only a servant. She had envisaged herself growing old there, but what would happen to her now? She wouldn't be able to hide her condition for much longer – but who could she say was the baby's father? Mr and Mrs Farthing would never believe it was their son. She knew that there were women who might be able to help her but she would never be brave enough to go down that road so what was she to do?

Once she reached Abbey Street, Bessie visited Cooper's, the ironmonger's, where she purchased a new tin bowl, the first item on Mrs Pegs's list. She moved on to the marketplace and went from stall to stall, adding each item from her list to the increasingly heavy basket. At last she had everything she needed but, rather than go straight home as she usually did, she headed for Riversley Park. Perhaps if she had a little time to herself to think a solution to her problem might occur to her.

The park was heaving with people enjoying the bright sunshine. Children rolled hoops across the grass or chased their balls as smiling mothers or nannies watched over them, but the light-hearted atmosphere was lost on Bessie. She was too sunk in misery to notice. When she came to a large weeping willow she scrambled beneath its overhanging branches and slid down the bank to the edge of the river where she took off her boots and dangled her feet in the slow-moving water. It was so peaceful there, away from prying eyes, that she wished she could just sit there for ever. The minutes ticked away, and then it came to her that there was only one solution to her dilemma. A calmness settled over her. Lifting her feet from the water she dried them on the hem of her skirt and put her boots back on before heading to the only place she had ever thought of as home, stopping just once to make one more small purchase from a stall in the market. Deep down she knew that the solution had always been there. She just hadn't allowed herself to accept it before now.

Late that evening, when all the work was done, Nell and Dilly sat together in the yard enjoying the cool evening air. Fergal had been asleep for hours and Niamh was painting another lovely picture of her grandparents' cottage in Ireland.

Nell seemed to have come out of her depression lately. She was one of thousands across the country who were having to come to terms with the loss of a loved one. In almost every street in every town and city, a mother, or wife, sweetheart or sister was mourning, but still the telegrams arrived with frightening regularity.

Earlier in the evening, Dilly had tackled the washing in the dolly-tub, run it through the mangle and pegged it onto the line strung between the two cottages. Now the women sat watching it flap gently in the balmy evening breeze.

Dilly's relaxed mood was shattered when Nell told her, 'I heard Peggy Davis sayin' in the shop earlier on that Stan Bunting had turned up back in town, like a bad penny. He's stayin' in one o' the courts along Abbey Street, by all accounts. He reckons he wants the police to reopen the investigation into who killed Madge apparently. All I can say is he must 'ave smelt a bit o' compensation or summat cos he didn't give a shit fer her while she were alive.'

Dilly thought back to the terrible time when Madge had been blackmailing her. It seemed so long ago now and she hadn't given the woman a thought for a good while. 'But it could have been anybody if she was on the game,' she said quietly.

Nell nodded. 'O' course it could, but good luck to 'em, I say. Between you an' me, I allus thought she'd come to a bad end. She had a lot of enemies, did Madge. Anyway, it's time I were turnin' in. G'night, lovely.' She stood up and went back to her cottage, leaving Dilly to stare thoughtfully off

333

into the night.

At the Farthings' house, Mrs Pegs was damping down the fire as she prepared to retire for the night. The kitchen was as clean as a new pin and now she was looking forward to her bed. She'd fetched a book from the free reading rooms that afternoon. It was *The Rainbow*, by D. H. Lawrence. It was completely different to the penny dreadfuls that she normally favoured but it was said to be a bit *risqué* so she was looking forward to starting it by the light of the candle in her room.

Bessie had been sitting quietly by the low fire without saying a word all evening, but now, as Mrs Pegs prepared to go to bed, she rose from her seat and kissed her tenderly on the cheek.

'What were that for?' Mrs Pegs said gruffly. She had never been very good at showing her feelings, although she was touched at this show of affection.

'It was just because I wanted to and because I wanted you to know how grateful I am to you for always being so kind to me,' Bessie said shyly.

Mrs Pegs flapped a hand at her as she snatched up her book but a little smile played about her lips. 'Yer daft little bugger, you. Yer don't need to go butterin' me up. Get yourself off to bed, lass. I don't want yer lyin' in in the morning.'

She marched towards the door and paused to look back at Bessie to find the girl's eyes still tight on her. For no reason that she could explain a shiver rippled up her spine. 'G' night, love.'

'G' night, Mrs Pegs.'

The cook shook her head and took herself off as Bessie settled back by the fire to bide her time.

Slowly, very slowly, the night darkened and the old house settled about her, its pipes creaking. Eventually Bessie glanced towards the clock, which she was just able to make out by the glow of the fire. It was almost one. Everyone should be asleep. Mr and Mrs Farthing had gone to bed hours ago, as had Miss Norman. She had heard Mr Samuel roll in just after midnight.

Creeping to the door that led into the main part of the house, she strained her ears. When only silence greeted her she went up the stairs to her room.

It took her just moments to change from her work clothes into her Sunday best and pack her few possessions into the battered old carpet bag she had arrived with. There were pitifully few: two calico skirts, two white cotton blouses, her one best dress, two aprons and a few items of under-wear. She lifted the note she had so carefully penned to Mrs Pegs. It was she who had taught Bessie to read and write, and although Bessie would never be a scholar, she could do enough to get by. She would leave it on the table where Mrs Pegs would find it first thing in the morning.

She put on the only hat she owned, a black straw boater with a wide brim that matched her best three-quarter-length flared jacket, which was also black, nipped in tight at the waist and fastened with a single button. Beneath it she wore an ankle-length blue skirt and a white frilled blouse. As she checked her reflection in the mirror, she was satis-fied with what she saw. She looked reasonably smart and respectable.

Glancing around the tiny room that had been

her sanctuary, she felt her resolution waver but then she straightened her back. She was no longer the little girl who had arrived here from the workhouse. She had proved that she could work for a living and that was what she intended to do. Samuel's brutal rape had affected her so badly that, for a time, she had considered taking her own life. But then she had realized that she would also end the life of the innocent child she was carrying and she could never bring herself to do that. Strangely, she was looking forward to seeing her baby and holding it in her arms. It would be the first person who had ever truly been hers. She loved the mite already and was determined to do right by it.

It wouldn't be so hard, she had decided. There were thousands of pregnant young widows all across the country, and after tonight that was what she would be. Lifting the brass ring she had bought from the market on the way back from her shopping trip, she slipped it onto her finger. There was still plenty of time to catch the mail train on its way to Liverpool's Lime Street station. Somewhere along the way she would get off and start a new life with the money she had saved. It didn't amount to much, but she had always been thrifty and there would be enough to survive on for a short time. Then one day when she had made something of herself, and she was determined that she would, she would come back and present the Farthings with their first grandchild. Revenge would be sweet.

She stole quietly away, and as soon as the house was behind her, she raised her head and straightened her back, leaving behind the only home she had ever known. The streets were deserted, as she had known they would be, but they looked different from how they appeared in the day time. Shadows seemed to jump out at her from every corner, startling her. She had rarely been out alone at night, or in the early morning as was now the case, but her steps never faltered.

At the station she found the ticket inspector snoozing in his office, a low gas lamp lighting his snoring features. 'May I have a one-way ticket to Liverpool's Lime Street, please?' Her request woke him, flustered to be caught napping.

'There ain't no passenger trains due through till morning.'

'Isn't the mail train due to stop here?'

'Aye, it is.' He stared at her, wondering what such a young lass was doing abroad all alone at such an ungodly hour. 'But if yer hopin' to get that one you'll have to sit in the mail van an' it won't be none too comfortable.'

'It'll do.' She handed him the money for her ticket.

Seconds later she was alone on the platform, staring along the track into the thick mist that had formed. Minutes later she heard a roaring noise and determinedly swallowed her apprehension. She had never set foot on a railway platform before, let alone been on a train, and her heart was hammering almost as loudly as the locomotive hurtling towards her. Then two lights appeared, like giant eyes, from the darkness and the huge beast hissed into the station.

A man appeared from a doorway further along

337

the platform and began to load sacks into the end carriage, then beckoned to her. Taking a deep breath, she walked towards him. This is it, she thought. The start of the rest of my life ... and my baby's. Her hand dropped protectively to her stomach as she climbed into the carriage.

Chapter Thirty

Dilly yawned as she poured tea into three mugs. Fergal was still sleeping but Niamh should be down any minute now. She had said the night before that she had jobs to do at the school before the children arrived so she would no doubt want to be there early.

'Niamh, I have some tea for you,' her mother shouted, from the foot of the stairs. Then she carried a mug across to Fergal. 'Come on, sleepy head. It's another new day.'

She knew he'd had a bad night. He had been sweating and muttering in his sleep but now he didn't respond so she shook his arm as Niamh appeared in the doorway, knuckling the sleep from her eyes, still clad in her long cotton night-dress.

'I can't seem to wake your daddy,' Dilly muttered, as she increased the pressure on Fergal's arm.

Niamh came to stand beside her and frowned. 'He looks very hot,' she said and after feeling his forehead she told her mother, 'He's burning up,

Mammy. Should I get dressed and run for Dr Beasley?'

'Aye, perhaps you should.'

While Niamh went back upstairs to throw on her clothes, Dilly hurried to the sink and poured some cold water from the large jug into a tin bowl, then returned to her husband. By the time Niamh reappeared she was sponging him down, but even the shock of the cold water on his skin could not rouse him.

'I'll be as quick as I can,' Niamh promised, and then she was off, running like the wind, as Dilly continued to wet the cloth and try to cool him.

A breathless Dr Beasley and Niamh returned twenty minutes later, and Dilly stepped away from the bed while the doctor examined the unconscious man. Niamh waited in the small scullery area.

'This is the problem,' the doctor told her gravely, and threw the blankets off Fergal's legs. Dilly winced. They were covered with bed sores, some so large she could have put her hands into them. They were clearly infected and weeping a poisonous evil-smelling pus.

'I – I had no idea they were so bad,' she croaked. 'Fergal always made me leave the room and insisted that he washed them himself when I'd fetched him the water.'

'And now you know why,' the doctor said gravely. 'He clearly didn't want you to know how bad they were. I think the poison from his legs has gone into his system, poor man. He must have been in absolute agony.'

'So what can we do?' Dilly was wringing her

339

hands as she stared at him hoping that the doctor would come up with a cure, but when he did it took her breath away.

'I'm afraid the only possible cure is to amputate,' Dr Beasley informed her. 'As you are aware that is a risky procedure, more so now because of his weakened condition. Also, there may be so much poison in his system that even amputation won't save him.'

As Dilly swayed, the doctor hastily pushed her into the chair at the side of the bed as Niamh came back into the room, wide-eyed with fear. 'I – is me daddy going to die?'

Dr Beasley sighed. 'I cannot truthfully answer that question, my dear. It's up to your mother to decide what you want me to do. I doubt he will waken, Mrs Carey, so if you wish to proceed with the amputations I shall go to the hospital and speak to the surgeon. Then I'll send an ambulance for him.'

'What will happen if he doesn't have the amputations?' Dilly asked. Fergal had fought against this so hard and for so long that it seemed unfair for her now to have to make the decision. 'Surely there's some way you could bring him round so that he can choose for himself.'

The weary doctor spread his hands helplessly. He had grown fond of this family over the years, particularly Dilly, who had worked so tirelessly to keep them together. 'In answer to your first question, well, you can see for yourself that he is desperately ill. As for the second, no, I can't bring him round, I'm afraid. I'm so sorry, Mrs Carey. I do know how hard this must be for you.'

Niamh had come to stand beside her now, and as tears spilled down her cheeks, she sank to her knees and wrapped her arms about her mother's waist, much as she had when she was a little girl seeking comfort. 'You have no choice, Mammy,' she whispered. 'If we don't let Daddy have the operation he'll die. At least this way he may have a chance.'

'You're right,' Dilly muttered brokenly, calling on every reserve of strength she had left. 'Organise it, if you would, please, Doctor, as soon as you can.'

The doctor placed his stethoscope in his bag, then snapping it shut. He hesitated for a second, then said, 'Perhaps you might like to call in Father Brannigan to say the last rites while I go and make the arrangements – just in case, of course,' he added hastily, as he saw their stricken faces.

'Yes ... you're quite right. We'll do that,' Dilly answered dully as he left the house.

'I'll go for him,' Nianth offered. 'And on the way I'll tell Nell what's happened and get her to come in to you.'

Moments later Nell appeared, clad in a long nightgown with a shawl about her shoulders and her hair covered with a nightcap.

'What's goin' on?' she asked, with a yawn. Then her eyes settled on Fergal and her face became serious. 'Give me a damp cloth an' all,' she said quietly, as she threw her shawl across a chair back. 'We'll both sponge him an' see if we can't get his fever down a bit, eh?'

They worked together, side by side, until eventually Niamh and the doctor reappeared. 'The ambulance will be here shortly,' the doctor said. 'They're preparing the operating theatre at the hospital.'

He had no time to say any more because Father Brannigan huffed into the room then, his face red with hurrying, looking like a big black crow as his long cassock slapped against his legs.

He shook his head sadly as he took an intricately embroidered white satin stole from his bag, kissed it reverently, then placed it about his neck and shoulders. He uncorked a bottle of holy water and, as he advanced towards the bed, the women silently stood aside.

He genuflected and made the sign of the cross, and they all bowed their heads and repeated the Lord's Prayer before he administered the last rites. He of all people knew how much this would mean to Fergal: he was aware that without these rites his soul would not be allowed into the Kingdom of Heaven and would be doomed to float in space for all time.

Dilly watched solemnly, her hands pressed tight to her waist, as the priest went through his ritual.

'This is the Lamb of God who takes away the sins of the world. May the Lord Jesus protect you and lead you to eternal life...'

His voice droned on, but Dilly hardly heard it until at last he summoned them to join him in more prayers, then he concluded with a blessing.

Two men bearing a stretcher had joined them, and as the priest nodded to them, they advanced on Fergal and began to lift him.

'Don't forget, pet. That were only a precaution,' Nell said, placing a comforting arm about Dilly's shoulders. 'There's every chance Fergal will come through this. Tough as old boots, he is.'

'I – I must get dressed and go with him,' Dilly said, as the stretcher-bearers carried him towards the door, but the doctor placed a restraining hand on her arm.

'There is no point,' he explained gently. 'All you could do is sit in the waiting room. I'll go with him, and I'll let you know how the operation has gone just as soon as it's over. You have my word.'

Nell nodded at her encouragingly. 'That makes sense. Sit down now while I make us a nice hot drink, eh? Then perhaps Niamh could run round to the Farthings' an' let 'em know you won't be in today.'

Dilly nodded. There didn't seem to be much more she could do than wait. In due course Father Brannigan left and Niamh arrived back from her errand, with Max Farthing. His face was grave as he asked, 'Is there anything I can do, Dilly?'

The use of her neighbour's first name was not wasted on Nell, but she didn't comment. Instead she poured a mug of tea and pressed it into the visitor's hand. 'I'll just slip away and get dressed but I'll be back presently,' she said.

Dilly answered his question. 'No... There is nothing more that anyone can do, but thank you for asking.'

Niamh slipped upstairs to get dressed properly – she had pulled on her dress over her nightgown when she had run for the doctor.

Max stood awkwardly, sipping his tea, not knowing what to say. Fergal had never made him particularly welcome on the occasions he had visited

343

but Max didn't hold that against him. From what he had heard Fergal had been an energetic, active man before his accident and he could understand how difficult it must have been for him to find himself a cripple. And now the poor devil was going to have his legs amputated.

The silence stretched between them. Normally he and Dilly could hold a conversation about anything and everything but today words seemed futile and he felt in the way. Perhaps he shouldn't have come.

He drained his mug and carried it to the sink, then said quietly, 'I'm going now, Dilly. You need your family and close friends around you at a time like this. But try to stay positive and remember that if there is anything – anything at all – you or Fergal need you must let me know immediately.'

He put on his hat and slipped from the room, leaving Dilly alone with her thoughts.

It was almost three hours later when Dr Beasley returned to find Dilly still sitting exactly where he had left her, with Niamh and Nell fussing over her. After removing his hat, he placed his bag on the table, his eyes downcast. There was no need for words: one look at his face had told Dilly all she needed to know.

'He's gone, hasn't he?'

The doctor nodded as a lump swelled in his throat. He had known Fergal ever since he was a little lad. 'I'm afraid so, Dilly. In his weakened state he didn't survive the operation. But you need to know that it was very peaceful. He never re-gained consciousness so he would have felt nothing, which is a blessing.'

'I – I must see Father Brannigan again to arrange the requiem mass and the funeral...' There were no tears. As she sat there she thought that the man who had just died was not the man she had married. She had done her grieving long ago for Fergal and the life they had once led.

'Of course,' the doctor said. 'But it doesn't have to be right now. I have already sent word to him and he will be here in due course. First, you must give yourself time to adjust to what's happened.'

Niamh was sobbing on Nell's shoulder but Dilly merely nodded. 'Thank you, Doctor. Let me have your bill and I shall see that it's settled immediately.'

Dr Beasley shook his head. 'There will be no bill for today's service,' he said, then slipped away.

'We shall have to send a telegram to Gran'ma and Granda,' Niamh sobbed. 'But how can we let the lads know what's happened? They won't even be able to come to their own daddy's funeral!'

'Hush, now, an' don't get worryin' about that, lass,' Nell soothed. 'They'll be able to pay their respects when they come home. Your daddy would have understood. He was proud that the lads had gone off to fight for king and country.'

'Eeh, what a day this is turnin' out to be,' Mrs Pegs said, when Max Farthing informed her of Fergal's death a short time later. She was sitting at the kitchen table, clutching the letter that Bessie had left for her the night before, tears streaming down her cheeks.

'And you say that Bessie has run away ... just

345

like that?' he asked disbelievingly.

Mrs Pegs nodded, the letter gripped tightly in her hand. What was written on it was for her eyes only, as far as she was concerned.

'But why would she do that?' He paced up and down, almost as disturbed as Mrs Pegs. It was he, against his wife's wishes, who had fetched Bessie from the workhouse when she was little more than a child and he had never regretted it. She had turned into a loyal and devoted servant and had been so happy, until recently. There seemed neither rhyme nor reason for her to run away.

'Happen the girl had her reasons,' Mrs Pegs said guardedly. She needed time to think about what Bessie had disclosed in her letter, although her blood was boiling.

'Well, I dare say I shall have to look for another maid,' Mr Farthing said. 'Now that Mrs Carey works part time and Millie has gone, there's far too much for you to do on your own, Mrs Pegs. Leave it with me, would you?'

'Of course, sir. And when you next see Dil– Mrs Carey, please pass on my condolences at her loss. Happen she won't be into work for a while.'

He inclined his head and, once he had left the room, Mrs Pegs again pored over Bessie's note.

Dear Cuck

Mrs Pegs smiled. Despite all her efforts, Bessie would never be the best at spelling and writing, bless her heart.

I'm sory to leave yu in the lurch but I cant stay ere any longer. Back in May yu may remember yu noticed me split lip. Well the nite before that Mr Samuel raped

346

me in the kitchen. He told me that if I telled on im he'd tell yu all that I encuragd it but I sware I didnt! I opes yu know me better than that. Anyways, the long an the short of it is that Im to ave a baby. For a start I thought of doin away wi meself but I weren't brave enuff an anyway it ain't the babys fault is it. So I've desided that the only thing I can do is leve. If I stay an tell the truth the missus'll ave me an the little un put back in the workouse an I couldn't bear that. She'd never take my word over Mr Samuels. Try not to wurry about me. Ill be fine. Ive got sum muny an when the baby is born Ill get meself a job. Thanks for all yuve dun fer me, Ill never forget yu. Yuve bin like the mam I allus wanted an one day when Ive made summat of meself I shall come back an show Samuel his child.

Take care an try to think fondly of me
Luv,
Bessie xxxxxxxxx

As the tears rolled faster, Mrs Pegs carefully put the letter into her apron pocket. Bessie's departure would leave a huge hole in her life. Over the years she had come to love the girl. And it was all because of that spoiled young man upstairs. But she would have her day with him, she vowed. It might mean biding her time but Samuel Farthing would get his comeuppance. She would see to that, if it was the last thing she did.

Chapter Thirty-one

Bessie was tired. She dropped down onto a low wall behind Liverpool's Lime Street station and rubbed her aching back. She had stepped off the mail train full of plans and dreams but already they had turned to dust. The small amount of money she had managed to save over the years she had worked for the Farthings was dwindling already. She had been forced to spend some of it on a cheap lodging house the night before and more on a loaf of bread she had bought from a local bakery to stave off her hunger. She was sure she must have walked miles and come full circle searching for a job. Now it was almost night time again and she didn't want to have to spend any more of her meagre savings on lodgings.

It was only the thought of the workhouse that made her set off again, heading for the back-streets this time rather than the main town.

She could feel the blisters on her heels rubbing against the backs of her shoes and was so cold and miserable she could have cried. There weren't so many shops here but she walked from one to the next, going inside and enquiring after work, but the answer was always the same, and she was beginning to despair.

Eventually as she turned yet another corner, she saw a shop ahead. As she drew close her heart began to race when she saw a sign in the window advertising for an assistant.

Straightening her skirt and taking a deep breath she entered. As the bell above the door tinkled, a man, who looked to be in his late forties, appeared from a door behind the counter. He had a kindly face and his hair, which was plentiful, was a salt-and-pepper colour. 'May I help you?' he asked.

'I – I've come to enquire about the job in the window,' she croaked, as she clutched her bag.

'I see.' He looked her up and down. She certainly seemed respectable enough. 'And may I ask if you've had any experience of shop work?'

Bessie was desperate now and gulped, 'Well not exactly. I er ... worked as a maid at a house in Warwickshire, but then my husband died and I – I–' It wasn't proving as easy to lie as she had thought it would be but she thrust the brass ring on the third finger of her left hand towards him anyway. 'The thing is I have nowhere to go and it's getting dark and I don't have much money and I–' Suddenly the words trailed away and, to the shopkeeper's horror, she burst into tears.

Quickly lifting the counter, he urged, 'Come through, my dear. I'm sure things can't be as bad as that.'

'Th-they can,' Bessie sobbed, as he took her arm gently and led her through to a pleasant room at the back. He pressed her into a chair and scurried away to put the kettle on as Bessie glanced about her. The room was nowhere near as luxuriously furnished as the Farthings' house had been but it was clean, comfortable and cosy. There was a lovely fire blazing in the grate, and thick curtains to keep out the cold hung at the windows.

The man returned minutes later and passed her a cup and saucer, saying, 'There you are, my dear. I'm sure you'll feel better with some nice hot tea inside you.'

His kindness only served to make the tears fall faster but he stood back until at last she became a little calmer when she muttered, 'I'm sorry. You're very kind and I'm afraid I've been lying to you.' And then the whole sorry story of the rape and the predicament she found herself in spilled out.

He listened avidly. 'Hmm, you are in a pickle, aren't you?' He stroked his chin thoughtfully before saying, 'I've a little room at the back where you could stay if you decided you want the job. It's not very big but it's comfortable enough. My late wife's sister used to sleep there when she came to stay with us occasionally.'

'You ... you mean I can have the job *and* stay here?' Bessie asked incredulously, hardly daring to believe her luck.

He nodded and held out his hand. 'I'm Malcolm Ward, and you are?'

'Bessie.' She smiled through her tears.

'Have you had anything to eat today, Bessie?'

An hour later, when he had encouraged her to eat some rather tasty ham sandwiches, he showed her to the little room that was to be hers. 'We'll discuss your hours and wages in the morning when you've rested,' he told her, and closed the door softly behind him.

When Maeve saw the telegram boy pedalling down the drive towards the farm, his legs going

350

like a piston, her heart did a somersault and she had to clutch at the draining-board with one hand as she pressed the other to her heart, which was pounding.

Daniel and Liam were out in the fields so Maeve crossed to the kitchen door, and shouted, *'Shelagh!'* A telegram could only mean bad news and she didn't want to be alone when she opened it.

'What is it? Sure you called loud enough to waken the dead.' Shelagh appeared with floury hands from her own kitchen doorway. The smile slid from her face as the boy on the bicycle skidded to a halt in the yard, sending the chickens squawking in all directions. Solemnly he held out the dreaded brown envelope to Maeve, then silently turned about and wheeled away as Maeve stared down at it.

'It – it's got to be Nipper,' she said, as Shelagh rushed towards her.

'Don't you be jumpin' to conclusions now,' Shelagh scolded, although her own heart was thumping. 'Those ships he'll be sailing on are built strong, so they are.'

'That's what they said about the *Titanic* an' look what happened to her! And on her maiden voyage!' Maeve had always had a terror of ships and the sea, just as she did about aeroplanes and flying. She was even terrified of the ferry she had forced herself to travel on from time to time. To her mind if the Good Lord had meant men to float or fly he would have given them fins or wings.

'Well, don't just stand there looking at it,' Shelagh said now, wiping her hands down the front of her apron as Patrick raced into the yard behind her. 'Give it here if you don't want to open it and let me read what it says.'

Maeve did as she was told, her hands shaking. When Shelagh had torn open the envelope she scanned the telegram and the colour drained from her face.

'It *is* Nipper, isn't it?' Maeve muttered.

Shelagh licked her lips. 'No, it isn't... It's from Dilly. It's your Fergal ... I'm afraid he's passed away.'

'*Fergal!*' Maeve didn't want to believe what Shelagh was telling her – but she had been expecting this for years. Each time she had seen her son since his accident he had seemed a little more shrunken, a little more hopeless.

'You keep an eye on the weans and I'll run up the field an' fetch Daniel an' Liam back,' Shelagh said, taking control. It was clear that Maeve was in no condition to do anything and the men needed to be told.

'So, that's what we'll do, then,' Daniel said, an hour later as they all sat around the table in Maeve's kitchen. 'Our Liam can keep his eye on this place and we'll catch the first ferry we can to England. Dilly can't face this alone, the funeral arrangements and everything, especially with the lads away at war. She and Niamh are going to need a bit of support. And when it's over we'll try to persuade them to come back here with us. There's nothing to keep them over there now, and we can get word to the boys somehow. I think it was only the fact that Fergal was too ill to travel

352

that stopped them coming to live with us years ago.'

'I hope you're right.' His wife nodded. Then, not wanting to waste a second, she hurried away to pack a suitcase.

The day of the funeral dawned bright and clear but within the Careys' cottage the mood was dark. Father Brannigan had been there since first light, saying prayers and sprinkling Fergal's coffin with holy water. Eventually, just before the hearse arrived, the family and friends were allowed to file past before the lid was hammered into place.

Dilly had dug deep into her savings, determined that Fergal should have the best send-off she could afford. Max Farthing had generously offered to pay for everything, insisting that money was no object, but she had politely refused. Fergal would have hated the man he had never forgiven for adopting his daughter to pay for his funeral.

Outside, four perfectly matched horses with plumed black headdresses pawed impatiently at the ground as Fergal's coffin was carried outside to be placed in the glass hearse they pulled.

The priest solemnly intoned the psalm *De profundis*. Then with a lighted candle he walked in front of the silent procession, while the family followed the hearse.

Dilly had made sure that she, Maeve and Niamh each had smart black coats and veiled hats to wear, and as the procession moved along, she kept her eyes firmly fixed on the fine mahogany coffin. When they reached the church, the men carried Fergal shoulder-high into the church and the first part of the service, the mass for the deceased, began. The church was packed to capacity with many of Fergal's old colleagues attending, even though they were not Catholics, and it brought it home to her what a popular man he had once been. Candles were lit to surround the coffin, and as the priest continued the prayers, Dilly's mind drifted back to happier times. It was in this very church in Riversley Road that Father Brannigan had joined them as man and wife. They had stood on the very spot where Fergal's coffin lay and made their vows. As the children had arrived they had been baptized here. Happy days, but they seemed so far away now.

Suddenly she was aware that the priest was giving the absolution. The service was almost over and somehow she had missed the requiem mass. There was just the ceremony at the graveside to face now, and at last it would be over.

Glancing around, she saw that Maeve was sobbing silently, her shoulders heaving. Even Daniel's eyes were wet, and yet she couldn't cry. Perhaps she had cried all her tears. And then they were outside, and she was glad of the fresh air on her face after the cloying smell of incense in the church. Fergal's coffin was carried to the yawning hole that waited for him and Dilly noticed Max Farthing standing well back from the rest of the mourners. It was good of him to come and pay his respects, she decided.

The graveside committal was mercifully short, and soon then they were all making their way back to the cottage where Nell had tea waiting for anyone who wished to go back with the family.

Luckily, because it was such a fine day, it shouldn't be too much of a squeeze. People would be able to stand outside in the lane and in the yard.

The rest of the day passed in a blur for Dilly as she mingled with her guests, accepting their condolences and making sure their cups and plates were filled.

'You gave him a fine send-off, so you did,' Maeve said approvingly, as the last of the mourners left. 'You've done me lad proud, lass.'

Dilly smiled weakly. She had the beginnings of a headache behind her eyes and she just wanted the day to be over.

'I'll just change into something a little more comfortable, if you don't mind, before I begin the clearing up.'

'Of course. Sure I might just do the same,' Maeve agreed. The coat Dilly had insisted on buying her was the finest she had ever owned and she didn't want to spoil it.

Dilly slipped upstairs still trying to get used to the fact that the bed was up there again. Daniel and the rest of them had carried it back to the room that she and Fergal had shared before his accident and the room downstairs was arranged as it used to be. It was strange to see the furniture set out instead of pushed back against the walls, but a lot felt strange at the moment and she had no doubt it would for some time. The bed felt enormous without Fergal to share it and she hadn't been sleeping well. Daniel and Maeve's presence had helped, though, and now she dreaded their return to Ireland, although she knew that was selfish. With the boys gone as well, she and Niamh

355

would rattle about the house but she would face that when she had to. For now she just had to get through this awful day. She had noticed that Max hadn't come back to the house and felt disappointed. No doubt he had not wished to intrude. Since Fergal had died he had popped in every day to make sure that she and Niamh were all right, that they had everything they needed, and she was grateful to him. He had proved himself a true friend, although she knew that Maeve had found it odd that a man of his standing should show such concern for an employee.

Opening the wardrobe to take out her work dress, her eyes were drawn to Fergal's one decent suit. He had worn it on the day they'd been married and it had been worn for every special occasion ever since, until he had become housebound. But he would not be needing it again. She supposed she should bundle his clothes together and take them to the rag stall in the market where they would do somebody some good... but not yet. While they were still hanging there, it was as if a little part of him remained. Anyway, she hated the thought of some stranger wearing Fergal's clothes. Perhaps one of the boys would want them.

'So will you consider coming back to Ireland with us now?' Maeve pleaded, the following day. They were due to catch the ferry the next morning but she felt guilty at leaving Dilly and Niamh behind. 'To be sure there's nothing to keep you here now, pet, is there? We could get word to the lads, and when the war is over, they could come and join us. Just think how grand it would be, all of us together.'

Dilly smiled regretfully. 'It's a fine idea, Maeve, but Niamh and I have our jobs to consider.'

'Huh!' Maeve said, aggrieved. 'I'm thinkin' Niamh will be joining us anyway when Nipper gets home, and what will you do then, here all alone, eh? Sure it makes sense for you to come, so it does.'

'Stop nagging the lass, Maeve,' Daniel said gently, seeing that Dilly was growing agitated. 'Doesn't she need time to get her head around what's happened?'

'But–'

A look from her husband silenced her and Dilly felt sorry for her. She knew Maeve was only trying to do what she thought was for the best, but how could she tell her the real reason why she would never leave the Midlands? That there was a grand-daughter she didn't even know existed! That would put the cat among the pigeons good and proper!

It was late afternoon when Max popped in. Removing his hat, he bowed to Maeve, and said pleasantly, 'How are you today, Mrs Carey? Well, I hope – or, at least, as well as you can be under the circumstances.'

'Aye, I'm bearing up,' Maeve replied politely, although her swollen red eyes told another story. Dilly had just popped to the shop to get something for their evening meal. There had been little time for shopping lately, and seeing his eyes dart about the room, Maeve told him, 'Dilly ... Mrs Carey has just gone out.'

'Oh, I see.' Max nodded towards Daniel, who was reading the newspaper in the chair that had been his son's beside the fireplace. 'Then please tell her I called. I wanted to check she had everything she needed.'

'We'll make sure of that before we leave, so we will,' Maeve answered, a little more sharply than she had intended to.

'Yes ... yes, of course you will. I didn't mean to intrude.' Max backed towards the door. 'May I wish you both a safe journey for tomorrow? Goodbye.'

'Well!' Maeve said indignantly, as the sound of his footsteps echoed down the entry. 'Can you believe the nerve of that man, Daniel? Our lad not even cold in his grave yet and he's calling around for all the world to see! I reckon he has his eye on our Dilly, so I do!'

'From what I can make of it, he's always visited – and Dilly does manage his shop, you know,' her husband responded. 'You have an overactive imagination, to be sure. The man is married.'

'Married or not, I can spot a twinkle in the eye when I see one.' Maeve sniffed before pushing the kettle onto the fire as Daniel smiled behind his paper. Daniel might be as blind as a bat when it came to matters of the heart but she wasn't and the sooner they persuaded Dilly to move to Ireland with them the better, as far as she was concerned.

When Dilly arrived home she found her mother-in-law in a strange mood.

'Max Farthing just called,' Maeve said innocently. 'He's a fine-looking man, is he not?'

The colour flared in Dilly's cheeks. 'I, er ... suppose he is. I've never really taken much notice.'

'Well, he takes notice of you, all right,' Maeve said, in her usual forthright way. 'Any fool can see he's taken with you.'

'Nonsense!' Dilly responded. 'Max – Mr Farthing is a married man and my employer.' She scuttled away to fill the water jug as Maeve watched her thoughtfully.

'What shall we do now, Mammy?' Niamh asked, after they had waved off her grandparents on the train.

'Well, I don't know about you but I've decided I'm going back to work tomorrow,' Dilly told her.

'But won't that seem a bit ... disrespectful? Aren't we supposed to be in mourning?'

Dilly shrugged. 'Mourning is all well and good for those who can afford it but we still have to pay the rent and the bills and put food on the table.'

Niamh was relieved that her mother felt that way. She was tired of sitting about moping and missed her job. She loved working with the children. She also still loved to paint and her granda had taken one of her paintings, trussed up in a towel, back to Ireland with him to hang on the wall of the farmhouse, declaring it was as good as any he had seen. The problem with some of Fergal's clothes had been solved too, when Maeve had asked if she might take some back for Liam. He was about the same size as Fergal had been before his accident and Dilly had felt happy to think he might enjoy wearing them. But now that the funeral was over, she was painfully aware that she needed to start earning again so she started to try and plan a future without Fergal.

Chapter Thirty-two

'Are you still so keen to join the Voluntary Aid Detachment now?' Camilla snapped, shaking the newspaper at Olivia one morning, as the family sat at breakfast.

'As a matter of fact, yes, I am,' Olivia replied calmly, as she cut the top off a soft-boiled egg and dipped a sliver of bread and butter into it. She would be fifteen soon and was keen to feel that she, too, was doing her bit for the country.

'Since I read about the German firing squad executing Edith Cavell I'm even more determined to become a nurse. Did you know that she helped many French and English soldiers to escape across the Dutch border? She was a heroine!'

Olivia had recently received letters from all three of her brothers but, surprisingly, it was Harvey who seemed the most dedicated to his job. He wrote of the love he felt for the horses he cared for and the sorrow he felt when some, indeed many, didn't come back from battle. It appeared that the mortality rate for horses was almost as high as it was for men. But he had always loved animals, and Olivia had no doubt that when the war was over he would pursue his dream of becoming a vet. Camilla wasn't happy about that but, then, as she was fast finding out, her children were growing up and making their own decisions. It seemed that nothing she could say would sway them. Max was no help at all, much to her disgust. He was content for them to do what they felt would suit them best, and she had long since stopped trying to get any backing from him.

Camilla glared at her, then turned her attention back to the meal in front of her. It was then that they heard a tap on the door and Mrs Pegs appeared, her face creased with concern.

'I'm sorry to disturb you, but this just come an' I thought yer'd want to see it straight away.'

As she held out a telegram, Camilla's hand flew to her throat. 'Y-you open it, would you?' she said shakily to Max.

Max took the telegram from the cook and tore it open. They all held their breath as he read it. 'It's Oscar. But don't panic. He's been wounded and is in hospital in Plymouth. It says there are more details to follow.'

'But how badly wounded?' Camilla asked, as a picture of a man sitting begging in the town centre with no legs flashed in front of her eyes. She couldn't bear it if he had been maimed for life.

'It doesn't say but I shall make it my business to find out,' Max said grimly, as he rose from his seat.

'Does it say which hospital he's in? We must go to him at once!'

'No,' he answered, scanning the telegram again. 'But I'm going to telephone now. There can't be that many hospitals in Plymouth, can there?'

He left the room as Olivia and her mother

361

stared fearfully at each other.

'I don't know what all the panic is about,' Samuel said heartlessly as he loaded a forkful of fried black pudding into his mouth without a care in the world. 'At least he isn't dead!'

Olivia glared at him with contempt, and followed her father from the room.

Within an hour, Max had located which hospital Oscar was in and had spoken to the doctor who was caring for him. 'He's been lucky, if you can call it lucky,' he told the anxious women. 'He was caught on the edge of a gas attack but, thankfully, he didn't get the full blast so he's expected to make a full recovery. In fact, they are planning to send him home this week to recover. His eyes were affected but the bandages are already off and they think he'll be able to return to the front within a month.'

Olivia wasn't too pleased to hear that – she had been hoping that the war would be over for Oscar. But at least he was coming home and she was grateful for that. 'How will he get here?' she asked. 'Couldn't we just go and fetch him?'

'I asked that but they prefer him to travel in an ambulance with some other soldiers who will be returning to the Midlands. They'd rather we didn't visit either. It's too upsetting for the patients, apparently. I'm afraid all we can do now is wait.'

She sighed, knowing that the next few days until Oscar was safely at home would pass very slowly indeed.

Three days later Oscar returned. His mother and Olivia rushed out to meet him as the driver helped him down from the ambulance. But he wasn't the Oscar they had waved off to war: he seemed to have aged ten years. His eyes were still bloodshot and swollen but he could obviously see because when Olivia raced towards him he smiled.

'Oh, it's so wonderful to have you home!' his sister cried, and hugged him so tightly that she almost knocked him over.

'Steady on.' Oscar grinned. 'I'm still a bit shaky on the old legs, you know.'

'Sorry.' Olivia took his elbow and began to lead him slowly inside as his mother thanked the ambulance driver and took Oscar's medication from him with instructions on how it must be administered. The eye drops were most important, and must be put in every hour for the next week at least.

Olivia was delighted to have her brother home but shocked at the change in him. She could feel the bones in his arms and his clothes were hanging off him.

He in turn was shocked by the change in his little sister. She seemed to have grown into a young woman in his absence and he suddenly realized how much he had missed her.

Mrs Pegs and Mrs Carey rushed to welcome him, but when Camilla came into the hallway and glared at them, they crept away to the kitchen as she hurried him into the drawing room and settled him by the fire.

'Stop fussing, Mother,' Oscar snapped, as she tucked a warm rug across his legs. Her face fell and instantly he felt guilty. At the hospital he had been one of the least injured patients. He had seen sights there that would stay with him for the rest of his life. Young men of his age with missing arms and legs or facial scars so horrific that he could barely look at them. Some of them had taken the full force of the poisonous gas and had had to be transferred to asylums. Others' lungs had been so badly affected that they had died without ever seeing their families again. Yet more had been permanently blinded. But he shouldn't take it out on his own family, he told himself, and tried to calm down. It was the quiet that took the most getting used to. He had become accustomed to the constant sound of machine-gun fire, exploding grenades and the screams of the dying, and suddenly there was nothing but silence. He was tense, waiting for it to begin all over again.

On the day he had been injured he had stopped to help a young private, who was lying face down in the mud, groaning with agony. He knew now that had he not stopped he would probably have taken the full force of the gas. He had turned the chap over, horrified to see that one of his arms was missing – the severed limb was sinking into the mud a few yards away, the fingers still twitching. Worse was the sight of the fat rat that had scurried out of the empty sleeve as the lad had looked up at him. It had been feasting on the bloody stump and Oscar had vomited violently. When he had next looked at the poor chap, he was almost relieved to see that, for him at least, the war and the pain were over. He had closed the staring eyes before crawling on through the mud, tears streaming down his face. He didn't remember much after that until he woke up in a field hospital with his eyes heavily bandaged. He had screamed in terror, thinking he was blind, but then he had felt the sharp prick of a needle in his arm and had sunk into blessed darkness again. Now he was at home, and he wasn't sure how he felt about it. Why had he been allowed to live when so many thousands of others had not? It was a question he could not answer.

'Now, Mrs Pegs has made you some nice chicken soup,' his mother fussed. 'We have to build you up and get you strong again.'

The thought of food made him feel nauseous but he smiled, wishing she would go away and let him sleep. It had been a long journey and he was tired.

'Would you like me to bring you some newspapers?' she asked. 'Of course you wouldn't. Sorry, darling, I wasn't thinking. You must rest your eyes. Now I'll just go and see where the soup has got to.'

As she bustled away, Olivia smiled wryly. 'She means well,' she whispered.

'I know... I'm just so tired.'

'Then I'll leave you to have a nap. And don't worry – I'll keep Mother out of the way until you wake up.'

She kissed his forehead tenderly and before she had even crept from the room he was fast asleep.

'He doesn't seem himself at all,' Camilla told Max worriedly over dinner that evening. Oscar had chosen to have his meal in his room on a tray.

'But surely you wouldn't expect any other,' Max said sensibly. 'The poor lad has been to Hell and back. He needs peace and quiet now. The doctor told me that rest is the best medicine he can possibly have.'

'Even so I've invited the Merrimans for dinner tomorrow evening. Dear Penelope can barely wait to see him.'

'You've done *what?*' Max thundered, incensed at her thoughtlessness. 'Haven't you heard a single word I've said, woman?'

Camilla had the grace to look uncomfortable. 'I thought it might cheer him up.'

'*Cheer him up!* Why, the way you're carrying on, you'll finish the lad off. Now I suggest you make our excuses to the Merrimans until Oscar is feeling stronger.' The tone in which the words were said left Camilla in no doubt whatsoever that if she didn't put them off, Max would, and probably none too subtly.

'Very well,' she said reluctantly. 'I dare say it won't matter if we delay it for a few days, although Penelope will be very disappointed.'

Max shook his head and glanced at Olivia, then turned his attention back to his dinner. There were times like now when he wondered where his wife's priorities lay.

Over the next week, Olivia took on the role of Oscar's carer and they were all pleased that he appeared to improve slightly with every day that passed. The swelling on his eyes went down, although they were still bloodshot and sore, and his appetite increased. In the afternoons Olivia would read snippets from the newspapers to him, or run backwards and forwards between his room and the kitchen, fetching tasty treats that Mrs Pegs had made. In the evenings they played cards together or sat chatting quietly, content in each other's company. She wished that this peaceful time together could go on for ever. They had effectively shut out the world.

'You're going to make a first-class nurse,' he told her one day, and she flushed with pleasure. She had endless patience with him, and nothing was too much trouble for her. The doctor called in every day at Camilla's request to check on his progress, and each time he called, Olivia would hover outside the door while Oscar was examined, terrified that the doctor might say he was well enough to return to his regiment. The only time Olivia left him for a few hours was when she attended a first-aid class.

Finally, Camilla suggested that now Oscar was on the road to recovery it might be time to invite the Merrimans to dinner. With a deep sigh, Oscar agreed. He supposed he might as well get it over and done with.

That evening the Merrimans were shown into the drawing room for drinks. Penelope made a beeline for Oscar and smiled at him shyly. 'I – I'm so pleased you're feeling better,' she stammered, blushing an unbecoming shade of brick red. 'I – I've been worried about you.'

Oscar peered at her over the rim of his glass, feeling almost sorry for her. She had clearly made a great effort with her appearance although it hadn't made a great deal of difference. She was very tall for a girl, almost as tall as himself, and she had attempted to pin her lank mousy, coloured hair up onto the top of her head in curls that were already escaping the pins and straggling around her plump face. The dark lilac bombazine dress she was wearing was clearly of a very good quality but it strained across her chest giving her the appearance of an all-in wrestler. He found himself staring at the thick-lensed glasses she was forced to wear and stifled a sigh. It looked set to be a very long evening indeed. Then Olivia breezed into the room like a breath of fresh air looking enchanting in a fitted cream gown that showed off her lovely copper-coloured hair to perfection and he couldn't help but compare the two girls. Even so, Penelope was a pleasant enough girl so he did his best to be polite to her and when Mrs Carey called them in to dinner he gallantly offered Penelope his arm knowing his mother would expect it of him. Dilly was kindly coming in to serve the food until his Father could find a replacement for Bessie and once everyone was seated in the dining room she rushed away to start bringing the food in.

'I – I thought perhaps you might like to come to dinner at our house,' Penelope whispered hopefully, somewhere between the first and second course.

Oscar almost choked. He was quite happy to be polite but he didn't want to give her false hope.

'Why, how kind of you to ask him. You'd like that, wouldn't you, darling?' Camilla butted in.

Oscar glared at her, as Mrs Merriman twittered, 'You would be very welcome, my dear. Would tomorrow evening suit you? Penelope might play a little piece on the piano for us after dinner. She's becoming quite accomplished now, aren't you, my love? But then Penelope has always been very talented. Her embroidery is quite remarkable.'

Clearing his throat, Oscar began awkwardly, 'It's very kind of you but I'm afraid I still get quite tired and I–'

Mrs Merriman waved aside his excuses, her plump hand adorned with so many sparkling rings that Oscar was amazed she could lift it. 'Oh, please don't worry about that, my dear,' she gushed. 'We will dine early and send the carriage for you. With this damned war on, it's getting more difficult to get petrol for the car, isn't it, Wilbur?' she said aggrievedly. Her downtrodden husband merely nodded. 'And when you're tired we shall be sure to have you delivered safely home.'

Feeling as if he had been backed into a corner, Oscar could only nod. But you just wait, Mother, until I have you alone, he thought angrily.

Penelope stuck to his side for the rest of the evening, and when she and her parents finally left, Oscar let out a huge sigh of relief. 'I thought they were never going to go,' he told Olivia irritably as his parents saw their guests to their waiting carriage.

'And it's not going to be many hours before you see them all again,' Olivia teased impishly.

With a grin he lifted a cushion from the sofa and hurled it in her direction.

From that moment on, Penelope Merriman became a frequent visitor to the house, despite Oscar's protests. She would turn up at the most unlikely times with the most unlikely presents. A dish of chicken soup made especially for him by their cook, and sweetmeats to tempt his appetite, she said.

'Does she think I don't get fed here?' he

369

groaned to Olivia.

'She's just being friendly,' Olivia told him, but Oscar knew differently. He also knew exactly what his mother was up to.

'I'll tell you this,' he stormed. 'It would take more than an arrow from Cupid's bow to make me fall in love with Penelope Merriman.'

Olivia said nothing although like Oscar, she thought her mother was wrong to keep pushing them together so blatantly. Deep down she felt a tiny bit jealous, although she knew she had no earthly reason to be. Oscar was her brother.

Finally the day Olivia had been dreading arrived, when the doctor proclaimed Oscar fit enough to return to the front. Once the doctor had gone she burst into inconsolable tears. 'But... you might not be so lucky next time,' she sobbed, as Oscar held her. 'And I really don't know what I'd do if anything were to happen to you.'

He stroked her hair, muttering soothing words as he stroked the tears from her cheeks. Then, as she looked up at him, their eyes locked, and before they knew what they were doing, their lips had joined and pure bliss coursed through every vein in Olivia's body. She felt as if she was floating on a cloud of delight until Oscar shoved her roughly away from him.

'Oh, my God – I can't believe we did that,' he gasped in horror. 'You're my sister, for Heaven's sake! You'd better leave my room, Olivia.'

She slid off his bed and, head bent, slunk away, mortified. She knew that in the eyes of God what they had done was wrong, so why had it felt right? And why was it that no other young man had ever been able to hold a candle in her eyes to Oscar? Confused, she crept away to her room to cry herself to sleep.

Three days later Oscar left to rejoin his unit. It was almost a relief to see him go: since that kiss they had been unable to look each other in the eye.

'Have Olivia and Oscar had a tiff?' Camilla asked Max, once Oscar had gone. 'They seemed to be avoiding each other. It took them all their time even to say goodbye to each other, and yet they've always been so close.'

'I've no idea,' he answered automatically. He had far more pressing things on his mind, like the war reports in the newspapers. Austria-Hungary had now gained full control of Serbia and he wondered where it would all end.

Chapter Thirty-three

In December, the War Office in London reported that the ill-fated Gallipoli expedition had been abandoned. Max was relieved. The last they had heard, Lawrence and Harvey had been in that vicinity so, hopefully, they had escaped unscathed. Every night when he retired to bed now he offered up a silent prayer of thanks that no telegram bearing bad news had arrived. No news was good news as far as he was concerned, and long may it continue.

Christmas came and went and the new year of 1916 began with little for the British people to celebrate. Food was still increasingly difficult to obtain, now that the ships were finding it so hard to dock, and in almost every street someone was mourning the loss of a loved one. There was no party to mark Olivia's fifteenth birthday, although Max and Camilla bought her a beautiful gold locket that she would enjoy wearing in happier times. Her biggest surprise came from Dilly, who waylaid her in the hall and slipped a small box into her hand.

'What's this?' Olivia asked.

'It's just something I'd like you to have,' Dilly told her, after glancing quickly about to make sure that no one could hear them. 'Fergal bought it for me when we were courting and it's such a special birthday I thought you might like it. But please don't mention to your parents that I've given it to you. They might not understand.'

Olivia opened the box to find a slender chain bracelet with a small silver heart suspended from it.

'But, Mrs Carey, I can't take this,' she objected. 'It must have huge sentimental value to you, particularly now that... Well, perhaps you should save it for your daughter. I'm sure she would treasure it if her father bought it for you.'

Dilly wanted to scream at her, *You are my daughter too!* But she remained calm as she answered, 'Niamh will have my wedding ring one day, so please take it and wear it.' She had never overstepped the mark before and was well aware that she shouldn't now, but how could she let this special day go unmarked?

'In that case, thank you very much. It's beautiful

372

and I shall take very good care of it.' Olivia leaned across and kissed Dilly's cheek, then skipped upstairs with her trinket.

Dilly fingered her cheek as tears welled in her eyes. Sometimes it was hard to be so close to Olivia, yet it was only seeing her so regularly that had made the years bearable. With a great effort she pulled herself together and went about her work.

That week Max visited the workhouse once again and returned with a girl of thirteen to take Bessie's place as kitchen-cum-general maid. He knew he should have replaced Bessie sooner as her absence had meant a lot more work had fallen to Mrs Pegs and Dilly, but he had hung on, hoping that Bessie might have a change of heart and come home. There seemed very little chance of that happening now so he introduced Gwen with a smile. 'This is Mrs Pegs,' he said. 'She'll tell you what your duties are and show you the ropes, won't you, Mrs Pegs?'

'I will that.' Mrs Pegs still desperately missed Bessie and constantly worried about how the poor girl was faring but she would be glad of an extra pair of hands. As she had told the master, she wasn't getting any younger. Mind you, looking at the lass he had chosen, she wondered if the girl would be up to it. She wasn't as far through as a clothes prop, and looked as if a puff of wind would blow her away. She was a pleasant little thing, though, with fair curly hair, scraped into a piece of string at the nape of her neck, and wide blue eyes. I shall have to get her some decent clothes, Mrs Pegs thought, staring at the ugly brown workhouse shift dress the girl was wearing. The trouble was, Bessie's uniform would drown her. Dilly came to the rescue, promising she would take it to the shop and alter it to fit her.

Gwen was a timid girl and said little but, then, Mrs Pegs remembered that Bessie had been much the same when she had first arrived. Perhaps when she started to come out of her shell, she would be good company. And I'll make sure I keep her away from Mr Samuel an' all, she thought grimly. He wouldn't defile her as he had Bessie.

'Did you see in the papers that the House of Commons has voted for military conscription?' Dilly asked Mrs Pegs, 'They reckon that more than half a million single young men, who are fit for service, haven't volunteered. They're going to take them first, apparently, and then the married ones.'

Mrs Pegs was rolling pastry for a hare pie but she paused and her face lit up. This news was like the answer to a prayer. 'If that's the case that 'un in there'll have to go, won't he? Mr Samuel, I mean.'

'Of course he will. I hadn't thought of that,' Dilly said. 'He isn't going to like it, is he?'

Mrs Pegs grinned. 'I dare say he ain't but it'll do him good. Between you and me he's the only one here I can't stand. He's such an arrogant little sod. Happen the army will make a man of him, wi' a bit o' luck.'

Could she have known it at that very moment Samuel was panicking as he read the very same article that they were discussing.

'But this means that they'll be sending for *me!*'

he told his mother, in dismay, as he threw the paper onto a chair and began to pace the room. He should have been working in one of his father's factories but as usual he had come up with some excuse not to be there.

'Calm down, darling. I'm sure we'll be able to come up with something to prevent you going,' Camilla soothed him. 'We'll talk to your father about it this evening.' Yet as the words left her mouth she doubted there would be anything Max could do to stop it. The law was the law, and it appeared that this damn war was going to claim all of her children. Just this week Olivia had made enquiries about becoming a VAD. Yet another bombshell had dropped when Miss Norman had informed her that she intended to leave. The government was calling for well-off families to cut back on their staff so she had decided to join her widowed sister in Brighton and work for the Red Cross.

'But who will run the house if you go?' Camilla asked.

Miss Norman's back stayed straight. 'We all have to do our bit, Mrs Farthing. And with three of the young men away, soon to be four,' she added pointedly, looking at Samuel, 'I'm sure you will be more than capable of doing it yourself.'

Camilla's shoulders sagged. Things were going from bad to worse and she wondered when the nightmare would end. She had always felt in charge of her home and family. Even when the boys had been sent to boarding school she had still had control of them when they were at home during their holidays. She had even hoped to arrange suitable marriages for them all. It seemed that this damn war was going to ruin all her plans and there was nothing she could do about it.

The third week in February found Lawrence crouching in a trench in Verdun. There had been a week of gales and storms and he had almost forgotten what it felt like to be dry. The troops were kneeling ankle deep in thick, sludgy water and many were suffering from trench foot, which was unbelievably painful. The German bombardment had started at seven fifteen that morning and since then a hurricane of shells had rained ceaselessly down on them, systematically demolishing the Allies' position line by line. Until now the bulk of the troops had been told to lie low to minimize losses, but those who had gone into the front line had been mown down mercilessly. Now Lawrence could only wait for the all-clear when the stretcher-bearers' work would begin.

'I wonder how long it will be before it's our turn,' a soldier, crouched next to Lawrence, said. Taking a packet of cigarettes from his sodden overcoat he offered them to Lawrence, then produced a box of matches that were, miraculously, still fairly dry.

'I reckon there'll be a fair few casualties and bodies for us to collect today,' Lawrence answered glumly. He thought he and the soldier might have travelled there in the same truck, although he couldn't be sure. Everyone looked the same in their mud-spattered khaki uniforms and their tin hats, although he noted that this chap wore the uniform of an officer.

'Where are you from?' Lawrence asked,

through a cloud of smoke.

'Dublin.' The stranger held out his hand. Lawrence shook it.

'And you?'

'The Midlands. Nuneaton, not far from Coventry. I'm Lawrence Farthing.'

'Nice to meet you, although it's a shame it couldn't have been under better conditions.' The chap smiled, and Lawrence thought he could possibly be quite nice-looking under the layers of filth. 'I'm Lionel McFarren. It'll be my turn to go up top again shortly.'

Lawrence was tired of it all now, tired of wondering if today would be the day he would cop it – the stretcher-bearers were not safe from the Jerries. He had seen so many men slaughtered mindlessly like cattle. He couldn't believe it wouldn't be his turn soon, but he was past caring. In fact, it would be almost a relief. He could see his own thoughts reflected in the eyes of his new comrade and thought that they could have been friends under other circumstances. But they had no more time to chat: suddenly the ladders were being propped against the sides of the trenches and the men were scaling them as best they could.

'Here we go again, then.' Lionel threw his cigarette butt into the mud, where it was gobbled by a large rat with bloodstained whiskers and evil yellow eyes.

'Good luck, mate, and thanks for the ciggy,' Lawrence said.

The man nodded. Seconds later he was climbing the ladder, his rifle slung across his shoulder. At the top he paused to get a foothold in the mud and salute Lawrence. Then he was gone and all Lawrence could do was wait.

There was no way that Lionel could run: the mud was trying to suck him down and it was like wading through quicksand. His rifle was trained ahead as he tried to see through the pall of thick smoke that hung across the field, moving on through the deafening roar of machine-gun fire. He had gone no more than a few yards when he jerked and dropped.

Much later that afternoon, as Lawrence and the other stretcher-bearers scoured the field for the wounded, he came across Lionel, lying face up in the mud, and groaned. 'Did yer know 'im, mate?' the man handling the other end of the stretcher asked.

Lawrence stared down at the corpse. There was a ragged hole in the man's jacket and through it Lawrence could see a gaping hole in his chest. Lawrence clenched his fists. 'Not really,' he muttered. 'I met him today, but he was a nice chap. Come on, let's get the poor sod out of here.'

They knelt to roll the body onto the stretcher, and it was as they were crossing the field some minutes later that the gunfire started up again and Lawrence was hurled into the air.

'You bastards!' he shrieked. 'Do your worst!' But his words were snatched away by the wind and he dropped like a stone.

Lawrence felt as if he was wading through a thick fog. There was something wet and annoying on his

378

face but when he tried to lift his hand to swat it away he didn't have the strength. With an enormous effort he managed to open his eyes and eventually a freckled face swam into focus. It was that of a young woman, wearing a tin hat, and for a moment he was disoriented.

'Wh-where am I?' he asked thickly. His tongue felt swollen and parched.

'You're in the field hospital,' she told him, and when he frowned, she smiled as she tapped her hat. 'We nurses have to wear these because we're so near to the front,' she explained. 'Now, come on, I bet you're longing for a drink.'

She lifted his head and tipped a trickle of water across his dry lips. He thought he had never tasted anything so sweet and tried to gulp it but she shook her head. 'Easy does it. We don't want you being sick, now, do we?'

Suddenly he became aware of the deafening sound of gunfire still going on all around him. He also noticed a cage-like structure across his legs and his heart thumped. 'M-my legs! Have I lost my legs?'

'No, you haven't,' she reassured him. 'But your ankle's a nasty mess. I thought you might have to lose your foot when you first came in but the surgeon's done a grand job of putting it back together.' She lowered his head to the pillow.

'Will I be able to walk on it?' He had seen too many men crippled by this damned war and didn't know how he would cope if it happened to him. He'd sooner be dead.

'The surgeon will be round later to tell you all about it,' she answered, as she tucked the sheets around him. 'But what you need now is rest.'

'I don't want to *bloody* rest!' Yet as the words left his lips his eyes closed and sleep claimed him once again.

It was dark when next he woke, apart from the flickering light from the gas lamps that were placed on tables along the length of the tent. The gunfire had ceased for now, and all he could hear was the groans of men lying in the beds at either side of him. The chap in the bed next to him had his head heavily bandaged. All that was visible were his lips and Lawrence shuddered. It must be awful to be cut off from the light like that. The man on the other side was sitting up with a cage like Lawrence's over his legs.

'You're back wiv us, are yer, matey?' He smiled. 'How yer feelin' now, then?'

'Not too bad,' Lawrence croaked. He peered up and down the tent for a glimpse of the young nurse who had spoken to him earlier. He had liked her. She had a nice face. A cluster of nurses were with a doctor near to the door, they were going over a patient's notes but after a while one glanced along the row of beds and, seeing he was awake, came towards him – she was the girl he had talked to earlier.

'Here we are again, then. Back in the land of the living.' Taking a thermometer from the end of the bed, she placed it in his mouth while she took his pulse. She checked the reading and smiled. 'That's normal. I'll get someone to bring you a cup of tea and a sandwich. I'm going off duty now but I'll be back in the morning. Goodnight.'

Lawrence watched her go. He was in discomfort now, and when he tried to move his injured foot, stabs of pain flared up his leg.

'The nurses can give you sumfin' to ease that, if it's painin' you,' the chap in the next bed said, as he saw Lawrence grimace. Then he smiled wryly. 'I ain't got that problem. Boff my bleedin' legs got shot off. Still, at least I'm still 'ere so I don't suppose I should complain. The war's over fer me an' I'll be goin' home to me missus an' kids soon. I'm Jimmy Mann, by the way, born wivin' the sound o' Bow Bells an' proud of it.'

Feeling as if he was caught in a nightmare, Lawrence screwed his eyes tight shut. Perhaps he had been one of the lucky ones, after all. What was a shattered ankle compared to what had happened to Jimmy?

The freckle-faced girl was back on duty early the next morning, although she couldn't have looked less like a nurse if she had tried. She still wore a tin helmet and a greatcoat that reached almost to her ankles over an unsightly pair of lace-up boots. 'There's nowhere for us to wash our uniforms properly,' she explained, as she saw Lawrence eyeing her outfit curiously as she gave him his first bed-bath. His face was glowing with embarrassment, but he didn't say anything. A lock of curly hair had slipped from beneath her hat and he saw that it was red, which explained the spattering of freckles across her nose. He'd heard somewhere that redheads usually had freckles, although he couldn't for the life of him think where.

'How long have you been a nurse?' he asked.

She giggled. 'Well, I'm not a proper nurse. I'm

381

just a VAD,' she admitted. 'But out here we all do whatever needs doing, whether we're fully qualified or not. I've been working in the field hospitals for about eight months now, although it feels a lot longer.' She sighed wistfully. 'I'm due some leave soon and I'm looking forward to going home and seeing my family.'

Suddenly, although he knew he was being selfish, Lawrence hoped her leave wouldn't happen while he was still there. From then on, his eyes followed her about the tent.

It was later that day before the surgeon found time to see him. He was a bald, middle-aged man with a stress-lined face and grave eyes, but his smile was kindly.

'So, how are you feeling, Farthing?' he asked, as he flicked through the notes that were hooked over the end of the bed.

'Not too bad, although this leg is giving me a bit of gyp,' Lawrence admitted.

'I'm not surprised. When they brought you in your ankle was shattered and there were bones where there shouldn't have been bones.' The doctor peered at him above the spectacles that were perched on the end of his nose. 'Luckily we managed to put everything back where it should be and, given time, it will heal enough for you to walk on it but I should warn you, you're going to have a very bad limp at best.'

'What happens now?'

'As soon as you're well enough, you'll be transferred to a proper hospital in France, and then, as soon as possible, you'll be shipped to a hospital in England where you will convalesce until you're ready to go home. The war is over for you, Private.'

Lawrence could barely take it in. He was going home and he wouldn't be coming back, but he would pay for the privilege, if what the doctor had said was true. He would be semi-lame for the rest of his life. And then he felt ashamed. Compared to Jimmy he had got off lightly.

Over the next few days he discovered that the little redhead was called Patty Newcombe and she came from Whitby, where she lived with her parents and siblings. She would chatter on about them until Lawrence felt he almost knew them. In fact, he found himself counting the hours when she went off duty until she reappeared, and when she did, butterflies would flutter to life in his stomach. She told him of the picnics they took up to the abbey ruins on the hill overlooking the sea and of the fish and chips to which they treated themselves while they watched the boats in the harbour. She told him how she had caught crabs with a tiny net in the rock pools the sea left behind, collected shells and swam in the clear blue water. It sounded so idyllic that he promised himself he would go there when the war was over and he was fully recovered. He had been to Whitby on a holiday once with his family, when he was just a little boy, and Patty's reminiscences brought back memories of happier times.

Jimmy had been sent to a hospital in France, and Lawrence got used to seeing the beds occupied by different men with varying injuries. Through the tent doors he had a view of the large tent that was used as a makeshift morgue, and every day he was saddened when he saw the stretcher-bearers carrying corpses into it. They would then dig shallow graves and the chaplain would say a hasty few words as the lucky ones were interred. The not so lucky were left on the field. As Lawrence knew all too well, there were far too many to reclaim them all so their resting place was the sea of mud in which they had fallen. The war seemed so futile and such a waste of so many young lives, and Lawrence felt relieved that he was no longer a part of it. He also began to dread the time when he would be shipped home, because that would mean leaving Patty. He knew then that he was developing feelings for her and wondered if he dare hope that she might feel the same.

Then one cold, murky morning, nearly a week after he had arrived, Patty approached his bed to tell him regretfully, 'Your name is on the transfer list. They'll be taking you to the main hospital later today, with some of the other men.'

He knew he should have been pleased to get out of such a Hell hole. The nurses did the best they could, an admirable job in such trying conditions, but there were so many shortages – not enough sheets and blankets, not enough medicine. They were short of everything, despite the regular arrival of supplies. There were just too many casualties for everything to go round. But he would miss Patty more than he cared to admit.

'I see... Will you write to me?' he asked suddenly, and when she blushed, his heart began to race.

'Er, yes, if you leave me your address. We shouldn't write to patients, really, but I won't tell anyone if you don't.'

She fetched him a pen and a piece of paper

while Sister was out of the way, and after he had scribbled down his address she shoved it into the pocket of her coat and smiled at him shyly.

'I shall miss you,' Lawrence said. 'Thanks for taking such good care of me.'

'It was a pleasure and ... I shall miss you too.' She reached out and squeezed his hand, then scuttled away to administer bed-baths and empty bed-pans. His eyes followed her as he tried to lock her every feature in his memory.

That day the telegram arrived at the Farthings' home. When Camilla saw the telegram boy cycling furiously up the drive her legs turned to jelly.

'Would you answer the door, please, Mrs Carey?' she asked, as she dropped heavily onto a little gilt-legged chair.

It was so rarely that she spoke civilly to Dilly that Dilly was surprised. 'Of course.' She had been dusting the highly polished sideboard in the drawing room but put down her cloth and went to the door.

When she came back she held out the envelope to Camilla, but she shook her head.

'No – no! I can't!... Would you open it and tell me what it says, please?'

Dilly slit the envelope, then sighed with relief. It wasn't good news exactly, but it could have been a lot worse. 'Mr Lawrence has been injured and is in hospital in France at the moment. He's going to be shipped home within the next two weeks and they'll let you know which hospital he's in here.'

Camilla gave a sigh of relief. She hated to think of Lawrence injured and so far away, but at least he was alive. That was two of her sons who had been injured now, but how long might it be before one was killed? It just didn't bear thinking about.

Chapter Thirty-four

'Samuel, do cheer up,' Camilla urged, as he stared morosely through the window. He had spent two nights at home following his training but the next day he was due to return to his barracks and then he would, no doubt, be sent to the front with the rest of his unit.

Samuel had always been vain and knew he looked handsome in his uniform, but today he took no pleasure from it. He wouldn't be handsome if he was a corpse, and there was every chance of him becoming one, once he was in the firing line.

'Why don't you go and see some of your chums?' Camilla suggested, then wished that she hadn't: most of them were away fighting. But there must be something she could do to cheer him. She had already asked Mrs Pegs to cook his favourite dishes for dinner and the succulent piece of beef that was roasting was sending tantalizing smells along the hallway. The day before, Samuel had travelled with her and Max to visit Lawrence, who was now recovering in a hospital in Portsmouth. With hindsight Camilla had realized it had been a mistake to take Samuel with them. It had done him no good whatsoever to see some of the poor injured souls in the hospital and he had come home in an even blacker mood, convinced he would be joining them before long.

She had been thrilled to see Lawrence, though. He was doing well and had chatted almost non-stop about a little nurse called Patty, who had cared for him in the field hospital. They were going to write to each other, he had informed her, and Camilla had an idea that her son had formed a romantic attachment to the girl. She hoped she came from a good family, but there would be time to address that when Lawrence was at home.

For now she had to come up with something to snap Samuel out of his black mood. The way he was behaving, she was afraid that he might disappear and everyone knew what happened to deserters. Then he surprised her. 'Actually,' he said, 'there is someone I'd like to see before I go away. Bye for now.'

'Will you be back for dinner? It'll be ready in a couple of hours,' she called after him, as he strode purposefully towards the door. Mrs Pegs would be none too pleased if she had gone to a lot of trouble for nothing.

'Probably,' he threw across his shoulder, as the door closed behind him.

His mother sighed. Samuel could be very difficult when he had a mind to be. Perhaps Max was right when he said that a bit of army discipline would do him good.

Samuel strode off in the direction of the Coton Arches. It had been a while since he had seen Niamh Carey but he hadn't given up on her yet,

387

and surely she would be nice to him this evening, knowing he was going away to fight for king and country tomorrow.

It was already after four o'clock and the darkness was drawing in. He hoped that Niamh wouldn't have left the school already, but he knew she often stayed behind after the children had departed so he had every hope of catching her. The lights were still shining from the classroom windows as he approached the school and through them, he spotted Niamh busily wiping slates clean and laying out chalks for the children to use the next day.

It was then that it occurred to him. When Niamh walked home alone she usually took the short-cut through the Pingles Fields and Riversley Park. She had always insisted on sticking to the roads when she was with him, but if he were to wait for her a little way into the Pingles, she would seem churlish if she were to turn back...

He hurried away, and by the time he had gone some way into the Pingles he was pleased to note that it was really dark now. Leaning against a tree trunk, he lit a cigarette and waited, hoping that his ploy would pay off. It was cold and he wished he had thought to put on his overcoat but perhaps it would be better if Niamh saw him in uniform. How would she be able to resist him?

At last the tap-tap-tap of footsteps sounded on the path, and seconds later Niamh appeared out of the darkness, starting as he stepped out in front of her.

'Well, blow me,' he said, in a friendly fashion. 'I'd just stopped to tie my bootlace. Fancy meeting you here. How are you, Niamh?'

She was wearing a very becoming beret and a fitted coat, although he couldn't see what colour they were in the darkness.

'Samuel,' she said, feeling mildly uncomfortable. 'I'm very well, thank you... and yourself?'

She moved on again, dismayed when he fell into step with her.

'Oh, you know, getting ready for tomorrow. Did your mother tell you I'm going to join my unit in the morning?'

'She did mention it.' Niamh had been delighted to hear the news, although she couldn't tell him so. They were approaching the long tunnel now that would lead them into the park and Niamh felt apprehensive. It was black as pitch in there and she didn't fancy walking through it with Samuel. Still, it was too far to walk back to the road now so, taking a deep breath, she plunged ahead.

The rounded walls of the tunnel were clammy and damp and their footsteps echoed eerily around them. Samuel was peeved that Niamh hadn't admired him in his uniform so now he asked, 'What do you think of me in my uniform? Will I pass muster?'

Niamh shrugged. 'I hadn't really noticed. But then there are so many men in uniform now, aren't there?' There was no way she was going to boost his ego, she decided.

Samuel's face twisted into a scowl. He grasped her arm, pulled her to a stop and demanded, 'Why are you always so horrible to me? You should be grateful that someone of my class is showing an interest in you.'

Niamh saw red and snatched away her arm.

389

'Then why don't you go and bother some other girl who *is* your class?' she flung at him. 'When are you going to understand that I'm not in the least bit interested in you? I've tried to be polite to you but now I'm telling you clearly – *I am not interested.* Go away and leave me alone! My affections lie elsewhere, and even if they didn't, I wouldn't look at you. I find you quite – quite *obnoxious,* so there you have it!'

She made to move on but Samuel was in a rage now. Catching her by the elbow again, he slammed her viciously against the tunnel wall, knocking the air from her lungs and cracking her head painfully.

'Why you common little whore!' he snarled, through clenched teeth. 'You need taking down a peg or or two and I'm the one to do it.'

As he snatched at the front of her coat she felt the button pop. Before she could say anything, he clamped his mouth on hers and ground his lips against her teeth. All the while his hand was yanking at her skirt and she panicked. She began to fight and struggle, and at one point she had the satisfaction of feeling her nails rake his cheek. Even more infuriated, he raised his hand and slapped her face, making her head snap back on her shoulders. She was crying now. Her strength was no match for his and she prayed that someone would come and save her, but she heard nothing except the harsh sound of his breathing as he bore her to the ground. Again the air was knocked out of her and as she lay there he flung her skirt above her waist and she felt the cold night air on the bare skin above her stockings. She couldn't see anything, but she was aware of him fumbling with his

390

trousers as he clamped the other hand across her throat, effectively stopping her from screaming. Suddenly he tore her legs apart and pulled her drawers to the side. When he rammed into her, the pain was so excruciating that she wanted to die. She felt as if she was being ripped in two and prayed for death. She knew she would never be able to bear the humiliation when this was over – if he didn't kill her, and she had no doubt that he was capable of it. A picture of Nipper floated before her eyes as tears of shame streamed down her cheeks. She was spoiled now. She would never be able to marry him after this, and all her dreams slipped away.

Samuel continued to buck and groan but she didn't fight any more. Somehow she knew there was no point. He had done his worst. Finally he made a deep animal growling sound, stiffened and rolled off her. Too terrified to move, she lay where she was. She heard him stagger to his feet. Then he gave an inhuman chuckle.

'See who'll want you *now*, little Miss Lah-De-Da,' he taunted.

Then there was nothing, save the sound of his footsteps walking away from her.

She lay there in shock for a long time, too rigid with terror to move until the cold bit into her. Finally, she got to her knees, then staggered unsteadily to her feet. She bent down again, feeling along the ground until she found her bag, which had fallen from her hand at the beginning of the attack. Her hat had come off, too, but that could stay where it was. All she wanted now was to get safely home in case he came back.

Dear God, let him die, she chanted, beneath her breath, as she felt her way along the slimy walls. She had no way of knowing what time it was. The attack seemed to have gone on for ever yet common sense told her it must still be early evening. Out in the open she took a great gulp of air. Her cheek was smarting and she felt sick, but now she knew that she must get home before her mother arrived back from work. No one must ever know what had happened this night. She wouldn't be able to bear the shame. Clutching her coat together, she walked unsteadily, keeping to the shadows wherever she could. There were quite a few people about but nobody seemed to notice her.

Oh, Nipper, I'm so sorry! She was crying inside as she thought of him. His latest letter, which she had read many times, was in the pocket of her coat but what would she write to him now? She was no longer the pure, innocent girl he had fallen in love with. It all seemed hopeless. By the time she reached the cottage door, tears were streaming down her pale cheeks but at least she was home.

Suddenly Nell's door opened and after glancing at the girl she exclaimed, 'Lord love us! Whatever's happened to yer, pet?'

'I, er, took a short-cut through the tunnel in the park and tripped up on the cobbles,' she said lamely.

'Well, I wouldn't mind bettin' yer goin' to have a right shiner on yer tomorrer,' Nell said quietly. 'Let me come in an' bathe that cheek for you.'

Niamh shook her head. The last thing she wanted was for Nell to see the state of her clothes.

Nell was no fool. She'd soon put two and two together.

'No ... thanks... I'm all right ... thank you,' she rambled, as she fumbled with the door handle. 'It's just shaken me up a bit, that's all. I'll be fine when I've had a hot drink. Goodnight, Nell.'

As she disappeared, Nell frowned into the darkness.

Niamh was in bed when her mother got in and shouted down the stairs that she had a headache. She wouldn't want a meal.

Immediately Dilly went up to her but Niamh was curled into a ball in the darkness so Dilly left her to it. She didn't go to work the next day, she didn't feel up to facing anyone, saying the headache was no better. The following day she still didn't feel up to facing anyone but Niamh knew she had to make the effort or questions would be asked. Samuel should be long gone, she reasoned, so there was no chance of bumping into him. She managed to conceal the worst of the bruise on her cheek with face powder but struggled to get through the day as she thought constantly of Nipper. Her future had looked so bright, but now everything was sullied. She wondered if she would ever feel clean again.

'Can yer believe the silly young bugger got into a fight the very night before he left to join his unit?' Mrs Pegs had moaned to Dilly. 'He had a big scratch all down one side of his face. An' I went to so much trouble cookin' his meal an' he never even bothered to come home to eat it till bedtime.

Roarin' drunk, he was. The missus weren't best pleased, I don't mind tellin' yer. Still, at least he's gone now, an' though I shouldn't say it, I reckon it's good riddance to bad rubbish. Let's just hope the army makes a man of him, eh?'

Dilly could only nod in agreement.

Chapter Thirty-five

'I know it isn't the best of jobs but we all have to do whatever needs doing, if we hope to get this place up and running,' a harassed Red Cross worker told Olivia as she handed her a mop and bucket.

It was the end of March, and now that Edward Melley, a local businessman, had secured the lease on Weddington Hall, Olivia was helping to transform it into a Red Cross hospital for wounded soldiers.

'I don't mind what I do,' Olivia assured her, as she took the bucket good-naturedly. She was excited to be a part of it all because when the doors were opened to the first influx of patients she would be working there as a VAD. The rooms on the first floor were already being converted into wards, named after local companies that were contributing to their preparation and upkeep. Edward Melley was paying for much of the equipment needed for the conversion, and Olivia's father had been happy to contribute. Now names such as Griff, Arley, Hall and Phillips, Birch Coppice,

Reluctantly Harvey stepped away from the horse as another young soldier ran forward to lead him to the temporary housing that had been crudely erected. Everyone had soon seen Harvey's devotion to the animals he cared for and had a good deal of respect for him.

It was only then that Harvey realized how tired he was and, with a last glance at the horse, he made his way wearily back to his tent, with the sound of explosions crashing in his ears. The noise no longer bothered him. It was the silence he found unnerving. It appeared that the horses did too: when it was quiet they would toss their manes and paw the ground fretfully, as if they were waiting for the command to attack.

During the last week Dilly had heard from Kian and Seamus. Each letter was much the same as the last, heavily censored and giving her little indication of where they might be, but at least she could draw comfort from knowing they had been alive at the time of writing. She stored each one to read time and time again. Funnily enough it was Niamh who was giving her the most cause for concern. She didn't seem herself at all and had become withdrawn and touchy. The least little thing would make her cry but every time Dilly tried to get to the bottom of what was troubling her she would stalk off to her room. She'd always been such a sunny-natured easy-going girl but now Dilly felt as if she was living with a stranger, as she remarked to Nell one evening.

'That's girls for yer,' Nell answered philosophically. 'They're known for bein' moodier than boys. Just leave her alone an' she'll come out of it.'

Dilly could only hope that she was right and put Niamh's moods down to worry about Nipper. Because he was at sea his letters came far more infrequently than the rest of the lads' so she supposed that Niamh was fretting about him.

At the end of May, spirits rose in the Farthing household when Lawrence was discharged from the hospital and brought home by ambulance. He was very thin and pale, still suffering considerable pain from his shattered ankle, but at least he could walk short distances now, with the aid of a stout stick.

'I'll soon fatten him up again,' Mrs Pegs declared, and Dilly smiled. She had no doubt the kindly woman would do just that.

Olivia was still working at the soon-to-be-opened hospital and loving every minute of it.

'When the war is over I shall go on to become a *proper* nurse, not just a VAD,' she told Lawrence, and he believed that she would. Olivia could be very stubborn when she'd set her mind on something. She had been wonderful to him since he had arrived home, and nothing was too much trouble for her. She would change the dressings on his ankle and rush about fetching and carrying for him until he suspected that she was using him as practice for when the first patients arrived at Weddington Hall Hospital. He had confided to her his feelings for Patty, but she had already guessed that he was in love and hoped that Patty would get through the rest of the war unscathed. It might be over for him, but Patty was still dangerously close to the front and Lawrence worried about her all the time. He had done a remarkably good job of putting a brave face on things since he had returned home, but one day, when Olivia carried a tray of tea up to his room mid-afternoon, she found him sitting in his chair by the window with tears streaming from his eyes.

'Why, Lawrence, whatever is the matter?' Full of tender concern, she put the tray on his bedside table and rushed across to drop to her knees beside him as he swiped at his eyes with the back of his hand.

'Take no notice of me.' He sniffed, looking awkward, but she wouldn't be put off so easily.

Taking his hand she stroked it. 'They say that talking about bad things helps sometimes.'

He stared up at the clouds scudding across the sky. 'I doubt talking about the things I've seen will make them any easier to live with.'

'But it's worth a try, surely.'

Seeing the concern in her eyes, he took a deep breath. 'Just before this happened,' he tapped his lame leg, 'I was crouched in a trench, when I got talking to another chap. He was from Dublin and we had a cigarette together...' He swallowed. 'He was a really nice chap. His name was Lionel McFarren and he was an officer. I doubt he was much older than me and it was the first time I'd spoken to him, although I thought I'd seen him about. Anyway, when the order to advance came he went up the ladder. It's like Hell there. You'd have to see it to believe it. Sometimes I had to step over corpses that had sunk partially into the mud. At the end of each day me and the other stretcher-bearers would go out to retrieve as many bodies as we could. If there were too many of them we'd just collect their dog tags so they could let their families know they'd been killed. Then we'd dig trenches and the bodies would be piled inside them in rows, one on top of another, and covered with mud. Not a very fitting end for heroes, eh? Some of the bodies would be missing arms and legs, even heads. Most times the air was so heavy with smoke that we could barely see. And the smell ... it was awful, blood and rotting corpses! Later that day I came across McFarren's body. I could see a gaping hole in his chest and after that I don't remember anything but racing ahead full of rage. And now all I can feel is guilt. I'm still here but he's dead. How can that be fair?'

'It wasn't your time to go,' she told him softly. Now she understood why she sometimes heard him cry out in his sleep. Why she sometimes found him in a tangle of damp blankets in the mornings. He had been to Hell and back, but somehow he had to find the will to go on.

A week later a letter arrived with a Whitby postmark on it and Lawrence eagerly tore it open.

'It's from Patty,' he told Olivia. 'She's on leave and at home with her family but she wants to come and see me. Do you think Mother might let her stay for a couple of nights?'

'I don't see why not,' his sister answered. 'We've plenty of empty bedrooms. Why don't you ask her?' She looked up at him but he was already so engrossed in Patty's letter that he hadn't even heard her. She crept away with a smile on her face.

Dear Lawrence,

I'm finally back in Whitby for a time with the family and I can't begin to tell you how good it feels. It's so nice to be clean again and to be able to sleep in a proper bed. Mum and Dad gave me such a welcome but already they are dreading me going back. I have a whole two weeks off and wondered if you'd like me to come and see you? It would be so nice to be able to see for myself how you are coming along. I've no doubt you'll be feeling much better now. The ankle should be healing if you've done as you were told. It seems such a long time since I last saw you. I really missed you when you left, although I was kept as busy as usual. Your letters have kept me going and I read them over and over when I am off duty. There's not much else to do out there, as you know, apart from sleep. My sister and I climbed to the abbey ruins on the hill yesterday, and just for a while I was able to forget there is a war on. It's so peaceful here at present, although Scarborough, which is not so far away as the crow flies, has suffered a lot more raids. I'm still trying to persuade my family to move a little inland from the coast but I suppose there is no guarantee that they would be any safer there, and they're reluctant to leave their home, which is understandable.

Please write straight back when you get this letter. I am so looking forward to seeing you again.

With love

Patty

Lawrence reread the letter twice more, then

reached for a pen and ink. There was no time like the present. If he hurried, Olivia might take his reply to the post office and it would go that day.

'Well ... I suppose we could manage a couple of days,' Camilla said grudgingly that evening when Lawrence told her he had invited Patty to stay. It would be her chance to see what sort of girl Patty was.

As Max helped himself to vegetables from the serving dishes on the sideboard he winked at Olivia over his wife's shoulder and the girl had to lower her head quickly to prevent herself from laughing aloud. She almost felt sorry for Patty.

Four days later Patty arrived at the station, where Olivia was waiting to meet her. She recognized her the instant she stepped from the train by her flame-red hair and was pleasantly surprised. The girl was neatly dressed in a navy two-piece costume and a white blouse. As she placed her carpet bag on the platform she glanced about nervously.

'Patty?' Olivia asked, as she hurried towards her.

The girl's face relaxed into a smile. 'Yes, and you must be Lawrence's sister, Olivia. He told me you would be here to meet me. It's very good of you. How do you do?'

'I'm very well, thank you, and very pleased to meet you.' The two girls shook hands and took to each other immediately. Patty had been very nervous about meeting Lawrence's family but if they were all as pleasant as Olivia she was sure they would get on famously.

'How is Lawrence?' Patty asked, as they left the

402

station together.

Olivia sighed. 'Well, his ankle is coming along nicely, although he still can't be on it for too long. He was very upset that he couldn't come to meet you himself, but I told him you'd understand. He's still having awful nightmares, but I suppose he wouldn't thank me for telling you that,' she admitted wryly.

'It's to be expected.' Patty's face clouded for an instant. 'The things the men saw – well, all of us saw, actually – were enough to give anyone night- mares. I don't think anyone will walk away from this war unscathed.'

'I can understand that just from what we read in the newspapers,' Olivia agreed. Then, hoping to lighten the atmosphere, she added, 'I'm so envious of you, though. Did Lawrence tell you I'm going to be a VAD?'

'Oh, yes, but I shouldn't go building up any romantic notions about the job.' Patty grinned. 'This is the first time Lawrence will have seen me without my tin hat and overcoat. The conditions were so appalling out there that we couldn't wash ourselves, let alone wash our uniforms.'

They chattered away like old friends until at last they reached the house. At first sight of it, Patty hesitated. It was very grand and suddenly she was nervous. She and Lawrence had known each other only a short time before he was transferred. What if she wasn't as he remembered her? What if the spark was no longer there between them?

As she stood there indecisively, Olivia took her elbow and marched her up the rest of the drive. 'Come on,' she urged. 'Lawrence is longing to see

403

you. Best not keep him waiting, eh? I bet you'll have loads to tell each other.'

Once they were inside Patty's eyes strayed around the enormous hall and her nervousness increased. Out in the field hospital, Lawrence had been just another wounded soldier, as filthy as the rest who were brought in. She had never dreamed he might live in a house like this.

'Put your bag on that chair there,' Olivia told her. 'In a minute I'll take it up to your room and show you where you'll be sleeping. First, though, we'd better put Lawrence out of his misery. He's in the drawing room.'

Patty smoothed her hair in a lovely gilt mirror and ran her hands down her skirt. Then she straightened her back and followed Olivia.

The room she was shown into was beautiful. Its large windows were covered with heavy velvet drapes, the furniture was clearly expensive. But she didn't have time to admire it for long because someone rose from a chair and hobbled towards her leaning heavily on a walking stick.

It was Lawrence, and she almost gasped at the change in him. He was dressed in a smart dark grey suit, under which he wore a crisp white shirt and a striped tie. With his hair neatly brushed, he barely resembled the young man she had tended in the hospital.

'Patty ... I can't tell you how much I've been looking forward to seeing you.' In his turn he was startled by the change in her. She looked quite different without her tin hat, oversized coat and ugly boots, and was even prettier than he had remembered. Her glorious red hair tumbled about her shoulders and her green eyes were sparkling as he took her hand and squeezed it. 'You look beautiful,' he muttered.

Suddenly feeling in the way, Olivia went off to the kitchen to make a tray of tea.

'You don't look so bad yourself,' Patty responded, once they were on their own. Suddenly all the nervousness was gone and they were at ease with each other again. By the time Olivia returned with the tea tray they were chattering away so much that they hardly noticed she was there so she placed it on a small table and discreetly left the room again.

'It's a case of two's company, three's a crowd.' She grinned at Mrs Pegs when she got back to the kitchen.

'What's she like?' the older woman asked.

'Really nice,' Olivia answered, pouring herself a glass of milk. 'And it's more than obvious that she and Lawrence are really taken with each other. I just hope Mother doesn't try to spoil it. I haven't seen Lawrence so happy since he came home.'

'Well, we'll have to wait and see,' Mrs Pegs said stoically. Unfortunately she couldn't see Camilla thinking anyone was good enough for one of her children unless she had handpicked them, but time would tell.

Camilla was out at one of her ladies' meetings but the minute she returned home she barged into the drawing room without taking off her coat to meet their visitor.

'How do you do? I'm Lawrence's mother,' she introduced herself.

Suddenly all fingers and thumbs, Patty rose so hastily that she almost overbalanced. 'It's very nice to meet you, I'm Patty,' she answered politely, feeling as if she should curtsy or something. Camilla was eyeing her critically from head to foot and she felt colour flame into her cheeks.

She looked towards her son then and said pointedly, 'I hope you aren't overdoing it, dear. You know the doctor said you must rest. Perhaps it's time you went to your room for a little lie-down. I'll be quite happy to entertain your guest for you.'

Give her the once-over more like, Lawrence thought ruefully, but he kept a smile on his face as he answered, 'I'm feeling perfectly fine, thank you, Mother. And Patty is a nurse in case you'd forgotten. I'm sure she wouldn't let me overdo it.'

Camilla's lips pursed into a thin line but she inclined her head before answering, 'Of course. Then if you have everything you need I'll go and have a word with Mrs Pegs about dinner.' She swept from the room and Patty let out a long breath.

'Oh dear. I don't think she's taken to me,' she told him worriedly.

'Don't let Mother concern you. She's like that with everyone,' Lawrence reassured her, and in no time at all they were chattering away nineteen to the dozen again.

Later that afternoon, Olivia showed Patty to her room so that she could freshen up and change for dinner.

'I'm not sure I have anything grand enough to

wear,' Patty fretted, as she opened her carpet bag and began to hang the few clothes she had brought in the wardrobe.

Olivia giggled. 'That skirt and blouse you just hung up will be fine. We don't usually make a fuss. Mother's just putting on airs and graces to impress you. Take no notice and be yourself. You'll get on fine with my father. He's much more down to earth.'

Olivia was proved right, and over dinner that evening Patty and Max got on well. Patty wasn't used to being waited on: she found it quite uncomfortable to have her food served, as she remarked to Lawrence later on.

'Mum always cooks for us and when I'm at home I give her a hand,' she told him. 'I don't think the whole of our house put together would be as big as half of the downstairs of this place alone. And Mum will never believe it when I tell her you have servants and even a cook!'

Lawrence wouldn't have cared if Patty had come from a slum. He had never been a snob.

The following morning at breakfast Camilla's inquisition began. Lawrence had been expecting it.

'So where in Whitby do you live, dear?'

'Down by the harbour in a fisherman's cottage. It's been in the family for years and my grandfather was a fisherman as is my father.'

'*A fisherman!*' Camilla tried not to look shocked. 'Then the war must have affected his livelihood badly?'

'It has,' Patty admitted. 'But my father can turn his hand to most things so we're getting by till he can go fishing again. He was a little too old to enlist or I'm sure he would have done so, especially now that conscription for married men has come in. At the moment he's working as a mechanic at a nearby military base. I dare say car engines are not so very different from boat engines.'

Camilla shuddered as she thought of all that grease and oil. 'And how many of you are there in the family?'

Patty smiled. She was proud of them all and they were very close. 'There's my mum and dad and then I have two sisters and two brothers, but I'm the eldest.'

'I see,' Camilla said primly. This didn't sound at all the sort of family she had had in mind for her son to marry into. But he was still very young and as yet he hadn't admitted to any romantic involvement with the girl. Perhaps he and Patty were just friends in which case she was worrying unnecessarily. 'What do you intend to do once the war is over?' she asked then.

'Continue with my nursing,' Patty answered, without hesitation. 'The war has changed everything for women. It's accepted that they work. In fact, they've had no choice. Someone has to do the jobs for the men while they're away fighting.'

Camilla opened her mouth to ask another question but Max stepped in. 'Camilla, Patty's breakfast will be stone cold at this rate.'

Camilla glared at him but fell silent and for the rest of the meal too, left the girl alone.

'I don't think your mother considers I'm good enough for you,' she told Lawrence later, as they sat in the library together.

He grinned and took her hand, turned it over and gently stroked the palm. 'I don't give a damn what my mother thinks,' he told her truthfully. 'From the moment I clapped eyes on you I knew that you were the girl for me. We're both still very young but do you think you could ever feel anything for me, Patty?'

She stared at him intently for a moment, then answered shyly, 'I already do. I've tended hundreds of wounded men since I was shipped abroad, but when you woke up and looked at me I was lost. I ... I love you, Lawrence, with all my heart.'

'So does this mean you'll be my girl ... for always?'

When she nodded his face lit in a smile. 'Then from this moment on it's official. When this damn war is over I'm going to marry you, if you'll have me, that is?'

'I'll have you.' It wasn't the most romantic proposal in the world but it was the only one Patty ever wanted to hear, and as their lips tentatively touched for the first time she knew their future was sealed.

Chapter Thirty-six

On 1 July the men approached the front under cover of darkness. They were heavily laden with their packs but marched along at a smart pace. Some were trying to keep up the spirits of their comrades by singing popular music-hall tunes and occasionally a mouth-organ could be heard. Ahead the flames from falling British shells stabbed at the darkness. Despatch riders on motorcycles scooted around the market squares of small French towns, and as officers passed in motor cars French sentries raised their arms in salute. *'Bonne chance, mes camarades,'* some shouted, and the British men touched their caps to them.

The long-prepared British and French offensive on the Western Front was about to begin astride the River Somme in Picardy. It would be the biggest British army yet sent into battle. There were twenty-six divisions on a fifteen-mile front. The French had hoped to send forty divisions but, after the savage five-month German attack on Verdun, had produced only eighteen.

The following morning at seven thirty the artillery barrage was lifted and the men went over the top of the trenches in waves. Each carried seventy pounds of equipment, which slowed his pace to little more than a crawl. All were laden with gas helmets, entrenching tools, wire-cutters, two hundred and twenty rounds of ammunition, sandbags, groundsheet, Mills bombs, haversack, water bottles and a field dressing, with the order from Field Marshal Haig to gain at least four thousand yards of enemy territory on the first day. But as they crept across no man's land thousands were cut down in the first five minutes by the relentless enemy fire.

Harvey Farthing watched the carnage from a distance as he tried to calm the horses in a field where yet more makeshift shelters had been erected for them. As he saw the men slain, tears rolled from his eyes. They were dropping like flies and there wasn't a damn thing anyone could do to help them. The horses were restless at the terrifyingly close and ceaseless roar of machine-gun fire, snorting and tossing their heads as he tried to calm them. The army vet was present. Harvey had asked him to come and look at one of the horse's legs. It had caught it some days before on barbed wire and now it was swollen and angry-looking and the poor creature was unable to put any weight on it.

The vet shook his head solemnly as he examined the quivering animal. 'Not much to be done for him, I'm afraid,' he told Harvey. 'Were we at home, with the right medication, I might be able to help him but out here it's useless. He'll certainly be unfit for battle any more so it would be kinder to put him out of his misery.' He took a revolver from his bag and as he loaded it with bullets, Harvey screwed his eyes shut and stroked the frightened creature's muddy mane. 'It's all right, boy,' he soothed, feeling helpless. He stepped away then, unable to look, and when he next opened his eyes, the horse was lying at his feet. It jerked just once convulsively, then was still. Suddenly Harvey was filled with rage. All this slaughter of men and beasts! When would it end?

Seeing the young man's deep distress, the vet patted his shoulder. He, too, was weary of having to kill magnificent animals that had done no one any harm, but out here in this living Hell he had no choice. 'Why don't you take a break?' he sug-

411

gested. 'You're here day and night to my knowledge. Go and get some rest. The animals will be all right for a while now.' Like everyone else, he knew how devoted Harvey was to the horses and admired him for his kindness.

'But what if some are brought back injured? No. I'll stay a while longer.'

The veterinary surgeon moved on. He had gone through veterinary school hoping to help animals but all he seemed able to do now was put them out of their misery. There were not enough medical supplies for the men, let alone the horses, and he felt as if he were fighting a losing battle.

Once alone again Harvey strained his eyes across no man's land, fighting the urge to scream for the men to retreat. They were dropping like ninepins. Then he saw a horse go down with an officer on its back. He had no idea if it was the rider or the horse that had been injured but before he could stop himself he was off, sprinting across the mud so quickly that his feet had barely time to sink into it. When he reached the animal he saw that there was a gaping hole in the side of the rider's head but the horse was still alive, although one of its legs was twisted at an unnatural angle.

He stood up and shook his fists in the direction of the Germans as his spectacles flew off his nose and landed in the mud. 'You *lousy* murdering bastards!' he screamed and then suddenly he jerked and looking down was shocked to see a hole had appeared in his tunic top. Blood seeped from it but as he sank to the ground he felt no pain, just an overwhelming sense of peace. At last he could rest.

By nightfall that day many battalions numbered scarcely a hundred men, and only parts of the barbed-wire obstacles had been destroyed. Because of the huge number of dead and wounded on both sides, the attack was suspended at midday until four o'clock to allow the stretcher-bearers to work in no man's land. The following morning saw another informal truce, but it was three more days before all the wounded had been collected and taken to the field hospitals. The British had sixty thousand casualties, 60 per cent of whom were officers, but the French had fared slightly better, with only light casualties reported; they had taken at least four thousand German prisoners. What was to become known as the Battle of the Somme had begun.

Two days later, as Camilla was arranging some roses from the garden in a vase in the hall, there was a tap at the door. She opened it to find the telegram boy outside holding an envelope out to her.

She took it from him without a word, wondering which of her sons had been injured now. She wished Max was there but he was at one of his factories, and Olivia was nursing the first patients to arrive at Weddington Hall Hospital. She slit open the envelope and, as her eyes slid down the page, the colour drained from her face.

REGRET INFORM YOU PRIVATE HARVEY JAMES FARTHING KILLED IN ACTION ON 1 JULY PICARDY STOP

The rest of the words swam out of focus as the telegram fluttered from her hand and she dropped into the nearest chair.

Some time later Mrs Pegs found her there, staring blankly into space. 'Dilly, fetch that bottle o' smellin' salts out o' the dresser drawer,' she shouted. Within seconds Dilly joined her, and once they had wafted it under Camilla's nose they helped her into the drawing room.

Mrs Pegs had found the telegram and read it. 'Could you go an' fetch Mr Farthing, Dilly? Mr Lawrence should be able to tell you where he is. Meantime I'll get him to sit with his mother. They might be a comfort to each other.'

Dilly nodded. She had never been fond of Camilla, although she could not fault her for how she had brought up Olivia, but now she saw her as a mother and felt a deep sympathy for her.

Lawrence was shocked to his core when he learned what had happened but managed to tell Dilly that his father should be at one of his mill factories in Attleborough.

She made the journey in record time, running all the way – she was sure that her lungs would burst. She found him easily, but deciding it wasn't her place to tell him what had happened, she said simply that he was needed urgently.

Niamh had been off work again that day, claiming she had a headache, and now Dilly decided to call into the cottage on her way back to the Farthings'. It would take her a little out of her way but she was worried about her daughter.

She found the girl crying pitifully, still in her night-

414

clothes, curled up in the fireside chair. Niamh had not expected her and started when her mother appeared in the doorway.

'Niamh, whatever is the matter?' Dilly asked. 'Surely your headache isn't that bad.'

Niamh jumped out of the chair crossing her arms tightly beneath her breasts – and it was then that her mother noticed the slight swell of her belly. She had to hold tightly to the back of a chair as a realization hit her.

'Niamh... you – you're having a baby!' She suddenly understood why the girl had been so out of sorts now. 'B-but how? Nipper has been away for months. It can't be his.' None of it made sense. Niamh adored Nipper and would never look kindly on anyone else. A second realization struck Dilly between the eyes. Someone had taken advantage of her – raped her! There could be no other explanation.

'Who *did* this to you?' she hissed, as a red mist appeared in front of her eyes. She would make sure they paid for bringing down her girl if it was the very last thing she did.

Niamh only sobbed harder. Crossing to her now, Dilly took her arms and shook her. 'Did you lie willingly with whoever is responsible for this?'

'N-no – of course not!'

'Then tell me who did it to you because I tell you now, my girl, I'll give you no peace until you do!'

Still Niamh's head wagged from side to side, and Dilly's anger grew as she shook her until her teeth rattled. Suddenly everything was falling into place, like the pieces of a jigsaw. Niamh coming home from work with a bruise on her face and going straight to bed; it must have been at least a couple of months ago. The night before Samuel Farthing had gone away. He had missed the special meal Mrs Pegs had cooked for him and come home roaring drunk with scratches on his face. He'd had his eye on Niamh for a long time.

'It was Samuel Farthing, wasn't it?' She released the girl so suddenly that Niamh almost lost her balance.

Niamh nodded miserably. The cat was well and truly out of the bag.

Dilly began to pace the room. What a day this was turning out to be – but what were they going to do?

'We shall have to write to Nipper and tell him you'll be married on his next leave,' she said suddenly, but Niamh shook her head adamantly.

'No, we won't. Why would he want me now, when I'm soiled goods and carrying someone else's child? It would stand between us the whole of our married life and I love him too much to do that to him.'

'But if he truly loves you he would accept that it wasn't your fault.'

Again Niamh shook her head. 'No. Whatever happens to me, I won't do that to him.'

'Then what *do* you intend to do?' Dilly rasped. 'You know what people round here are like. Your name will be mud.'

'I – I could go away and have it. Father Brannigan might know of somewhere. There are convents where girls in my position can go to have their babies.'

'Huh! And terrible places they are,' Dilly said.

416

'Half of the girls that go in those places never come out so you can forget that idea.' More than anything she longed to storm to the Farthings' and tell them what their son had done, but how could she today of all days, when they had just been told that one of their sons had been taken from them?

'I shall have to think about this,' she told Niamh. 'But now I must get back to work. Stay here meantime, and we'll talk about it more this evening.'

Niamh could only nod as her mother swept out of the room.

When she got back to the Farthings' house the doctor was arriving. Mrs Pegs had asked Mr Jackson to fetch him, and he went straight into the drawing room to see what he could do for the grieving parents. Dilly joined Mrs Pegs in the kitchen.

'It's terrible,' the older woman said, as she blew her nose noisily on a large white handkerchief. Then turning to little Gwen, she said, 'Make us a nice brew, would yer, pet? This has right knocked me for six.'

Gwen hurried away to do as she was told as Mrs Pegs shook her head. 'He were a nice lad, were Mr Harvey, not like that brother o' his, Samuel. Still, they always reckon the good Lord takes the best 'uns first.'

Dilly couldn't have agreed with her more and wished that Fergal was there. He would have known what to do about Niamh's predicament.

Camilla stayed in bed the next day, and the day after, and Max was concerned about her.

'It's her way o' dealin' with it,' Mrs Pegs told him, when he expressed his anxiety to her in the kitchen early one morning over breakfast. He would never have dreamed of doing that if his wife had been up and about. She considered it wasn't right to mix socially with the servants but he enjoyed the informality. It was cosy in the kitchen with Mrs Pegs and Gwen.

Dilly was working in the shop that day and he was looking forward to seeing her, but when he arrived later that evening, as she was tidying up, he didn't get the welcome he normally received and thought perhaps it was because of what had happened to Harvey.

'Are you all right, Dilly?' he asked, removing his hat.

Straightening, she clenched her hands at her waist, a posture he had noticed she favoured when something was troubling her. 'I – I'm afraid not, sir.'

She cleared her throat, wondering how best to begin, but then, barely able to control her fury, she decided just to get it over and done with. 'The thing is ... I know the timing is awful, not that there could *ever* be a good time for what I'm about to tell you ... and I do appreciate that you must be feeling so sad after hearing about young Mr Harvey... but I'm afraid I have more bad news for you.'

He sank down on one of the machinists' chairs. 'Let's have it, then,' he said quietly wondering what the hell was coming next. She never normally called him 'sir' when they were alone together now, and her eyes were flashing with suppressed rage.

Dilly avoided his eyes. 'I've just discovered that my daughter, Niamh, is going to have a baby.'

'*What?*' He could hardly believe his ears. Niamh had always seemed such a good, pleasant girl. He couldn't imagine her being loose with her favours. 'And is the person responsible prepared to stand by her and marry her?'

'It isn't as simple as that. You see, she was raped and doesn't know what to do. She's in a terrible state.'

'*Raped!*' Max was appalled. 'But didn't you tell me she had a young man?'

Dilly nodded. 'Yes, I did, but Ben, or Nipper as he's known, has been away for months. This happened back in March... The night before Samuel left to join his unit.'

He stared at her uncomprehendingly, trying to work out what relevance Samuel could have to this conversation and then as comprehension dawned he gasped. 'You're not trying to tell me that it was *my son* who raped her, are you?'

When Dilly nodded and began to pace up and down he covered his face with his hands. Had anyone else told him such a thing he would have defended Samuel to his last breath, but he knew that Dilly would never lie about such a terrible thing.

'He was waiting for her in the Pingles Fields as she made her way home from work that evening,' she muttered, as tears flooded her eyes, 'and when they got to the tunnel that leads into the park he—' Unable to go on she started to cry in earnest then. 'She did try to stop him – in fact

419

she scratched his face – but he hit her and threw her down and–'

'I think I get the picture,' Max interrupted as fury coursed through him. He had known that Samuel was going off the rails for some time before he had been forced to join the army, but he would never have believed him capable of such an act, the worst possible thing that a man could do to a woman. He was ashamed.

'Is her young man prepared to stand by her?' he asked after a time, in a clipped voice.

Dilly shivered. 'She's too ashamed to tell him,' she whispered. 'In fact, I don't think she's even replying to his letters and I don't know what to do. Niamh is adamant that she won't saddle Nipper with someone else's child, but if she doesn't, what will become of her? You know how unmarried young girls are ostracized in these parts.'

Max's lips set in a grim line. 'Then the person who is responsible for this will have to make an honest woman of her, won't he?'

'Niamh ... marry *Samuel!*' she gasped. 'But Mrs Farthing would never allow it. I'm her servant. And, anyway I don't think Niamh would want to.' Neither would she wish to see her daughter joined to him, she could have added. Just the thought made her want to retch.

'I don't see what other choice she has,' he said flatly. 'And I shall make sure he shoulders his responsibilities. I shall also ensure that Niamh and the child get the best of care. As for Camilla, you will leave her to me. This will be our grandchild, after all.'

That was the last thing Dilly had expected and

she wasn't at all sure how her daughter would react to the idea.

As Max saw the despair in her eyes he had to stifle the urge to take her in his arms there and then, but of course he was far too much of a gentleman to do that. Instead he told her, 'Go home and talk to Niamh. I'll deal with Camilla. I can contact Samuel's unit and speak to the officer in charge and hopefully he'll give him a few days' compassionate leave. I'll tell him we have a family crisis. I know the officer in question so it shouldn't be too hard to arrange.'

Her shoulders sagged and, unable to stop himself, he reached out to squeeze her hand. 'It won't be so bad,' he said. 'And, Dilly ... remember that our families have already been linked for many years.'

It was the first time he had openly referred to Olivia's adoption and now Dilly's tears flowed faster. If she had not been forced to give up her daughter on that far-away night none of this would have happened. She blamed herself.

'It'll be all right. I promise.' With that he left the shop as Dilly's chin dropped to her chest and sobs racked her body. Part of her wanted to blame Max – Samuel was his son – but she couldn't. He had always tried to steer his children in the right direction and maintain discipline, but his wife had always overridden him. This was the result.

Chapter Thirty-seven

It was a lovely balmy evening in Enniskerry and, with the meal out of the way and all the work done, Maeve had carried her chair into the yard and was knitting socks for the troops. Wool was becoming harder to get so she'd unravelled the menfolk's old jumpers to reuse the yarn. It made her feel she was doing her little bit towards the war. Patrick and Bridie, who was now a plump toddler, were chasing the chickens around the yard and Maeve sighed with contentment. If only Nipper was home everything would be perfect. She had received a letter from him the day before and in it he had sounded concerned because Niamh had stopped writing to him. She had no doubt it was down to the post. Niamh loved him, Maeve was sure of that, but the mail delivery service was haphazard nowadays. He'd probably get a batch of letters from her all at once.

Suddenly, above the noise of the cattle and the children's giggling, she heard a horse's hoofs. Glancing up, she saw a pony and trap with a smartly dressed woman in it bowling down the dusty drive towards her. The woman reined in the horse just outside the gates leading into the yard, tethered him then opened the gates and came towards her. She was a fine-looking woman, Maeve noted, impeccably dressed in an outfit that had probably cost more than the farm earned in a month. Her two-piece costume was in a deep purple, heavily edged with black braid, as was her feathered hat. Her shoes were fashioned from soft black leather and her hands were encased in black kid gloves that made Maeve almost drool with envy.

'Hello, lass, can I help you?' Maeve asked. The woman had probably lost her way and stopped to ask for directions. 'Got lost, did you?'

'No. I've come to see you, if you can spare me a few moments of your time.'

Patrick and Bridie had come to stare at the stranger curiously but their grandmother shooed them away before saying, 'Sure I can. Why don't you come in and I'll make us a brew? Or perhaps you'd prefer a sup o' poteen?'

'Oh, no, tea would be lovely. Thank you very much,' the woman said hastily, as Maeve ushered her into the kitchen. She was glad that everywhere was gleaming – this woman clearly had class.

'Sit yourself down while I put the kettle on,' Maeve said, more curious by the minute. Why would a well-spoken English lady be seeking her out?

The woman perched awkwardly on the very edge of a hard-backed chair as Maeve bustled about, preparing cups and spooning tea into the pot. Meanwhile the woman was glancing about the room and said, 'You have a lovely home, Mrs Carey.' Maeve's chest swelled with pride, although she wondered how the lass knew her name. It was all getting more mysterious by the minute and she was intrigued to know what the woman might want with her.

At last she joined the guest at the kitchen table and as she strained the tea into her best china cups, the woman cleared her throat nervously. 'You must be wondering who I am and why I'm here.'

'I am, to be sure,' Maeve answered, as she placed the tea in front of her.

'I suppose I should introduce myself and start at the beginning. My name is Elizabeth McFarren.' The woman then launched into the story she had once told Father Doherty some time ago.

As the tale unfolded Maeve's eyes stretched wide. 'So was it *you* who left all that money here for Nipper?'

Elizabeth sighed. 'Well, it wasn't me personally but I sent it,' she admitted. Her violet eyes were full of tears now as she went on, 'I know I've behaved abominably, and I doubt you have any time for me, but do try to understand the position I found myself in. I have never forgiven myself for abandoning Benjamin, and the guilt I have felt over the years is indescribable. It was almost like a physical pain at times. When my husband died I saw a way to make sure that he was at least financially stable but since then...' She took a great gulp of air as a solitary tear slid down her pale cheek... I have received a telegram saying that my other son, Lionel, has been killed in battle.'

Maeve's heart went out to the woman and she felt her pain as she slid a hand across the table to her. As a mother herself, she could only imagine how the poor woman must have suffered over the years for that one ghastly mistake.

'I'm sorry to hear that, so I am,' Maeve said,

with true sympathy, 'but I don't quite understand what has brought you here now.'

'My husband and my son are dead now. I cannot hurt them any more by revealing what I did all those years ago so I was hoping .. that Benjamin might agree to meet me. Do you think he would?'

Maeve frowned. 'I have no idea,' she said eventually. 'And the worst of it is that he isn't here. He joined the navy you see and he's at sea.'

The woman paled even further. Her only living child was now also at risk. What would she do if anything were to happen to him before she had had time to meet him and apologize? She wanted desperately to explain why she had abandoned him, as she had, and try to make things up to him; but perhaps she had left it too late.

'I suppose I could tell him about you and ask him if he would wish to meet you when I next write to him,' Maeve suggested. She knew that at one time all Nipper had wanted was to know who his real parents had been, but he was almost a man now and had long since given up hope of finding them. This would come as a shock to him.

'You would do that for me?' Elizabeth said incredulously. 'Knowing how I have let him down? You have been much more of a mother to him than I ever have.'

'It was my pleasure. He's turned into a fine young man you can be proud of. And as for letting him down... Well, life deals us all a bad hand from time to time and we all make mistakes, so we do. You've paid dearly for yours over the years. But, of course, I can't guarantee anything,' she added hastily.

'Thank you. I would be most grateful if you would do as you suggested, and then perhaps you would let me know what he says. Whatever he decides, I have named him as the sole beneficiary in my will so at least I will have peace of mind in knowing that he will be provided for when anything happens to me.'

'I'll do what I can, I promise,' Maeve told her. She handed Elizabeth a piece of paper and a pencil. 'You write your address down for me and I'll be in touch as soon as I've heard from him.'

A few moments later, glancing at the address Elizabeth had scribbled down, she saw that the woman lived in a wealthy part of Dublin.

Elizabeth was rising from her seat now. The meeting had gone far better than she had dared hope although she was bitterly disappointed to find that her son wasn't there. Still, all was not lost and, after so many years, she supposed having to wait a little longer to see him wouldn't hurt her. 'I should be going,' she said. 'I've taken up quite enough of your time already, but thank you for listening to me and being so understanding. I half thought you might send me away with a flea in my ear. After all, you have far more of a claim on Benjamin than I have, with everything you have done for him. I thank you for that too.'

Maeve shook the hand the woman extended, noting how soft her skin was. Nothing like hers, which was prematurely aged from all the scrubbing and cleaning she did. But then, she supposed it wouldn't do if everyone was the same, and the woman seemed genuine.

Maeve saw her out, then she stood staring

thoughtfully from the kitchen window, wondering how Nipper would feel about the development. Only time would tell, but wouldn't she have something to tell the men when they came in from the fields!

Chapter Thirty-eight

That evening Niamh was waiting in the chair for her mother when she got home from the shop and Dilly saw at a glance that she had been crying again.

'I've spoken to Max Farthing,' she told the girl and saw the fear flame in her eyes.

'Did he believe what you told him?'

'Of course he did. Max ... Mr Farthing knows I wouldn't lie about such a thing,' Dilly responded. Her head was thumping and she was longing to go to bed and lose herself in sleep. Everything was such a mess.

'Has he made any suggestion?' Niamh asked.

'He certainly has, but I'm not sure how you will feel about it.' Dilly pressed a hand to her aching brow. 'He thinks Samuel should marry you.'

'*Marry me!*' Niamh's lip curled with contempt. 'Why, I wouldn't marry him if he was the last man on earth!'

'Well, if you won't marry him and you won't marry Nipper, what *do* you intend to do?' Dilly snapped. 'I would *never* turn you from my door but I've no need to tell you that if you go ahead

427

and have this wean without a ring on your finger you'll be known as a scarlet woman. You'll never be able to hold your head high again, and your child will be branded a bastard. Is that really what you want for him or her?' Then, as tears rolled unchecked down her daughter's cheeks, she softened. 'I know none of this is your fault, lass, and I'm heart-sore for you, but I don't see any other way out of it. But you must do as you think best. Are you quite sure you don't want to tell Nipper? I'm sure he'd understand, loving you as he does.'

Niamh shook her head determinedly. 'No, I could never saddle him with another man's child. I would rather die.'

'Then we'd best let Mr Farthing get in touch with Samuel and see what he intends to do about the mess he's created,' Dilly said quietly and for now the subject was closed.

She went to bed thinking that things couldn't possibly get any worse.

A hammering on the front door fetched Dilly from her bed early the following morning. She had thrown a shawl over her nightgown but, after struggling with the bolts on the door, which were stiff from lack of use, it slid from her shoulders as she opened it. The telegram boy was standing outside.

'Mrs Carey?'

When she nodded numbly he pressed a brown envelope into her hand. As he cycled away, she stared down at it in the early-morning mist. Presently she closed the door, made her way to the kitchen, sat down heavily and forced herself to

428

open it.

Some time later Niamh came down the stairs to find Dilly staring absently into the fire with the telegram still clutched in her hand. She was deathly pale but, surprisingly, her eyes were dry. She would shed a million tears for Kian in the years ahead but for now her pain went beyond them.

'What is it?' When her mother didn't answer her, Niamh took the telegram and read it, then dissolved into tears.

'Oh, no ... not Kian,' she whispered brokenly, but Dilly continued to stare straight ahead. For now she had retreated into a place where nothing could touch her. Not sure what to do, Niamh ran for Nell, who had always been their first port of call in trouble. Pots of tea were duly mashed, poured and pressed on Dilly. It seemed that Nell thought a strong sweet cup of tea was the answer to all ills. Eventually, she sent for Dr Beasley, who administered a sleeping draught and packed Dilly off to bed with instructions to rest. Every day he was called out to people in Dilly's position, and it was becoming unbearable, with all the young lives snuffed out so needlessly – but that was war. And there was still no end in sight...

Father Brannigan was duly sent for and said a prayer for Kian's soul, assuring his family that he would go straight to Heaven even though he had not received the last rites, for didn't he die admirably fighting for his king and country? He promised that a mass would be said for him but Dilly took no comfort from it. She would not even know where his grave was or have somewhere to visit where she might lay flowers. That was almost as hard to bear as the loss of her son.

It was almost a week later that Max Farthing drew Dilly aside in the kitchen at his home. During the last weeks they had both lost a son to the war, but now they had to deal with the result of his other son's misdemeanour.

'I have spoken to Samuel's commanding officer and told him bluntly what has happened,' he informed her. 'He is going to speak to Samuel, then get back to me, but in the meantime I must know if Niamh is prepared to marry him.'

Dilly nodded miserably.

'Then I shall tell Camilla what has happened,' he said, not relishing it one little bit. Dilly merely shrugged. She felt drained and unable to deal with anything at present, so she would leave it up to him.

Max approached his wife as she sat in bed, breakfasting from a tray.

'Can you truly believe what that little whore is saying?' she screeched. 'Why, the bastard she's carrying could be anyone's! Yet you would consider saddling our son with the likes of her for life!'

'The *bastard*, as you refer to it,' Max told her, with icy calm, 'will be born to the flesh-and-blood sister of the baby we adopted all those years ago, in case you had forgotten. And it will be our first grandchild. Could you really turn it away?'

Camilla opened and shut her mouth, then said, through clenched teeth, 'Keep your voice down. What if Olivia were to hear us?'

'Olivia left for the hospital some time ago.'

'B-but what would we tell everyone?' she said in panic.

Max sighed. 'There you go again, worrying about what people will think. What do we care? There's a war on and people have more pressing things on their minds than wondering why our son should marry so suddenly. Many young men are marrying their sweethearts sooner than they had planned in case they don't come back.'

Camilla still wasn't happy about it but she could see the wisdom in what he said. 'So has Samuel agreed to marry the girl?'

'The *girl* has a name. It's Niamh, and I don't know what he's agreed to yet. His officer will speak to me today. But if he refuses to do the honourable thing I shall disown him without a penny to his name.'

'You *wouldn't!*' she gasped.

'Oh, yes, I would.' Max stormed from the room, leaving his wife in no doubt that he had meant every single word he had said.

'Your son will be allowed a week's compassionate leave and he will arrive home with you two weeks today,' Samuel's sergeant informed Max on the telephone later that day. 'Will that give you time to arrange the wedding, sir?'

'Yes, it will. Thank you,' Max replied. He hurried away to tell Dilly. It wasn't until much later that he wondered why he hadn't gone to tell his wife first.

Niamh bowed her head when her mother told her the news that evening but she didn't object. She

431

had accepted that this was the only way out of her dilemma. It was time to write to Nipper and tell him she was going to marry someone else. She feared it would break his heart, but rather that than him be forced to bring up another man's child. She began the letter later that evening but found it far harder to write than she had thought it would be. She threw sheet after sheet of tear-stained paper into the fire as she tried to let him down gently.

Finally she took a deep breath and wrote the words that would change the course of her life.

Dear Nipper,

I am writing with some news and I hope you will forgive me when you have read this letter. The thing is I realize now that what we thought we had between us was nothing more than a foolish fancy. Since returning home I have met a young man and I have agreed to marry him. We are to be wed in a couple of weeks' time so please don't contact me again. It will be much better for both of us if we make a clean break now. I pray that you will stay safe and hope that in time you will meet a girl who is worthy of you. I know you will be happy living in the little cottage behind the blacksmith's and I shall remember you fondly. We may even still see each other from time to time when I visit my grandparents but now we shall meet, I hope, as friends.

Niamh

It seemed so short, so abrupt, but how did you write a letter that put paid to two people's hopes and dreams for ever? With a weary sigh, she laid

432

the letter on the mantelpiece. She would post it first thing tomorrow and then it would be done.

In the hospital Olivia was rushing about, emptying bedpans and straightening sheets ready for the ward inspection. The only fully trained nurse in the whole hospital was Sister Carrington, who had come from Burton-on-Trent. There were also two medical officers, Dr Wolfendale and Dr Edward Nason. The rest of the staff consisted of ninety-five VAD nurses from the Nuneaton and Hartshill detachment of the Red Cross. A few were married but the majority were single; the unmarried daughters of local families, like Olivia. When the doors to the hospital had finally opened, fifty-five beds were available for patients but already forty-two had been filled.

Olivia was enjoying her new role. After months of preparation it was good to be tending patients rather than wielding a paintbrush or cleaning, but the work was exhausting. Sometimes when she got home at night all she wanted to do was fall into bed.

Home was not a happy place since news of Harvey's death had reached them, and Olivia couldn't see that the impending wedding would be a happy occasion either. Her father had informed her coldly that Samuel would be marrying Mrs Carey's daughter as soon as possible and Olivia had been shocked but, with the mood in the house as it was, she didn't like to ask questions. She had never seen the two of them together, and from little bits Mrs Carey had dropped, Olivia had thought that Niamh had a young man in Ireland.

It was all very strange but perhaps they had fallen in love secretly, though she was surprised anyone could fall in love with Samuel. And she also thought it disrespectful that they should arrange the wedding so soon after Harvey's death.

Camilla hadn't moved from her bedroom since the loss of her son, and Olivia wondered now whether the wedding would tempt her from her bed. It was to be a very low-key affair, apparently, in the register office, which had shocked Olivia even more. Her mother, who was a frightful snob, had always frowned on such weddings, saying they were not binding in the eyes of God, but she supposed it might have something to do with Niamh being Catholic and Samuel Church of England. There was no time for either of them to conform to the other's faith so perhaps a register office was the speediest way of getting the job done. Whatever the reason, no one seemed to be looking forward to it – but that was hardly surprising. Both families had lost a son very recently and were still grieving.

Moving into the sluice room, she wrinkled her nose as she placed the pans in the enormous sink. Her thoughts raced on. She and Oscar had not written to each other since his last leave but she still thought, with confusion, of the kiss they had shared. They were brother and sister, yet she knew that the feelings she had for him were not those that a sister should harbour for a sibling and the knowledge brought shame. Perhaps she was unnatural. He was due some leave soon and she wondered if he might be home for the wedding. She was looking forward to seeing him with mixed feelings. Half of her couldn't wait and the other half dreaded it. She knew that the meeting would have to come some time and hoped they might be able to put the kiss behind them and carry on as they had before.

'Nurse Farthing, if you have finished in there, could you please roll some more clean bandages?'

Sister Carrington's voice brought Olivia's thoughts sharply back to the present. She washed her hands thoroughly and rushed away to do as she was told. She had rolled so many bandages since the first patients had arrived that she was sure she could do it in her sleep but at least it kept her mind occupied and off Oscar ... for a short time at least.

'So where will the happy couple be living after the wedding?' Olivia asked her father at dinner that evening. Her mother was taking hers in her room, as had become usual.

Max paused as he looked at the lovely girl who had stolen her way into his heart. It had been Camilla who had insisted on the adoption after losing Violet, yet Max had come to love her as his own. He wondered if he could trust her. He decided he could and that she deserved to know the truth. 'I'm looking at houses for them now. There's quite a nice little detached one on Abbey Green, which I will be taking Niamh to see tomorrow, but even if she likes it, I dare say they'll have to stay here until I can finalize everything. At least, Niamh will. Samuel will be returning to the front. But I feel I should tell you, my dear, that this is no love match.'

Olivia remained silent as Max put down his knife and fork and went on, 'Samuel raped Niamh on her way home from work one evening. Apparently he had been pestering her for weeks but she refused him. She has discovered that she is to have a child. Samuel refused to stand by her until I told him in no uncertain terms that I would cut him off without a penny if he didn't.'

'I see.' Olivia tried to take it in. Samuel had always had a cruel streak but she had never dreamed he would sink so low. She felt sorry for Niamh – she couldn't imagine having to marry someone you didn't love. At that her thoughts turned again to Oscar and the familiar guilt flooded through her.

'At least we shall have the baby to look forward to,' she replied, hoping to cheer her father. But the words didn't have the desired effect, if his glum face was anything to go by, and they finished their meal in silence.

In the cottage the mood was no lighter as Dilly sat sewing by the light of a candle. She was determined that Niamh should have a new outfit for her wedding and had managed to get hold of a length of fine royal-blue material. She had sewn the main part of the dress on a machine in the workshop and now she had only the finishing touches to complete. The dress had leg-o'-mutton sleeves, a high neckline, heavily trimmed with lace, and a row of tiny pearl buttons all the way down the front to the dipped waist. The skirt was fairly straight, as was the trend now, although Dilly had allowed room for Niamh's slightly swollen tummy.

She had copied the pattern from one of Camilla Farthing's fashion magazines and, under other circumstances, Niamh would have been thrilled with the dress, but she could scarcely bear even to look at it. Ever since posting her final letter to Nipper she had sunk into a deep depression and had come to loathe the child that was growing inside her. Could she have torn it out of her body she would have done so. She knew she would never be able to love it, which made her feel guilty. It wasn't the child's fault, but she couldn't control how she felt. Samuel was due to arrive home any day and she was dreading that too. Still, the arrangements were in place and the time to change her mind was gone. Somehow she would have to go on with the rest of her life as best she could, with a man she loathed and a child she could never love. It was a daunting prospect.

The following evening, as Dilly prepared to lock up the shop, Max Farthing appeared. After removing his hat, he told her, 'It's time we had a little talk, Dilly. You must know that things cannot go on as they are. Do you have any plans for your future?'

'What do you mean?' she asked, as she picked up a roll of khaki-coloured thread that had fallen to the floor.

'Very soon now your daughter and my son will be married. It will be odd for you to work in my house as a maid once the families are joined. I thought perhaps you might have decided to go to Ireland to your in-laws.'

Dilly clutched at the edge of the nearest machine. He was going to sack her – but then how would she pay her rent? With Kian gone, and Declan, Seamus and Nianth away from home, she would be on her own for the first time in many years.

'No,' she said quietly. 'I have no intention of leaving Nuneaton.'

They both knew why, although neither voiced it. Dilly would never leave Olivia.

'In that case,' he went on, interrupting her troubled thoughts, 'I think it might be best if you no longer worked at the house but came here full time.' She opened her mouth to object but he rushed on: 'Furthermore I'd like to sign the business over to you.'

'*What?*' Dilly thought she must be hearing things. Surely he couldn't be serious.

'You would make a go of it, I know you would,' he told her. 'The government pays good money for the uniforms the shop turns out. Once the war is over it will revert to dresses and you could put your own stamp on the place. You have a flair when it comes to fashion, and to be honest you would be doing me a favour if you'd take it over. It's not easy to keep so many businesses going, with so many men away at war, although of course the women are doing a sterling job in holding the fort, so to speak.'

Dilly had always dreamed of owning a little dress shop but pride reared its ugly head as she told him primly, 'I appreciate the offer but unfortunately I cannot accept it. Can you imagine what people would assume if they knew that you'd given the business to me? They would say I was your bit on the side or something equally awful. It's bad enough as things are, with your son forced to marry my daughter.'

To her amazement, he laughed. 'Oh, Dilly, you're a tonic, you really are. But surely you see why things cannot go on as they are.'

'I can,' she admitted. 'So, now I have a proposition to put to you.'

He was intrigued as he stared back at her.

'I have always dreamed of owning a dress shop so I could buy the business from you,' she said calmly. 'Of course, I don't have the money to buy it outright but I could pay you so much a month out of the profits. I wouldn't need much to live on – in fact, there are three small rooms upstairs that we use for storage where I could live. Then I wouldn't need to pay rent on the cottage. I could make one into a small sitting room and the other two into bedrooms for me and Seamus when he comes home. I'd use the little kitchen at the back here and there's a privy in the back yard. I could live here very comfortably.'

'Let's go up and have a look at the rooms,' he suggested, swallowing his surprise. Dilly had never hinted before that she harboured a dream, but then he supposed that until now a dream was all it could ever have been. She had always been too busy working, seeing to the needs of her family, for her own wishes. They climbed the steep, narrow staircase, their footsteps echoing hollowly on the wooden treads. Max saw that she was right. The rooms were small but he was sure that Dilly could make them comfortable.

'But where would you store all the material if these rooms are lived in?' he asked.

439

Dilly had thought of that too. 'We could use the old fitting rooms for storage until after the war.'

He nodded. 'I dare say you could,' he agreed. Then, holding his hand out: 'It seems you've thought of everything, Dilly. Do we have a bargain?'

'We do.' They smiled at each other as they shook hands and the deal was struck.

Downstairs again, he picked up his hat. 'I shall have my solicitor draw up the contracts immediately and I shall ensure that you get the business at a reasonable price.' He was suddenly reluctant to leave her.

'I shall be happy to pay market value,' she answered, her chin held high. Everything had happened so fast that she barely knew if she was coming or going.

He inclined his head and left and once alone Dilly gazed about in wonder. The shop was going to be hers!

Niamh was shocked when Dilly got home and told her the news.

'Who would ever have thought you'd have your very own business, Mammy? At least something good will have come out of this mess.'

Dilly put her arms around her and fought the overpowering urge to throw some things into a bag and whisk her away to Ireland. Then common sense took over. Niamh would never go there. She wouldn't want to face Nipper. And if Dilly left she wouldn't see Olivia. At least this way she would still be close to both her daughters.

Chapter Thirty-nine

The following day Oscar was at home when Olivia returned from work. It was all she could do to stop herself flinging her arms about him, but something in the cautious way he looked at her held her back.

'You're looking very smart in your uniform,' he said politely, as she unhooked the cape from her shoulders revealing the crisp white apron with a large red cross on the front.

She smiled as she took the pearl hatpin from her nurse's cap and flung it onto a chair. 'So do you,' she answered, equally as politely, feeling as if they were skirting around each other. They had always been so at ease in each other's company but now they were like strangers.

'It's a bit of a rum do about Sam and Mrs Carey's daughter, isn't it?' he said, for want of something to say. 'And our poor Harvey, of course.'

Olivia nodded but before she could speak, he went on, 'Mother has invited the Merrimans for dinner this evening so I expect you ought to get changed. She won't appreciate you turning up at the table dressed like that, smart as it is.'

Olivia was shocked. 'You mean Mother is actually out of bed?'

He nodded. 'She certainly is and she's dressing even as we speak. I suggest you go and do the

441

same. They should be here at any minute.'

Olivia frowned as she went upstairs to her room. Poor Oscar had barely set foot through the door and Mother was pushing Penelope at him already. It was enough to make him turn tail and run, but he wouldn't, of course – Oscar was far too well-mannered for that. He would grin and bear it.

An hour later the Merrimans were there when Olivia appeared. She had brushed her hair until it shone and was wearing a lilac dress with a string of pearls. Oscar glanced at her briefly before offering his arm to Penelope and steering her into the dining room. Throughout the meal he was attentive to Penelope and the girl positively glowed as Olivia seethed with jealousy. She and Oscar hadn't seen each other for months and she had so much to tell him, but she might as well not have been there.

Camilla and Max were in mourning black for Harvey but Camilla looked elegant and sophisticated, and made a special effort to be charming to her guests.

Once the meal was over the men went to the drawing room to enjoy a glass of port and a cigar but Olivia made her excuses and retired to her room in a very bad humour. Oscar's homecoming had been nothing like she had expected it to be and she could only hope that he would spare a little more time for her the next day.

However, the next day, which happened to be Sunday, saw the return of Samuel. Within minutes of his arrival the whole house was in chaos.

He was in a foul temper and confronted his

father immediately. 'You can't *really* expect me to marry the Carey girl, Father? I'll be a laughing stock. Her family are *servants*.'

'Perhaps you should have thought of that before you raped her,' Max said angrily.

'I didn't *rape* her! She was begging for it!'

Max didn't believe a word of it and struggled to contain his rage. At that moment there was nothing he would have liked more than to punch his son's nose.

'That child could be *anybody's*,' Samuel ranted. The wedding was getting a little too close for comfort and every time he thought of it he broke out in a cold sweat.

Camilla, who had left her bedroom to greet him, was clearly upset and wrung her hands.

'Perhaps he's right, Max,' she said, with a note of desperation in her voice.

Her husband merely glared at her. 'The matter isn't up for discussion,' he answered coldly. 'It's about time Samuel learned that there are consequences to his actions.' With that he walked out of the room, not prepared to discuss it for another moment.

A few days before, Max had taken Niamh to view the little house on Abbey Green. She had been politeness itself, but she had been unable to hide how unhappy and terrified she was at the prospect of marrying Samuel. He had felt sorry for her.

Under other circumstances, Niamh would have felt a thrill of excitement at the prospect of owning such a home. It was a small detached house that stood in its own little gardens and there were three good-sized bedrooms. It even had an indoor bath-room, with a pump that could bring the water upstairs from a boiler in the kitchen, and a lavatory. Downstairs there was a fine kitchen, with a deep Belfast sink, a small drawing room and a dining room, yet as she walked from room to room she was thinking of Nipper. He would have received her letter by now, and she felt as if she had betrayed him. Sometimes she tried to imagine how she would feel if it had been Nipper's child she was carrying. She knew she would have loved it and been impatient to hold a part of her man in her arms, but she was dreading the birth – dreading the rest of her life. Even so, she still felt that she was doing the right thing. It wouldn't have been fair to saddle Nipper with someone else's child, especially one that had been conceived in that way. From now on she must try not to think of him and get on with her life as best she could, but it was hard.

As well as buying the house Max would also give them a sum of money to furnish it with the essentials they would need, but even this had not put a smile on Niamh's face. Deep down, he felt he was condemning her to a life of misery, although he had no idea what alternative he could offer.

Eventually the day of the wedding dawned bright and clear. Niamh allowed her mother to help her get ready without protest but Dilly's heart was breaking as she saw the dull look in her daughter's eyes. A wedding should be a joyous occasion, and yet Niamh looked as if she was preparing to go to a funeral. Once she was ready, Dilly stood back to admire her. The fitted royal-blue dress looked stunning, and Dilly had trimmed her hat with the same white braid that was on the dress and attached a little veil to it. Half an hour before the pony and trap that would take them to the register office arrived, a bouquet of cream roses and sweet-smelling freesias was delivered from Max, and Dilly was touched by his kindness.

'It will be all right, you'll see,' she told Niamh, taking her hand tenderly. 'These things have a way of working out.' She didn't believe it for a moment but what else was there to say?

Niamh merely stared at her, unable to raise a smile. Already this was the worst day of her life. Her clothes had been taken to the Farthings' house the evening before, and now she looked around the cottage that had been her only home with regret. Nell appeared then, all done up in her Sunday best, and Dilly was grateful that her friend was trying to put a brave face on things.

'I don't think I've ever seen a lovelier bride,' she said admiringly. 'That outfit, Dilly – you've ex-celled yourself. But come along now. Me hubby's waitin' outside an' I reckon I just saw the pony and trap draw up at the end of the entry as I crossed the yard. Best not keep the groom waiting, eh?'

Dilly saw the girl flinch but, without a word, Niamh lifted her bouquet and walked from the room. Anyone seeing her might have thought she was about to face a firing squad rather than go to her wedding.

When they arrived at the register office they were

in time to see a young man in army uniform emerge with his bride hanging proudly on his arm. Their families were showering them with rose petals and the man was staring down at his new wife with such open adoration that it brought a lump to Niamh's throat. Nipper had looked at her in that way.

The Farthings were waiting for them – Max, Camilla, Olivia, Lawrence and Oscar. Samuel was standing slightly apart, with a thunderous look on his face. He didn't glance at Niamh as Max helped her down from the trap.

'You look lovely, my dear,' he said kindly, but got no response. 'Right... Shall we go in and get this over with?'

They all trooped inside with not a smile between them.

Twenty minutes later they were outside again, and Nell muttered to Dilly, 'Blimey, that were quick – and not very personal, was it? There weren't even a flower in the place to brighten it up apart from the ones Niamh's carryin'.'

Dilly shrugged helplessly. She had given up trying to inject any joy into the day. Now as she glanced towards Samuel all she could feel for him was hatred. Father Brannigan was most upset because Niamh had refused to call into the church on the way back and have her marriage blessed. In his eyes she was committing a sin in marrying outside the Catholic Church but to refuse to have the union blessed was even worse.

'You'll not be married in the eyes of God,' he had warned, but Niamh had said nothing and he had stalked away. He wondered what Fergal would have thought of it, God rest his soul. And to marry when she was still in mourning for her poor brother! He would have expected a little more respect from her ... but, then, the world was changing.

'We'll get back to the house shall we?' Max said then, as they stood about, looking as if the end of the world was nigh. Niamh was with her mother and Samuel was a distance away, his hands thrust into his pockets and a mutinous look on his face.

Mrs Pegs had prepared a meal for them, and Max supposed that the least they could do, after all the trouble she had gone to, was make some show of enjoying it. Camilla had not smiled once throughout the short ceremony but had clung to Olivia protectively as she glared at Dilly. Now she dragged the girl to the nearest carriage. Samuel climbed reluctantly into the second carriage with Niamh, Dilly and Nell, but they noticed he kept as much distance between himself and his new wife as he could, which suited Niamh down to the ground.

Gwen and Mrs Pegs rushed to meet them as soon as they arrived back at the house and proudly showed them into the dining room, where Mrs Pegs had prepared a buffet fit for the King. No one understood how she had managed it, with food so scarce, but they all complimented her and she raised a smile although, deep down, she was seething. What would Camilla say if she were to tell her that Bessie was somewhere out in the world caring for Samuel's child as well? Not a day went by when Mrs Pegs didn't think of Bessie, and now Dilly had confided in her that he had got young

447

Niamh into the same position. It just made her wonder how many more poor innocent girls he had taken down. They couldn't all have become pregnant but they were probably too afraid and ashamed to admit what he had done. The dirty little sod wanted horsewhipping, but she couldn't say that.

Instead she said, 'If you need anythin', just pop along to the kitchen.' And with that she and Gwen hurried away as Samuel crossed to the whisky decanter and poured himself a large measure. His father frowned at him as Camilla headed for the door.

'I have the most awful headache coming on,' she told them, not prepared to be a part of this farce for a moment longer. How could her husband have tied their son to a servant's daughter? She knew she would find it very difficult to forgive him.

Max's mouth set as he watched his wife leave but then, forcing a smile, he told his guests, 'Do please help yourselves, as Mrs Pegs said. She has clearly gone to a lot of trouble.'

Niamh knew that anything she tried to eat would lodge in her throat, and sank down onto one of the spindly-legged chairs.

'Don't mind if I do,' Nell said heartily, and she and her husband loaded their plates with all manner of treats.

Dilly tried to eat too, although everything tasted like sawdust. She wanted to shout and scream at the injustice of it all, but that would only make things worse.

It was then that Oscar told them, 'I hope you

448

don't mind but I've asked Penelope to join us. It is a wedding, after all, and I don't believe she gets out much. I thought she might enjoy it. She should be here any minute.'

Olivia stared at him, aghast. He had virtually ignored her since arriving home and now he was inviting Penelope Merriman when, only months before, he had been trying desperately to avoid her. She was confused and hurt as she watched him leave the room, no doubt to wait for Penelope. She allowed a few moments to elapse, then slipped into the hall to join him. Sure enough she found him sitting on the chair beside the front door.

'Don't you think it's time we had a talk and cleared the air?' she challenged him. 'If this is about what happened between us before you went away I–'

Someone banged the door knocker, which stopped her going any further, especially when Oscar leaped out of his seat and hurried to answer it.

'Penelope,' he said, as he ushered her inside. 'Let me take your coat and then you must join us in the dining room.' He hung it on the coat-stand and waited patiently as she removed the pin from the unbecoming brown felt hat she was wearing, then handed that to him, too. He whisked her away without so much as a glance in Olivia's direction and all she could do was follow them.

Everyone greeted Penelope when she entered the room as Max went around filling everyone's glasses with wine. Then he smiled in Oscar's direction and said, 'May I have your attention, please? I

449

believe Oscar has something he wishes to tell you all.'

Olivia was more confused than ever.

'We wanted you all to know,' Oscar said, 'that I have asked Penelope to be my wife and she has accepted. I have already spoken to her father, who has given us his blessing.'

Olivia felt the room swim and clutched at the back of the nearest chair. This must surely be a joke? Oscar didn't love Penelope, she would have bet her life on it, yet even as the thoughts raced through her mind everyone was stepping forward to offer their congratulations to the newly engaged couple. Just for a second her eyes locked with Oscar's and she saw in them the same helplessness that she knew was shining in hers. Suddenly she knew why he had done it. He loved her as she loved him, but it was hopeless because he was her brother. Without a word she left them with what dignity she could muster and went upstairs. Once she reached the privacy of her room, she threw herself onto the bed and sobbed into the pillow. Why was life so cruel? Niamh had married Samuel, whom she clearly loathed, and Olivia was in love with her own brother, which was a sin.

Downstairs, Dilly was staring worriedly into her glass. She had seen the look that had passed between Oscar and Olivia and, in a blinding flash, the truth had come to her. She had always known they were close but now she knew they loved each other, and not as a sister and brother should. They were not related but, of course, they didn't know that. As she glanced at Max she saw that he was thinking the same thing. What were they going to do? She decided that all she could do was speak to him about it at the earliest opportunity. For now she had the afternoon to get through. They had to face one problem at a time.

As the afternoon lengthened, Dilly knew that she and Nell should take their leave, although she dreaded the thought of leaving her daughter at the Farthings' house. Never one for social get-togethers, Fred Cotteridge had left some time before and, had it not been for abandoning Niamh, Dilly would gladly have gone with him. Samuel had been drinking all afternoon so now he was glassy-eyed and almost cheerful.

'Thank you,' she told Max stiffly, although she didn't know what she was thanking him for. It just seemed the polite thing to say. Nell was more than a little merry, and Dilly hoped she would get her home safely.

'Perhaps you would like to see your mother to the door, Niamh,' Max suggested tactfully.

Niamh followed Nell and Dilly into the hallway where she started to cry. Max had had a room prepared for her and Samuel on the first-floor landing although he was hoping she would be able to move into her own house within the next couple of weeks.

'Now, don't cry,' Dilly urged, putting on a brave face. 'Mr Farthing is a kind man and he'll make sure that Samuel treats you right.'

Niamh sniffed as she clung to her, and Dilly felt as if her heart was breaking. But it was done now for better or worse. Niamh was officially Mrs Samuel Farthing. It would take some getting used to, especially as everything had happened so fast.

'You could come round and help me do some packing tomorrow. Unless Samuel is planning to take you out somewhere, that is,' she told the girl. She had already started to pack in preparation for moving to the rooms above the shop. She should have been dancing with excitement at the prospect of having her very own dress shop, but her heart was heavy with grief for Kian and for her beloved Niamh.

Niamh nodded miserably. Now that they were man and wife, she was dreading the night ahead. Would he treat her as brutally as he had before?

As it happened, she had no need to worry on that score; after Dilly and Nell had departed, Samuel staggered out of the house telling them he was going to see a friend. He was not seen again until the next day, when he turned up midmorning, unshaven and reeking of cheap perfume.

Niamh had spent her wedding night alone and was eternally grateful for it.

Chapter Forty

'That's about it, then,' Dilly said, a week later, as she looked around the empty room. Everything she wanted to take to the shop with her was loaded on the cart that Max had sent with Mr Jackson. All the things that she wouldn't have room for were now in Nell's home.

It was funny to think she would never enter the

cottage again, and a wave of sadness washed over her. Once upon a time, when the children were little and Fergal was well, it had been a happy home that rang with laughter, but that seemed so long ago. So much had happened since then, and now Fergal and Kian were gone for ever.

To add to her worry, she had received another telegram, just days before, informing her that Seamus had been injured in action. At present he was in a hospital in Southampton but Max had arranged for him to be brought to the Wedding-ton Hall Hospital within the next few days where Olivia would keep her eye on him. The telegram had told her that he was suffering from trench foot and shell-shock, and she had felt relieved. Neither of those things could be too serious, surely. And at least he would be close so that she could visit him regularly.

Nell was sniffing quietly into a rather grubby handkerchief and Dilly grinned as she hugged her. 'You daft thing,' she scolded. 'I'm not leaving the country, you know. I shall only be a couple of streets away and you can pop in to see me whenever you want.' But, despite her brave words, she was feeling tearful too. Nell had been her rock and confidante over the years.

'I almost feel as if I'm leaving Fergal and Kian behind too,' she said wistfully, which triggered a memory in Nell. She remembered the letter that Kian had left, with instructions that she should give it to his mother if anything happened to him. Still, today might not be the day for it. She would find it, and take it to the shop when Dilly had had time to settle in. She had more than enough on her plate at present.

'Now, are yer sure you don't want me to come and help yer?' she offered, yet again.

Dilly shook her head. 'No, I shall manage. Mr Jackson will carry the heavy things upstairs for me and then I can decide where I want everything to go.'

Arm in arm, they walked down the entry and Dilly kissed Nell's cheek before climbing up to sit on the front seat of the trap with Mr Jackson. Then they were off, and as she watched her friend leave, Nell knew she would miss her. They had gone through a lot together over the years.

Back in her own kitchen, Nell tapped her lip thoughtfully. Now, where had she put the letter that young Kian had left with her? She hurried across to the sideboard drawer where she kept her best tablecloth, only ever used on high days and holidays, and felt beneath it. Yes, it was exactly where she had left it. As she stared down at it, the strangest feeling of foreboding stole over her, although she had no idea why. She put it down and went about her business, but every now and then her eyes moved back to it and the bad feeling intensified. Finally she trusted her instincts and, holding the envelope above the kettle that was bubbling on the fire, she steamed it open and sat down to read it. Dilly would have shared the contents with her anyway, and wasn't she only checking it to make sure it contained nothing that would upset her?

Dear Mammy,
  If ever you receive this letter I shall be gone. I am not

brave enough to confess what I have done to Father Brannigan so I am telling you now and hope that you will forgive me and pray for my soul for I've done something grievous. On the night that Madge Bunting died I overheard you both talking in the yard and realized she was blackmailing you. I had no idea why, but even so I was filled with rage that she could do that to you when you were working so hard to try and keep the family together. Later that night I followed her with one of her fancy men. She took him under the Cock and Bear bridge and when I saw him leave her shortly afterwards I went down to the canal and confronted her. She was clearly very drunk and she got really angry and started to lash out at me saying I should mind my own business. Then she asked if I wanted a good time and I felt sick and told her so. She came at me then and I hit her back. She fell against the wall of the bridge and cracked her head. It was dark but I could see she was badly hurt from the blood coming out of the side of her head. I panicked then and rolled her into the water. It wasn't until I was almost home that I realized fully what I'd done. I swear I didn't intend to kill her, but saying that, I have no regrets. She was causing you grief and I couldn't allow that. Pray for my soul and try to understand my actions. Murder is a mortal sin, but I would do the same again to protect my family. I wish you a long and happy life, Mammy, and know that I died loving you with all my heart.

Your loving son,
Kian xx

Nell's eyes flooded with tears as she read the young man's confession. So Kian had killed Madge Bunting. But hadn't he done the community a service? The woman had been rotten to the core and no one had missed her. Even so, Nell knew that once Dilly read his letter she would feel honour-bound to report her son's actions to the police. That was the sort of woman Dilly was, and then, instead of having died as a hero fighting for his country, Kian would be branded and remembered as a murderer.

Nell stared at the letter indecisively. Then, with a flick of her wrist, she flung it into the heart of the fire and watched the flames lick around it, turning it into ashes. There. It was ended. Dilly had suffered more than her share of heartache and should be allowed to remember her son with pride. Nell didn't feel even a pang of guilt for what she had done. Kian's secret would go to her grave with her and may the good Lord let him rest in peace.

When Dilly and Mr Jackson arrived at the shop, the kindly man carted all the heavy furniture upstairs for her. It was no easy task as the staircase was steep and narrow and it took some manoeuvring, but at last it was done and there were only the boxes left to bring up.

'I'll pop down and put the kettle on,' Dilly told him. 'I reckon we've earned a break, after all that hard work.'

The gentleman didn't argue, as she tripped off down the stairs, but sat heavily on one of the chairs he had just carried up to rest for a while. He wasn't as young as he used to be, although he didn't regret the time he had spent helping. Dilly was a good lass. Mr Jackson and his wife thought she'd had a raw deal of it, one way or another, what with losing her husband and son, and having to see young Niamh tied to Samuel Farthing. Neither of them had much time for that young man, but they weren't paid to have opinions about their employer's son so they wisely never spoke of it. Samuel would get what was coming to him in due course. His sort usually did.

When Dilly reappeared with a tray, she said apologetically, 'I'm afraid I can't offer you anything to eat, Mr Jackson. I haven't found the box with the food in it yet.'

'Not to worry, lass. The missus will have me dinner on the table when I get back, but make sure as you eat summat, now, won't yer?'

Dilly promised that she would, and after they'd had their tea break they lugged the rest of her things upstairs. Considering she had brought only a fraction of the cottage's contents, Dilly was shocked at how much there was to find a home for. Still, while she was busy she wouldn't have time to fret, so after she had thanked Mr Jackson and waved him off, she set to. By bedtime she had made her bed and put away her clothes in the wardrobe. She had also hung some curtains at the window so at least one of the rooms was beginning to look like home. By then she was so tired that she could barely keep her eyes open. Deciding that the rest could wait until tomorrow, she went downstairs into the kitchen, boiled a kettle and, after having a wash at the sink, she retired for the night.

She had imagined she would be asleep the instant her head hit the pillow, but sleep eluded her. St Mary's Road had been in a fairly quiet area but here she was on the main street in the town and the sound of people leaving the inns and clattering by in the street below made her feel lonely and vulnerable. She tossed and turned until the early hours, then eventually drifted off. There could be no going back now. The shop was in her name, and from now on this would be her home, for better or worse.

In the Farthing household Niamh had been fast asleep too when the bedroom door banged open and Samuel fell into the room. He was clearly very drunk. Her heart skipped a beat as she fumbled with the matches on her bedside table and lit the oil lamp.

'What do you want?' she asked abruptly, as he stood at the end of the bed and leered at her. Up to now he had stayed away or, if he had returned, he had slept on the sofa downstairs, which suited her.

'Now, ish that any way for a wife to talk to her husband when he'sh going off to fight the war in the morning?' he slurred.

Niamh's lip curled. 'I am your wife in name only,' she responded coldly, pulling the blankets up to her chin. 'Go away and leave me alone.'

'I don't think so!' Samuel began to unbutton his jacket. 'You've tricked me into marrying you so the leasht you can do ish show me how grateful you are before I leave.' His jacket was flung into a heap on the carpet and now he was struggling to undo his flies and stay upright.

Revulsion flooded through her as she hopped out of the bed and faced him. 'If you try to come one step closer to me I'll scream the place down,' she warned. 'And what do you think your father will do about that, eh? I certainly don't think he'll ignore it. Let's get something straight here and now. You raped me and the only reason I agreed to marry you is for the sake of the child I am carrying. I don't want it any more than you do but it didn't ask to be born so I have to do the best I can for it. But make no mistake. I *despise* you, and though we will be forced to share the same house, I will *never* be a true wife to you, *ever!* Do you understand me?'

Something about her stance and the cold way she spoke told him she had meant every word she said and he hesitated. He was already in his father's bad books, and if the silly bitch started screaming blue murder now he was likely to carry out his threat and disinherit him. But it wouldn't always be like this. Once they were in their own home, courtesy of his father, there would be no one to hear her scream.

'Suit yourself,' he said and snatched up his jacket, almost toppling over in the process. 'I was only going to shleep with you out of a sense of duty anyway. After all you're not even of my class; you're just a *common* little trollop. But have it your own way, there's plenty more fish in the sea, *wife!*' And with that, he staggered out of the room.

Niamh let out her breath on a great sigh of relief. This time tomorrow he would have returned to his unit and she could hardly wait to see the back of him.

The following week Seamus arrived at the hospital in Weddington and Dilly was impatient to

459

see him. The day in the shop seemed interminable. She glanced at the clock every ten minutes and was finding it difficult to concentrate on her work. Eventually, in the late afternoon, she gave up and went upstairs to get changed for visiting hours.

Already the three bare little rooms she had moved into had been transformed. She had whitewashed the walls and gay curtains now hung at the windows. In the room that she had chosen to be her small parlour a fire now burned merrily in the grate and the hearth was surrounded by a gleaming brass fender. The floorboards had been scrubbed until they were almost white and colourful peg rugs made the place look warm and cosy. Two comfy chairs covered with cushions stood at either side of the fireplace, between a small sofa, and in the corner was the table she had brought from the cottage and two sturdy chairs. Unfortunately there had not been enough room for four but she managed comfortably enough. Some of Niamh's paintings were dotted about the walls and drew admiring remarks from everyone who saw them. The other two rooms had become comfortable bedrooms, with bright patchwork quilts on the beds. Usually Dilly felt a little rush of pride every time she went upstairs but today her thoughts were so full of Seamus that she barely noticed her surroundings.

By the time the women had finished their shifts she could hardly wait to see him. She set off for the hospital with a spring in her step and once there she found her way to Griff Ward where Olivia had told her she would find him. The dear girl had called into the shop yesterday, when she had received their list of admissions due, and Dilly was grateful for her thoughtfulness. But then Olivia had always been a girl any mother could be proud of.

As Dilly waited anxiously in the corridor she was shocked by the transformation. The last time she had visited, Olivia and the rest of the workers had been busily cleaning and painting it. Now the tiles on the floor in the corridor shone, and through the glass in the ward door Dilly could see rows of neatly made beds. The whole place was sunny and comfortable, and the staff who hurried past her looked highly efficient. A number of visitors were waiting to be admitted. Some were clutching bags of apples, others newspapers or flowers, and Dilly was annoyed with herself for not thinking to bring anything. But there was always tomorrow. She could make it up to him then. At last a bell sounded and the double doors were opened by the sister, who told them, 'Two to a bed and please don't overtire the patients.'

A sea of people pushed past Dilly as she stared down the ward, searching for her son.

'Who are you looking for, dear?' the woman enquired kindly.

'Seamus Carey … I'm his mother,' Dilly told her. She saw a flicker of something in the nurse's eye.

'Ah. Perhaps you would like to follow me. Seamus has his own room at the far end of the ward.'

Dilly frowned as the first fluttering of apprehension stirred deep in her stomach. Why would Seamus be given a room to himself?

She followed the sister past the rows of beds, trying not to see the cages that covered legs or the heavily bandaged faces of burned men. The smell of flowers was cloying in the confined space and Dilly felt nauseous. But perhaps she was worrying unnecessarily. Perhaps all the new patients were kept apart for a time.

'Mr Carey is in here.' The sister stopped abruptly in front of a door that had a glass panel in the top half. 'But perhaps I should warn you... He is badly shell-shocked. He may not know you straight away.'

Dilly inclined her head as the woman opened the door and ushered her inside. The room was tiny with space only for a bed, a locker beside it and a chair. Her eyes were immediately drawn to the young man lying there. Or was it a young man? His face was lined and haggard and he looked nothing like the handsome son she remembered.

'Just sit by him, hold his hand and talk to him until he wakes up,' the sister encouraged, seeing the shock on Dilly's face. 'We are keeping him sedated for now so that he can get the rest he needs but he should wake up soon. Ring this bell if you need me.' The sister left the room, closing the door quietly, as Dilly swallowed her tears and stared down at her son. He was so thin that he was almost skeletal, and his once-thick hair stood up in clumps about his head.

'Oh, my poor boy,' she muttered, as she sank down beside him and gently took his hand. She could feel the bones beneath the skin and a tear rolled down her cheek. 'It's all right. You're back in your home town now,' she told him. 'We're going to get you well again, never you fear.' She talked on as the minutes ticked away until suddenly she felt a slight jerk in his hand and his eyes blinked open.

'Seamus, it's Mammy. I'm here, pet,' she told him soothingly, but he didn't seem to hear her. 'We have to get you strong again so you can come home.'

His head turned slowly towards her, but as she smiled at him there was no recognition whatsoever in his eyes. They were blank and staring, and Dilly's pulse began to race. His hands plucked at the counterpane and then, without warning, he let out an animal howl that went right to the heart of her. *'No! No! Go away!'* He began to thrash about as Dilly stared in horror.

The door burst open and suddenly two VADs were holding him down while a doctor in a white coat rushed forward to administer an injection. Within minutes Seamus had calmed down as Dilly looked on helplessly.

'May I have a word, Mrs Carey?' the doctor asked.

Dilly nodded numbly.

'Your son is suffering from a severe case of shell-shock,' he informed her, when Dilly had followed him out into the corridor. 'I'm afraid it will take a lot of nursing and many weeks before he starts to recover, but he will in time, I'm sure.'

As Dilly glanced worriedly towards the bed through the glass in the door she found it hard to believe. She hardly recognized Seamus, and the fact that he hadn't known her had almost broken her heart. Declan was in Ireland, Kian was dead, Niamh was married, and Seamus was all she had

463

left. She couldn't bear to lose him too. What if he stayed in that dark place and never came back?

As if he knew what she was thinking, the doctor patted her arm sympathetically. 'Many of our men are suffering from this condition,' he told her gravely. 'But they do recover eventually, I promise you, although I cannot guarantee that he will ever get over completely what he's been through. It takes time and patience, but for now I suggest you leave. The sedative I've given him will have him out cold for hours. Rest is the best cure, but you can come back tomorrow if you wish.'

Dilly walked woodenly towards the ward doors, feeling as if she was caught in the grip of yet another nightmare. There had been so many. She wondered how much more she could take.

Chapter Forty-one

Leaning heavily on the rail of the frigate, Nipper stared into the dark waters churning below him. His ship had been in the port for two days and he had come back to a stack of mail. That was the trouble with being in the navy: you only got your post when the ship docked. He had eagerly sorted his by the dates on the envelopes and settled down to read each letter in order. The first had been from Maeve, telling him what was going on at the farm. He had smiled as he read it feeling suddenly homesick. The next had been from Niamh, and his heart had raced as he had seen her familiar handwriting. He found one from Liam and Shelagh, telling him about Patrick and Bridie's progress. Bridie was into everything now, they informed him, and making a great nuisance of herself as she chased the chickens about the yard. He had smiled as he read it, picturing Bridie's mischievous little face and hearing the chickens squawk indignantly. The majority of the letters had been from Niamh until they had suddenly stopped abruptly some months before. Then he had come to the last she had written, and his world had turned upside down.

I have met a young man ... we are to be wed in a couple of weeks ... now we shall meet, I hope, as friends...

As snatches of the letter came back to him now he closed his eyes against the sharp pain in his heart. It had been written some time ago. Niamh would be married to someone else by now. It had been a bitter blow. His first instinct on reading it had been to reply to her, to beg her to reconsider, but then common sense had taken over and he had known it would be useless. It was too late.

Then he had come to the final letter from Maeve and had received yet another shock when she informed him that his birth mother had made contact with her and wanted to meet him. He still hadn't decided what to do about that. Part of him wanted desperately to meet her, yet another felt deeply resentful for all the years she had abandoned him without so much as a word. It would take him a while to make a decision, and he had told Maeve so in the reply he had posted to her the day before. One thing he was sure of: his name now was Ben Carey. Nipper was dead and buried, a part of his childhood. It was time to grow up and plan a future without Niamh. Most of his shipmates had gone ashore for a couple of days to let their hair down, find themselves a woman, get roaring drunk and try to forget some of the dreadful things they had witnessed at sea, but Ben didn't have the heart for it and preferred to stay on board. The rosy future he had planned had been snatched away from him and, as he turned away from the rail to make his way back to his hammock, his heart was heavy.

In September the spirits of the British people were raised when it was reported that a new weapon, conceived and built in strictest secrecy under the code name 'Tank', rolled over the German lines at the Somme scattering machine-gunners and crashing through strong points to gain ground. Within two hours the British and Canadian troops had taken more than two thousand prisoners and had gained seven miles of the thirty-mile front.

'We've got the buggers on the run now,' Mrs Pegs said gleefully, as she enjoyed a cup of tea with Dilly one evening in the rooms above the shop. 'Let's hope this is the beginnin' o' the end. Everyone's had enough of the bloody war now. But how are young Niamh and Seamus doin'?'

'Well, Niamh is still working although she'll have to stop soon. Her ankles are swelling quite badly with her being on her feet so much. And Seamus... All they'll tell me is he's doing as well as can be expected. It's going to be a long job but I hope he'll get there in the end.'

She smiled then as she shared more news with Mrs Pegs. 'I had a letter from Declan this morning. He's engaged by all accounts to a lass from Enniskerry called Róisín and he wants me to meet her soon. I'm really looking forward to it.'

'Why, that's grand,' Mrs Pegs said approvingly. It was good to hear of something nice happening, instead of the usual doom and gloom in the newspapers. 'And how is the shop doing?'

'Very well,' Dilly told her. She was living frugally, keeping only enough to meet her bills so that she could pay off her debt to Max Farthing as soon as possible. He had let her have the shop for what she knew was a ridiculously small amount, but when she had pointed this out to him, he had insisted that it was all he was owed so she had accepted it with good grace. Sometimes she would daydream about what she would do with it when the war was over and they were no longer sewing army uniforms. She intended to make it the classiest dress shop in town. There wasn't another like the one she intended it to become and she felt it would do well. And that wouldn't be the end of it, she had decided. Eventually she would own a string of shops, and she wouldn't stop pushing herself until she did. While she was busy she didn't have time to be lonely.

Chapter Forty-two

On a cold, blustery night in late November Dilly was woken by someone pounding on the shop door. Flinging her feet over the edge of the bed, she grabbed her dressing-gown and fumbled her way downstairs, then through the shop in the darkness. She cursed as she cracked her toe on one of the machines.

'All right, all right, I'm coming,' she snapped, as she fiddled with the key. At last the door was open and she blinked to find Max Farthing standing there.

'It's Niamh,' he told her, without preamble. 'She's having the baby, Dilly, and I thought you might like to be there. I've left her with the doctor and the midwife, but don't panic. They say she could be hours yet.'

'I'll go and get dressed,' she told him, and rushed back upstairs, leaving him standing on the pavement. His motor car was parked at the kerb. It was rarely used now because petrol was hard to find.

'Mrs Pegs popped in to see her earlier and she was having twinges,' Max informed her, as he steered the car into the road, 'so I got Mr Jackson to go round before he left this evening. When he came back and told me she was having pains, I sent for the doctor and the midwife.'

Dilly clung on for dear life. She wasn't keen on motor cars but tonight she would gladly have gone

468

in an aeroplane if it had got her to her daughter more quickly. Most of the women thereabouts relied on a local midwife to deliver their babies. Max had insisted on the best medical care for Niamh and Dilly was grateful.

When they arrived at her daughter's house she leaped from the car almost before it had stopped and shot through the front door. Niamh was in bed, and when she saw Dilly she held her hand to her and started to cry.

'I don't *want* this baby, Mammy,' she choked.

'Now, now, that's no way to talk, is it? Just do as the doctor and the midwife tell you and the baby will be here before you know it,' Dilly soothed.

And so began one of the longest nights of her life.

As Niamh's labour progressed, Dilly felt her pain as the girl clung to her hand and screeched.

'I – I can't do it! It won't come! Make it stop,' she implored, but Dilly remained calm and encouraging.

'Of course it will come. Didn't the midwife just tell you that you were almost there? Now, push when she tells you and breathe between the pains, there's a good girl.'

With the last of her strength, Niamh put all her efforts into bringing the child into the world, and as the first streaks of dawn lit the sky, a baby's weak cry echoed around the room and Niamh sank back onto her pillows.

'Why it's a fine baby girl and she's bonny,' the midwife told her approvingly, as she separated the baby from its mother and wrapped her in a towel. She lifted the red-faced scrap aloft as Dilly began to cry.

Niamh turned her head away. 'I don't want to see it,' she said tiredly.

Dilly and the midwife exchanged a glance.

'If you'll show me to the bathroom, I'll get this little madam bathed and dressed while the doctor examines you to make sure that everything is as it should be,' the midwife said. Dilly pointed to the tallboy in the corner. 'You'll find what you need in there.' It was full of the most beautiful baby's layette she had ever set eyes on, again thanks to Max.

The midwife bustled away with the baby, as Dilly looked on anxiously but after a thorough examination the doctor smiled at her reassuringly. 'Everything is just as it should be. The afterbirth should come away any minute now but the midwife can see to that. Now, if you will excuse me, I shall away to my bed and try to snatch a couple of hours' sleep before my morning surgery begins. It's been rather a long night.'

Dilly saw him to the bedroom door, thanking him profusely, as the midwife reappeared with a clean baby in her arms.

'Take this little mite down to see her grandfather while I get our new mother washed and changed, would you?' she said to Dilly. 'Then the little one will be ready for her first feed.'

As she placed the new little life into Dilly's arms her heart swelled with love. The baby was a replica of Niamh shortly after her birth and for a moment she felt the years melt away, and wished wholeheartedly that Fergal could have been there to see his first grandchild. 'Hello, little one,' she whispered, planting a gentle kiss on the baby's brow.

'Welcome to the world.' Suddenly it didn't matter any more how she had been conceived. She was there, a brand-new person, and Dilly loved her already.

When she entered the drawing room, where Max was anxiously pacing the floor, she told him shyly, 'Here is someone you may like to meet.'

His pacing stopped and he crossed to her. Instantly his face softened.

'B-but she's truly beautiful,' he muttered in awe.

Dilly laid the precious bundle in his arms. She was surprised to see Gwen there, but Max told her, 'I went back to the house earlier on to fetch her. She can stay here to look after Niamh and the baby during her lying-in period. I don't want her overdoing things and making herself ill.'

'But I was going to do that,' Dilly objected.

'I'm sure you were,' he said, with a wry grin, 'but you have a shop and, no doubt, you would run yourself into the ground, dashing between here and there. I know what a stickler you are for everything being done just so.'

Once again Dilly was touched by his kindness. It seemed he had thought of everything.

Gwen duly admired the baby. 'I've got some tea ready and some rounds of hot buttered toast. I thought you might all like something to eat and drink now.' She disappeared into the kitchen then, leaving Dilly and Max to coo over their grand-daughter.

'It seems that we have yet another strand to bind our families together now, Dilly,' he said softly and she could only nod in agreement as

471

their eyes momentarily locked before she swiftly looked away.

When the midwife was ready to leave, Dilly carried the baby upstairs to her mother but again Niamh refused to look at her.

The midwife frowned. 'You must be firm with her,' she told her, in a no-nonsense voice. 'The little one will be crying for a feed soon and this is the time when bonding between mother and baby should take place.'

'But how can I force Niamh to look at her or feed her?'

'Put the babe in the crib at the side of the bed and leave her to it,' the woman told her. 'She'll soon get fed up with the baby's crying and put her to the breast.'

'But what if she doesn't?'

'She will,' the midwife said, with certainty. 'I've seen this many times, and the only way you'll get past it is to do what I say. If you pander to the new mother, you'll be doing the baby no favours and just prolonging the problem, trust me.'

Dilly looked at her uncertainly but she supposed the woman knew what she was talking about so she went back into Niamh's room and laid the baby in her crib beside her.

'The little one will want her first feed soon,' she told her daughter. 'I'm going to fetch you a nice cup of tea now. Gwen has made you some hot buttered toast as well. You need to keep your strength up now.'

'Take her away,' Niamh muttered, her eyes fixed on the ceiling, but Dilly ignored her and left the baby exactly where she was.

Minutes later she returned and put down the tray, then left the room again and soon after the sound of the baby's cries floated down the stairs to them.

'*Mammy! Mammy!* Come and take the baby!' they heard Niamh call.

Steeling herself, Dilly ignored her although it was one of the hardest things she had ever had to do. She could see that Max was tense but tried to smile reassuringly. 'She'll see to the baby soon,' she told him. 'I'm sure the midwife knows what she's talking about.' Then, to Gwen, she said, 'You go and hop into bed, lass. You may as well try to get some rest. The bed is made up in the spare room.'

Looking worried, Gwen did as she was told, leaving Dilly and Max to listen to the baby's cries. Max looked more and more distressed as time went by, but held his tongue. Dilly was doing what she hoped was for the best.

'It seems that you and I will always have something to worry about, doesn't it?' Dilly said wryly.

He nodded wearily. 'When you have children it's constant, isn't it?' He sat on the sofa next to her and confided, 'I'm rather concerned about Oscar's engagement to Penelope Merriman, although Camilla is delighted. I'm sure he doesn't have feelings for the girl. Olivia has taken it very badly and hasn't been herself at all – sometimes I've worried that she and Oscar were *too* close for a brother and sister.'

'I know what you mean,' Dilly said sadly. 'I've noticed the bond between them too. But they're not brother and sister, are they? Not that we could

473

ever tell them so. Camilla could never bear the shame if it were ever to come out that Olivia is my daughter.'

'Quite, but she's another I'm worried about. She barely comes out of her room since we lost Harvey. Sometimes she acts very strangely, talking about him as if he's going to come home.'

'Grief affects people in different ways,' Dilly said wisely. 'And they do say that time is a great healer. I've been out of my mind with worry about Seamus too, although he does seem to be recovering, albeit very slowly. I doubt he'll ever be as he was before the war, but I'm just grateful that he came home.'

She realized that she was talking as openly to Max as she had once spoken to Fergal. Suddenly confused, she clamped her lips together and stared at the ceiling.

Upstairs in the bedroom, Niamh had placed the pillow over her head to drown the baby's cries but it seemed there was no escape. Why didn't someone come to take her away? Her mammy knew full well that she didn't want it.

'Shut up,' she snapped, in the direction of the crib, but the baby only cried harder. Eventually it sank in that no one was going to come to her aid and Niamh dragged herself into a sitting position. She had no alternative but to feed the child, although the very thought filled her with revulsion. She dragged herself to the edge of the bed as dizziness washed over her. Then she forced herself to stare at the tiny form swaddled in a warm shawl. Suddenly the strangest thing happened – a rush of feeling such as she had never experienced before swept over her. She had tried not to think what the baby might be like but she had certainly not expected to be confronted with such a perfect little being.

'Don't cry now,' she said, before she could stop herself. She lifted the bundle tenderly and gazed in awe at the perfect little face. She was beautiful and in that moment the child's mother fell in love with her.

The baby had quietened and was staring up at Niamh as she opened her nightgown and put the child to her breast. The baby's rosebud mouth opened and searched. Seconds later she had latched onto her mother's nipple and was suckling contentedly, as Niamh wonderingly stroked her downy hair.

'Everything has gone quiet,' Max said, as he stopped pacing. They both looked at the ceiling. There was nothing to be heard but the birds in the garden. They waited for half an hour before creeping up the stairs side by side. Dilly cautiously inched open Niamh's bedroom door and as they both peeped into the room a smile appeared on their faces. The baby was lying contentedly on her mother's chest in the protective circle of her arms and they were both fast asleep.

'Well, would you look at that,' Max whispered. 'I don't think I've ever seen a more beautiful sight.'

Dilly smiled as tears welled in her eyes. 'I don't think we'll have to worry now,' she said softly. 'I suggest you get yourself off home. Camilla will want to know about her new granddaughter and

I dare say you ought to let Samuel know he's a father as well.'

Max didn't think either of them would care about the new arrival, but he followed her down the stairs, then wearily made his way home.

The following morning Niamh told her mother, 'I'm going to call her Constance Louise. What do you think?'

'It's a beautiful choice,' Dilly assured her fondly.

Niamh could hardly take her eyes off her new daughter and Dilly had an idea that at last things might improve for her girl. She had her baby to love now, and as long as she had her, she would be able to take whatever life cared to throw at her.

As she closed the door softly, leaving the new mother and baby to get acquainted, she felt a measure of peace settle in her heart. Perhaps now that Niamh was happier she could concentrate on her own hopes and dreams for the future.

Chapter Forty-three

1917

In April 1917 the United States declared war on Germany and the British people took it as a good sign. When Max visited Dilly one evening, he told her, 'I reckon we stand a chance of winning this war now the Americans have come on board.'

Dilly prayed he was right. It seemed to be dragging on and on. Since moving into the shop she

476

had made every penny count and already she was well on her way to paying him back what she owed, which was why she had another proposition to put to him.

'Were you aware that the ironmonger's next door will be coming up for sale soon?' she asked, as she poured him a glass of sherry in her little sitting room above the shop.

'No. Why is that?'

'Mr and Mrs Bradshaw want to retire. They don't seem to have any heart for the business since their son was killed at Ypres,' she told him, handing him the glass. 'As you know, I have every intention of extending the dress shop when the war is over and this seems a heaven-sent opportunity. I was wondering... If the bank is prepared to lend me the money to buy the shop would you stand as referee for me? I know I could manage the payments and I wouldn't let you down.'

Max had always known Dilly was a hard worker but while she still owed him money, he doubted the bank would lend her any more. Even so he had the perfect solution. 'Why don't I buy it and you repay me?' he suggested.

Dilly shook her head. 'I appreciate the offer, but you've done more than enough for me already.'

'Nonsense.' He sipped his drink. 'I'm only thinking that this might be the easiest way round it. You've almost paid for this place already so you could just carry on with the payments on that shop too.' He would gladly have written off the outstanding debt but knew better than to suggest it. Dilly was fiercely proud.

The month before, when she had attended

Declan and Róisín's wedding in Enniskerry, Max had missed her – far more than he had thought he would, although when she came back she had clearly had a wonderful time. She had happily informed him that Róisín was a delightful girl, a true Irish colleen, with a mop of dark curly hair that no amount of brushing would tame and sparkling green eyes. She had a little snub nose and her cheeks dimpled when she smiled. She and Dilly had taken to each other immediately. Seamus had been well enough to go with her and was still there – Maeve had insisted he would recover much more quickly in Ireland than in the sooty Midlands air where there was so much more chance of raids. Dilly hadn't been able to argue with that and was forced to admit it had made things easier for her. Seamus had needed constant nursing since he had left the hospital – racing up and down the stairs to tend him and keep the shop running smoothly had almost worn her out.

The wedding, in the picturesque church perched high on the hill in Enniskerry, had been beautiful, and whenever Dilly remembered the look on Declan's face as his bride had floated down the aisle to him on her father's arm, it never failed to make her smile. That was one son she had no need to worry about now: Declan and Róisín were perfect for each other, and she knew that Maeve and Daniel would take good care of Seamus.

The day had been made even more perfect when Ben, as he preferred to be called now, had appeared just before the service, handsome in his naval uniform. As his ship was in dock, he had wangled two days' leave. He had looked older and wiser but seemed to have come to terms with the fact that he and Niamh were over. He had even hinted that he would agree to meet his birth mother after the war was over, and Dilly hoped that he would.

Niamh was doing well too. She was besotted with sevenmonth-old Constance, who was now a bright-eyed imp, who was already crawling and getting into all sorts of mischief. On the rare occasions when Samuel came home for a short leave he would stay at his club in town or at his parents' home, which suited Niamh. Now, at last, as she had hoped, Dilly felt she could concentrate on her own future.

She looked at Max uncertainly as she considered his offer. She knew there was a good chance that the bank would refuse to lend her the money and it would be awful to miss the chance of owning the adjoining shop. She already had great plans for it. The only indulgence she had allowed herself over the last few years was her monthly Paris fashion magazine. She would pore over the designs greedily, taking in every detail of the fabrics and cuts.

'I suppose it would simplify everything,' she said quietly, and watched his lips slide into a smile before rushing on, 'I *know* I can make a success of what I plan to do, Max! There is such a need in this town for a fashionable ladies' shop and I could make designs very similar to the Paris ones for a fraction of the price.'

'I believe you could.' He didn't doubt it. Many women would have folded after all that Dilly had gone through over the last few years, yet here she was, full of enthusiasm and determined to make something of herself. She really was a remarkable woman, and a beautiful one into the bargain, both inside and out.

His thoughts turned to Camilla and the smile died. She had deteriorated rapidly since they had lost Harvey, and he now employed a full-time nurse to care for her. Her mental state was questionable and she rarely ventured from her room except for meal time. It had begun when she had started to address Olivia as Violet. Max had found it disturbing but Olivia had taken it in her stride and been patience itself. Camilla had then started to scold Mrs Pegs for not setting Harvey's place at the dining-table and was often heard speaking to him as if he was in the room with her. She wandered about the house at night, her coat over her nightgown, demanding to know why Jackson wasn't there with the pony and trap to take her shopping, and Olivia would lead her back to her room, explaining that it wasn't time to get up yet.

The doctor had suggested she might be better off in a home that catered for people with conditions such as hers. Max had known that the 'home' was really an asylum and, although there was no longer any love between them, he couldn't bring himself to do that to her. Sometimes he felt it was only his visits to Dilly and her down-to-earth common sense that kept him going. 'Will you permit me to make a few enquiries then?' he replied. 'If I see the shop owner directly, we may be able to agree on a reasonable price and save the cost of a house agent.'

Seeing the sense in what he said, she nodded as a little shiver of excitement raced up her spine.

The shop would need stripping out, of course, and would need to be completely redecorated and redesigned, but she could save a lot of money if she did some of the work herself.

'Then let's drink a toast.' He raised his glass. 'To the finest dress shop in the Midlands.'

Dilly's eyes shone like stars as she touched her glass to his.

Chapter Forty-four

In the cosy kitchen above the shop in Liverpool, the girl who was often in Mrs Pegs's thoughts was staring in shock at the papers she held.

In the months that had led up to her baby's birth, Bessie had worked hard to repay the man who had taken her in off the streets for his kindness, and a warm friendship had sprung up between them. Bessie gauged that Malcolm must have been at least thirty years older than her but she didn't care. He was the nicest man she had ever met and she tried not to think of what might happen when the baby was born. She knew they were both the subject of gossip as her pregnancy became more visible, but Malcolm didn't seem to care so she lived for each day as it came, even happier than she had been at the Farthings' in the days before Samuel had raped her.

Finally one night as she lay in her bed she felt warmth between her legs followed by a sharp pain. Somehow she had managed to stumble to the bottom of the stairs and scream for Malcolm. He had raced off to fetch the midwife, then spent the rest of the night pacing up and down in the small corridor outside her bedroom door, like an expectant father.

When the child, a boy, screaming lustily, put in an appearance, the midwife duly allowed Malcolm in to see him, and Bessie was shocked to see tears glistening on his lashes as he stared tenderly at the child he was cradling in his arms. The midwife obviously thought that the baby was his and Malcolm didn't bother to enlighten her. As he said afterwards, it was none of her or anybody else's business for that matter.

'My wife and I were never fortunate enough to have children,' he told Bessie, when the midwife had taken her leave. 'So it will be grand to have a baby about the place.'

Bessie watched him with tears in her own eyes as confusion coursed through her. She had longed for this moment, to have someone in her life who was truly her own, and yet now that the child was born she felt nothing but revulsion for him because he resembled his father. She hoped that soon she would feel differently and be able to put behind her the terrible way in which he had been conceived. But in the days and weeks that followed, although she fed and changed him, she found she couldn't bring herself to do any more than that. It was Malcolm who made time to rock him and show him tenderness, and Bessie realized eventually that she was falling in love with him. Malcolm made her feel safe and cared for, and she blossomed like a flower. Despite the difference in their ages, when he asked her to marry him, two months later, she was overjoyed. They wed in a small register office ceremony, and from that moment on, Malcolm treated Roderick, as they had called the baby, as his own and Bessie felt blessed.

Malcolm was kind and considerate, and Bessie hoped that Roderick might be blessed with a playmate.

'Why don't you write to your Mrs Pegs, my dear?' Malcolm had suggested one day. Bessie often spoke kindly of the woman.

Bessie shook her head. 'I've thought about it,' she admitted, 'but I don't need to go back into my past any more. I have everything I could want here with you.'

She knew all too well that some believed she had married Malcolm for his money, but she didn't care what anyone thought and blessed the day she had met him. It would be easy to love a child of Malcolm's. But then he had suffered his first heart attack and Bessie was terrified. She had never been truly loved before, and the thought of losing him was inconceivable. She had nursed him with such tenderness that people had begun to see she genuinely cared for him and had come to accept her. Then had come the fateful morning when she had woken to find Malcolm cold beside her in their bed. He had slipped away peacefully in his sleep, with a smile on his face, and Bessie was bereft. Why? she asked God, over and over again, in the days before his funeral.

Now he had been laid to rest and the solicitor was telling her that Malcolm had left everything

483

he owned to her. She could scarcely believe it.

'May I offer my condolences for your loss.' The solicitor's voice sliced into her thoughts. 'You are now a reasonably wealthy young woman, but please don't hesitate to contact me if there is anything you don't understand. All should be clear in the documents you have. Good day, Mrs Ward.'

She saw him out in a daze, and once the door had closed behind him, tears streamed down her pale cheeks. She had thought there could be no more tears left to cry but still they kept coming. Malcolm had provided a future for her but what good was it without him? He was everywhere she looked. No amount of money could ever take his place.

And then she began to feel angry. She was all alone now, left to care for Roderick by herself. Why should Samuel get away with what he had done? The decision came out of the blue. She would go back to the Midlands and confront him. But not yet. Shops were not easy to sell in wartime, but the war couldn't last for ever. When it was over she would return to Nuneaton and make Samuel pay for what he had done to her. Revenge would be sweet.

In August that year the third battle of Ypres unfolded, to the accompaniment of ceaseless bombardments and remorseless mud. The fields around the Passchendaele ridge were turned into a quagmire. The newspapers reported fierce fighting in the air and slowly the Allies were gaining ground, but at what cost?

Olivia was beside herself with concern as the reports unfolded. Oscar was out there somewhere but all she could do was try to stay positive.

Max was worried, too, although Lawrence was now a huge help to him. He still walked with a stick and would always have a severe limp, but he had taken a lot of the work from his father's shoulders and had turned into his right-hand man.

Patty had agreed that after their wedding, which would take place as soon as the war was over, they would stay in the Midlands and Max was glad of that. The Merrimans were planning their daughter's wedding to Oscar, and it appeared that it would be a very grand affair, although Oscar seemed detached from it all.

Max was also concerned about Olivia. Although she was still working at Weddington Hospital, she was now talking about joining the nursing VADs on the front line. On the odd occasions when Oscar came home on leave, Max couldn't fail to notice that they were like polite strangers with each other. Olivia's sparkle was gone, and while Max and Dilly thought they knew why, they could never speak of it. If ever the two were to discover they were not brother and sister, all of their lives would be changed for ever. Dilly shared his concern about Olivia leaving for the front but hoped that she would change her mind. Weddington Hall Hospital was now catering for at least three hundred men with wounds of varying degrees, ranging from shell-shock, shrapnel, missing limbs to severe burns, and the nurses were rushed off their feet. All they could do was wait to discover what Olivia would do.

Olivia and little Constance bound Dilly and

Max together more surely than any chains, but they went on with their separate lives as best they could, waiting for the war to end.

Time passed slowly but it was in November 1918 when the women in the dress shop sat sewing at their machines that the church bells suddenly started to peal and a commotion was heard in the street outside.

'What's goin' on, then?' one of the machinists said looking towards the door. One by one the machines became silent, as Dilly threw it open, only to be lifted to her feet and swung about as if she weighed no more than a feather by a ruddy-cheeked farmer, who had been on his way to the cattle market in town.

'What's happening?' She laughed when he put her down. People were rushing about, throwing their hats into the air. Traffic had come to a stand-still and horses, carts and motor cars were backing up along the street.

'It's *over,* lass,' he crowed delightedly. 'The bloody war is finally *over!* The armistice was signed at eleven o'clock this mornin'!'

The women had spilled from the shop to stand beside her on the pavement and now they shrieked with glee and danced about, hugging and kissing each other, like a gaggle of excited schoolgirls. Many had sons and husbands away fighting, and it was the best news they could have had.

'No more work today,' Dilly told them, and after snatching up their coats and bags, they scattered like bees to share the news with their families.

Dilly made her way back into the shop and

stared at the rows of empty machines, with yards of khaki fabric laid beneath the silent needles. Her pleasure was laced with pain; there would be no homecoming party for Kian but one day she would find out where he was buried and go to lay flowers on his grave.

In her comfortable house on Abbey Green the news had also reached Niamh and as she cradled her baby daughter to her she experienced mixed emotions. While thrilled that the war was over, she was also trying to imagine what it would be like when Samuel returned home for good, yet her concern over her own future faded into insignificance with the relief she felt when she thought of Ben, as everyone now referred to him, returning to Enniskerry safe and sound. She could never be a part of his life but that didn't stop her loving him. And as she thought of him, tears slid down her cheeks at the cruel blow Fate had dealt her.

An hour later Max burst into the shop, his face alight, to find Dilly in the ironmonger's next door, which he had recently purchased. It felt natural to want to celebrate with her. Since he had bought the neighbouring shop, Dilly had done little to it, apart from taking down the empty shelves and sweeping it out, but now she could begin to live her dream.

'At last!' He laughed. 'It's all over and we can get on with our lives!' Grabbing her about the waist he danced her about the room and she giggled, until they came to a breathless halt. Fireworks were going off and laughter floated in to them from the road.

Her face became straight then as she surveyed her little empire and told him, with determination, 'I'm going to make a go of this, Max. And not only *this* shop. This is only the beginning.'

'I rather believe you will,' he answered, as his eyes followed hers. Then, taking her hand he told her softly, 'I might never have told you this before but I think you are a truly remarkable woman, Dilly.'

They were facing each other now. He was playing with her fingers as he went on, 'I also ought to tell you that I lo–'

Placing her finger gently on his lips, she stopped his flow of words then. 'Don't say any more,' she implored. 'We know there can never be anything but friendship between us. If we leave things as they are, everything can go on as before. We have our families to think of, and I have my dreams.'

He lowered his head, knowing she was right. Her friendship would have to be enough.

Dilly's head, meanwhile, was full of plans for the future. It was time to make her dream come true and turn her little shops into what would one day become an empire.

Acknowledgements

I would like to say a big thank you to Rebecca, my editor, for all her patience and support during the writing and editing of this book.

Also to my husband and family who never complain when I disappear off into my study at the drop of a hat!

This Large Print Book for the partially sighted, who cannot read normal print, is published under the auspices of

THE ULVERSCROFT FOUNDATION